a funny thing about
LOVE

Also by Erin Downing

Kiss It

And for more romantic stories:

Endless Summer
by Jennifer Echols

Love, Love, Love
by Deborah Reber
and Caroline Goode

Royally Crushed
by Niki Burnham

a funny thing about

LOVE

Dancing Queen
and
Prom Crashers
and
Drive Me Crazy

Erin Downing

Simon Pulse

New York London Toronto Sydney

SIMON PULSE

An imprint of Simon & Schuster Children's Publishing Division

1230 Avenue of the Americas, New York, NY 10020

This Simon Pulse paperback edition June 2011

Dancing Queen copyright © 2006 by Erin Soderberg Downing

Prom Crashers copyright © 2007 by Erin Soderberg Downing

Drive Me Crazy copyright © 2009 by Erin Soderberg Downing

All rights reserved, including the right of reproduction in whole or in part in any form.

SIMON PULSE and colophon are registered trademarks of Simon & Schuster, Inc.

For information about special discounts for bulk purchases, please contact Simon & Schuster Special Sales at 1-866-506-1949 or business@simonandschuster.com.

The Simon & Schuster Speakers Bureau can bring authors to your live event. For more information or to book an event contact the Simon & Schuster Speakers Bureau at 1-866-248-3049 or visit our website at www.simonspeakers.com.

Designed by Mike Rosamilia

The text of this book was set in Garamond 3.

Manufactured in the United States of America

2 4 6 8 10 9 7 5 3 1

Library of Congress Control Number 2010942826

ISBN 978-1-4424-0645-2

These books were previously published individually by Simon Pulse.

Dancing Queen

*For Milla, my little rock star,
and for Greg, who rocks*

Acknowledgments

Huge thanks to my fabulously fun editor and friend, Michelle Nagler, as well as the amazing Bethany Buck and the rest of the crew at Simon Pulse for taking a chance on me with this book.

This book wouldn't have been possible without my husband, Greg, who makes me laugh and appreciates my quirks.

Many hugs (hee hee!) to Robin Wasserman, my writing buddy extraordinaire.

And cheers to my incredible mom, who eagerly read and praised every draft of this book (even the really bad first round); my dad, who is just supercool and who forgave me for not using my maiden name (Soderberg) on the cover of this book; Sarah, who has been a superstar friend for twenty years and who made that first trip to London phenomenal; and Josef, Anna, Anders, and Stockholm—for helping to bring this book to life in Sweden and introducing me to the Eurovision Song Contest.

Also, hooray for ABBA, whose music makes me happy!

Super Freak

Olivia Phillips's first-ever celebrity sighting was going all wrong.

She had just landed flat on her butt, her long legs splayed at awkward angles across a busy sidewalk in the middle of central London. She had a discarded cigarette butt stuck to her jeans, her face was splotchy, and her curly brown hair was stuck to her lip gloss. Though she didn't want to look, she was pretty sure the bottom of one leg of her jeans had crept up above the cuff of her athletic sock and gotten stuck there.

Liv—as her friends called her—couldn't remember a time in recent history she had looked *less* fabulous.

Tragically, it was at this very moment that Josh Cameron, International Pop Star and *Celeb* magazine's Hottest Guy, was staring straight at her. *The* Josh Cameron, whom Liv had fantasized about a million and three times, was standing less than two feet away, casting a shadow from his perfect body onto Liv's disheveled figure on the sidewalk.

Why, Liv wondered, *do things like this always happen to me?* She had arrived in London from Ann Arbor, Michigan, less than two hours earlier . . . and she had already made a complete fool of herself in front of the world's biggest celebrity. *How is this even possible?!*

Because Liv was Liv. And she had a tendency to turn ordinary embarrassing moments into extraordinarily embarrassing ones—which meant this moment could get a whole lot worse. And it did.

Looking up at Josh Cameron, Liv was unable to stop a goofy, uncomfortable sort of smile from spreading across her face. She lifted her hand in a little wave and—very much against her will—blurted out, "Cheerio!"

Three hours earlier . . .

Gazing out the airplane window at London's sprawling suburbs miles below her, Liv couldn't believe she was actually here. In her sleep-deprived state, it *still* didn't feel real that she had been selected as one of Music Mix Europe's summer interns. But now that she was settled into a cramped window seat and minutes away from landing on the other side of the Atlantic, she finally let it sink in: She would be living in London!

Liv had spent every waking minute since she had gotten her acceptance letter daydreaming about days surrounded by rock stars and nights out tra-la-la-ing from club to club. Of course, deep down, she knew the Music Mix internship would be a lot of work, too. But she had somehow managed to avoid thinking about that part. Why not focus on the good stuff?

When the plane landed, Liv grabbed her black wheelie from baggage claim and followed airport signs to the Gatwick Express. Hustling through the terminal with her suitcase and overstuffed carry-on tote, Liv's excitement bubbled into giddiness. She heaved her stuff onto the train into the city, and a chirpy English voice wished her a good day and a pleasant journey. She just loved the British accent. It always sounded so civilized and kind.

The train began to roll toward downtown London as Liv flipped through the on-board magazine, reading about London's neighborhoods. Music Mix was setting her up with an apartment as part of the internship—she couldn't wait to find out where her roommates would be from, and where they would be living. Notting Hill, Chelsea, Greenwich . . . they all sounded fantastic.

Since she had never been anywhere more exotic than Ely, Minnesota, they all sounded a little intimidating and foreign, too. She had only lived away from home once before (Liv always gagged when she thought about that terrible summer her dad had decided to send her to an all-girls camp on Lake Michigan), so this was definitely going to be an adventure.

Paging through the magazine, Liv quickly studied British lingo and discovered that if she wanted to fit in, her roommates would actually be flatmates, the subway is the tube, and she absolutely must eat something called bangers and mash.

Eventually the train heaved out one final puff, and the doors sighed open to let Liv out into central London. She had arrived!

Making her way into Victoria train station, Liv scanned the signs overhead, looking for the London Underground. Dodging through the crowd, she found an open ticket booth and bought a monthly travel card. Studying the tube map in her guidebook, Liv found the route to Oxford Street, home of Music Mix Europe's central office. She had been told to "pop by" the studio to pick up keys to her flat.

Hustling through the corridor toward the tube, Liv eyed the advertisements pasted on the walls. Next to an ad for Cadbury chocolates (*Yum . . . must get some of that*), Liv spotted a poster of Josh Cameron. She slowed her walk slightly, scanning the advertisement for details.

JOSH CAMERON: SPECIAL APPEARANCE, LIVE IN LONDON! Liv stopped briefly—her eye had been drawn to a small detail in the lower corner of the ad: "Sponsored by Music Mix Europe." Liv wondered if she would get to help with the concert. . . . That certainly wouldn't be a bad way to spend the summer. She was just the tiniest bit obsessed with Josh Cameron, and would give pretty much anything to meet him in person. There weren't a lot of celebrities floating around Ann Arbor.

Liv could hear the subway train rolling into the station just ahead of her, and she hustled to catch it. She pulled her suitcase and carry-on clear of the doors just before they swooshed closed and the train roared out of the station. Two stops later the train's doors slid open and she stepped onto the platform as a freakishly polite mechanical voice reminded her to "mind the gap." Liv passed through one of the arches leading her away from the platform and rode the long escalator up and out onto the street. Red double-decker buses breezed past, stuffed with passengers out for a day of shopping. People packed the sidewalk, hustling past Liv, who stood rooted to her spot just outside the Underground exit.

The noise and speed of the crowd was overwhelming. The time difference had started to catch up with her, and Liv realized that it was the middle of the night back in Michigan. Hit with a wave of sleepiness, Liv glanced down Oxford Street and spotted the glowing Music Mix sign.

She applied a coat of gloss to her lips and hastily made her way toward the sign. She lifted her suitcase, slinging her carry-on tote over a shoulder, and pushed into the office's revolving entrance doors.

Liv's reflexes had slowed from lack of sleep, and she realized too late that she had forgotten to get out of the revolving door on the inside and was back out on Oxford Street. Blushing, she made another turn around in the door and stepped out into the large, open lobby, tucking a stray curl behind her ear. She looked around quickly to make sure no one had seen her mistake. Coast clear.

Liv smiled widely as she approached the security desk. "Excuse me . . . I'm one of Music Mix's summer interns. Can you tell me where should I go?"

The security guard looked up briefly, then returned to the tabloid he was reading. "Third floor, miss." Liv muttered a quick thanks, resisting the urge to curtsy, and took the escalator up. She stepped into a round, colorful sitting area whose walls were filled with floor-to-ceiling television screens playing a variety of music videos.

As Liv approached the circular desk in the center of the room, she could hear the receptionist chatting animatedly. Peeking up over the edge of the tall desk, Liv could see that the receptionist's dyed blond hair was formed into a dozen long thick dreadlocks and was pulled back from her face with a hot pink scarf. She was wearing a short strapless dress and an armful of silver bangles that set off her dark skin perfectly. She motioned to Liv to wait, and quickly finished up her conversation.

Looking up at Liv, she smiled. "Welcome to Music Mix. Here to check in?"

Liv grinned. "Yes, I am. My name is Olivia Phillips."

"It's lovely to meet you, Olivia. I'm Gloria. Here's the scoop: I give you keys to your flat, and you're on your own for today. Settle in, meet your flatmates, get some sleep. Just be back here at nine tomorrow morning. Simon Brown can be a bit testy in the morning, so don't be late—it's best to stay on his good side."

Liv recalled that her acceptance letter had come from a guy named Simon Brown—she now realized he must be the one in charge. What a fabulous job.

Gloria shuffled through a box on her desk and plucked out a small yellow envelope. She pulled out two keys and a card with an address printed on it. Scanning the card, Gloria passed it across the desk to Liv, along with the keys. She pulled a pocket-size London Underground map out of her desk drawer and circled one of the stops in hot pink marker.

"You're sharing a flat with two other girls," Gloria explained. "They have both checked in with me already, so they should be at the flat when you get there. Think you can find it?"

Liv nodded again and turned toward the escalator. "Thanks a lot. I'll see you tomorrow." Gloria smiled and pushed a button to answer the phone that had just started ringing.

Riding the escalator down, Liv could see that the Music Mix lobby had become much more crowded since she had arrived just a few minutes earlier. She scanned the faces and chic outfits as she passed, wishing she were dressed just a little cuter and didn't have her bulky wheelie and carry-on—she knew she looked like a tourist.

Liv glanced down to study the tube map as she made her way into the revolving door to leave the building. Distracted, she didn't notice someone step off Oxford Street and into the door as she exited.

Suddenly, Liv was jolted backward. As she lost her balance, both Liv and her wheelie toppled over onto the sidewalk. Though she had come out on the right side of the door this time, her bulky carry-on bag had not been so lucky. The strap of the bag was still attached securely to Liv's shoulder, but the bag itself was stuck on the other side of the glass in the compartment behind her. The revolving door had come to a complete standstill.

Liv pulled her arm out of the bag's strap to release it and craned her neck around, hoping no one was stuck in the door. Her face reddened as she realized that someone was definitely standing—trapped—in the other glass compartment. The person turned to face her, and Liv's mouth dropped open.

Staring at her from the other side of the glass, stuck in a revolving door between Oxford Street and the Music Mix lobby, was Josh Cameron.

Back to the Future . . .

It felt like hours had gone by. Josh Cameron had quickly freed himself and Liv's bag from the door and was now standing—staring—at Liv on the ground. And was it her imagination, or had she just shouted "cheerio" to the world's biggest pop star? Liv straightened her legs, but continued to sit on the sidewalk, stumped and horrified. *Nice first impression, Liv. Suave.*

Josh Cameron smiled as he held Liv's carry-on out to her. "I believe this is yours. . . ."

"Um, thanks." *Um, thanks? Really great response . . . very witty and charming.*

Josh Cameron tilted his head to the side just slightly and looked at Liv with concern. "Are you okay? That looked like a pretty bad fall." She scrambled to her feet and took her bag from him, groping for the right words.

Come on, supersexy girl within, Liv begged inwardly, *say something clever and alluring! Oh God, you're just staring. . . . Say something!* "Yeah, I'm fine. Just a little embarrassed. You don't think anyone saw that, do you? Hah hah hah!" Liv laughed too loudly at her own non-joke, quickly straightening her hair and brushing the cigarette butt off her jeans.

"I'm Olivia, by the way. And I'm really sorry. It's just that, well, my friends always say this is the kind of thing that I do, uh, you know, when I guess I want to meet celebrities, or, um, make a winning first impression, or uh . . . hah hah hah," *Shut up, just SHUT UP! What are you talking about?!*

Josh Cameron was smiling at her, clearly amused. He patiently ran a hand through his gorgeous curls as Liv stuttered through her ridiculous monologue. By the time she finally had the self-control to shut up, he had begun to laugh.

"Well, Olivia, I better be off. It's been lovely meeting you. I really do hope you're not hurt." As he made his way back through the revolving door, Josh Cameron turned once more and looked at Liv. He smiled his famous smile, and walked into the lobby toward the waiting crowd.

Liv stared after him for a few seconds, then backed away from Music Mix's front doors. She was pleased to see that her white athletic sock was definitely poking up over the cuff of her jeans. *Really cute, Liv. Very chic.*

As her mind replayed the past five minutes over and over—coming up with about twelve significantly more glamorous ways she could have met the biggest pop star in the world—Liv made her way back to the tube and toward her new home. She had been in London less than three hours, and had already managed to fit in a lifetime's worth of humiliation. And, much as she hated to admit it, Liv suspected this wasn't the end of it.

She Drives Me Crazy

Emerging from the subway, Liv detected the faint odor of urine. She covered her nose and hurried out onto the sidewalk, turning left and heading toward the address listed on the card she had gotten from Gloria.

She couldn't help feeling a little concerned as she took in her surroundings. Liv's image of London had come from movies like *Bridget Jones's Diary* and *What a Girl Wants*. This wasn't quite the same. All the buildings looked shabby, and there were more fish and chips shops than people.

She stopped at a medium-size gray building at the end of the block. The iron gate led into a small flowerless court-yard, with three huge garbage cans resting at the foot of a set of stairs that led upward.

Liv double-checked the address on her card and pulled the keys from her pocket. The biggest key worked, and Liv made her way into the courtyard and toward the stairs. Hers was apartment 523. She looked for the elevator, but immediately realized she wouldn't find one. Climbing slowly with her suitcase, Liv got to the fifth floor sweaty and out of breath. She figured the walk up was a good thing—her butt would look fantastic by the end of the summer.

As she made her way down the hall, Liv's heart began to beat faster. She was about to meet her new flatmates. *Where will they be from?* she wondered. *Paris? Milan? New York?* Liv turned the key and pushed open the door.

She was greeted with three enormous, obscenely expensive-looking Armani suitcases. Each was propped open, displaying a treasure chest of Gucci and Zac Posen, a pile of cashmere, and several very real-looking alligator pumps. Caught off guard, Liv stood silently in the doorway for a few minutes before stumbling into the room and pushing her generic wheelie against a wall.

Breathing heavily from her climb, Liv glanced around the room. It wasn't exactly charming, but it would certainly do. The room was mostly naked of furniture, which was a pretty good thing considering that the three huge suitcases took up most of the floor space anyway. Directly across from the front door was a slim counter, which overlooked a tiny kitchen. There were three small bar stools squeezed under the countertop. Along the right wall was an ironing board, jammed in next to an antique-looking stereo.

Liv quickly scanned the rest of the room. Her eyes came to rest on a short threadbare couch along the wall. It looked like it might have been flowered once, but was now just a pale shade of green. Liv realized that there was a wisp of a girl perched delicately on one arm of the couch. The girl was looking Liv up and down without any hint of subtlety.

Liv bellowed out a very loud "hi there" to hide her surprise and discomfort at (1) realizing someone was sitting on the sofa looking at her, and (2) realizing that that someone was very obviously studying her for flaws.

After an awkward moment of silence, the girl introduced herself as Rebecca, a self-described "Texas Honey." Liv quickly stated her name in response, and then Rebecca released a delicate sigh and launched into a list of house rules, nearly all of which related to Rebecca's clothes and what Liv could and couldn't touch (the "Could" list was blank, as far as Liv could tell).

"And most important," Rebecca explained in her thick Texas drawl, "Ah am to be called Rebecca—that is Rah*beh*kaw. Not Becky or Becks or Becca or any other fun little nicknames you might devise. My father taught me that this manner of coziness is tacky." A quick hair flip, and then Rebecca lifted her tiny body off the couch and swayed down a hallway.

Liv had said nothing more than "hi there," and already she felt like a goon. *Just my luck,* Liv thought, watching Rebecca retreat down the hall. *I come all the way to London and get stuck with* that.

Luckily, Liv's other roommate (*flatmate*, she reminded herself) was good-ol'-Becky's polar opposite. Anna, a calm, gorgeous blonde from Sweden, appeared a few minutes after Rebecca had closed her glossy lips and swept away.

Anna introduced herself by confessing that she would have come out sooner to say hello, but she had been avoiding Rebecca since the two of them had arrived at the apartment a few hours earlier. "She promised to show me the photo album from her last beauty pageant," Anna said simply. "I just couldn't deal." Liv could already tell she was going to like Anna.

"So," Liv said, grabbing the handle of her wheelie. She was dying to get out of her jeans—she'd been in the same clothes ever since she left Michigan more than twenty-four hours before. "You guys probably already picked rooms, right? Which one is mine?"

A sweet, high-pitched voice came trilling down the hall. *Rebecca.* Liv cringed as the tiny blonde came swaying back into the living room. Rebecca smiled, visibly glowing as she said dramatically, "Li-uhv, *this* is your room."

Anna glanced around the living room. "I'm sorry, Liv. There are only two little bedrooms, and the couch pulls out. . . . I'm sure it won't be that bad."

Liv turned slowly, surveying the couch. "Right . . . ," she said. She sat down on the couch and felt her butt squish a full two feet through the fabric until it was resting only a few inches off the floor. "Great. Well then, I'm just going to get settled." She smiled weakly.

Anna studied Liv carefully before turning and heading down the hall to her room. She called out, "Let me know if you need anything, okay? I mean it . . . anything."

Rebecca just stood there, arms crossed, batting her cold eyes at Liv. "You're such a good sport, Li-uhv. Ah think you'll be so comfy out here." And then she winked—yes, winked—and trilled a high-pitched laugh as she skipped down the hallway toward her bedroom.

Liv hoisted herself out of the couch and pushed one of Rebecca's suitcases out of her way with her foot. She would have much rather jumped inside the suitcase and stomped on all the clothes, but she realized that probably wasn't the first impression she wanted to make. It wasn't *Rebecca's* fault she was stuck sleeping on a fold out couch. Though Rebecca *had* seemed to get an unnatural thrill from breaking the news.

As she pulled her wheelie out of the corner, Liv spotted a small British flag embroidered on the bottom corner of her suitcase. *Uh-oh,* she thought. She turned the suitcase over and lifted the flap that hid the nameplate. The name Millie Banks stared back at her.

Nooooooooooooooo! Reality very quickly sank in: her bag, and with it all of her carefully chosen outfits, was gone. She must have taken the wrong suitcase from baggage claim, and now she was stuck with this one. It was identical to hers—except for the little flag.

The good news was that Millie Banks lived in London, and there was a phone number. Liv could only hope she and Millie had made an even swap so they could easily trade back and laugh about how funny this all was. Though at this moment Liv didn't find anything about the situation amusing.

She eagerly pulled the stranger's suitcase into the middle of the floor and tugged at the zipper—she figured it couldn't hurt to look. As it was, Liv had the jeans and T-shirt she had been wearing for two days, and that was it. She needed *something* to wear on her first day of work, and she quietly prayed that the suitcase would be stuffed with a fabulous selection of designer duds.

It wasn't.

Looking up at her from inside the stranger's black suitcase were seven little white dogs, each embroidered on a different color sweater. She unfolded the turquoise sweater with a dog-in-a-bonnet design and sighed.

As she sat staring at the half-dozen doggies and wondering what to do next, Rebecca breezed into the living room. Little Miss Texas was going full-speed ahead on a one-sided conversation—Liv suspected that Rebecca enjoyed hearing herself talk, and didn't really care whether anyone was listening or responding.

"Oh, Li-uhv, those are just such cute little sweaters. One doggie sweater a day. Precious. Very chic." Rebecca tinkled out a laugh and swept a pile of Armani from the ironing board into her arms.

"Yeah, they're just adorable." Liv bit her lip and continued. "Rebecca, I don't suppose there's any chance you have anything in one of your suitcases that I could borrow for work tomorrow? I picked up the wrong suitcase at the airport, and as cute as these little collies are, I just don't think they'll cut it."

"Oh, Li-uhv." Rebecca sighed. "Those are westies, not collies. And no, I'm afraid I just don't have anything that will work on you—you're too big. Maybe Anna has something in your size?" She tilted her head and smiled. "Besides, Ah just don't think I have anything I can spare. I get oozy about people borrowing my clothes. Stains and such . . ."

"Great," Liv said sarcastically, ignoring Rebecca's jabs. "That's just great. I'll talk to Anna."

"About what?" Anna had just walked into the living room with an enormous apple. She plunked down into the couch, took a bite, and folded her legs up under herself.

"I was just asking Rebecca if I could borrow something to wear to work tomorrow, but she doesn't have anything she can spare." Liv cringed and held up the purple sweater with a dog-in-a-basket design. "I swapped bags with someone at the airport. I'm not sure this is going to go over well at Music Mix. Help?"

"Of course." Anna stood up quickly and headed to her bedroom. As she turned and beckoned Liv to follow, she briefly made a face in Rebecca's direction. "Let me show you what I have."

An hour later Liv and Anna finally stopped laughing long enough to pose for a photo next to the living statue in Leicester Square. When they had first approached the silver figure, Liv thought the statue was metal—but realized it was actually a live person after the mouth released a loud screech and the statue's joints shifted position.

Liv popped a ten-pence coin into the hat in the figure's outstretched silver hand, and jumped when the human-statue robotically shifted position to say thanks. Laughing again, she grabbed Anna's arm and moved toward the center of the square.

"I still can't believe Rebecca thought I was going to be excited about that velour thing." Liv and Anna had spent the whole tube ride from their apartment to central London dwelling on Rebecca's unwillingness to share her clothes. Liv was even more stumped by the fact that after her original no, Rebecca had apparently changed her mind and generously offered Liv a zip-up crushed velvet jogging suit, saying it was "all she could spare."

"I know! She spent the whole morning bragging to me about how she had packed three suitcases so she would be prepared for anything." Anna shook her head and giggled. "There must be *something* she can part with for a day."

"Well, let's celebrate the fact that we got out of the apartment tonight. I have no doubt we would have been stuck watching a fashion show if we had stuck around." Liv switched to a thick Southern drawl. "Ah mean, what on earth is she goin' ta wa-uhr ta-mah-row?"

Anna laughed, and suddenly Liv felt a little bad about making fun of Rebecca. But on second thought, Liv had gotten no signs of kindness from her at all. And life was too short to bother with people who were going to treat her like a second-class citizen. She was just lucky she had Anna to laugh it off with.

They settled onto an empty bench in the center of Leicester Square. Anna had arranged to meet up with two Music Mix interns she had met that morning when she was checking in, and had invited Liv to tag along.

As they sat and waited, Liv leaned back into the bench and gazed around at the pigeons and camera-happy tourists who filled the square. Breathing in the damp London air, Liv couldn't help but think about her mom, Isobel, who had grown up in London. Though her mom had died more than ten years earlier, Liv could still hear her voice—with its lovely, lilting English accent—saying that London was the best place on earth.

What was it that made her believe that? Liv wondered. *Did she ever sit in this square with her friends, looking at the same buildings I am now, when she was a teenager?* After her mother died, Liv had sworn to her father that she would live in London someday. She intended to find out what her mother's life had been like and what had made her love England so much, even years after she had moved away.

"How did you convince your parents to let you come to London?" Anna asked, pulling Liv out of her memories.

"Well, my mom died a long time ago, so it's just me and my dad," Liv explained. "My dad is a photographer, so it helped to play up the whole developing-my-inner-artist thing. And I don't think it hurt that he was offered a gig doing a photo shoot for some rich Italian businessman this summer—he gets to spend the summer on Lake Como in Italy. He seemed to like the idea that we'd be on the same continent. It all just worked out, I guess."

"You're lucky—it sounds like he was pretty cool about it," Anna said, lowering her eyes. "I had the hardest time getting my parents to let me come. My mom is certain I'll be a doctor, and this is about as far from med school as you can get. She told me I could have this summer to 'play,' as she calls it, but I had to promise to re-evaluate my priorities when I get back to Sweden." Anna sighed. "I just wish she would back off some. I mean, I'm nineteen. I should be making my own decisions." Anna shrugged and smiled weakly.

"You're nineteen?" Liv couldn't believe it—Anna was two years older than her, and already out of high school. "Actually, I guess I'm surprised that my dad let me come at all. But he moved out on his own when he was sixteen to take pictures of rock stars and 'live the seventies life.'" Liv made little quotation marks in the air. "I think he feels like he owes it to his childhood self to trust me."

"Wow. Your dad sounds fabulous. The complete opposite of my parents."

"Remember, this is all in theory." Liv smiled, picturing her dad struggling to mix his liberal ideals with his idea of what a good dad should be like. "In reality, he's pretty strict. But we have a lot of fun together." Liv smiled, suddenly missing her dad. "What do you want to do, if you're not into med school?" Liv asked Anna, wishing she had even the slightest idea of what she wanted to do when she graduated from high school next year. She had tried to avoid thinking about it, but realized decision-time was coming way too soon.

"I'm not sure," Anna said, frustrated. "Honestly, I've been dying to work at Music Mix for ages. That's really all I've ever wanted. If this summer goes the way I hope, I'll get a job offer at the end—which I'm sure will devastate my mom." Anna sighed and looked around the square before continuing. "But it's not going to happen, so there's no point in getting my hopes up. I just know I don't want to go to med school—yet. I guess I need some time before I'm forced to figure my life out."

"Does your mom know that?" Liv asked, noticing how upset Anna had gotten while talking about her future.

Anna shook her head. "I've already been accepted into a few great schools for next year, so Mom's taken it as a sign that I'm supposed to go right on to university. Unless something major happens this summer, I'll be at Oxford or Stockholm University in the fall." Anna suddenly broke off, and lifted her arm to wave across the square.

Liv followed her gaze and spotted two guys heading toward them. The taller of the two was looking right at her, and the way his smile spread slowly across his face as Liv looked up made her stomach crinkle into a little ball and somersault around inside her belly.

"Hey, guys!" Anna stood up and gave each of the two guys a hug in turn. "This is my roommate, Liv."

The shorter guy quickly leaned over and kissed Liv on each cheek. "It's lovely to meet you," kiss, "I'm Francesco Cipriani," kiss, kiss, "from Italy." Liv blushed, in shock from the cheek-kisses. Definitely not the way things work in the Midwest.

"Uh, hi. Olivia Phillips. But call me Liv. From Michigan. Ann Arbor. Near Detroit. You know—Motor City?" Liv laughed, and she could feel her cheeks turning redder. This was so weird. She *never* blushed. But for some reason, she had become a full-on dork in the past day, and kept saying the weirdest things. *Motor City? Where did that come from?* As Liv bumbled through her introduction, the taller guy kept looking at her, and finally stopped her rambling by cutting in to introduce himself.

"I'm Colin Johnstone. From merry old England. God save the queen, yeah?" He winked slyly at Liv. Was he making fun of her?

"I am in the mood for a gelato," Francesco declared

loudly in his sugary Italian accent. With a wave of his hand, he motioned across the square. "Join us?"

As they walked over to Häagen-Dazs—ice cream would have to satisfy Francesco's gelato craving—Liv couldn't stop casting glances at Colin, and thinking about her stomach's little loop de loop. Twice in one day she had fumbled through an introduction—Josh Cameron, and now this guy.

Blaming her dysfunctional social skills on jet lag, she decided to give it another try. She and Colin were walking a few steps behind Anna and Francesco, and Colin didn't seem to be much of a talker. Liv found silence unnerving, and often ended up babbling just to avoid it.

"So . . . where in England are you from?"

"Stratford-upon-Avon." Colin cast a sideways glance at Liv, grinning. "Shakespeare's birthplace."

"I guess that's a little more poetic than Motor City, huh?" Liv giggled. "I've always wanted to go to Stratford. I bet it's beautiful there. So much history. And I just love Shakespeare."

"Are you a tragedy or comedy girl?"

"Comedy. Definitely. They're so fun to watch. I've never actually seen Shakespeare live, just the BBC versions on TV. Hopefully I'll get a chance while I'm in London." Liv paused—was she coming across as a total loser, talking about the BBC and Shakespeare?

When Colin didn't say anything, she decided another question might help. "I guess you've probably seen a lot of theater, being from the Land of Shakespeare?"

Colin nodded. "I actually played Demetrius in *A Midsummer Night's Dream* at school. Twice."

"You're an actor?"

"No. Both times the play was awful. I'm not sure why I even bothered the second time." They both laughed, then more silence. Finally he continued, "There's a show playing now that looks really good. *Deception,* I think. It's a modern version of *King Lear.* Have you heard of it?" Liv shook her head. "If you're interested, maybe we could see if . . ."

Colin broke off midsentence as Anna grabbed Liv's arm and pointed at a billboard overhead. She had burst into a fit of laughter. Josh Cameron's soft brown eyes were twinkling down at them from overhead. As embarrassed as she was about The Incident from earlier in the day, Liv loved that Anna already felt comfortable enough with her to laugh at her dorkiness. The story *was* pretty funny.

Liv's face flushed as she was forced to share the details of her run-in with Josh Cameron once again. She shrugged casually at the end of the story, hoping Colin and Francesco wouldn't see how truly mortified she was.

As Liv followed the others inside Häagen-Dazs—Anna

was *still* giggling—she couldn't help but wonder what might have happened if she and Colin had finished their conversation. *Did he just almost ask me out?* Liv wondered, desperate to know what he had been *this* close to saying. Sighing, Liv realized the moment had passed.

Don't Worry, Be Happy

The next morning, Liv woke to find Rebecca staring at her from the kitchen. She was leaning against the edge of the counter, slicing a grapefruit. She greeted Liv with a chirpy "Good day, sunshine!" and an off-key rendition of the classic Beatles' song.

Liv murmured something rude under her breath and rolled over, checking the time. Seven on the dot. She briefly debated whether to give herself the additional fifteen minutes until her alarm was set to go off, but decided against it. Not a good day to risk it, especially since the time difference—and jet lag—was really messing with her sleep schedule.

Liv hustled past Rebecca toward the shower, eager to

get ready and get out of the apartment. She and Anna had avoided saying it out loud last night, but neither of them wanted to show up at their first day of work with Rebecca in tow.

An hour later Liv had squeezed herself into the slightly too small black skirt and light blue T-shirt Anna had lent her the night before. Her green sneakers would have to do—her feet had topped out at a massive size ten in ninth grade, so they were about twice the size of both Rebecca's and Anna's.

With an hour to spare before she had to be at the Music Mix offices, Liv peeked into Anna's room to see if she was ready to go. Anna, only half dressed, made a face and agreed to escort Rebecca to work. "Save yourself," Anna said quietly. "No need for both of us to be stuck with her. But you owe me."

Liv smiled gratefully at her roommate, grabbed her bag, and headed for the door. A coffee at one of the cafés around Oxford Street should make her feel like a real Working Girl. She closed the door behind her and skipped down the stairs.

When Liv arrived at Music Mix at ten to nine, Gloria was singing at the front desk. She greeted Liv with a little wave and a spin that made her frilly orange dress spin out around her.

"Good morning!" Liv waved back. She was in a great mood—it had been a fabulous morning. She had found a perfect little café just around the corner from the Music Mix offices, and had spent the past half hour relaxing at a quaint table by the window.

Gloria directed Liv to the orientation conference room, where Liv collected a folder with her name on it, then grabbed a free doughnut and cup of tea. As she paged through the folder and munched her doughnut, Liv took inventory of some of the other people entering the room. Some people were *too* cool, and skulked into the room without saying hello (the James Dean guy in leather pants and the snobby purple-haired girl in striped tights were immediately on Liv's "to avoid" list—they didn't even lift their eyes to acknowledge that anyone else was in the room).

Others nodded or smiled in her direction, and looked around uncomfortably. Liv later learned that the pretty Asian-American girl wearing six-inch platform boots just looked grumpy because her shoes were pinching.

Liv was the most impressed with the few people who came in and actually said something. Francesco was the most outgoing, bounding into the room like an electron and kissing everyone. Colin slid into the room behind him, shyly shooting Liv a cute little smile as he took a seat against the wall.

Just a few minutes before nine Anna showed up with Rebecca, who was decked out in an all-white pantsuit with a bright green tank under it. Liv had to admit that it was pretty hot, and definitely daring. Anna didn't look happy, but perked up when Liv pushed a doughnut her way.

Rebecca quickly introduced herself to everyone in the room, starting with James Dean, who was forced out of his one-man world to make eye contact. Rebecca seemed to have learned personal skills overnight, since she made her way deliberately around the room, dishing out compliments and witty little remarks to each person in turn. As she swept past Liv, Rebecca flashed her a gleaming smile. Confused, Liv just stared back.

A loud, raspy sigh from the doorway broke through the awkward small talk, and everyone turned to see who had entered the room. A shortish, thirtysomething guy with tan teeth and pants to match was staring around at the twenty-five people gathered in the conference room. He moved to the head of the table and began to speak.

"Brown. That is what you'll call me. Not Simon. Not Mr. Brown. Just Brown." *So this is Simon Brown,* Liv mused. *Interesting rule.* She wondered if he knew his tooth color matched his name. "I am the head of this program, and I expect that each of you is prepared to work as hard as I do. You have been given an opportunity that many would die for. Consider yourselves lucky to be here." *A bit over-dramatic, isn't he?* Liv thought. "Now. Inside the information folder each of you has received, you will find your summer project assignments. You're welcome."

There was a rustling as people sifted through their folders. Liv pulled a sheet of paper from the back of her folder that said "ASSIGNMENT: Olivia Phillips." Scanning it quickly, she spotted what she was looking for. Three little words that would shape the outcome of her summer: "Coordinator, *Hits Parade*."

Liv couldn't believe it. *Hits Parade* was *the* hottest show on TV. The most fabulous celebrities all swung by Music Mix Europe to promote their latest movies or albums, and the supersexy Andrew Stone played the day's biggest video hits. She read further:

**The *Hits Parade* Coordinator will
assist in the following:**
Audience Control *(Bouncer Liv. Nice.)*
Celebrity Attendance *(What does that mean?!)*
Booking Confirmations
Production Support, including
   time-management *(uh-oh)*
Segment Writing
Administrative Duties, as needed

"What's your assignment?" Anna was reading over Liv's shoulder. "*Hits Parade*?! That's so great! You are going to have so much fun."

Liv agreed. She had definitely gotten lucky. "How about you?"

"Wardrobe in the Features Department. Sounds good to me. I like clothes—" Anna was cut short by a squeal coming from the other side of the table. Rebecca was glowing, and flapping her paper around in the air. She had successfully turned all eyes toward her, and she took the attention as her cue to share.

"Events Team. First Assignment: Josh Cameron Concert! Oh, my dad is going to be so excited." Liv wanted to puke. The thought of listening to Rebecca gloat about the Josh Cameron concert for the next month was sickening. And the way Simon Brown was smiling at Rebecca as she flipped her hair and drawled on was infuriating and kinda gross. He seemed to be taken with her. For that matter, so did all the other guys in the room. Liv had to admit, Rebecca *was* pretty. But she was also so *weird*, and apparently bipolar.

"You. *Hits Parade* Coordinator." *Oh God,* Liv thought, *is Simon Brown talking to me?*

"Yes, Mr. . . . uh, I mean . . . yes, Brown?"

"You're the lucky one this year." Simon Brown huffed

out a wheezy laugh. "The *Hits Parade* coordinator has the profound good fortune of serving a unique duty. You'll be at the heart of the action." He paused for dramatic effect. "My assistant."

Was he serious? She was going to be his assistant? Things had just gone from best to worst. Anna grabbed Liv's hand under the table and squeezed. Liv managed a weak smile and muttered a tiny "thanks" before following her new boss out of the room to settle in at her summer desk.

"You. Here." Simon Brown was beckoning to Liv from the inner chamber of his office. She was finally getting settled in at her desk—just outside his door—and pretended she hadn't heard him.

Though she was positioned in a prime location near the *Hits Parade* studio, her "desk" was really just a small table jutting out into the hallway, en route to the coffee machine. She had to suck her belly up against the table edge every time someone needed to get past her. She felt like a toll-booth operator. Maybe she would start charging.

As Brown called out again—only slightly louder this time—Liv decided she really couldn't ignore him, though she couldn't imagine what on earth he needed, considering it was ten o'clock in the morning, she had just fetched him a coffee, and he had been snacking on doughnuts since nine.

He thought he had been sly about the doughnuts, but she had noticed. He was one of those people who took three of the best doughnuts before anyone else had a chance to take one. Inevitably, this meant that some poor, patient soul who had waited his or her turn would get stuck with the crusty, oozy leftover cherry-filled messes while people like Simon Brown gorged on the good stuff.

She slid out of her chair and approached his door. "Yes, Brown?"

"I need you to fetch the contract I just printed." He didn't look up. Liv stood in the door, trying to decide how to tell him that she had no idea where the printer was.

"Uh, Brown? . . ."

"GO, GIRL!"

Yowza. That guy could yell. *Okay, I'll be going now.* Liv smiled slightly and slid back out the door and into the hall. *Well, where to begin?*

Liv shuffled down the hall, gazing into each empty room. The Music Mix office was laid out in a weird, maze-like octagon. Every time Liv thought she had made a complete circle, and expected to see her tollbooth around the next bend, she was in a new wing altogether. She hadn't found a printer, but if anyone ever asked her for the inflatable gorilla costume, she now knew where to find it.

Turning the thirty-seventh corner (how did this building have so many hallways?!), Liv bumped into a familiar figure—Colin. His expression mirrored Liv's own panicked face. Looking at him, Liv couldn't help but laugh.

"What are you looking for?" she asked, realizing she probably wouldn't be able to help.

Colin held up his hands. "The watercooler. How big *is* this place?"

Liv pointed behind her. "I spotted a watercooler three turns back. Left, then right, then right again. You can't miss it." She giggled. *Am I flirting?* she wondered, noticing that her stomach was doing flip-flops and she had just *giggled*! "What department are you working with?"

Colin scratched his chin. "The Department of One: Andrew Stone. I think my production internship is really just a fancy way of saying 'personal assistant.'" Colin had barely looked at Liv as he spoke—he seemed focused on something just over her shoulder.

"Ooh . . . I'm the *Hits Parade* coordinator." Liv couldn't conceal her enthusiasm. *Yep, definitely flirting.* "We'll be working together!"

Colin shifted from foot to foot and gave her a thin smile.

He glanced quickly over Liv's shoulder again. "Right. I, uh, have to get going. See you later, yeah?" He breezed past her and turned the corner.

Did I just say something stupid? Liv wondered, watching Colin hustle off down the hall. Confused, she continued her quest for the printer. The next left led Liv into the round Music Mix front lobby. She stood in the center of the hundred television screens, confused and not sure how she'd gotten there.

"What's wrong, Olivia?" Gloria looked up from her desk. She looked genuinely concerned.

"Hey, Gloria. I'm looking for the printer. Mr., uh, I mean, Brown wanted me to fetch a contract for him. You can call me Liv, by the way. Everyone else does."

"Oh, Liv. I'm so sorry." What did that mean? Gloria's face morphed into a pitying smile. "Brown's printer is in his office. He does this every year. Some sort of power thing."

Liv groaned. "You're serious, aren't you?" Gloria nodded. "Great. That's just great. Thanks for the tip."

"No problem." Gloria shot Liv the same pitying look again. "Let me know if it gets too bad. I think I can help."

Okay, that wasn't exactly reassuring, but Liv appreciated the offer. "Thanks. Just one more thing—how do I get back to his office?" Gloria laughed, and pointed to one of the many doorways leading out of the lobby.

Back at Simon Brown's office, Liv knocked quietly at the door and made her way inside. He was sitting at his desk, feet up, tan teeth flashing an arrogant smile. She walked over to his desk and plucked five printed pages from the printer in plain view. As she handed them to him, he lifted a glazed doughnut in a salute and pointed to the door.

This could be a very long, very annoying summer.

9 to 5

Liv quickly came to realize that her idealized notion of what a Music Mix internship would be—days joking around with celebrities and nights spent at fabulous clubs and parties—was way off base. The reality was that her days were long, and she rarely got home before nine. A lot of the other interns had been going out after work, but Liv was stuck at her desk most nights until at least eight, finishing busywork for Brown.

Liv spent much of her first week doing meaningless errands: fetching Brown candies every thirty minutes, bringing him paper towels from the "loo," even being called in to press play on his CD player. She had almost no time to eat lunch, let alone mingle in the halls to get details on parties that—even if she did know about them—she would surely need to *sneak* into.

All the interns quickly learned that the Music Mix office was jam-packed with staff employees who thought they were the stars of the music industry, and who did everything in their power to keep interns from thinking too highly of themselves or getting invites to anything. Liv never failed to be impressed by the cool exterior these industry divas maintained. But eventually she realized that they were just as desperate to talk to celebrities as any of the interns were— they were just a little better at hiding it.

Liv's first (disappointing) brush with fame at work was meeting the supersexy Andrew Stone. He dropped by Simon Brown's office Tuesday morning, and on his way to the *Hits Parade* studio he swung through Liv's tollbooth for a cup of coffee. In person, Andrew Stone reminded Liv of a caricature of his TV persona. He was all winks and thumbs-up and smooth hair. Like a good TV star or slimy politician, he stopped to introduce himself and ask a few generic questions.

"Tell me, Olivia," he said, leaning toward her, all intense and faux interested, "what's *your* music style?" As Liv deliberated, Andrew Stone gazed past her with a polished smile on his face, mouthing "hiiii" to everyone who passed. Liv had to think quickly.

She couldn't really admit the truth to Mr. Pop himself,

could she? Would it be a faux pas to reveal that her music obsessions were mostly limited to seventies and eighties stars? She had grown up listening to old albums and light FM radio with her mom, and she couldn't help it—she was addicted. Of course, she had a few current faves (top of the list: Josh Cameron), but the real deal would be an opportunity to time warp and work at Music Mix in the days of ABBA or The Bangles.

She decided to risk it and go with the truth. It looked like he wasn't really listening anyway. "I really like Josh Cameron, but I'm also a big eighties junkie."

"Well, that's great, Olivia." Bingo. Not listening. "I'll see you on set later, yeah?" He pointed little finger guns at her and strutted toward the studio.

On her first afternoon of work Liv found out what one of her assignments—Audience Control for *Hits Parade*—meant. She was sent into the studio and told to "get things under control." Easier said than done. She opened the door to the small set and was greeted by fifty screaming fans. They had all been herded into a large roped-in area, and were jostling to get to the front of the fence.

As soon as she walked toward the ropes, people began shouting and gesturing at her. She heard it all—from the desperate and jealous "Hey you, how'd you get on that side of the rope?" to "Yo, sexy girl! Hook me up, yeah?" It was Liv's responsibility to quiet the screaming group and get them seated. The task gave Liv a good idea of what a shepherd would have to go through if his flock could talk.

Once she had them in their seats and had turned them over to the amateur stand-up comedian (who was brought on set each day to "get the peeps in the mood"), Liv had to hightail it back to the celebrity holding tank (aka Green Room), where she was responsible for the comfort of that day's guest star.

Initially Liv had been psyched about Star Control—she would get to meet and assist all of the celebrities who came by the set. Wrong-o. Turned out the real stars all have their own entourage, and Liv was left to deal with the overstressed and strung-out Personal Assistants To The Stars.

On Wednesday she had to deal with both Assistant One and Assistant Two to Kevin Landeau. Kevin insisted that there be two liters of completely flat, room temperature Sprite waiting in the Green Room (apparently he had had a rough night on Tuesday, and had already lost his lunch on a panicked and near-tears Assistant Two). That alone wouldn't be bad, but he had insisted that the flat Sprite be in sealed, unopened one-liter bottles.

Liv spent forty-five minutes working with Assistant One on the logistics of flattening the soda, then remelting the safety seal so Kevin could hear the *click* upon opening his Sprite. Liv celebrated her job-well-done later with a flat Sprite in a resealed bottle—Kevin had opted for orange juice instead.

One of the big perks of Liv's position—which was directly related to one of the worst aspects—was her responsibility to clean up after the celebrities and their entourages. Initially Liv had been horrified by the disaster the Music Mix guests left behind in the Green Room. But once she realized that the leftovers were fair game, she came to appreciate the full platters of food and snacks that were almost always sitting untouched in the midst of strewn trash, bottles, and cigarette butts.

Because she rarely had time to grab herself anything for lunch—thanks to Simon Brown's irritability around noon every day—Liv quickly found that the Green Room leftovers were a welcome treat. That first week of work, she pulled Anna out of the wardrobe department several afternoons so they could sneak into the Green Room to devour the tasty leftovers.

"Is it pitiful that we've resorted to eating someone else's trash?" Liv asked Anna as she bit into a forkful of mashed potato Wednesday afternoon. "It just feels wrong—and kinda depressing."

Anna shrugged, stabbing a piece of chicken from the barbecue platter that was laid out in front of them. "Maybe a little pitiful," she agreed. "But delicious."

"True." Liv buttered a piece of corn bread, relishing the taste of American food. She couldn't help but miss some of the comforts of home—she had never been much of a cook, and her internship didn't pay enough to eat out in London. "So, what do you think? We're halfway through the first week. Is Music Mix everything you thought it would be?" Liv and Anna hadn't gotten any time alone to talk since Monday—Rebecca was always within earshot—and Liv was eager to finish the conversation they had started in Leicester Square a few days before.

"Honestly, yes, it is," Anna said passionately. "Liv, this is exactly what I want to do. I mean, I always sort of knew that, but I didn't really want to give up everything to get a job here until I gave it a try. But now that I'm here, I don't ever want to leave."

"That's good, isn't it?" Liv asked, studying her roommate's reaction.

Anna flinched slightly before answering. "Yeah, it's great."

"Okay, roomie, that wasn't very convincing. Want to try that answer again?"

Anna leaned back into the brown leather couch. "I'm glad I know what I want to do. What I'm not happy about is how hard it is to get a job here. And I just don't think I can give everything up—college, scholarships, my mom's dreams—on the off chance that this might work out."

"Anna, your mom's dreams aren't the same as your dreams. What do you want?"

Anna released a deep sigh. "It's not that simple. My mom has done everything in her power to make sure I've gotten everything I wanted my whole life. Now, if I postpone college and pursue this dream, it would be like stabbing her in the back. She really wanted to be an actress when she was younger, but she gave everything up to make sure our family would be comfortable and happy. So I don't think it's fair for me to go all selfish now and say, 'Hey, thanks for everything, but I just don't care what you think or want.'" She broke off, winded. "Sorry, Liv, didn't mean to go off. . . . I'm just frustrated."

"That's okay. I wish I could do something. I feel totally useless." Liv couldn't imagine the pressure Anna was dealing with, and she didn't really know what to say.

"Can we change the subject?" Anna said, flustered. "I really hate talking about it."

"If that's what you want. But know that I'm here for you whenever."

"Thanks," Anna said, smiling. "But I'll be fine. Now, let's talk about something more pleasant."

"Okay . . . ," Liv said.

"I don't mean for that to sound rude—I guess I just need to figure out how to deal with this on my own."

"But you shouldn't have to deal with it on your own. That's what I'm here for." Liv grinned.

"Thanks, Liv." Anna rubbed her belly contentedly. "I should probably get back soon. I'm stuffed anyway."

Liv had completely forgotten about work. She had no idea how long she'd been gone from her desk, but suddenly realized Simon Brown was probably wondering where she was. He never actually wanted her around, but he liked to know she was available whenever he needed her. She usually tried to saunter past his office or cough loudly at least every thirty minutes—it seemed to comfort him. "Yeah, I should get back too. Thanks for lunch."

"No, thank you. Same time tomorrow?"

"It's a date."

That night Liv got home from work at nine, completely pooped and ready for bed. When she walked through the front door, she almost ran into Rebecca, who was sitting cross-legged in the middle of the living room, staring into a giant bright white screen. Liv, stuck somewhere between amused and mildly frightened, stood and stared.

Rebecca turned around and instructed with a sigh,

"Oh, Li-uhv, please stop staring. Haven't you seen a sun lamp before?" She went on to explain that the sun lamp had been shipped in by Rebecca's father to "prevent the saddies." Liv just shook her head and holed away in Anna's room until Rebecca announced that she was a "new woman." Liv took that as her cue that it was safe to return to the living room.

"Ah feel so much better," Rebecca purred to Liv as she floated down the hall to her bedroom. "It's so important that I stay sunny and rosy. You know, Li-uhv, Ah'm in charge of the Josh Cameron concert, and there are just so many people who are depending on me."

Liv mustered up a thin smile. *There it is,* she thought. Liv knew this wouldn't be the last time she would have to listen to Rebecca talking about her überimportant role organizing the Josh Cameron concert. They had only been at Music Mix two days, and already Rebecca had taken every opportunity to make sure everyone knew just how critical her internship assignment was.

Anna and Liv were forced to endure the worst of it, since they had to listen to Rebecca ramble on both at work and at home. But what made it worse was that Rebecca seemed to have mastered multiple personalities, and her sweet Texas Belle character from the office was usually replaced by a self-centered, somewhat evil Crazy at home. Anna and

Liv had realized their best coping strategy was just to keep their distance.

The unfortunate dilemma was that Rebecca loved to hear herself talk, and often sat in the living room waiting for her flatmates to come home so she could lock them in to one of her famous one-sided conversations. Liv had exhausted her patience for Rebecca's little "quirks" already, but Rebecca didn't seem to get the hint, and things at the apartment continued to spiral from bad to worse.

Exhausted, Liv arrived home from work on Thursday night only to find herself stuck outside the apartment door. When Anna finally heard her banging and came to let her in, Liv discovered that a huge treadmill had made its way into the living room. Liv didn't even bother to question how on earth this monolithic structure had found its way through the door—she knew it had something to do with Rebecca. The monstrosity was stuffed into the corner of the room next to Liv's couch-bed, and it was jutting out over the first seven inches of the front door, preventing it from opening.

Liv carefully approached Rebecca for an explanation, and was greeted with a frustrated sigh. "Oh, Li-uhv, haven't you noticed? The heels in Europe are just so much higher than they are in Texas." Liv stared back at her blankly. Another *don't-you-get-it?* sigh, and Rebecca continued her drawl. "Ah have to practice walking in my heels *somewhere*. You know, Li-uhv, you're welcome to use it. Ah'm sure you're eager to get yourself some pretty heels one of these days—those sneakers are so late nineties."

Ah, yes, Liv thought, once again pointedly ignoring Rebecca's insult. *This is a perfect explanation. She is going to practice walking in heels on a treadmill. Completely logical.*

Liv's bedroom was slowly being taken over by Rebecca's strange, creepy obsessions. And to top it off, a peculiar smell had started to invade the living room, and was getting worse by the day. But Liv didn't have time to figure out what the smell was, since she had finally gotten ahold of Millie Banks, the westie sweaters owner, who was so excited to get her "darlings" back that she was on her way over to Liv's apartment to make the suitcase swap.

Millie stayed for two hours, giving Liv a full background on the origin of the sweaters. Tired and weirded out, Liv finally got her to leave after handing over her Ann Arbor address so the woman could send Liv a personalized thank-you sweater for the suitcase's safe return.

By the end of her first week of work, Liv was completely worn out. She was frustrated from dealing with Rebecca, cranky from lack of sleep, and angry with her boss. Simon Brown had grown increasingly smug and arrogant throughout the week. He was constantly hurrying Liv out of his office with a harsh "Go, Girl!"

Friday morning Liv woke with a splitting headache and an attitude to match. Rolling out of bed twenty minutes before she had to leave for work, she kicked her leg straight into the treadmill. She released an enormous growl and limped to the bathroom with a huge scowl on her face. The scowl stuck through breakfast and the whole tube ride into work. When she stomped into the office at eight, Gloria looked up from her newspaper and whistled, "Whoa, girl, remind me to stay out of your way. . . ."

Liv stopped for her mandatory morning check-in at the boss's office, where she was greeted by a surly-looking Simon Brown. He pushed his coffee cup across the desk at her, and barked, "Go, Girl!" without looking up from his newspaper. Liv spotted the headline—CHRISTY BITES BACK!—and perked up slightly. Simon Brown only read the gossip pages when he was in a good mood.

Settling into her desk a few minutes later, Liv tried to throw herself into her work. She didn't even bother to look up when she felt someone shuffle to the coffee machine just before nine. She usually muttered a quick hello or chatted for a few minutes (Liv had gotten to know most of the other interns during their morning coffee runs), but that day she just flipped through the pile of nonsense Simon Brown had left on her desk to "deal with," and sucked in her belly to let the person pass.

A few minutes later the same person approached her desk from the other side, coffee in hand. Whoever it was was looking at her, lurking around the side of her chair. Annoyed, she squeezed in even closer to her desk. The person didn't pass. Clearly, whomever it was expected that Liv would move completely out of his or her way.

She had just about had it with Music Industry Divas; the übercool nobodies who worked at Music Mix all thought they were somebody, and treated interns the way they themselves were treated by real stars. It was a vicious cycle. With an enormous sigh, Liv stood up and violently pushed her chair back, shooting the lurker a look that could kill.

"Olivia." Gulp. The lurker was none other than Josh Cameron. "I thought that was you." Liv panicked. *He remembers me? Is that good or bad?*

"Oh. Hi. Um, sorry about that." Liv didn't quite know what she was apologizing for, but she babbled out something to mask her discomfort. What did one say to Josh Cameron? "So, uh, how are you?"

Josh Cameron laughed. "I'm doing well. It seems the

same can't be said for you." His eyes twinkled, brightening her mood. "Bad day?"

"Not anymore." No! Liv could not believe she had just said that. "I mean, you know, I'm not really a morning person." She smiled slightly. "But I guess you figured out the other day that I'm not really an afternoon person either. Sorry about the revolving door thing." *That's just perfect,* Liv thought. *Remind him about what an idiot you were on Monday. You wouldn't want him to forget.* "So, uh, what are you doing here?"

"I'm meeting Andrew Stone for breakfast."

Yum, Liv thought. *Breakfast of Champions.*

He smiled and continued, "I'm scheduled to play my new single on *Hits Parade* next week."

"Oh, that's great," Liv answered with a very uncharacteristic giggle. *Stop talking NOW!* "Well, I guess I'll see you then—I'm the *Hits Parade* intern this summer."

"I'll look forward to it," Josh Cameron said, smiling. "Are you just in London for the summer?"

Liv stared unblinkingly at him. *Is he actually interested in what I'm saying?* "Yeah, just the summer. Of course, they want me for longer—but I'm in huge demand, so I'm only willing to give them the summer." *What?!* Liv's eyes widened as her mouth spilled out more and more nonsense. *Are you trying to be funny?*

She smiled weakly, torn between wanting him to stay near her forever and wanting him to go so she couldn't humiliate herself any more. "Are you living in London now?" she asked, though she already knew the answer.

"Yeah, just for a while. I find it enchanting. You?"

"Mmm-hmm, enchanting," she repeated. "Sooooo . . ."

He looked down at his watch. A dark curl fell over his right eye. "I should get going."

"Right. Great. Have a good breakfast." Liv lifted her hand in a little salute. She realized she probably looked like a member of Dorks on Parade, and promptly returned her hand to her side.

Josh Cameron laughed, and his eyes lingered on her face for a few nerve-wracking seconds. She instinctively rolled her tongue over her teeth to check for stray food.

"Olivia, you intrigue me." Was he serious? Why was he looking at her like that? "Join me for a night out." He studied her face for a reaction. She stood silent, for once, dumbfounded. The day had just gotten a whole lot better.

"Yeah, sure. Anytime." Liv felt like her heart had pounded its way right out of her chest and was now thumping away on her desk.

"How's tonight? I'm meeting some friends at a fabulous little club. Come along—you'll have a great time." He scribbled out some details and glided off down the hall. As he turned the corner toward the studio, Liv broke into a celebratory dance. *What just happened?!?* Liv hustled off in search of Anna. This was an emergency.

Life in the Fast Lane

Flushed and sweating and starting to freak, Liv threw her hip against the door to her apartment for the third time and pushed. She was able to nudge it open a full ten inches, and quickly squeezed her arm and right leg through.

As her butt lodged itself into the tiny opening between the hall and the apartment, she was suddenly hit with unsympathetic images of Winnie the Pooh waving and giggling at her from where he was stuck in Rabbit's front door hole. With an unflattering squeeze and a grunt-thrust, Liv eventually wiggled through. Slamming the door shut, she cursed Rebecca and her monstrous treadmill, which was still blocking the front door. *I hate her fit, freakish, stilettoed self.*

Though Liv shouldn't have been surprised at what she found waiting for her in the living room (she realized that she would *never* understand Rebecca), the sight that greeted her was the last thing she ever would have imagined.

The smell that had been growing in the living room— her bedroom—for the past few days had hit an all-time bad. Liv finally understood why. Sitting in the middle of the living room floor, perched atop Liv's silver strappy shirt, was a teeny tiny not-a-dog-not-a-cat creature.

Brown and sort of see-through, the dog (yes, looking again, she could confirm that this odd little creature was definitely a dog) was shaking in its ratlike skin. Its tail, which Liv had to go all squinty-eyed to see, was formed into a curlicue next to its minuscule little butt, perfectly framing the itty-bitty poop that had landed smack-dab in the center of Liv's favorite shirt.

Liv and the dog stared at each other for a good ten seconds, and then Liv broke the standoff to look around the rest of the room. Her eyes scanned from chair to couch to treadmill, taking a quick inventory of the damage. Her pink scarf, her perfect-blue sweater, her backup jeans, her (*noooooooooooo!*) little black dress, her soft green jammie pants, and the silver strappy shirt—complete with curlicue poop—were strewn around the room.

Her suitcase was exactly where it had been that morning, safely zipped and tucked into the corner of the room under Rebecca's sun lamp. But in the corner of her suitcase, there was now an itsy-bitsy hole. This horrid little creature had clearly decided that a thinly chewed hole was the best way to extract the items in her suitcase one by one, just like a tissue box. Her favorite black skirt—which, along with her silver shirt, was on the roster for tonight's date—was half in the hole, half out, winking at her.

Heaving a huge sigh, Liv kicked off her shoes—briefly considering whether this was a safe move with Hell Dog in the living room—and flung herself on her bed-couch. Staring at the dog, which had been following her movements with its eyes, like one of those freaky Victorian paintings, Liv was startled by the clanging of the church bells outside the window. One, two, three, four, five, six, seven, eight . . .

OH NO! She had just an hour until she was supposed to be back on the tube to make it to her maybe-date-but-*not*-getting-any-hopes-up meeting with Josh Cameron, Superstar.

As she rifled through her suitcase for suitable underwear, Liv caught a whiff of something across the room that was almost more disturbing than her ruined silver shirt— Rebecca's Gucci eau de parfum. *She* was home. Looking up, Liv fixed Rebecca with her angriest stare. Liv suspected she looked more constipated than angry, but it was the best she could do.

"Oh, Li-uhv, A'm just so glad you're getting along with My Rover. Isn't he just the cutest thing you ever did see?" Liv could only imagine that Rebecca was referring to Liv's new best friend, Hell Dog, who was now curled into a brown dot on Liv's shirt. She had, naively, been under the impression that Rebecca was not yet home, as all of Liv's clothes were still strewn about the room as chew-toys. *Ah, yes,* Liv realized, *this is Rebecca. Is it really safe to assume she would do the normal thing and CLEAN UP?!*

"Rebecca . . ." Liv strained to keep her voice calm, hoping that if she played the part of normal, it would somehow inspire normalcy in Rebecca. "Is this your dog?" Stupid question, but somehow necessary given the circumstances.

"Ah just couldn't stand the thought of being without my perfect little pooch this summer, so I bought myself a new one. You know, they put dogs in a little holding cell for months when you fly them across the ocean? I wouldn't have gotten my puppy back until the end of the summer, so I figured it was just better to get a new one." Rebecca lowered her voice to a whisper and looked sideways at the freakish creature on Liv's shirt. "Isn't he just darling?"

It was official: Rebecca had just crossed yet another line

into Crazy. "When did you buy this thing, Rebecca? And where is it going to live?"

Rebecca's eyes frosted over, giving Liv the look that she had grown so accustomed to over the past week. "My Rover has been here since Tuesday. How on earth have you not noticed?" Rebecca sneered, and rambled on. "Ah've already potty trained him. We keep his little wee-wee pad over in the corner, next to the couch. He just piddles on there, and I replace it when he tells me it's time. Ah hope you don't mind." With that, she turned and swooped up the little see-through creature and strutted back to her room.

Was she serious? This creature would be here for the rest of the summer? Peeing in her room? *Well,* Liv thought, as she rooted around in her suitcase, *I guess that explains the smell.*

Glancing quickly at the clock, Liv decided she would have to deal with Rebecca when she got home. Now was not the time to get into a battle. She only had half an hour to find a new shirt and get herself out the door.

She pulled her black skirt the rest of the way out of her suitcase and assessed the damage. No harm done. Balling the skirt, a pink ruffly bra, and her underwear in her arm, she ran to the bathroom and flew through her shower.

Returning to the living room half-dressed, Liv was relieved to see Anna was home and sitting on the couch, looking just as confused as Liv had been a few minutes before. Anna looked at Liv's panicked face, and her eyes darted to the silver shirt still crumpled in the middle of the floor. "Don't ask," Liv blurted out, more harshly than she had intended. "I have to leave in five minutes to meet Josh Cameron and win him over with my charm and grace, and I now have nothing to wear. Help."

Anna stood up, gave Liv a quick hug, and leaned down to press play on the CD player. "Music therapy," she explained, as ABBA's "Dancing Queen" came pouring out of the tinny speakers.

"Dancing Queen" was undoubtedly Liv's favorite song. She sort of liked to think it was her theme song—she *loved* to dance, and loved that you could totally lose yourself on the dance floor. It was the one place where you could reinvent yourself, act goofy and just go with the music.

"Okay," Anna continued, as Liv danced around the living room. "What look are you going for? Sex kitten? Confident seductress? Naive nobody? All of the above?"

"Anna, you're European—just make me look like I fit in."

Anna thought for a second, then darted off to her bedroom closet while Liv shimmied around the living room singing, *"Dancing queen, young and sweet, only seventeen . . ."* Anna returned a few seconds later, holding a silky, shimmery, icy pink sleeveless shirt. "Try this on. It's perfect."

Liv grabbed the shirt and slipped it on over her pink bra. As it slid over her next-to-nothing breasts and down past her slender tummy, Liv could tell it was perfect. It clung in all the right places, revealing just enough that she looked sexy, yet left enough to the imagination that she looked demure and sophisticated.

Anna breathed out a sigh, and grabbed Liv's hands. The two of them spun around the living room, singing along to the last notes of "Dancing Queen." Just as the church bells outside chimed nine times, they collapsed onto the couch in a fit of laughter.

Liv scanned the crowd gathered near the fountain at Piccadilly Circus. As expected, no Josh Cameron. He had told her to meet him at Meat, some new nightclub in Soho.

Liv had secretly hoped that he would surprise her at the subway and escort her there, but she knew she was being totally unreasonable. He was busy and famous. And this was, after all, not a date. She headed across the street and followed the directions Anna had written for her back at the apartment as Liv had strapped herself into the World's Most Uncomfortable Shoes Ever.

Turning onto the club's street, she spotted a long line that snaked around a brown rope outside an unimpressive brick building. A small sign verified that she had arrived at Meat. Uncertain of what to do next, she mingled around the crowd, half in line, half out. There didn't seem to be any real rules or order, since the bouncers were just randomly picking people out of the crowd and ushering them in. Just when Liv's stomach had begun to curl at the idea of standing on the outside of the rope, smiling and flirting in the hope that she would be chosen to enter, a skinny guy in a suit approached her.

"Olivia." He stated her name so matterof-factly that she immediately nodded and smiled. "He's inside. He asked me to escort you up. Follow, please." Liv had no idea who this guy was, but just assumed that "he" was none other than Josh Cameron.

Liv followed as Skinny Guy made a tunnel through the waiting crowd and toward the door. He snapped twice, and a bouncer quickly pulled the rope aside to let them pass. Liv smiled at the bouncer. He narrowed his eyes and released what Liv could only assume was a growl.

Skinny Guy hustled through the low, narrow entrance to the club, while Liv struggled to stay upright on her shoes. She wondered if her feet were bleeding yet.

She looked around, trying to take everything in as she trailed behind the suited stranger into the main room of Meat. There were about thirty brown leather booths packed around the perimeter of the room, each one lit by a bare, plain white light bulb hanging from a cord extending all the way down from the superhigh ceilings.

The center of the club held a dark, crowded dance floor. Some sort of R&B music was being piped, quite literally, from pipes that extended out of each corner. A bar at the far end of the room was lit by flickering red lightbulbs. The club left Liv feeling creeped out, but she knew she would never admit that to anyone. This was, after all, one of London's hottest clubs, and the site of her first date with *Josh Cameron*.

She and Skinny Guy had made their way past the booths and were now standing in the back corner of the club, next to the bar. They were directly under one of the pipes, so when Skinny Guy turned to say something to Liv, all she could hear was "ung, uh uh snu." She just nodded her agreement (hoping he had asked something reasonable), and followed as he pulled a curtain aside, moved past a bear-size bouncer, and up an unlit staircase.

They emerged into a dim, thickly carpeted room that reminded Liv of her grandparents' small downstairs den. She suddenly wished she were there now, watching movies and giggling with her cousin Luke while their parents played cards and drank cheap wine at the folding table upstairs.

But she wasn't. She was in London. Standing in front of an L-shape couch packed with no less than fifteen people, all of whom were visibly drunk. Judging from the security guards positioned around the room, and the fact that two of the women on the couch had been on the cover of *Us Weekly* last month, Liv could only imagine she had entered some sort of VIP section at Meat.

Skinny Guy disappeared, and Liv suddenly felt very alone. She stood in the doorway for a few minutes, letting her eyes adjust to the low light. She could feel beautiful faces scanning her own, trying to determine why she was here, with them. Among the stars.

Just when she was about to turn and flee, realizing this must all have been a horrible, cruel joke, she spotted Josh Cameron walking through an archway toward her. She could feel the eyes on the couch watching as he breezed up to her and took her face in his hands, giving her a kiss on each cheek.

"You," Josh Cameron whispered in her ear, "look stunning. Thank you for joining me."

Blushing, Liv allowed him to take her hand. She squared her shoulders and followed as he led her through the archway and pushed aside another velvety curtain that masked a small hidden room. Apparently, this was the VIP section of the VIP section—Liv was overwhelmed.

Josh Cameron gave Liv's hand a quick tug, and he pulled her toward the other side of the curtain, behind him. As she passed through he let the curtain fall back into place, and it knocked heavily into the side of Liv's head. She grunted rather loudly and pushed it off, trying to act natural.

Tucking a stray curl behind her ear, Liv was relieved to see that Josh Cameron hadn't seemed to notice. His attention had turned away from her and on the people crowded into the long, low booth sprawled out in front of them. Liv quickly scanned the faces around the table—she recognized just about everyone, but had never imagined she'd ever be this close to any one of them.

Taking a breath, Liv managed to muster up a thin, nervous smile. Josh Cameron had moved away from her and slid into a corner of the booth, kissing a few people on the other side of the table as he passed. For a few awkward seconds Liv stood alone again. Her heart was racing, and her stomach was flipping up and down.

This was just too much. Not only was she out with Josh Cameron, but she was living in a picture from *People* magazine's Star Tracks section. Directly across from Liv, in the far corner of the booth, It Girl Christy Trimble was wobbily standing on the table in her stilettos, arms out to the sides, dancing with her eyes closed. Several jaw-droppingly gorgeous guys were holding her hands while she flipped her body in time to the music.

Liv noticed that the song currently piping out of the

wall was a dance remix of Josh Cameron's recent single, "Split." The song was amazing, and rumored to be inspired by his recent break from Christy Trimble's best enemy, Cherie Jacobson.

As Liv stood there, starstruck, Bethany Jameson—who was, quite possibly, the hottest starlet in Hollywood— nimbly hopped up on the end of the table and danced alongside Christy. Bethany's thong rested a comfy two inches above the ultralow waistline of her Joe jeans. The two women giggled and shimmied, clearly hamming it up for the benefit of the rest of the table. Both of their mouths were wide open, singing loudly and laughing. Josh Cameron looked delighted.

They finished their routine with a quick hug, and Bethany scooted off the table and onto the lap of one of the guys who had, only moments before, been holding Christy's hand. Christy leaned over to plant a quick kiss on Bethany's cheek (obviously there were no hurt feelings about the guy swap) before taking a long sip from her drink.

Josh Cameron motioned Liv toward him in the corner of the booth, and she adjusted her skirt as she slid in beside him. A few of the Star Tracks subjects glanced up briefly to greet her, then went back to their cigarettes and conversations.

"Drink?" Josh Cameron was pouring himself a short

glass of vodka from the center of the table, where a buffet of booze sat in icy buckets next to a platter of mixers.

"Oh, um . . ." Liv hadn't really had a lot of opportunity to drink in Michigan. In fact, she had had a total of one nasty incident involving some sort of licorice liqueur that left her facedown on the toilet seat. Her dad had not been impressed, and frankly, Liv hadn't been so impressed with the morning after.

So, she wondered, *is this the time to give it another whirl? With a table full of It Girls and Josh Cameron?* "Hmm, you know, I think I'll pass for now. I had kind of a weird dinner, and my stomach is a little iffy."

Liv realized her excuse sounded pretty lame—and, on second thought, kind of gross—but figured it was better than the alternative. She already had a visual in mind that involved Bear Bouncer dragging a passed-out Liv from the VIP section with her skirt wrapped around her armpits. *Cute.*

"Olivia, you are astoundingly charming. So All-American Girl." Josh Cameron's dimples deepened as he smiled at her. His eyes were deliciously green. Liv couldn't believe she was here, with him. And it *did* seem a little like a date. "Tell me all about *you*."

"Oh," Liv said, her tongue tied. "Well, what do you want to know?"

"Everything. I want to know what moves you." Josh stared into her eyes, his expression identical to the front of his last CD cover.

Liv was caught between laughing and crying. *Is he serious?* "Well, okay, um, I, ah, I'm from Michigan. Hmm, and uh, I live with my dad?" *Is that a question?! What's wrong with you, Liv? Say something remotely interesting.* "Oh! I know. My mom actually worked as a VJ at Music Mix in New York before I was born. That's something!" Though it was true, Liv wasn't sure why she had decided to mention that, of all things, to Josh Cameron. Although, her mom's music background did make her feel more worthy of sitting at this table, with all of these celebrities.

"I'm in awe, Olivia." Josh Cameron continued to stare at Liv with a poster boy sort of expression. "You are fascinating."

"Okay," Liv said, averting her eyes from his constant stare. "Well, thanks. But tell me about you! I guess I know a lot, but, well, I s'pose a lot of the stuff I read in magazines isn't really true." She laughed awkwardly, hoping to turn the topic of conversation away from herself.

Josh Cameron's eyes twinkled in the low light as he murmured, "It's all true. If you want it to be." Liv swallowed hard, wondering what, exactly, that meant.

In fact, Liv wasn't quite sure what she wanted to be

true. The Josh Cameron sitting next to her was a little intimidating . . . and rehearsed. She wasn't sure why, but she sort of felt like he was reading from a script. *But,* she reminded herself as he smiled at her again, *you're on a date—in a VIP room—with Josh Cameron! So who cares?*

Liv let herself melt into the booth while Josh Cameron entertained her with stories of his recent tour, gossip about other celebrities, and his plans for the fall. She couldn't believe the life he led. It seemed so fascinating. And as she sat there, he seemed more and more normal. She soon realized that when her mouth was zipped tightly shut, Liv felt a thousand times more comfortable with him.

So for the next several hours Liv let Josh chatter on and enjoyed the insider gossip. As they stood up to dance sometime long after midnight, crowded among the other celebrities, Liv just smiled silently as Josh Cameron leaned in to share the details of his last party at Chateau Marmont. His hands wrapped around her waist, talking all the while—he never even noticed that she hadn't uttered a word.

West End Girls

"Hang on ... Christy Trimble, Bethany Jameson, *and* C.J. Jackson were there? And you talked to all of them?" Anna stopped to pick up a strand of handmade beads, checking the price.

Liv had promised to spill all the juicy details of her previous night's date if Anna would spend the day wandering around Portobello Road, Notting Hill's outdoor shopping market, with her. Liv had only gotten as far as dishing the scoop on celebrity sightings from Meat, and already Anna was impressed.

"Yeah, they were all there. And it's weird, because Christy is actually really nice. You know how the tabloids say she gets in catfights with people all the time? Well, she was totally friendly to me."

Actually, Liv thought guiltily, *maybe that isn't exactly true.* In reality, most of the other people at Josh Cameron's table had been pretty self-absorbed and virtually ignored her. But Christy had kissed Liv on the cheek when she left and said how "absolutely stunning" Liv looked, which seemed totally unnecessary and had been a really sweet gesture for a stranger.

"Enough. Stop making me jealous with the guest list— get on to the good stuff." They had made their way to a scarf vendor, and Anna poked her head around a rack to find Liv modeling a purple tiger-striped fur.

"Well, dah-ling, it was simply mahvehlous. . . ." Liv strutted down the aisle with her huge fake fur. "Okay, so there I was, standing alone in the middle of this weird little room with half the models from Vogue staring at me. I seriously thought I was going to die. Thanks for the shirt, by the way. It was perfect."

"No problem. You looked hot. Go on. . . ."

As Liv spilled the details of her date to Anna, she relived each second in her head. She could still smell Josh Cameron's cologne, and she could feel his touch on her hand from when he had led her out of the club at the end of the night. He hadn't kissed her, but she sort of suspected he probably would have if Christy Trimble hadn't stumbled out of the club to throw up just as Liv's taxi pulled around the corner.

Liv smiled as she thought about how Josh Cameron had handed her taxi driver a twenty-pound note and opened the door for her, saying, "I'm so glad you could join me, Olivia. I hope you'll be willing to grace me with your presence again soon." *Okay,* Liv thought, grinning. *Maybe that line was a little cheesy. But it was really sweet.*

"Here's the thing," Liv said, watching Anna wrap a long silk skirt around her jeans and model it in the mirror. "The things he said were almost . . . lame . . . sometimes." She cringed. She didn't really want to ruin her memory of the night with a confession that Josh Cameron was less than perfect—but she couldn't withhold any details.

"Ooh," Anna said, lifting her eyebrows. "Do tell."

Liv quickly shared the "I hope you'll be willing to grace me with your presence again soon" line, as well as some of their other conversations. She gritted her teeth after being forced to say it aloud.

Anna burst out laughing. "Are you serious? He actually said that?"

Liv nodded. She had sort of been hoping Anna would say it was sweet and romantic. But who was she kidding? Liv could only hope Josh Cameron would be a lot less scripted if they went out again. After all, she reasoned, he did have to live up to a certain pop star image, and she wondered if maybe his lame, over-the-top lines were partly because he was in London? Maybe his publicist forced him to say junk like "lovely time" and "grace me with your presence." Maybe there was a book of etiquette that celebrities lived by that she just didn't know about?

"I guess the good news is, it sounds like I'll see him again sometime," Liv flashed Anna a quick, coy smile. She leaned down and picked up a fringed lampshade. As she did, she blurted out, "I just don't want to get my hopes up. Let's be realistic. This is Josh Cameron. Isn't it a lot more likely that he'll never call?"

"He'll call," Anna said confidently. "If he's feeding you lines like that, he's obviously trying to be a gentleman. And it sounds like you had an amazing time. Why *wouldn't* he call?"

"You're right." Liv nodded, though she definitely wasn't so sure. But it couldn't hurt to *hope*. Liv linked arms with Anna as they continued their path up Portobello Road. "So," she asked. "What did you do last night? I feel like I've been hogging the last hour with my story. Dish."

Anna began to speak, but was cut off as her cell phone started to ring. She answered, murmuring something in Swedish to whoever was on the other end of the line.

Liv didn't feel too guilty listening, since she couldn't understand anything anyway. All she could tell was that Anna definitely wasn't enjoying the conversation—whomever it was with. After a few more minutes Anna flipped her phone closed and exhaled.

"Who was that?" Liv asked nosily.

Anna look flustered. "My mom," she said simply.

"Everything okay?"

"Fine," Anna said, walking slightly ahead of Liv. Liv got the hint—Anna's mom had called several times since they'd arrived in London, and every time Anna had refused to talk about it. Liv knew something was going on, but it obviously wasn't any of her business. As usual, Anna quickly changed the subject. "To answer your question about last night—I did absolutely nothing. It was super-relaxing, since even Rebecca went out."

"She did?!" Liv couldn't hide her surprise. *Who would date Crazy?* "With who?"

"You're not going to believe this, but . . . Colin!"

Liv's stomach sank. "Are you serious?" she asked, hoping Anna was joking. There was still a little part of her that couldn't stop thinking about the sweet, kind, funny Colin she had met on her first day in London. She hadn't seen that guy resurface since that first evening in Leicester Square, but there was *something* about him that made her insides clench every time she saw him. But, she reasoned, if Colin was dating Rebecca, maybe she had gotten the wrong impression.

"Completely serious," Anna said. "I have no idea how it happened, but I guess they've been hanging out. I'm trying to get the dirt from Francesco, but he claims there's nothing going on."

This just didn't seem right. But maybe Rebecca was more normal around Colin than she was around her and Anna. She had mastered multiple personalities, so maybe there was a sweet, seductive side that Liv just hadn't witnessed yet. "Well, this should be interesting to watch, if nothing else."

Anna nodded. "Yes, indeed."

"Oh, Li-uhv, why are you so pushy?"

Rebecca was not taking Liv's anger about My Rover's behavior very well. In fact, she had interpreted Liv's request to move Hell Dog's wee-wee pad out of Liv's bedroom as a personal attack. Liv was still astonished that Rebecca hadn't yet apologized for the whole curlicue poop incident from the previous evening, but as Rebecca angrily yammered on, Liv realized that there would be no apology forthcoming.

"Sometimes, Olivia," Rebecca continued, "people need to *compromise.* You are living with three other people now—

me, My Rover, and Anna—so maybe you should stop being so concerned about you, and think about other people's feelings for once. *Ah mean*, how do you think My Rover feels about all of this?" Rebecca stopped chiding for one dramatic moment, then stormed on. "He's devastated, Liv. Just devastated. He's ashamed that his wee-wee pad is causing you problems. He's been curled up in his little blanky in the corner of the couch all afternoon, pouting. Doesn't that just break your heart?"

"Does *what* break my heart?" Liv blurted out, astounded. "The fact that your dog is currently curled up in *my* blanket on *my* bed? Yes, that does break my heart!" Liv took a deep breath and continued. "Rebecca, I am very sorry that your dog is devastated. But I think it's reasonable for me to ask that you find a nice, cozy place for his *potty mat* in *your* room. Sound good?" Liv crossed her fingers, hoping for a break.

"Oh, Li-uhv." Rebecca swept her see-through dog into her arms and sidled down the hall. "Ah pity you." With that, she delicately closed her bedroom door and left Liv alone in her living room.

Liv rolled her eyes and fell back on the couch. Clearly, logic and rational discussion weren't going to work. Liv leaned over the arm of the couch, gathered up Hell Dog's wee-wee pad, and strolled down the hall. She plunked the mat right in front of Rebecca's door and returned to the living room.

A few seconds later Anna poked her head out of her bedroom door. "Is it safe?" she mouthed, tiptoeing over to the couch. "Feel like going out tonight?" she whispered conspiratorially.

"Did you hear that conversation?" Liv grumbled. "I'd rather spend the evening at Simon Brown's flat than deal with another second of Little Miss Don't-Mess-with-Texas in there."

"Great!" Anna squealed, before quickly covering her mouth. "I just got off the phone with Francesco," she continued, whispering. "Apparently Colin got tickets to a show from Andrew Stone earlier this week. It's some hot new band that's playing at a club in Shoreditch. I've already laid out a shirt for you on my bed. Throw on your cute jeans, and let's get moving."

"You . . . and I. Were meant . . . to be. But you . . . took the low road, baby . . ."

This is absolutely awful. Liv quickly glanced around the club to see the reaction on other people's faces. Nodding heads and swaying hips surrounded her. *Apparently, I just don't get it.*

Liv had been feeling that way for the past two hours—

basically, since she and Anna had met up with Colin and Francesco outside Presence. Presence was a dimly lit, Asian-inspired club that reminded Liv of a China Buffet restaurant. Slightly tacky and oddly fragrant, it gave her the willies.

Anna had seemed completely at ease walking into the club, but Liv felt her stomach clenching much like it had when she'd arrived at Meat the night before. The scene was very much *not* Michigan. Tiki lamps dotted the walls, and people lounged on the floor around a battered stage.

As the foursome had moved farther into the club in their quest for a table, Liv's eye was drawn to an enormous fish tank decorating the center of the room. After looking more closely, Liv could see human faces peering back at her from *inside* the fish tank. She had stared at the faces until Colin leaned over and explained with a grin, "Men's room."

"Of course," Liv had responded, horrified. She found it disconcerting that everyone else was acting so normally. Were they oblivious to the fact that there was an enormous see-through *toilet* slicing through the center of the room?

Now, several hours later, Liv was stuffed between Anna and a large bearded man, listening to—quite possibly— the *worst* music she had ever heard. As Liv's eyes wandered around the club for *any*one else who shared her pain, she felt a hand brush her arm. Tensing, she turned. Colin was leaning forward, a smile teasing the corners of his mouth.

Liv felt her chest tighten as his mouth moved toward her ear. "This really is astoundingly awful, yeah?" His lilting English accent made the criticism sound almost dignified. Liv nodded, then started to laugh. "Shall we head out, then?" he asked. Giggling uncontrollably now, Liv nodded again. She grabbed Anna's arm while Colin pulled Francesco toward the door. Outside, Liv burst into laughter.

"What's so funny?" Anna asked. "Why did we leave?" Laughing, she continued, "Is it because of the song about pancakes?"

"Hmm, I sort of liked that one," Francesco mused, then chuckled. "I think the song that really got to me was the one about getting stuck in a scuba suit. It was very romantic, but also odd."

"Okay, so I wasn't the only one who didn't *get* that?" Liv asked, still laughing. "Colin, you got those tickets from Andrew Stone?"

Colin nodded. "I'm starting to think my boss may have been playing a joke on me. . . ."

"Hey, Liv." Anna was grinning in Liv's direction. "Maybe you should suggest a few of those lyrics to Josh Cameron. After last night I'm sure he would be happy to get your creative input."

Liv shot her roommate a faux-angry look. "Very funny,"

she said. Blushing, she quickly gave the group a shortened recap of her date while they walked toward a fish and chips shop for a late-night snack.

"So you are . . . dating Josh Cameron?" Francesco asked in his soft Italian accent. Though he was asking Liv the question, he looked at Colin as he waited for the answer.

Liv shrugged. "No. I don't think you could call it that. But I guess I'll see what happens." Francesco was still looking at Colin, and Liv sensed there was some weird unspoken thing going on, but she couldn't figure it out.

You hardly even know Colin, Liv thought, rationalizing the awkwardness. *He's obviously not interested—he's hanging out with Rebecca! Besides . . . Josh Cameron, Colin, Josh Cameron, Colin . . . Do you really have a choice if there's even a* chance *with Josh Cameron?*

Liv linked arms with Anna, still perplexed by the exchange she had just witnessed between Colin and Francesco. *Am I missing something?* she wondered. *Am I making a huge mistake?* She studied Colin's form strolling down the sidewalk in front of her. He stopped and turned, holding the door to the fish and chips shop open. As a smile spread across his face, Liv desperately tried to unravel the knot that had formed in her stomach. *Uh-oh,* she thought, recognizing the crush feeling all too well. *What am I going to do?*

I Will Survive

Simon Brown's feet rested comfortably atop his desk, his coffee cup empty next to them. He was trying to read the morning paper but was distracted by his empty mug.

Glancing at the door every few seconds, Brown briefly considered slipping his feet off the desk and back into the loafers sitting at his side. He was tempted to fetch himself a fresh coffee. But he was comfortable, and he enjoyed the fact that he had an excuse to be angry.

It was eight fifteen Monday morning, and Liv was running late.

As she hustled past the security guard and swept past Gloria in reception, she knew she was in for it. Simon Brown did not tolerate lateness, and his morning coffee was not a game. Liv knew she had effectively *"ruined his life"* by showing up fifteen minutes late.

After throwing her bag and umbrella in a heap at her tollbooth, Liv adjusted her skirt and cautiously approached his door.

"Good morning, Brown. Did you have a nice weekend?"

"I'm not sure if you're stupid or arrogant," Simon Brown mumbled, "but I believe we agreed that eight would be an appropriate starting time?" He didn't lift his head from his morning paper, but Liv could feel his beady little eyes narrowing.

"Now. You," he continued. "I will take a coffee, as usual, and ask if you might be so kind as to prepare the conference room for our Monday morning meeting. Will you need help, or do you think you'll be able to manage?" Brown tilted his face up and flashed a tan smile in Liv's direction. She suspected there wasn't a lot of love behind those pearly not-so-whites.

"Not a problem, Brown. Consider it done."

"I'll consider it done when I have a coffee in my hand. Please don't play games with me." As Liv made her way to the door, Brown continued. "Now, I assume you sent a meeting reminder memo out to all interns on Friday?" *Hello. Memo?!* "All interns will be in the conference room at ten?"

This was the first Liv had heard of either the Monday morning meeting or a memo. "Yes, sir—uh, Brown. We'll all be there! I'll be back with your coffee in a sec."

"Go, Girl!"

As Liv zipped through her tollbooth toward the coffee machine, she racked her brain for any memory of this meeting.

She couldn't come up with even a glimmer of what he was talking about. But last Friday had been a little scattered, considering the evening's "date" with Josh Cameron. As she pressed the brew button on the coffeepot, Liv formulated a plan. With Gloria's help, she should be able to catch most of the interns on their way in. A little help from her friends should guarantee word would get out to the rest. No worries.

"As I've already made clear, each of you is living a once-in-a-lifetime experience. I trust you have no complaints?" Brown scanned the meeting room, and looked pleased to see no heads shaking.

Amazingly, word about the meeting had spread in twenty minutes flat. Liv had filled Gloria in on the situation, and Gloria had immediately kicked into action. Apparently, the "forgotten memo" trick was a regular in Simon Brown's book of intern gags. Gloria had a plan to counteract this and several other Brown crises. Liv was grateful to have Gloria's help—she imagined the receptionist could get pretty feisty, and she wouldn't want to be on her bad side.

After pausing to ensure all twenty-five interns were focused on him, Brown continued his pep talk. "You may not believe it, but this summer will soon be even more remarkable for one or several of you." Brown's mouth curved into an uncomfortable smile. "This year, each of you will have the opportunity to participate in Music Mix's VJ for a Day contest. With the cooperation of our very own Andrew Stone, we have arranged an audition date later this summer. This will be your opportunity to show us if you have what it takes to be on-air talent, or if you can effectively work behind the scenes on one of the production teams.

"Perhaps . . . ," he continued, "if you really blow us away, there may be a job offer for one of you at the end." Brown puckered his lips and smugly sat down.

Andrew Stone, who had been slouched seductively in the corner, stood up and cleared his throat. "Right. Are you ready?" He paused. Liv was temped to pump her arm in the air and shout out, "Yea-uh!" but figured it wasn't a good bet.

"The auditions will be held in August, and the winning team's segment will go on the air that same day. We'll include it as part of the *Hits Parade* lineup." Andrew Stone was beaming. "I'm sure you've all watched my stuff, so you know the deal. Your role, as VJ, will be to hold the audience's attention throughout the video countdown, and keep them coming back for more. Obviously, I've mastered it—feel free to look at some of my earlier work for examples of great novice VJing. You can do a skit, a game—hey, you can strip if you like—just come up with the best gimmick, and prove that you've got what it takes to be on the Music Mix VJ team. Someone in this room will be a Music Mix VJ for a Day. Excited?"

Liv glanced around the room. This was crazy. One of these people could possibly *be* a Music Mix VJ? Now this—*this*—was exactly what she had been hoping this internship would be. She wanted to do *real* TV work—not just Simon Brown's grunt work.

Everyone was grinning ear to ear, and chattering nervously with the people next to them.

Simon Brown quickly wrapped up the meeting and sent all the interns back to their departments. As Liv headed off to her tollbooth, Anna caught up with her.

"Liv, we are going to rock at this. Team?"

"Of course!" Liv grinned. "What are we going to do? I'm up for anything except getting naked—that's going a little far, even for me." Anna laughed as Liv quietly mocked Andrew Stone's stripping suggestion.

"Liv, I think this might be my chance," Anna said seriously as they moved away from the conference room.

"You think if we won the audition, you could get a job offer?" Liv inquired. She wasn't so sure—Brown didn't seem like the type of guy to make things so simple.

"I know he said it was only a possibility, but I just have a feeling. We *have* to win this competition. You're in, right?" Anna looked so desperate.

"Absolutely." Liv gave her roommate a quick, reassuring hug—she knew how much Anna wanted this. "We *will* get you a job."

As Liv and Anna wandered back through the halls, they could hear Rebecca's distinctive voice behind them. Liv stopped and glanced over her shoulder. Rebecca was walking with Colin and discussing the competition. From the sound of it, Rebecca was pretty sure she would win. And she seemed to think it would boost her chances if she told everyone how much she wanted it.

"We *must* work together on this, don't you think?" Rebecca purred to Colin. "Of course, I have to focus on the Josh Cameron concert first—Joshie is so sweet, so I just want to make sure everything's perfect—but after the concert we'll focus every ounce of our energy on this. What do you say, Colin?" Rebecca giggled, casting Liv a sidelong glance as she linked arms with Colin and slid past Liv and Anna down the hall.

Colin murmured something quietly in response, and Liv felt a little like throwing up. Though Liv had begun to get used to the idea of them dating—Rebecca and Colin had spent all day Sunday together, and Rebecca had made sure Liv and Anna were informed about *all* the details—Liv felt queasy seeing them together. She couldn't shake the feeling that had swept over her when her eyes had met Colin's on Saturday—but obviously, she was the only one who had felt something. So she was doing everything she could to forget it.

"Jemma *always* meets and greets one fan at appearances. It's the way she keeps it real." Jemma Khan's personal assistant, Sam, was standing at the door of the *Hits Parade* studio. Liv was inside the studio, arranging ropes and chairs for that afternoon's show.

Sam had been trailing Liv most of the day, announcing things at random. Liv knew Sam wanted her to do something with each of these announcements, but she was never quite sure what. She had found that if she waited a second, Sam would usually expand. This time was no exception.

"Soooo," Sam said slowly, "can you find a fan for Jemma to spend a few minutes with? You know, to keep it real with . . ." Liv smirked. Sam had delivered that line with complete sincerity. She had clearly been well trained.

"No problem, Sam." Liv pulled the velvet rope taut in front of the audience seats. She had to make sure it was clear that the rope was a barrier—yesterday she had come into the studio just before taping to find a girl sitting in the center of the *Hits Parade* stage. Liv had to literally drag the girl back into the fan section, where she spent the rest of the show sulking and shouting out obscenities. Eventually the girl was removed from the set, but not before grabbing a nice, thick chunk of Liv's hair. The audience control portion of Liv's job was truly a delight.

"Liv, you're the best," Sam gushed, relieved she didn't have to mingle with the "regular people" to find her boss a token fan. "Please make sure you don't find a Crazy. Or it's my butt on the line—you know how it is."

"Yes, Sam," Liv sighed. "I know how it is."

And she did.

Liv had spent much of the past week getting to know the *Hits Parade* fans. She studied them, trying to figure out how *not* to act in a celeb-dense situation. The *Hits Parade* audience was a captivating combination of several types of fans—Criers, Desperate Wannabes, Psycho Stalkers— many of whom fell into the "Crazy" category. But she knew who Sam was looking for—a Regular Fan.

Regular Fans were the non-Crazy folk. Regular Fans usually consisted of tourists, preteens, and groups of girl-friends. They were psyched to be on set, and respected the rules of the game.

The Criers could almost be considered Regular Fans, but not quite. They were the people who got teary-eyed and panicky when they could sense that a star was near. The Criers didn't need to *see* the star—it was enough to know the star was close. The thrill of being in or near the Music Mix building could even send them over the edge. Most days Liv found a Crier in meltdown mode just outside the studio. They were unable to go any farther, suddenly over-come by the possibility of a brush with fame.

The Desperate Wannabes, on the other hand, terrified Liv. Desperate Wannabes dressed and acted like stars, and embodied a presence that shouted, *I'm Somebody!* They went to abnormal lengths to get into the studio, because they felt they *deserved* to be there. And they wouldn't take no for an answer. Every moment in the audience was an opportunity to be "discovered," and Liv would *not* be the one to take that away from them. Liv had seen one Desperate Wannabe actually brush off a C-list reality TV star because the reality star was "beneath" her. The star's ego was severely damaged, and Liv had to do some major pampering to prevent a diva moment.

The real Crazies were the classic nut job fans—the Psycho Stalkers. On Tuesday one Psycho Stalker had found his way into a performer's dressing room and rested nonchalantly on the couch. When the star had returned from rehearsal, the Psycho Stalker was sitting there, sipping a Perrier, and chatting with the star's dog. He greeted the star with a chirpy "g'day," then continued his conversation with the dog. Needless to say, security had him removed from the area.

In addition to audience control, Liv had spent her week attending to various errands for Personal Assistants to the Stars, like Sam. Most of the errands, she guessed, were tasks being shirked by said Personal Assistants so they could grab a cigarette, a coffee, and a break. Liv's job description had listed "celebrity attendance" and "booking confirmations" as her responsibilities; she was pretty sure that didn't mean "dog walker" or "stain remover." However, she was quickly realizing that *Hits Parade* coordinator made her the go-to girl whenever a dog "piddled" on the Green Room carpet or a cup of organic chai spilled on a cashmere tank.

The only thing getting Liv through the workweek was the fact that Josh Cameron was scheduled to perform on *Hits Parade* on Friday, and he had been around the studio all week rehearsing. She hadn't seen or talked to him since their maybe-date the weekend before, but she had spotted him from afar, chatting with Andrew Stone or rehearsing in the *Hits Parade* studio. She was dying to know if Josh Cameron had been genuine when he told her he wanted to see her again.

As she passed the studio one day, casually peeking to see if Josh Cameron was around, Liv spotted Colin and Andrew Stone in a conversation. She paused, waving to Colin through the window. He looked up, ignored her, and turned in the other direction. Andrew Stone glanced over his shoulder to see who was at the window, and—without the slightest hesitation or acknowledgment—returned to his conversation with Colin. Feeling like a total nuisance, Liv hustled down the hall and back to her tollbooth.

Liv wanted to believe she was imagining it, but almost every time she had seen Colin in the office that week, he had quickly turned and gone in the other direction. She wasn't sure what she had done to offend him, but she got the impression that he was avoiding her. Between Colin and Josh Cameron, Liv was starting to wonder if she was invisible.

One afternoon she ran into Colin at Tully's, the coffee shop around the corner from the office, and lingered long enough so they could take the short walk back to Music Mix together. He stayed mostly silent as they made their way up the escalator, and as soon as they passed Gloria's desk he quickly hustled off, casting glances over his shoulder and generally acting weird. *Rebecca must be getting to him,* Liv thought, smiling.

When Friday, the day of Josh Cameron's *Hits Parade* session, finally dawned, Liv's nerves were out of control. She was frustrated that she hadn't talked to him all week, but she knew he was busy promoting his single. There were a million good explanations. So, positive attitude in hand, Liv dressed herself in her Friday best and glided off to work, hopeful that today would be the day.

She arrived at her tollbooth a few minutes before eight and found a note from Simon Brown that read:

2 Sheepskin throws
14 Red Bulls (NOT 13)
Stuffed pig

After rereading the note a few times, Liv finally gave up and walked to the lobby to find Gloria. Gloria was sitting at her desk, twisting one long dreadlock around her finger while she sang along to "Split."

"Hey, girl. What'd he do this time?"

Liv passed the note across Gloria's desk. "I need you to help me translate. Any idea what this means?"

Gloria glanced at the note, and then passed it back. "Josh Cameron is on *Hits Parade* today?"

"Yeah," Liv responded. "Why?"

"That's his usual request. Brown must want you to get the Green Room ready. You can get the sheepskin throws from Andrew Stone and buy the Red Bull at the market on the corner." Gloria paused, then reached under her desk. "And here"—she triumphantly held up a worn purple pig—"is your stuffed pig." She smiled. "Good?"

Liv just nodded. "Thanks. Again." This was too weird. Why did Gloria have a stuffed purple pig under her desk? And more important, how scary was it that Josh Cameron wanted a stuffed pig waiting for him in the Green Room when he arrived?

Liv spent the rest of the morning preparing the Green Room and getting the studio ready for that afternoon's audience. Her stomach did a little backflip each time the door to the Green Room opened or someone entered the *Hits Parade* studio—she was constantly on pins and needles waiting for Josh Cameron to arrive.

Finally, around one, Josh Cameron breezed into the studio. A small entourage of PR people, personal assistants, and a crew from the *Star* accompanied him. He glanced in Liv's direction, and then instructed one of his assistants to clear the room so he could rehearse in private. Liv and several other interns were shooed out of the way as Josh Cameron began singing his scales.

Around two, just before *Hits Parade* went on air, Liv was summoned to the Green Room. *This is it,* she thought. She was bummed that Josh Cameron hadn't said hello earlier, but she figured things had been hectic. *Whatever,* she thought. *Now is better than never.*

When she knocked at the door a few minutes later, Skinny Guy (her buddy from Meat) greeted her. He was wearing a suit again.

She could see Josh Cameron in the background, strumming his guitar on the couch. He briefly looked up, gazing through Liv with a blank expression. She smiled in his direction, but Skinny Guy moved slightly to block her view.

"Yes," Skinny Guy began. "He will need Gummi Bears and a toothbrush. That will be all."

Liv stared for a moment. *Is this for real?* The look on Skinny Guy's face suggested that yes, this was for real— and that she had better hop to it. Liv nodded, casting a quick glance over Skinny Guy's shoulder, then turned to leave. She headed out onto Oxford Street in search of Gummi Bears.

Forty-five minutes later, Liv sat at her tollbooth, weary and disappointed. She had delivered the requested items to the Green Room and received nothing more than a short thanks from Skinny Guy. No "hello, nice to see you, have a good one," nothing. She was near tears and incredibly embarrassed.

She didn't know what she had expected. Did she want Josh Cameron to embrace her and sing to her, announcing their love to the *Hits Parade* audience? *Um, no. Creepy.* But she had expected a glimmer of recognition from him. At the very least, he could have said hello. She was humiliated that she had apparently read too much into their date. She should have realized how stupid she was being—really, did she think that she and an international superstar would start dating? Seriously, why would he waste his time with a nobody from Michigan?

Liv was pulled from her depression by Simon Brown's loud bark. "You. Here." She dutifully made her way to his open door.

"Yes, Brown?" She could barely muster up the energy to be polite.

"I need my sweater." *Details? No? Okay . . .* "Go, Girl!"

Liv trudged off in search of Brown's sweater. She hadn't the faintest idea where he could have left it, but he rarely dragged his lazy butt farther than the *Hits Parade* studio or the Green Room, so she figured she might as well start there. As Liv passed the studio, she could hear the rumblings of the crowd. Checking her watch, Liv noticed that there were still a few more minutes left in the show—she would have to come back. Postshow crowd was the *last* thing she could deal with today.

She turned right and moved toward the Green Room. As she approached the door, she could hear a few faint guitar chords coming from inside. Knocking softly, Liv pushed the door open.

Josh Cameron was alone, sitting on the couch and strumming his guitar, looking more fabulous than ever. One dark curl brushed his cheek. He looked up and smiled. "Olivia."

Liv braced herself. So he did remember her. What was *with* him? "Hi. Um, great show." *Great show? He ignored you all day, made you feel like a complete idiot, and sent you off on errands to fetch little treats. And all you can say is "great show"?*

"Olivia, I need to apologize. I haven't been myself today. I'm afraid I've given you the wrong impression." He laid his guitar on the couch and stood up to approach her. He leaned forward to kiss her on the cheek. As he did, Liv could smell the cologne that had haunted her all week. *Mmmm. Yummy.* "Have you had a good week?"

"Me? Oh, um, yeah. Sure. It's been . . . well, it's been okay. A little strange, maybe, but you know . . ." Liv trailed off. There she went again. Blah, blah, blah. "So . . ."

"Olivia, I feel terribly about how I've treated you today. I'm afraid you must hate me."

This guy is good, Liv thought, smiling. "Not at all. Don't worry about it. I know you're busy and distracted."

"That's not an excuse. But you understand, don't you?" Josh Cameron smiled, exposing his dimples. "I've been looking forward to seeing you all week. I hope you know that."

Liv swallowed. Hard. She did not know that. "I've been looking forward to seeing you too. I had a great time on Friday. Thanks again for inviting me. And don't worry about today. Really. I understand." *Shhhh, Liv,* she begged herself. *Stop now.*

"Listen, let me make it up to you. Are you free tonight?" Liv nodded. She was now. "Would you join me for dinner?" Liv nodded again.

Just then she spotted Simon Brown's sweater sitting atop the chair in the corner. *Thank you, Simon Brown,* she thought, grinning. *One of your meaningless errands has finally been worth it.*

Wake Me Up
Before You Go-Go

Please don't let this be happening to me.

Please don't let this be happening to me.

Please don't let this be happening to me.

Like a mantra, Liv repeated her internal plea again and again. She stared at the unforgiving bathroom door, studying its blank façade. She pressed her nose up against the opaque glass door and tried to get a view into the exterior of the hotel room.

There had to be an emergency door handle somewhere. *Come on . . . where is it?!*

Pushing gently against the muddy glass, Liv studied her wiggly reflection in the door. She suddenly pictured herself dying a slow, miserable death, alone in Josh

Cameron's hotel bathroom. She could see the *Sun* head-line: STRANGE GIRL DIES HORRIBLE, SQUISH-FACED DEATH IN AN ATTEMPT TO WOO JOSH CAMERON. Liv peeled her face off the door's glass. Smushing her face against the door was not helping matters.

"Abracadabra!"

"Open Sesame!"

"Supercalifragilisticexpialidocious!" *Oops. That's something else.*

Trying to think of few more magic words, Liv slouched against the wall and stared at the indigo toilet taunting her from the opposite wall in the dark red bathroom.

When Liv had turned up for her date with Josh Cameron that evening, things had seemed so promising. The plan was to have a quiet dinner in his hotel suite. Apparently, Josh Cameron was fed up with the paparazzi and had been trying to lay low. That was fine and dandy with Liv—she was more than happy to check out a superstar suite at the Ñ Hotel.

The Ñ was famous for its übercool, sparse rooms and state-of-the-art technology. Retinal scanners instead of keys. Voice-activated elevators. Automated dumbwaiters that dispatch room service orders through little tunnels in the walls ("Like a drive-up ATM!" Liv had lamely pro-claimed when their champagne had arrived).

And touch-free bathroom fixtures, which were, Liv now realized, *not* a good thing.

When she had arrived, Josh Cameron had greeted her at the door and ushered her into his suite. He had produced a bottle of champagne from the room service receiving berth, and poured deep glasses for each of them. The bubbly champagne shot straight to Liv's head, combining with nerves to make her dizzy and flustered.

After a few minutes of awkward conversation about his suite (during which, Liv recalled with a twinge of discomfort, Josh Cameron had smiled smugly at each of Liv's gushing remarks and nodded, saying, "I know, I know," over and over again), Liv had excused herself to the bathroom.

Which is where she remained, ten minutes later.

Near tears, she decided to give it one more go. She could only imagine what Josh Cameron was thinking, waiting for her out in the suite. Really, what could a person do for ten full minutes in the bathroom? It was not a pretty thought.

Liv stood up and moved toward the door again. Its smooth, glassy surface was unmarred by a handle. She studied the walls around the door for the umpteenth time, looking for any opening device. She ran her hand along the tiles, stopping when she felt one tile tilt slightly. It looked just like the rest of the bathroom's dark red tiles. Hopeful,

Liv gave it a hesitant poke. The door swooshed open, revealing the interior of Josh Cameron's hotel suite. Liv released the breath she had been holding and stepped out of her bathroom prison.

"Well, hello there." Josh Cameron swept across the room toward Liv, holding her champagne flute in his hand. "Everything all right?" He tilted his head and smiled.

Liv took a deep slurp of her drink and felt her face blush a bright crimson. Whether it was from embarrassment or the champagne, she didn't know. "I'm amazing," she said, feigning a seductive purr. As her voice garbled out, she realized she sounded pretty stupid, and decided not to experiment with seduction again.

"I'm going to guess," Josh Cameron said, lifting his glass in a toast, "that you had some problems with the door. Am I right?" Liv nodded sheepishly. "Not to worry," he continued. "It took me a while to find my way around in here. The first time I ordered room service, I waited for two hours not realizing my order had been cooling in the wall panel the whole time."

Liv laughed, and—unsure of what to say—drained her glass.

"Tell me, Olivia," Josh Cameron said, filling her glass with more bubbly trouble. "What is it that makes you so incredible?"

"Well," she began, her confidence bolstered by her glass and a half of champagne. "Perhaps it's my understated grace and elegance?"

Josh Cameron's dimples deepened. "Let's see . . ." He took Liv's arm and led her to a chaise in the corner of his suite's living room. "I don't think it's that. But you are exceedingly charming."

For obvious reasons, Liv cracked up. *Charming?* Liv's champagne was dancing around inside her head now, causing her words to spill out a few seconds before she had a chance to consider them. "What *do* you see in me? Seriously? I mean, I've done nothing but humiliate myself every time I've seen you, and yet you insist on calling me 'charming.'"

Josh Cameron laughed. "It's just *that*, Olivia. I admire your incredible ability to say everything that crosses your mind. It's refreshing to meet a real girl." He took her hand and leaned in close. "You're different."

Liv sucked in her breath. "I see." Her hand was resting lightly in Josh Cameron's palm, sweating. She regretted not swiping Lady Speed Stick across every exposed surface of her body. *Is he holding my hand? Is this real?*

As Josh Cameron stroked the top of Liv's hand with his thumb, she relaxed into the chaise. "Can I ask you something?" she asked, smiling slowly.

"Anything."

"Why did you ask for a stuffed pig at Music Mix?" Liv giggled.

Josh Cameron leaned in closer. She could feel his breath on her cheek as his lips moved toward her ear. "Because," he said with a smile, "it's always fun to see how far people will go to make me happy."

Liv giggled again. In her slightly drunk state, his answer made her laugh. "So the purple pig was what, like a challenge or something?"

"I guess you could say that. Now, Olivia," Josh Cameron pulled away from her and smiled. "I just heard our dinner arrive. Shall we?"

"Let's," she said with a nod. She was starting to feel sleepy, and was suddenly nervous that if she didn't get some food in her stomach, she could be curled up in the corner passed out in a matter of minutes. Or worse, she would be forced to use the bathroom again. And Liv definitely didn't want to get trapped in there a second time.

Josh Cameron led her to the table that had been set for them in the corner of the suite. Liv studied the table, counting no fewer than seven forks and four plates in front of each of their seats. *I guess I should have watched* Pretty Woman *more carefully—the fork lesson would have come in handy.*

"A toast." Josh Cameron was standing at Liv's side, one hand resting on her shoulder, the other holding his glass toward her. "I feel so lucky to have met you. To what's next," he finished, squeezing her shoulder.

Liv lifted her glass to her lips, but carefully monitored her intake. "To what's next," she repeated, groaning inwardly at his lame line. "Josh, do you always use canned lines like that?" Liv's left hand flew to her mouth to cover up what she had already said.

Josh Cameron spluttered champagne as he pulled his glass quickly away from his mouth. "Canned lines?"

"I'm sorry. I shouldn't have said that."

"No, please, explain. I'm intrigued."

"It's just that, well, uh," Liv had dug herself into a big fat hole, and now she wished she could slide a door right over the top of it and never come back out. "When you say things like 'I feel so lucky to have met you' and 'To what's next,' it's maybe just a little, uh, cheesy?"

To Liv's relief, Josh Cameron started laughing. His dimples were deeper than she had ever seen them, and his eyes had started to tear up. *This* was not the response she had been expecting. "Olivia, that's priceless," he stammered, gasping for breath. "No one has ever said anything like that to me before."

"I'm really sorry. I shouldn't have said it. Your toast was very sweet." She couldn't believe she had just criticized Josh Cameron. *What is* wrong *with you, Liv?*

"No, please, don't be sorry. It's nice to hear the truth. Frankly, I get tired of the nonstop adoration from fans. Don't get me wrong, it's flattering to have people love you, but it's also nice to be brought back to earth from time to time." He smiled at her. "My apologies for the cheesy line. Mind if I try again?"

Liv shook her head, smiling meekly. She couldn't believe he wasn't furious she had just criticized him. This was too weird.

"To you, Olivia," Josh Cameron said, smiling widely. "The most refreshingly honest woman I have ever met."

Cheers to that, Liv thought, tipping her glass back. *Cheers to that.*

Yawning contentedly, Liv stretched her leg and wiggled her toes. She rolled over, eyes closed, and replayed the previous evening over and over in her head.

Things had gone a little fuzzy in the middle of dinner, but Liv could still remember most of her amazing night. She couldn't believe how incredibly sweet and sexy Josh Cameron was. After Liv had teased him for being cheesy, things had gotten much easier between them.

Liv thought back to the rest of their dinner conversation, and still couldn't believe that Josh Cameron, International Pop Star had opened up to her. "The thing is, sometimes you just want to be *normal*, you know?" he had said at one point during their meal. "That's why I appreciate your honesty so much, Olivia. You're not worried about what I'll think—you just say it like it is." He had smiled at her. "There's something unique about you—and I don't want that to sound like a line." Liv flushed as she remembered the way his eyes had lingered on hers.

Her memory of the rest of their meal was a bit of a blur, but she clearly remembered their dessert (some sort of gooey chocolate volcano) out on the balcony. The fresh air had revived her.

Liv had swaggered onto the balcony and moved to one of the glass walls to steady herself. She remembered leaning against the wall for support, and then strong hands circling around her waist like a safety net.

"Olivia," Josh Cameron had sighed, moving toward her. "I've had an amazing evening." His right hand had tightened around her waist as his left pushed a stray curl from her face. Liv congratulated herself on doing a quick tongue-check for food lodged between her teeth. She hadn't *expected* him to kiss her, but she wanted to be ready, just in case.

She could still feel the moment his lips first touched hers. Gently, cautiously at first, then expertly pressing into her more urgently. He delicately let his hand run through the length of her hair, then wrapped his soft hand around the back of her neck. He leaned back slightly to study her face in the moonlight as his thumb lazily traced a line across her jaw. Cupping her chin in his hand, he tilted her face upward gently before kissing her chin, each of her cheeks, and . . . finally . . . settling on her lips again.

She relived that kiss several more times before slowly opening her eyes. Yawning, Liv scanned the room, squinting to see her alarm clock. It was still dark, so she figured she had a few more hours to sleep, but wanted to make sure. As she searched in the dark for her clock, she suddenly became very aware that she was not alone. And she was very much not asleep on her couch-bed.

Where am I? Freaked out, Liv bolted upright and looked around. Her mind frantically raced through the rest of the previous night's date, desperately searching for an ending. *Oh no,* she thought, horrified. *Oh no. There was no ending. I don't remember an ending! I kissed him and then . . .* Nothing. Her memory was refusing to go beyond that kiss.

Racking her brain for details, the rest of the evening suddenly started trickling back into focus. After their balcony kiss, Josh Cameron had escorted Liv back inside the suite and they had settled into the corner of the couch. He had been talking about his ski trip to the Alps, and then . . . *Noooooo! I fell asleep!*

Liv squeezed her eyes shut, willing herself back in time. When she opened them, she hadn't moved. She realized she was sprawled out on the couch in the corner of Josh Cameron's hotel suite, covered in a fur blanket. She hadn't moved from the night before—even her shoes were still securely attached to her feet. She was feeling more than a little sheepish about her present situation. *How long have I been here?*

Looking across the room, Liv could see the outline of Skinny Guy, who was seated on a low footstool, his chin in his hands, watching her. When he saw that she was awake, he stood abruptly and moved toward her. "Mr. Cameron has retired for the evening," he explained briefly, helping Liv to her feet. "He has asked that I arrange for a car to take you home. He felt it best that you sleep here for a while, considering."

Considering what?! Liv wondered, suddenly nervous about what she had done or said. *How much did I drink?* She scolded herself for getting so out of hand. *I will never drink again. . . .*

"I took the liberty of ordering you a sandwich. Please feel free to bring it along for your ride home." Skinny Guy held a small pouch in her direction and made his way to the door. "Come along. Quickly."

Liv followed as Skinny Guy bustled down the hallway

and led her into a dark, narrow elevator. She peeked into the sandwich pouch as the elevator descended, and groaned as her stomach protested. She had definitely had too much champagne if the sight of plain old ham and cheese was causing her stomach to curl.

Poking around inside the sandwich pouch, Liv found a small note next to the wrapped sandwich. "Olivia," it read, "Thank you for an incredible evening. I can't wait to see you again. Soon. Fondly, Josh Cameron." Liv smiled. He still had a way to go before he lost all of his cheesiness ("fondly" was just the tiniest bit old-fashioned), but at least he was sweet. She smiled as she reread his words. Soon, she thought, happily.

When the elevator reached the ground floor, Skinny Guy led Liv through the nearly deserted lobby. As they made their way past the frosted glass doors of the swanky hotel bar, though, she heard laughter and the clinking of glasses coming from within. The doors had whooshed open to welcome a stunning couple into the late-night gathering.

Liv craned her neck to try to get a glimpse of the inner reaches of the bar as Skinny Guy hurried her through the lobby. For a split second her heart caught in her throat— was that Josh Cameron on the other side of the bar's sliding doors? *Nah,* she thought, *impossible. Skinny Guy said he "retired for the evening"—and he wouldn't have left me in his room alone to go out.* Shrugging it off as her own overactive imagination, Liv smiled. *One amazing kiss, and I'm already paranoid,* she thought, giggling to herself.

Stifling a yawn, Liv made her way out of the lobby. With a sigh, she slid into the limo waiting outside the hotel—her limo!—and bit into her sandwich as the car sped her toward home.

Afternoon Delight

"Monet's inspiration for this piece . . ."

Blah, blah, blah-ba-di-blah. Liv plopped down on one of the hard, backless benches in room thirty-four of the National Gallery and stared up at the famous Monet above her. She was only vaguely listening to the description. Her self-guided tour headphones had given her a headache, not to mention the fact that they had squished her ears flat and left one side of her hair panked tightly against her head.

When Liv had gotten up that morning, the weather was dreary and drizzly. After dragging herself out of bed and into the shower, Liv had returned to the living room and discovered that Rebecca's mood apparently matched the weather—she had settled herself in front of her sun lamp with a stack of fashion magazines, her iPod Nano, and a sneer. Hell Dog was by her side, snuggled tightly into Liv's blanket, soaking up the bright faux sunshine.

So Liv decided to get out of the apartment and do some London exploring. First stop: the National Gallery. Truth be told, Liv didn't really like museums all that much. In theory, she loved art—in reality, it got old really quickly.

So now, an hour after arriving, she was bored and weary—and hadn't yet made it out of the nineteenth-century wing. Leaning back on the bench, Liv turned the volume down on her headphones and focused on the crowd. This, she realized, was her favorite part of the museum. So many people from so many places. People who had seen so much more of the world than she had. She loved listening to the different languages, seeing their faces, studying their body language.

After a few minutes of people watching, Liv stood up and headed for the front hall. The rest of the museum would have to wait—she was ready to explore the city, and old art was getting her nowhere fast.

Breezing down the main stairs of the gallery, Liv plucked her visitor's tag off her T-shirt, returned her headphones, and slung her bag over her shoulder. She pushed the front door open and made her way out toward the lions in Trafalgar Square. The sun had burned through the clouds while she was in the museum, and the rain had cleared. It was a beautiful day.

"Liv!" Hearing her name, Liv turned back toward the gallery. A few steps behind her Colin was standing with his arm raised in a slight wave. "Sorry," he said breathlessly, "I thought that was you."

Liv's stomach flipped nervously. She was surprised to see Colin. And even more surprised he had stopped her— they hadn't spent much time together since he had started dating Rebecca. And at work he was always so distant and busy. "Hey, Colin. Were you at the gallery?"

"I was just on my way in—this is one of my favorite places in London. They make a fantastic cup of tea, and it's free admission." Colin shrugged. "But you look like you're off, then. See you at work tomorrow, yeah?"

Liv considered her options. She could walk away and spend the day alone, living out a solo adventure in London. Or she could be bold and invite herself to join Colin for a cup of tea. It certainly couldn't hurt to try to be friends. "Do you mind if I join you?"

Colin looked surprised, but—Liv noted happily— pleased. "Of course."

They walked up the steps of the museum together in silence. Liv didn't know what to say, but she felt compelled to fill the silence with unnecessary commentary. While

Colin guided her through the halls to the museum café, she asked him endless questions about his flat, afternoon tea, and what it was like to grow up in Stratford-upon-Avon.

By the time they finally settled into a small table in the corner of the café, Liv had exhausted all of her generic questions and was almost out of things to say. Colin had barely uttered a word.

"Can I ask you something?" Liv silently vowed that this would be her last question. She *had* to stop talking.

"Isn't it a bit late to ask me that?" Colin smiled. *Aha,* Liv thought. *So he has noticed my endless chatter.*

"Sorry," Liv said, embarrassed. "I tend to talk a lot. I've never been very good with silence. It makes me uncomfortable."

"Yeah, I noticed," Colin said, immediately looking like he regretted being so honest. Liv laughed, noticing his embarrassment. "But it's a good thing," Colin said, by way of apology. "I tend to clam up around new people. Or I scare people off with my sarcasm. Go ahead—ask me anything."

"I sort of get the impression that you kind of avoid me at work." Liv could not believe she had just said that. But she was desperate to know what she had done to offend him.

"You do?" Colin furrowed his brow. "Sorry about that. I guess I've been a bit distracted. Andrew Stone is literally around every corner, and he doesn't like to see me not working. Rebecca has been stopping by my desk a lot lately, and he's sort of scolded me for—how does he put it?—'wasting his time.' So I try to stay focused, yeah?"

"Oh. Right." Now Liv felt bad. She should have figured Rebecca had something to do with his weird behavior. "It was rude of me to ask you that. I don't have a very good filter—really, pretty much everything that goes through my head comes out my mouth. I guess it's just a curse of being an only child. You can say whatever you want, and no one is there to hear you. So you just keep talking."

Colin laughed. "Don't worry about it. I like honesty—it's refreshing. My family tends to bottle up most of our issues and pretend all's well. So I like when people can express themselves. It's a nice change."

"Do you have a big family?"

"There you go with the questions again," Colin teased. "Kidding. I have two little sisters. So it's a pretty big family, yeah. You?"

"It's just me and my dad." Liv paused. There was something about Colin that made her feel safe. She *wanted* to tell him things. "My mom died in a car accident when I was little."

"I'm sorry," Colin said quietly. He paused, waiting for Liv to continue.

"It's okay. She was English. From London. So that's a big part of why I'm here. I'm trying to figure out what her life might have been like. Being here makes me feel so much closer to her." She paused, sipping her tea.

"Have you met anyone from your mom's family?"

"She was an only child, and her parents died before she did. I didn't know my grandparents at all. So there isn't really anyone left." Liv shrugged. "It's enough for me to soak up a little of her culture. I just want to feel like I've lived a part of her life. *Lived London,* you know?"

"That makes sense." Colin folded his napkin and set it on the table. "Well then, that's settled." Liv looked at him curiously. "I think it's time for us to get out and explore. Live some of the London life. Have you walked along the Thames yet? Visited Big Ben? Westminster Abbey? Buckingham Palace?"

Liv shook her head. She had done very little besides sit at her tollbooth and fetch Brown cups of watery coffee.

"Then I'll be your guide. We have a lot to see." He came around behind her and pulled her chair away from the table. Liv stood and followed as Colin guided her out of the museum, across Trafalgar Square, and down the Mall toward Buckingham Palace.

Hours later, after darkness had fallen and they stood together in the grainy light illuminating the turnstiles in the Charing Cross tube station, Liv was at a loss for words for the first time all day. "Colin, thank you," she finally said.

He smiled. "It was my pleasure. Have you had a good day?"

Liv and Colin had spent the afternoon chatting and laughing as they walked through St. James's Park and around Buckingham Palace, before eventually turning and going back toward Westminster Abbey and the River Thames. Colin led Liv past Big Ben and the Houses of Parliament, stopping only briefly for a second cup of tea in a small shop off Parliament Square. They had walked for hours, but Liv had hardly noticed.

"Amazing." Liv glanced at him. "I hope we can do it again sometime?"

"Me too." With that, he raised his hand in a little salute. "I hope you liked the tea at the museum. It really was the perfect cup, yeah?" Laughing, she waved as Colin backed out of the station, and then she turned and went down the escalator and toward home.

"I was starting to get worried about you," Anna greeted Liv from her position on the couch. "You've been gone all day."

"I ran into Colin outside the National Gallery," Liv said, throwing her bag into a heap in the corner of the living room. "We spent the day wandering around London."

"Sounds scandalous," Anna said, sitting up.

"It's not like that!" Liv insisted, swatting Anna as she settled into position on the couch. "But I think we can be friends." As she said it, Liv realized it was true. She had never actually pursued a friendship with a guy, and that afternoon had helped her realize how much fun it could be. She felt absolutely no pressure around Colin. She could be herself, and didn't have to worry about flirting or trying to figure out what to say so she didn't sound foolish. It was so easy and comfortable—it was actually a relief that he was taken, so she didn't have to worry about impressing him.

"Liv, seriously. Friends? He's hot. Maybe he's into you." Anna tucked her legs into a pretzel and fixed Liv with a stern stare.

Liv giggled and sat down next to her roommate. "Seriously. Friends. Yes, he's hot, but it's not like that. At all. I felt completely comfortable around him, and I don't want to ruin that by even thinking about hooking up with him. And hello—" Liv gestured down the hall and lowered her voice. "Rebecca. Though I did completely forget to ask him what's going on with them. He only mentioned her once, and I guess I wasn't so keen on bringing it up a second time."

Anna didn't look convinced. "Is this about Josh Cameron?" She frowned. Anna had been cautiously optimistic about Liv's date the night before. She said she couldn't help but feel suspicious of celebrities, and "needed to see what Josh Cameron's next move would be" before she would let Liv get too hopeful.

"No. And yes. Come on, Anna—you have to admit that things are going really well with Josh Cameron. I wouldn't say we're a 'couple,' but there's definitely hope, right?"

Anna nodded and grinned. "It's looking good."

"Trust me," Liv said. "I think Colin and I will be friends. But that's it. I'm not getting in her"—Liv gestured toward Rebecca's room— "way. Colin is clearly taken, so no matter what might have been, I'm not going there. Get it?"

"Got it."

"Good."

Sweet Dreams
(Are Made of This)

Though she had meant it when she'd said it, Liv was finding it impossible to stick to her vow. She'd sworn she wasn't even the tiniest bit interested in Colin, but throughout the next week, Liv couldn't stop thinking about their weekend adventure.

She would recall funny stories Colin had told her about Andrew Stone as she filled Simon Brown's cup in the coffee room. She would catch herself smiling about how he always said "yeah?" like he was asking a question at the end of almost every sentence. And as she walked from the office to the tube every night, her mind flashed back to the way his eyes shone in the light of the Charing Cross tube station.

What she found most perplexing was the fact that she

was obsessing about her totally normal afternoon strolling around London with Colin, but had spent almost no time dwelling on her steamy and fabulously chic dinner with Josh Cameron. *What's wrong with you, Liv?* She didn't like the tricks her emotions were playing on her. *You made out with the world's most coveted celebrity, and you're obsessing about some random guy from Stratford-upon-Avon? Some English dude who is crazy enough to go out with your psycho roommate?*

Liv could only hope this Colin nonsense was her mind's way of trying to prevent her from obsessing about Josh Cameron. Luckily, stuffing Colin to the back of her mind became much easier after she caught a glimpse of his hand on Rebecca's back as they wandered down the Music Mix hallway deep in conversation one afternoon—yuck! So she focused her energy on willing Josh Cameron to call and ask her out again.

Simon Brown was particularly gruff and surly all week, so Liv didn't have too much time at the office to focus on anything but his bizarre needs. Brown had developed an unexpected addiction to Nicorette—the stop-smoking gum—and had begun to send Liv out to fetch three or four or twenty packs most afternoons. The gum didn't seem to do much for Brown, since he still went through at least two packs of cigarettes a day—usually lighting up as he stuffed a fresh piece of Nicorette into his mouth. This dual habit resulted in breath that smelled like a public bathroom, so Liv was relieved that she rarely needed to get close enough to be hit with the full effect.

On her way back into the Music Mix building one evening, her arms loaded with packs of Nicorette and Dunhill cigarettes, Liv spotted Anna pushing her way out of the revolving door. Anna quickly rushed over to relieve Liv of some of her packages. "Hey," Liv said, breathless. "Thanks. You going home?"

"Yeah," Anna said quietly. "Rough day."

Liv tilted her head, confused. Anna didn't have a lot of rough days—her Music Mix assignment suited her perfectly, and her whole department loved her. So most days, Anna came home glowing with happiness. "What's up?"

"Nothing major. It's nothing, really." Anna looked up defiantly and smiled.

"Hmm," Liv responded, studying Anna carefully. She didn't believe that for a second. "Are you sure?"

Anna smiled weakly. "I promise."

"You know what? I think I can get out of here—let me just run this stuff up to Brown and grab my bag. We can go home together." Liv always ended up riding the tube home alone, since she usually worked hours later than any of the other interns. But she wasn't going to let Anna go home alone—to Rebecca—when she seemed so upset.

"Really? You can leave at . . . ," Anna said sarcastically, glancing at her watch, ". . . seven thirty?"

"Crazy, isn't it? Yeah, just hang out here for a sec and I'll be right back. Promise you'll wait?"

Anna nodded, so Liv gathered up all her packages and made her way up the escalators to deliver Brown's goods. Luckily, Brown was engrossed in watching an episode of *Footballers' Wives* and just grunted when Liv dropped the bags on his desk and announced that she was leaving. So she breezed back down the hall and out the door to her waiting roommate.

Anna filled their walk to the tube with superficial stories of what had happened at the office that day. Liv listened and nodded, but couldn't help wondering what was going on. Anna was clearly trying to keep talking to prevent Liv from asking any more questions. Finally Liv couldn't stand it anymore and just blurted out, "If there's something going on—if there's anyone whose butt needs kicking—you know I'm your girl, right?"

Anna laughed.

"I'm serious," Liv continued. "I don't want to force you to tell me what's going on, but I'm not pretending that everything's dandy. You're clearly avoiding something. . . ."

They had reached the tube station and were riding down the escalator to the tracks. Liv and Anna both pressed to the left side of the escalator, allowing hustling Londoners to walk past them on the right. Liv had quickly learned that this was an unspoken rule of the tube that people were *very* serious about. . . . Never stand on the right side of the escalator.

Anna turned to face Liv as they descended underground. She explained, "Everything's fine. Things are just stressful with my parents right now. But I really don't want to get into it."

"Your mom? Are there new developments?"

"No, same old stuff. She's just really been on me lately, and it's sort of sucking the fun out of this summer. She hasn't even asked me how the internship is going—we just avoid talking about it. She only calls to tell me what she's buying for my dorm room next year."

"So she hasn't relented at all, huh?"

"It's gotten worse. And the more she talks about my plans for school, the more I'm convinced I'm not ready to go yet. I'm loving this job so much, and know that if I just had one year to pursue this, I would be so much happier with the next ten years of my life being committed to Oxford and med school or whatever." Anna sighed as they boarded their train.

Liv began to respond, but Anna cut her off. "Can we talk about something else? Make me laugh," Anna begged. "I want to take my mind off this."

Realizing she meant it, Liv thought for a second before pulling her iPod out of her bag. She scrolled through the song list, then stuck one earbud in Anna's ear, and the other in her own. "Music therapy," she explained, pressing play on the dial. "If the sight of me gettin' down in the tube doesn't make you laugh, nothing will."

As ABBA sang out, *"You can dance, you can jive, having the time of your life . . ."* Liv wiggled her butt and waved her arms in the air. Passengers in the train looked up from their newspapers to stare at her. Anna started to laugh, and a flush of red crept up her cheeks.

"Okay, okay! Stop—this is mortifying." Anna continued to laugh as Liv drew even more stares.

"Did I take your mind off it?" Liv whispered as she continued to shimmy more subtly in time to the music. Anna nodded. "Then it was worth it." The doors opened at their stop, and Liv and Anna hustled out, still joined at the ear by the iPod.

The next morning when Liv walked into the Music Mix lobby, Gloria stood up from her desk and whispered, "Look out . . . he's on the hunt."

Liv paused. "Brown?"

"Who else?" Gloria asked, nodding. "He's in rare form today—be prepared."

With a groan, Liv pressed through the door leading out of the lobby and braced herself for a fun day. As she passed Brown's open door, he shouted "Oy!" and waved her over.

"Good morning," she said, trying to start their conversation out on the right foot.

Brown just stared at her and launched into a list of instructions. "This will need to go," he said, gesturing toward two large boxes in the corner of his office, "as will this. I've arranged for a courier to pick you up and take you there. Don't irritate me with nonsensical questions. Go, Girl!"

Right-o, Liv thought, more confused than ever. *You got it.* She clumsily gathered the two enormous boxes in the corner of Brown's office into her arms and made her way back out to the main lobby. Setting the boxes on the corner of the reception desk, Liv just looked at Gloria and broke out laughing.

"Here's what I figure," Gloria said, without Liv's needing to ask. "The Josh Cameron concert is coming up. They're in the final prep stages, and Brown is starting to freak out. I'm guessing the car service that just called from downstairs is here to pick you and those boxes up and deliver you to the stadium. Make sense?"

"I'd say that's as good a guess as any. I suppose it can't hurt to get in the car and see where it takes me." She thanked Gloria, hoisted the boxes into her arms again, and made her way down the escalator. Outside, a driver was waiting next to a black car. Liv moved toward the backseat, and the driver whisked the door open for her. *So far, so good,* she thought.

Twenty minutes later Liv's car stopped outside the service entrance to a huge stadium. She made her way inside and wandered around aimlessly for a few minutes before running into Rebecca, who was bustling through the hallway with a clipboard and walkie-talkie, shouting things to stagehands and mechanics. When she spotted Liv, Rebecca came gliding over.

"Oh, Li-uhv, are those the dog beds?"

Liv just grunted. She had no idea what was in the boxes, but really hoped that a private car hadn't been hired to deliver a bunch of dog beds to the stadium. "No clue," she responded. "I was just told to bring these boxes here." Liv set down her packages and opened up one of the boxes. *You've got to be kidding me,* she mused. *Rebecca was right.*

Rebecca smiled smugly and directed Liv to one of the rooms behind the stage. "Just unpack the beds and make it nice and comfy in there, won't you? We want to make sure all our special guests are taken care of during the concert. Thanks, sweetie."

Liv spent the next hour and a half unpacking and fluffing dog beds in a small, rectangular room down the hall from the stage. She wasn't sure why she was preparing this little doggie hotel, but she had come to realize that her summer job entailed doing as she was told, and understanding later.

Liv finished quickly and decided to take a peek around the stadium—she had heard so much about the concert from Rebecca, but hadn't gotten to check things out for herself. Now that she was maybe-dating the star of the show, she felt like she deserved a little peek.

She made her way down the hall toward the stage, pulling aside the curtain that blocked off the backstage area. Liv's breath caught in her throat when she spotted Josh Cameron's familiar curls at the back of the stage. She hadn't really thought about how she would respond the next time she saw him, but now that he was so close she was suddenly panicked at the thought of seeing him again. *He kissed me, he kissed me, he kissed me*—that was all she could think about as she stepped onstage and walked toward Josh Cameron.

As she approached, he turned to her, his face a blank slate. He stared at her for a few seconds before a smile spread across his face. "Excuse me," he said, motioning to the sound engineer he had been talking to. "Olivia."

"Hey," she said, still nervous. "Hi." She grinned awkwardly. "How are you?"

Josh Cameron moved toward her, his eyes penetrating hers. "I hope you made it home safely on Friday."

"Oh! Yeah, fine. No problems. Thanks for the sandwich."

He looked confused. "Oh," he said. "Right. So tell me, Olivia. To what do I owe this surprise?"

"You mean, why am I here? I brought the dog beds." *That's great, Liv. Reeeeeally charming.*

"Right. The dog beds." Josh Cameron was smirking at her. "I don't suppose you have some time before you have to get back?"

Liv was definitely not in a hurry to get back to Brown, and she figured her task had taken less time than expected. "Sure, I'm free. Why?"

"I was just on my way to the Berkeley Hotel for tea. Care to join me?"

Forty-five minutes later Liv was still waiting on a plastic folding chair by the stage door. She had happily agreed to tea, and he had told her he would be "just a mo'." Many, many mo's later, she was starting to get impatient. She was also a little nervous about how long she'd been gone from the office. Finally, almost an hour later, the pop star emerged from the stage area. He approached Liv and offered her a hand, making no comment about the time that had passed.

But the wait was worth it. When Josh Cameron's limo delivered them to the door of the Berkeley Hotel, they were quickly ushered inside to a private table tucked into a corner. Liv wasn't offered a menu, but their table was almost instantly filled with towering platters of pastries, cookies, and sandwiches, steaming pots of tea, and cucumber wedges. The pastries and cookies were stunning, one-of-a-kind masterpieces. Josh Cameron watched her with an amused expression as she bit into a deep chocolate cookie with white trim.

"You know," he said, "that cookie was inspired by a classic Chanel dress."

"Am I supposed to eat it?" Liv asked, only half-joking.

Josh Cameron laughed. "Of course. But each of these cookies takes hours to design. That's what makes this place so inspired." Liv nodded, self-consciously nibbling at the cookie.

At the next table over, Liv could hear two ladies gushing about the service and, of all things, the table linens. Then one of them gasped and too-loudly whispered, "High tea at this hotel has more than a monthlong waiting list."

Liv giggled and looked across her table at Josh Cameron, who raised an eyebrow and smirked. "One of the benefits of dating a celebrity, wouldn't you say?"

Liv nodded, her cheeks flushing at what he had just

said—Josh Cameron had defined them as "dating"! Giddy with the knowledge that she was officially dating the world's most eligible bachelor, Liv floated through the rest of the afternoon.

Yet for some strange reason, her dreamworld didn't feel quite as perfect as she had always envisioned.

Girls Just Want to Have Fun

At six o'clock on Friday morning, Liv was jolted awake by a loud, tinny rendition of the Black Eyed Peas' "My Humps." Moaning, she rolled over on her couch-bed and covered her head with a pillow, cursing herself for changing Anna's ring tone from *Für Elise*. As she lay there, trying to muffle the sound of Anna's cell phone, she snuck a peek at her clock—*it's really early*, she mused sleepily. *What could be this important?*

She could hear Anna's door open, and she felt the thumping of her roommate running for her phone. Anna snapped open the phone in the kitchen and murmured a quiet "Mama" into the phone. *It's her mom?* Liv wondered, starting to worry. *Whose mom calls at six in the morning?!*

Anna spoke quickly and quietly in Swedish. Liv listened to her lilting voice, noticing a tense, agitated tone. There was a brief pause, and then Liv heard Anna flip the phone closed. Her roommate stood in the kitchen for a few minutes, while Liv pretended to be asleep. She wanted to sit up and ask what was going on, but she knew that Anna would let her know if and when she was ready to talk.

"Everything okay?" Liv asked sleepily.

She had minded her own business for less than thirty seconds, and she just couldn't help it—Liv *had* to know that Anna was okay.

"Yeah," Anna said, lying down beside Liv on the couch-bed and flopping her head back into a pillow. "That was my mom." Long silence. "She's coming to London tomorrow morning. Apparently we 'need to talk.' And I guess it's an in-person conversation. She's flying in from Stockholm on the first flight in the morning. She'll be here by eight."

Liv breathed out. "Are you okay with that?"

"I guess I have to be, don't I?" Anna said bitterly. "She hasn't exactly given me a whole lot of options."

"Any idea what inspired this visit *now*?"

Anna groaned. "I have a pretty good idea."

Liv rolled onto her side, facing her friend. "Do you want to tell me?"

"I don't know why I haven't told you this yet," Anna

said sheepishly. "I guess I didn't really want to say it out loud, because it makes it more real." She exhaled. "I turned down every university I was accepted to for the fall. I sent letters out earlier this week, and I guess they already got them and have started calling my house to find out why I'm declining their offers.

"I know I made the right decision," Anna continued, closing her eyes. "But I still need to justify that to my mom. I know I'll go to university sometime—I'm just not ready right now. I need to figure out what I want to do with my life first. I just need a year or two to try things and figure out what fits, you know? And if there's the tiniest chance I could get a job at Music Mix, I *need* to try."

"So your mom is coming to try to change your mind?"

"I guess," Anna said, flopping her hands at her sides. "It's not going to work, so it seems like sort of a useless trip. It's not like I just—*poof!*—made the decision. . . . There was some thought involved," she continued bitterly. "But I guess we need to get it out into the open. I couldn't have really hidden the decision from her. She would have found out eventually, so this conversation is probably inevitable."

"Probably," Liv mused. "If it helps, I think you made the right decision."

Anna sat up suddenly, swinging her legs off the side

of Liv's bed. "Thanks. Can we go get a yummy breakfast before work to clear my head?"

"Do you want me to make you breakfast?" Liv offered, secretly hoping Anna would say no. She could cook pancakes from a box and that was just about it. A scone from a café sounded much more appealing.

"Liv, get real. I've seen you cook. That's almost more of a punishment than my mom's visit." Anna grinned. "Move it. If we hurry, we'll escape before Rebecca even wakes up."

An hour later Anna and Liv had settled into a window seat at Tully's, which had become Liv's favorite coffee shop. The staff had become friendly with Liv, thanks to all the lattes and cappuccinos she fetched for *Hits Parade* celebrities and their assistants.

When they had arrived a few minutes after seven, they were given a pot of tea and scones with clotted cream—on the house. Liv grinned through a mouthful of scone and said, "Simon Brown has his benefits, doesn't he? There's nothing like free breakfast to make all those coffee runs worth it. Feel better?"

Anna nodded. "Much."

As she slurped her tea, Liv asked, "Do you want to talk about your strategy for tomorrow morning?" She had been a little hesitant to remind Anna about her mom's visit, but Anna still seemed distracted.

"Nah, I'm good. I promise. Thank you for asking, though—and talking me through it this morning." Anna waved her hand dismissively and set her face in a playfully stern scowl. "Here's what I want. . . . I want to sit here and eat until I'm sick, and then spend the night dancing it off. Tonight's club night, remember?"

"That's tonight?" Liv asked. With all the excitement of the past week, Liv had sort of forgotten that all the interns were going out that night. Anna and Francesco had been planning it for weeks. Apparently, the wardrobe department was way more into work-life balance than Simon Brown was—Anna's boss had even forced her to take one afternoon off to go check out a potential club for their intern outing. "I totally forgot. Wow, Anna, I'm losing my mind."

Anna smiled for the first time all morning. "You're distracted. But I still love you for helping me with this mom stuff. Now, no more serious talk. I'll deal with tomorrow, tomorrow. Tonight, we dance.

"Ah just don't know if I should wear my Jimmy Choos or my Manolos. Which of them makes me look more precious?" Liv and Anna were sitting in the living room, trying desperately not to laugh.

Rebecca had tried on no fewer than six outfits, each of which had a matching ensemble for My Rover. She had finally settled on a small pink dress and a silver clutch, outfitting My Rover in silver booties and a pink cape. Hell Dog was now scratching madly at the booties while Rebecca debated between five-inch peekaboo-toed stilettos and six-inch silver pumps.

"We have to leave," Anna said in reply, sending Rebecca over the edge.

Near tears, Rebecca looked at Liv with a look of desperation. "Ah just can't decide," she said, her lip quivering.

"The pumps," Liv said matter of factly, desperate to calm Rebecca down and get them out of the apartment on time. "Definitely the Manolo pumps. It totally coordinates your look with Rover."

"*My* Rover," Rebecca clarified, narrowing her eyes at Liv. "This precious darling's name is *My* Rover." Her tears had been replaced with a steely, stern voice. "The Jimmy Choos it is." She slipped on the heels, swept My Rover into her arms, and headed out the door.

Anna and Liv exchanged a look. "Perfect. Great choice, Rebecca," Liv yelled loudly after her. "You look perfect."

Thirty minutes later the three roommates emerged from the tube and made their way toward Runway, a swanky club that Anna promised Liv she would love. Anna had booked a table, and the other Music Mix interns were meeting them there.

When they walked in to the club, Liv could hardly believe it was real. The rectangular room was draped in deep red furs, and awash in understated white light glowing from within a long, fashion show–like catwalk that jutted out into the center of the room. Tables were arranged along the length of the runway, and frighteningly thin waitresses and waiters strutted up and down the length of the catwalk to deliver drinks.

Liv's mouth hung open, her face an expression of pure disbelief. Club owners went to such bizarre lengths to create a unique and glamorous atmosphere. Back in Ann Arbor, the high school gym outfitted for prom had always been considered exotic. Anna looked at Liv and burst out laughing.

Rebecca lifted one eyebrow and studied her nails. Clearly, this scene was very familiar to Rebecca—or she was playing the part very well.

As they walked toward the hostess, Anna shouted, "I picked this club because I heard it's pretty fabulous. Later they open the runway up to the crowd and you can vamp it up, supermodel-style. Sounds fun, doesn't it?"

Liv leaned in to Anna. "This is incredible. I assure you that there is no way I'll be walking that catwalk, but this is truly awesome. You picked a great place."

Anna took Liv's hand and led her toward their table. Rebecca trailed a safe distance behind, trying to look like she wasn't with them. The group squeezed through the crowds lingering near the front of the club and moved toward the runway.

Liv spotted Francesco bounding up from a table right alongside the center of the runway. He ran over and gathered her and Anna into a tight hug, planting kisses on their cheeks. "Welcome, welcome!" he shouted, his Italian accent more pronounced than usual.

Francesco moved to the table and pulled chairs out for both of them. Rebecca crossed her arms as best she could (My Rover was tucked delicately under one arm) and cleared her throat. Colin stood up from his place at the table and offered his chair.

The table was packed with Music Mix interns, some of whom Liv knew only from their daily trips to the coffee machine. Others—like Katia, one of the other Americans, and Alex, from Russia—she had snuck into the Green Room for lunch a few times. Liv settled into her seat and looked up at the runway, soaking in every possible moment.

Realizing that all eyes were on her, Liv adjusted her jeans just slightly and steadied herself on Anna's heels. She inched forward in time to the music, trying desperately to sedate her nerves. She still didn't know exactly how she had gotten here.

In an effort to look confident, Liv wiggled her butt and curtsied, soliciting cheers and whistles from the crowded club. She held Anna's sweaty hand tightly by her side, clutching it like a life raft. Looking to her left, Liv could see all the Music Mix interns sitting at the table smiling and laughing, urging them on. Liv glanced at Anna, who was grinning ear to ear beside her. She winked at Liv as they took a step down the runway.

Before Liv had accepted Anna's dare to hop up on the catwalk, she made Anna promise to join her. Double humiliation felt much better than going it alone. The catwalk looked like it was a mile long, and they had only gone two steps. But it was too late to turn back now.

Liv steeled her nerves as she and Anna moved forward again. Suddenly the music (which had been some cheesy, uninspiring Rick Springfield song) changed, and the first notes of ABBA's "Dancing Queen" came flowing out of the speakers lining the runway.

"You can dance, you can jive, having the time of your life . . ."

Anna and Liv looked at each other as they recognized the familiar lyrics and burst out laughing.

"See that girl, watch that scene, dig in the Dancing Queen . . ."

"This is definitely becoming our theme song, isn't it?" Liv yelled in Anna's ear.

Anna nodded, grinning. "Feel better about doing this now?" she yelled back.

Putting all shame aside, the two strutted down the runway in unison and shimmied in time to the music. They knew they looked completely ridiculous, but they were having so much fun that it really didn't matter.

As they hammed it up on the runway, Liv caught a glimpse of Rebecca dancing next to Colin on the floor. In fact, when she looked around, everyone in the club was dancing. No one was laughing at them—instead, everyone looked like they were having an incredible time. When the last notes chimed out of the speakers, both Liv and Anna slid to their knees, arms raised, and struck a pose. Everyone in the club was cheering, and the Music Mix interns all ran to the end of the runway to help them off the platform.

"That was incredible!" Katia screamed.

"Hilarious," Francesco chimed in.

Liv and Anna looked at each other and cracked up. "I can't believe we just did that," Anna said, giggling and gasping to catch her breath.

Laughing, Liv responded, "You *said* you wanted to dance tonight. You rocked!"

The rest of the night went by in a blur. In no time they were being whisked out of the club and into a taxi home. Liv settled into the backseat and leaned against Anna. She smiled and closed her eyes as "Dancing Queen" ran through her head over and over—*You can dance, you can jive, having the time of your life* . . .

I am, Liv thought happily. *I am having the time of my life.*

Should I Stay or Should I Go?

As promised, Anna's mom arrived early the next morning, and her knock at the door startled Liv from a deep, contented sleep. Anna hustled out of her bedroom, dressed and ready. She hurried through an introduction while Liv sat snuggled up under her covers in her couch-bed. She had made a motion to stand up for a proper handshake, but Anna's mom insisted she stay in bed.

Anna hastily showed her mom around their apartment, and less than five minutes later, Anna declared they were leaving. She and Liv had decided during the previous night's taxi ride home that Anna should take her mom out shopping and for high tea at Selfridges to soften her up a bit.

Liv hoped everything would be okay—she couldn't imagine the pressure Anna must be feeling. The phone calls and arguments had really taken their toll on her. Liv hoped Anna and her mom could sort things out so Anna could enjoy the rest of her summer guilt-free.

Though she would never admit it to Anna, Liv did sort of envy her roommate's parents' involvement in her life. Liv's dad was incredible, but she sometimes wished he paid more attention to what she was doing. She wouldn't even mind if he got a little more angry when she screwed up. He was often so wrapped up in his photography that Liv sometimes wondered if he noticed she was growing up. She only had one year left at home before she went off to college.

But now that she'd seen Anna's situation, she was beginning to realize that her dad's lack of involvement in decisions about her life was probably just his way of letting her know he supported her. He never said it, but maybe his silence was his way of encouraging her to make her own choices. *Hmmm,* she thought. *Interesting trick.*

Pulling herself out of bed, Liv realized she had the whole day to herself. Rebecca was in the shower, and seemed to be getting ready to go out. So Liv happily lazed around the apartment—under the careful watch of Hell Dog—before deciding how best to spend the day.

She was still surviving almost exclusively on Green Room leftovers, and she felt like she deserved a tasty lunch at one of the neighborhood pubs. She could hole away in a dark corner and work on ideas for the VJ for a Day competition. Things had been so hectic at work that she and Anna had had almost no time to think about their audition. They still had a month before the competition, but Liv knew how crazy things were going to get around the office with the Josh Cameron concert coming up.

Around noon she wandered out into the rainy early afternoon and into a pub just a few blocks from her flat. She was instantly comforted by the warm, dark interior, and she spotted a small open table in the back corner. The cozy restaurant made her feel very literary and Shakespeare-esque—she hoped the environment would inspire great ideas for the audition.

As she passed through the dark room, Liv's stomach dropped. Sitting in one of the deep red booths along the side wall was a way-too-familiar blond head. *Rebecca,* she groaned inwardly.

Rebecca spotted Liv just as Liv was deciding whether she could make a quick getaway, or if she had to stop and say hello. She realized that running off wasn't the most adult thing to do, but she didn't know if she could handle spending her lunch with Rebecca. *Maybe I'll get lucky and*

Rebecca will be with someone, Liv mused. *Maybe she doesn't want to see me any more than I want to see her.*

Just as quickly as she had hoped Rebecca wasn't alone, Liv took it back. Because Rebecca was very definitely having lunch with someone . . . and that someone was Colin. Sure, Liv had vowed that she and Colin were just friends—and she was dating Josh Cameron, International Superstar—but she still cringed when she saw them together.

"Oh," Liv blurted out. "Hi, Rebecca. Hi, Colin."

"Li-uhv," Rebecca purred coldly. "How marvelous to see you here." *Is she joking?* Liv thought, her stomach churning.

Colin shot Rebecca a look, and said quickly, "Liv, join us."

Now, Liv could think of *nothing* she would rather *not* do at that moment than join Rebecca and Colin for lunch. But she could see no escape.

"So, what are you guys up to today?" Liv asked, though she wasn't entirely sure she wanted to know the answer.

"We're just—," Colin began, but Rebecca quickly cut him off.

"Oh, Li-uhv, Colin is just so sweet," she said, leaning in conspiratorially toward Liv. "He's taking me all around London today, showing me all of the sights. Isn't that just the sweetest thing you've ever heard?" She beamed across the table at Colin as Liv willed herself not to puke.

Although she was being totally unreasonable, Liv just couldn't stop herself from feeling pangs of jealousy. For some dumb reason, she thought Colin's tour around London had been for her alone. She now realized just how silly that assumption was.

What's wrong with you, Liv? Did you think Colin might be interested in you even though he knows about you and Josh Cameron, and he's clearly dating Rebecca? Did you think he was going to wait around for you?

"Yeah," Liv said, after a moment's silence. "That's really sweet, Rebecca." She glanced at Colin, who was focusing on the table in front of him.

"Are you alone today, Liv?" Rebecca asked with a smirk. "Where's Josh Cameron?"

All right, Liv thought bitterly. *Is that question really necessary?* Out loud, she said, "Oh, I'm not sure. You know how it is—preparing for his concert and everything. He's a busy guy." *Lame, Liv. Totally lame.* Liv had tried to keep the details of her relationship quiet, but her close friends knew she was "hanging out" with an International Superstar. Rebecca, however, was convinced Liv was making it all up.

"Yeah, Ah definitely know how it is. The concert is going to be fab-u-lous, by the way," Rebecca said with an air of superiority. Liv thought she noticed Colin shoot Rebecca a weird look across the table, but she couldn't be sure.

After a moment of awkward silence, Colin spoke. "We should probably get going, yeah?"

"Right," Rebecca said cheerfully. "Big day. Liv, you should definitely try the shepherd's pie. Ah tried some of Colin's and it was absolutely dee-lish."

Liv muttered something and hastily said good-bye. As Colin and Rebecca headed for the door, she noticed Colin lean over and mutter something quietly to Rebecca. Rebecca frowned, then turned to look back at Liv. She broke into a huge pageant grin and waved. Liv managed a thin smile, then slid further into the booth.

"Urghhhhhh."

Liv looked up from her book as the door slammed. "Didn't go so well?" she asked, as Anna threw herself onto the couch.

"You could say that," Anna said, clunking her head against the back of the couch.

Liv folded down the corner on her page and tossed her book on the floor. "Details, please. If you want to share."

"Yeah, I'll share. I think I need to." Anna stood up and went to the fridge. She returned a moment later with two glasses of black currant juice and a packet of biscuits. "Let's just say, she isn't happy with me."

"Did high tea help?" Liv asked, smiling.

"Uh-huh," Anna mumbled, tearing open the cookies. "That was a good idea—she totally loved it. But she's still *really* upset with me. She says I broke our agreement."

"Yikes."

"I mean, I did say if she gave me this summer, I'd get back on track this fall. But I agreed to that when I didn't think there was really a chance I would be putting off college for a few years. But, Liv, I just can't do it." Anna had tears welling up in her eyes. Liv set her glass on the floor and leaned forward to give her roommate a hug.

Anna continued. "I don't know what I am going to do. I *know* I'll go to school—there's even a good chance I'll apply to med school—and that's part of the reason I feel like I have to take a couple years to explore now."

"What did your mom say to all that?" Liv asked.

"It was the first time I'd ever really mentioned any of this to her, so I think it came as a surprise. She just assumed I wanted everything she wanted. But I want to work at Music Mix! Not forever, but for a little while. . . ." Anna smiled weakly.

"I know you do." Liv didn't really know what to say. So she just sat and waited for Anna to continue.

"I know it's unlikely that I'll get a job from Simon Brown at the end of the summer, but I need to try," Anna said resolutely. "And if that doesn't work out, then I'll figure something else out. It feels so good not to have a plan—I know that sounds silly, but my whole life has been completely planned out, and I love that it could be a blank slate for the next few years."

Liv nodded. Everything Anna was saying made complete sense. But she couldn't stop thinking that the situation Anna was dealing with was the complete opposite of the one she would be dealing with in a year. She'd gotten so little pressure, and had so few ideas of what she was going to do, that college seemed like the only option for her. She was looking forward to the structure.

Anna guzzled the rest of her juice. "You know, even though today was awful and painful and really, really unpleasant, I'm glad I had a chance to talk to her about it. I think that she might sort of get it. Even though she's upset, I'm sort of hoping that on some level she understands what I've been going through. It's possible she might ease up for a while. At least until application season comes around again," Anna broke off, laughing.

Liv was happy to see Anna's mood brightening. "So you think you guys are good now?"

"Not good. But maybe better. I understand where she's coming from, and she understands that I need to do what I'm going to do, and forcing me to do something else isn't going to accomplish much." Anna grinned. "Even though I'm stubborn, I'm not stupid. . . . She knows I'll make the 'right' choices"—she made little quotes in the air—"eventually."

"You will *definitely* make the right choices," Liv said. "You have up until now, so I don't think there's much risk of that."

Anna stood up and turned on some music. "Now we just need to focus on getting me a job at Music Mix so I'm not homeless and penniless at the end of the summer," she laughed. "How was your day, dear?"

Liv groaned. "Not as terrible as yours, but definitely not good."

"Why?" Anna asked. "What happened?"

Liv quickly told Anna about her run-in with Colin and Rebecca. "It was just so awkward," she finished.

"You are totally into him," Anna said simply.

"What? No."

"I don't know—that's what it sounds like to me."

"That's crazy." Liv shook her head. "What about Josh Cameron? And what about the fact that Colin is dating *Rebecca*? There's something really wrong with him if he's attracted to her."

"Mmm-hmm." Anna grinned. As Liv reached over to

swat her roommate with a pillow, the door to their apartment flew open and Rebecca floated in.

"Hi, girls," she said, winking. The look on Rebecca's face told Liv everything she needed to know. And it was then—Josh Cameron and Rebecca aside—that Liv realized Anna may have been more than a little bit right.

I Think We're Alone Now

The next week flew by.

Liv hadn't heard anything from Josh Cameron since their tea at the Berkeley Hotel. She hadn't *really* noticed over the weekend, but as soon as she was at work on Monday, she became obsessed. She was, of course, hoping he might call or pop by her tollbooth at Music Mix. She held on to that hope throughout Monday and into Tuesday morning, eventually suffering a mild case of whiplash from looking up quickly every time someone came near her desk.

On Tuesday afternoon she convinced herself that this sort of behavior was normal for a pop star, and obviously she couldn't expect him to drop everything to make time for her.

By Wednesday she had rediscussed the situation with Anna so many times that Liv was starting to suspect Anna was avoiding her.

On Thursday she began to question whether she had totally misinterpreted their relationship.

By Friday, however, she was mad. Still no call.

Liv would never receive the Lifetime Achievement Award for Dating, but she did know that this sort of behavior was strange, to say the least. And something deep down was telling her that she should run as fast as possible the other way, pop star or not—this guy was not worth waiting for.

Finally released from the office at five o'clock on Friday with a hearty "Go, Girl!" Liv decided to drink away her Josh Cameron paranoia with a large café mocha and a side of treacle pudding at Tully's. Several minutes later she settled into a window table, shrugged off her sweater, and dug into her dessert.

She pulled out a notebook, hoping the caffeine kick would inspire some great ideas for the VJ for a Day audition. Liv had been thinking about the competition almost constantly, but had still come up with a grand total of zero good ideas.

Liv and Anna swore they would spend every night the next week planning. They were desperate to win, but they knew they had very little chance if they didn't get to work soon.

As she stuck her pen in her mouth, accidentally suctioning the cap to her tongue, Liv felt someone brush up behind her. Turning, Liv noticed Colin sitting down at the table behind her.

"Hey," she said, lifting an arm to wave.

"Hello you. All right?" Liv nodded and smiled. She loved how the English simply said "All right?" rather than "Are you all right?" or "How are you?" It just seemed so much simpler.

"Did you just get off work?" Liv closed her notebook and unsuctioned the pen cap from her tongue. A little raised bump had been left in its place.

"Long day, yeah? Mind if I join you?"

"For sure." Liv reached her leg out and pulled a spare chair to her table. "Have a seat."

"Ta." *Aha,* Liv thought, *another good Britishism—"ta."* The simple, short version of "thanks." She sometimes thought British English could be more difficult to follow than a foreign language. "So," Colin continued. "What are you working on?" He motioned to her notebook.

Liv shrugged. "Nothing, really. I was hoping to get started on our VJ for a Day audition stuff." She took a sip of her drink. "Anna and I are working on it together, but we're sort of having a hard time figuring out what to do."

"Well, don't they always say you're supposed to play to your strengths?" Colin said, sounding like Liv's high school guidance counselor. "What do you like? What are you passionate about?"

Liv considered Colin's question. "Lucky Charms. I really like Lucky Charms cereal. But you can't get it in England."

"Lucky Charms. Interesting." Colin nodded seriously. "Could be a good angle. But what I meant was, what are your music passions? You know, what kind of music do you like?"

"Ohhhh." Liv grinned. "Okay . . . honest answer, or appropriate for Music Mix answer?"

Colin laughed. "Honest answer."

"I love the seventies and eighties. I grew up listening to ABBA, The Bangles, Blondie, U2, stuff like that. And I know the lyrics to every single Eagles song. No joke."

"Impressive," Colin said, nodding. "Maybe you should just do an Eagles sing-along? Showcase your unique talent," Colin suggested.

"I'm sure that would go over well," Liv said, laughing. "Thanks for the help. We'll figure it out eventually, I'm sure." She grabbed her bag and stuffed her notebook into it. "Did you know," she asked, smiling, "that today is the

Fourth of July? If I were home, I would be getting ready to go to a picnic at the lake to celebrate."

"Obviously," Colin cut in, "here in London we won't be celebrating America's Independence from England."

"Obviously," Liv agreed.

"Though, the English are glad to be rid of you." Colin smirked. "Happy Independence!"

"Funny," Liv said, smiling. She felt so relaxed around him—his humor was weird, but somehow it seemed to match hers perfectly. "Now, just because it's not a holiday here doesn't mean we have to mope around like it's some regular day. I think we should celebrate something. Say, for example, our independence from Music Mix—good-bye, Simon Brown and Andrew Stone. If only for the weekend."

"I'm up for it," Colin said, downing the rest of his Ribena juice box. "What do you have in mind?"

"I'm thinking hot dogs, sodas, blockbuster movie—your typical Fourth of July stuff." She grinned. "Some traditions are hard to break. Sound good?"

"Delicious. Very American." Colin nodded. "However . . . seeing as this is England, how would you feel about doing something a little more British?"

"Sure," Liv said, shrugging. "I'm up for anything."

"It's not exactly the movies, but there's this place I think you'll love."

Several minutes later Colin and Liv were strolling down Oxford Street, en route to Covent Garden. While they walked, they talked nonstop about everything—their families, the VJ for a Day audition, Music Mix. They easily slid back into the same natural conversation they had during their last London walk. Liv felt giddy and lighthearted as they approached the Millennium Bridge.

"Where are we going?" Liv asked as they crossed the Thames. She could see the Tower of London off to their left, but had no idea where they were or where they were going. It was getting dark, and Liv suddenly realized they had been walking for almost two hours.

"You'll see. I just hope my uncle is there."

"Your uncle?" Liv said, stealing a glance at Colin. "Please don't tell me we're going to some sort of family picnic."

"We are not going to a family picnic. I promise." Colin smiled suspiciously and led Liv along the river. The river walk was almost deserted, and Liv was starting to feel slightly creeped out. *Does he know where he's going?* Liv wondered. Just as she was about to steal a subtle look over her shoulder to look for weird stray dogs and other creepy things, Colin turned down a short ramp and stopped. "We're here."

They were standing in front of a large round building that Liv immediately recognized from pictures as

Shakespeare's Globe Theatre. "I've been dying to come here!" Liv exclaimed as Colin led her toward the entrance.

"I thought I remembered you saying how much you liked Shakespeare the first day I met you," Colin said, mirroring Liv's excitement. "I've been meaning to come here for a while—my uncle is one of the theater's prop masters, and I promised him I would pop by for a visit."

Colin led Liv inside the Globe's lobby, stopping briefly to talk to one of the staff. The clerk nodded when Colin introduced himself, and he ushered Liv and Colin through the building to the theater at the back. Liv's eyes widened as they passed replicas of Shakespeare's original Globe Theatre. Then they moved through an outdoor corridor toward the stage.

They passed the main audience door and stepped into a bustling backstage area. A rosy, round man stood in the center of a circle of people, waving a sword. He looked up as Liv and Colin walked into the room, then threw his hands (which, frighteningly, still held swords) into the air and came barreling toward them. Clearly, this guy was Colin's uncle.

"M'boy!" the man exclaimed, gathering Colin into an awkward, roly-poly hug. Colin was nearly half a foot taller than his uncle, and only half as wide. Blushing, Colin introduced Liv to the man, who was—oddly—called Ginger

(Colin later explained that Ginger got the nickname thanks to his red hair).

Ginger had an impossibly thick accent, and Liv—if she was being honest—couldn't understand more than ten words he was saying as he showed them around backstage. She just nodded and smiled, hoping she didn't look too stupid. Finally Ginger excused himself; a performance was under way, and he needed to outfit the cast of Romeo and Juliet with their swords and daggers. He explained, "It shan't be a bit of a tragedy without the swords, eh?"

Colin turned to Liv, laughing, as Ginger walked away. "You didn't understand anything he said, did you?"

Liv shook her head. "Not a word. Did I say anything stupid?"

"Nothing much," Colin said simply. He smiled secretly and looked like he was about to say more. But he didn't. He just motioned for her to follow as he led her into a quiet corner that was stuffed with trunks and dusty shoes. Liv suspected he was withholding something, and worried about what she might have said.

"What are you doing?" Liv whispered as Colin pried one of the trunks in the corner open. "Colin, seriously, I don't think we should take stuff."

"Not to worry, ma'am," Colin said, winking. "You're going to have to trust me. Now . . ." He studied Liv carefully as he rustled through the trunk. "I think this will suit you nicely, yeah?"

Liv broke out laughing as Colin pulled an enormous red . . . thing . . . out of the trunk. He held it up, motioning for Liv to take the material from him. "You want me to put this, um, *frock* on?" she asked incredulously, eyeing the Renaissance-style dress.

Colin nodded and grinned, chuckling as he pawed through the trunk again. "It should fit over your clothes quite nicely. And for the gentleman . . ." Colin had pulled a long piece of checkered wool out of the trunk. "A kilt!"

"You're going to wear that?" Liv asked, giggling as Colin wrapped the material around his waist, forming a thick, unflattering skirt. She studied her dress curiously, giggling as she pulled the fabric over her head. It slipped over her T-shirt and jeans easily, and Liv poked her arms into the puffed sleeves. "How do I look?"

Colin looked up—he had been trying to secure his kilt with a large diaper pin—and burst out laughing. "I think it's missing something." Colin held up a finger as he stepped over to a rack against the wall. "A hat should complete the look." He held an enormous, wide-brimmed hat out to Liv and moved toward her to fasten the ties under her chin.

Liv studied Colin's face as he stood in front of her. His

brow was furrowed, and he had pushed his lower lip out while he concentrated on unknotting the chin strap on Liv's hat. He looked up at her in the dim backstage light and smiled. His eyes were bright with laughter.

Liv broke into a smile. She felt completely silly and comfortable with Colin. Standing there in her enormous dress, watching Colin tie an Elizabethan hat around her head, Liv suddenly felt a flip in her stomach. *No!* she instructed herself. *Things are only this easy because you're friends. Nothing more!*

"There you go. All set," Colin said, moving away from Liv. "A hat for me," he said, quickly pulling a floppy felt hat from the rack, "and we're on our way!"

"On our way where?" Liv said, envisioning her and Colin strolling down the river walk in full costume. She hoped that wasn't what he had in mind—Colin was turning out to be even stranger than Liv.

"The theater, of course," Colin answered, poking a feather into the brim of his hat.

"We missed the first act, but I believe you said you have never seen Shakespeare live?"

"I haven't. But how . . . ?"

"While you were busy nodding at everything he said, Ginger offered us seats to tonight's performance. You nodded, so I just figured . . . unless you don't want to go?

It's not a comedy, but . . ." Colin tipped his hat at Liv and waited for a response.

"Of course I want to go!" Liv couldn't believe Ginger had offered them seats and she had hastily accepted. She felt really greedy, but was relieved she had been nodding, rather than shaking her head. "Shall we?"

Decked out in their silly costumes, Liv and Colin made their way through the back corridors of the Globe. Ginger had arranged a secret backstage platform for them to watch the show from. They were slightly behind and to the side of the action onstage, but Liv couldn't have been happier. She was wearing goofy clothes and watching Shakespeare from backstage at the Globe Theatre. In all her life, she could never have imagined she would *ever* be doing this.

As the curtain rose to start the second act, Liv turned to smile at Colin. "Thank you," she whispered.

He tipped his hat again. "Happy July Fourth," he whispered back. He settled into his seat and spread his kilt out around him. "You look lovely in a frock."

Love Is a Battlefield

"You!" Simon Brown bellowed in the general direction of the hallway. "Here!" Liv smiled. She had grown accustomed to Brown's no-nonsense ways, and was even starting to warm to his brusque way of summoning her to his office. It probably helped that she had been in a particularly good mood since her trip to the Globe on Friday too.

"Yes, Brown?" Liv popped her head into Brown's office and greeted him with a big smile. He looked up from his newspaper with a surly expression and cringed when he saw Liv's smile—Brown didn't like positive moods.

"Take that ridiculous expression off your face. Are you tipsy?" Without waiting for an answer, he gave a dismissive wave. "I don't care. Anyway, you need to do something for me." He scanned a pile of papers on the corner of his desk. "We are producing a ridiculous program about the eighties. Complete rubbish, but . . ." He trailed off, muttering.

Liv waited patiently in his doorway. When a full thirty seconds had passed, she prompted him. "What can I do for you, Brown? I'm happy to help any way I can." Liv couldn't believe those words had just come out of her mouth. She sounded like a robot.

"Oh, yes, you. Right. I need you to do some research. Get me up to speed on some of the songs that made the eighties 'so bloody great.'" He made little quotes in the air. "Put something together, pull some information. Make me look good. The regular nonsense." He glanced up at Liv to make sure she was paying attention, then sighed dramatically.

"Okay," Liv said happily. "This sounds great. Do you—?"

"Go, Girl!"

Liv spun on her heel and moved away from Brown's door. Apparently there would be no further explanation. Even still, Liv could hardly contain her excitement. *Yesssss!* she thought giddily. *A real project! And it's perfect!* She had finally been asked to do something meaningful, to show Brown that she could do more than herd a roomful of freakish fans into their seats. Of course, she needed a little translation from Gloria (she had no idea what "make me look good" or "the regular nonsense" meant), but that should be no biggie.

A few minutes later Liv was standing in the Music Mix lobby, explaining the assignment.

"This is huge, Liv," Gloria said, after Liv finished reciting Brown's instructions. "He must really trust you."

Liv beamed. "Really?"

"Trust me, I would know," Gloria said, rolling her eyes. "You know I was his intern a few years ago, right?"

"For real?" Liv said, curious. "I had no idea. Was he this hard on you, too?"

"Oh, yeah. The thing is, he's actually a pretty great fellow if you can see past his creepy, self-centered exterior." Gloria laughed. "But seriously—this research he's asked you to do . . . it's a big deal. He never let me do anything more than make copies and file." Liv listened carefully as Gloria elaborated on Brown's hasty instructions—she wanted to make sure she got this right. And Gloria was an expert on Brown translation.

At the end of the following day, Liv returned to Brown's office, report in hand. She had spent two days gathering every interesting factoid about the eighties she could find. She had included little biographies of each of the major producers from the era, as well as photos and bios of each musician who had earned a number one spot on the Billboard charts.

She had also downloaded a bunch of music from iTunes (using Gloria's corporate card, which she hoped wouldn't get her friend in trouble), and burned CDs that featured each of the weekly chart toppers. Liv was excited about her report and CDs, and she stood in Simon Brown's door with a smile plastered across her face.

"Yes?" Brown didn't look up.

"I finished the report you asked me to do on the eighties," Liv said, moving toward his desk.

"Leave it," Brown said, motioning to the corner of his desk. Liv did as she was told, then retreated to her tollbooth to wait for his thoughts. The phone was ringing when she got there. Liv assumed it was her father calling to check in—he was the only person who ever called her at work. Seeing that her caller ID was an outside number, she hastily picked up the receiver and prepared herself for a long conversation.

"Hey, dad," she said, twirling her hair with her free hand.

"Well, that's an interesting nickname," the voice on the other end said, teasing. "Most girls just call me Josh, but you've always been a little different, Olivia."

Liv blushed, relieved that Josh Cameron couldn't see her at that moment. "Hi," Liv said, grinning. "I thought it was my dad. But, um, it isn't. It's you. So. How have you been?"

"It's been a while," Josh Cameron responded. Liv could hear the smile in his voice. "I've missed you."

"Me too," Liv said honestly. "Where have you been?" Liv groaned, realizing how needy and stalkerish that may have sounded.

"I've been in the States. But I'm back now. When can I see you?"

Liv's throat was dry. *Um, now?* she answered silently. "How about this weekend?"

Josh Cameron agreed, and they settled on Saturday night. He was going to call her on Friday to work out the details—and he had given Liv his cell phone number, just in case. Hanging up, Liv couldn't stop smiling. She was going out with him again. She was going out with *Josh Cameron. Again!*

As she sat at her tollbooth, giddily reflecting on the conversation, Simon Brown sauntered over. He had *never* come to Liv's desk—his laziness prevented him from leaving his office—so she didn't really know what to do. Could she just sit there, or did she need to stand? Was she supposed to offer him her chair?

Brown solved the mystery by perching on the edge of Liv's desk, forcing her to back her chair up against the wall to give him room.

"Well done," Simon Brown said at last. "I'm impressed with your efforts." Liv could tell it had taken all of Brown's energy to dole out a compliment, which made his praise even more valuable.

"Thank you, Brown," she said, restraining herself from screaming with excitement.

"One more thing," Brown said, studying the contents of Liv's desk. "Will you be auditioning for the VJ for a Day contest?"

"Yes, sir . . . uh, Brown. Yes, Anna and I are planning to audition."

"Very well, then," Brown said, smiling slightly. His tan teeth glinted in the fluorescent light. "Very well."

As Brown sauntered off, retreating again to the confines of his office, Liv did a little dance at her tollbooth. She had done a good job. And unless she was totally misreading him, Liv was pretty sure Simon Brown had—in his strange, confusing way—just endorsed her VJ for a Day audition. At the very least, he wasn't totally against her auditioning.

And that alone was something.

That Friday, Liv was still floating. Brown had retreated back into his crabby shell, but now Liv knew that he wasn't totally out to get her. He hadn't stopped acting crass and rude, but at least he had shown Liv—if only for a minute—that he was the tiniest bit human inside.

She was distracted all morning, obsessing about her date with Josh Cameron the next day. She couldn't prevent her nerves from going crazy every time she thought about hanging out with him. She assumed things would get more natural between them soon—at least, that's what she was hoping. *I won't be intimidated by his celebrity status forever, right?* she wondered over a midmorning latte. *He's the same as everyone else—just a little more . . . famous. But I know that doesn't really mean anything.*

Liv had started to realize her obsession with celebrity was silly—now that she had spent a few weeks surrounded by stars and their entourages at Music Mix, she had seen firsthand how *average* most of them were. Usually they just had a touch more attitude.

Celebrities are just people who got lucky and had their talent turned into fame. So why did they deserve her respect and admiration so much more than, say, someone like Anna did? When she thought about it that way, Liv realized that she would much rather spend an evening with Anna than with someone famous just because they're famous. At least with her friends, she was comfortable being herself. She didn't worry about whether she was doing and saying the right things.

Liv realized she had been nervous around Josh Cameron for all the wrong reasons. When she let herself just *be*, things were always so much smoother and less awkward. She needed to let down her guard and hang out with him as an equal—not as Josh Cameron, *Superstar,* and Olivia Phillips, *Who?*

But before she could test out her new theory, Liv was forced to deal with one more celebrity ego—and this one made it tougher for her to remain calm and natural. Friday afternoon, Liv was summoned to the studio where Cherie Jacobson, Josh Cameron's ex, was in rehearsal. Cherie was scheduled to perform on *Hits Parade* in just a few hours, and Liv was dying to see what she was like.

Part of Liv didn't want to meet her new boyfriend's ex, but the other part of her was desperately curious. Liv figured there was no way Cherie knew about her and Josh Cameron's relationship—it's not like they'd been out in public together after that first date—but her stomach was in knots nonetheless.

Cherie's new single was a response to Josh Cameron's single, "Split," and rumored to be harsh. Their breakup had been smeared through the tabloids, and Cherie had gotten most of the bad press. Apparently, she had gone psycho, and frankly, Liv was a little scared of her.

When Liv got to the studio, she quietly poked her head

in to catch the attention of one of Cherie's assistants. A tall, rail-thin woman came to the door and ushered Liv inside. Cherie stood in the center of the *Hits Parade* stage, red hair flowing down her back as she belted out the last notes of her song. When the music ended, she returned the microphone gently to its stand and smiled at Liv.

"Hi, sweetie," she said, her voice dripping kindness. "Thanks for coming by. I hear you're the girl to go to when I need something?"

That's me, Liv thought, already annoyed. *Waitress, dog groomer, maid—at your service. There's that celebrity attitude.* Out loud, she said, "Yep. What can I do for you?"

"What you can do," Cherie said, all kindness stripped from her voice, "is lay your hands off my boyfriend." Liv's knees buckled. "I have friends everywhere, and they tell me everything. Just to remind you, you're nobody. And I can make your life miserable."

Liv stared at Cherie Jacobson. "Excuse me?" Liv said, much more boldly than she had intended. For some reason, she suddenly wasn't intimidated.

Cherie's smile returned to her face, and the false charm that had been there earlier snuck back into her voice. "What I mean to say is," she said, putting her hand on Liv's arm, "be careful. You don't know what you're dealing with." And with that, she spun on her heel and returned to the Green Room.

Liv headed out of the studio. As she walked down the hall, she considered Cherie's warning. She was a little flattered that Cherie was threatened by her, but equally freaked out. She didn't want anything to put a damper on the next day's date with Josh Cameron. . . . but what had Cherie meant when she said, "You don't know what you're dealing with"?

You're So Vain

Liv stood in line at the half-price theater ticket booth at Leicester Square, soaked and miserable. She hadn't realized that the ticket office didn't open until eleven, and she'd been waiting to buy tickets for almost two hours.

Stupidly, she hadn't brought an umbrella. And shortly after she had settled into her place near the front of the line, the sky had opened up and poured for twenty minutes straight. She had nonchalantly tried to duck under her neighbor's umbrella, but when the man in front of her saw her inching closer and closer, he had freaked out and vacated the line. The bad news was that she had lost her only hope of staying dry. The good news was that she had moved up in line.

The rain had eventually slowed to a drizzle, but the damage was done. Liv was cranky, dripping wet, and completely devoid of any remaining patience. Finally, a few minutes after eleven, the booth opened and she approached the window.

"Two tickets to *As You Like It*, please." Liv smiled at the booth attendant and waited.

"I have two tickets in the first row of the second balcony. Okay?"

Liv wasn't sure. The truth was, she didn't know why she had agreed to do this in the first place. Why, when Josh Cameron had called and asked her out again, had she insisted on planning the date? He was a multimillionaire, and she was . . . well, *not* a multimillionaire. In fact, these tickets were going to cost her an entire week's salary. She could only hope that he would pay for the rest of the date.

But, she thought, *this way I can show him what I like to do.* She was confident Josh Cameron would love Shakespeare just as much as she did, and she couldn't wait to see one of her favorite plays live onstage.

"That's fine. The first row of the balcony is fine." Liv

paid, and wandered away from the half-price booth, tickets in hand. She was worried that he would be disappointed with their seats. He probably only ever sat in the first row. Or some sort of luxury box. *Whatever,* she thought, shrugging off her paranoia. *I'm sure he's not that shallow. And he said he liked me because I'm "normal."*

Nine hours later, dry and umbrella-ed, Liv stood outside the theatre, waiting for Josh Cameron's limo to arrive. She had gotten there a few minutes before their planned meeting time, and had been waiting for twenty minutes. The play was supposed to start in less than five minutes, and Liv was starting to get nervous . . . and wet again.

Only moments before the theater doors closed, a limo came zipping around the corner. Josh Cameron hopped out of the backseat and embraced Liv in a quick hug. Several passing tourists stopped to stare and point, and a small herd of paparazzi materialized out of nowhere. Liv was taken aback, but Josh Cameron deftly stepped away and smiled for the cameras. He waved, then took Liv's arm and moved quickly into the theater.

"As usual, you look incredible," Josh Cameron said as Liv silently led him up the stairs toward their seats. She was still stunned by the scene outside—she had never been near paparazzi before, and she was freaked that she might be *in* the pictures. "I apologize for my lateness," Josh Cameron continued.

Liv waited for a further explanation, but none was forthcoming. "It's okay," she said simply. "But we should hurry. The show's about to start."

As they settled into their seats in the second balcony, Josh Cameron looked around. People were staring, and he shifted nervously in his seat. Smiling uncomfortably, he whispered to Liv, "We're an awfully long way from the stage, aren't we?"

Liv's stomach dropped. She couldn't believe she had been so stupid as to try to arrange this. He was probably horrified that he was stuck in the back of the theater with normal people. They could barely see over the balcony edge, and they were sitting a million miles above the stage. "I'm sorry. It's all they had," she explained quietly, studying her program to avoid his eyes.

"Not to worry, Olivia," he murmured in her ear. "I just appreciate you making the effort. Like I told you before, it's nice to be normal every once and a while. And it's refreshing to go on a date that my assistant didn't plan." Then he slouched down in his seat to hide from curious onlookers. As the curtain rose, Josh Cameron slid his hand into Liv's and left it there through the rest of the play.

Liv could barely focus on *As You Like It*. Fortunately,

she had read the play at least five times and easily followed the plot. But she was antsy and distracted, worrying about whether Josh Cameron was having a good time. He kept shifting anxiously in his seat, and hadn't laughed at any of the obviously funny parts.

When the final curtain dropped, Liv clapped and cheered with the rest of the crowd. Josh Cameron took his cell phone out of his pocket and quickly tapped out a text message. Liv glanced at him, and he stuffed his phone back into his pocket. When the cast took their places on the stage for the curtain call, Josh Cameron stood and led Liv out of the theater. He hurried them down the stairs and into the lobby, just as the crowds started to fill the main level of the theater.

"Let's get out of here," he said, weaving through the crowd as Liv struggled to catch up. She didn't know why they were in such a rush, but just assumed this meant that he had not liked the play. He held Liv's hand tightly as they moved through the crowded lobby and toward the front doors. Just as they were about to exit the theater, Liv's stomach lurched when she spotted a familiar face near one of the side doors.

"Colin!" she shouted, eager to be heard above the noisy crowd. Liv waved as Colin looked up and spotted her. Squeezing Josh Cameron's hand to get his attention, she leaned toward him and said, "Hang on one second—a friend of mine is here. I just want to say hi."

Liv crossed the lobby toward Colin with her date in tow. Her heart skipped a beat when she saw that Colin also wasn't alone—rather, he was with a gorgeous girl. *Who is she, and where is Rebecca?* Liv wondered.

Liv forced herself to shove aside the instant jealousy by focusing on Josh Cameron's hand in hers. *You are on a DATE,* she reminded herself. *With Josh Cameron. So stop being stupid. Now.*

"Liv," Colin stated simply. Liv thought he looked a little pale and uncomfortable, but couldn't be sure. "Did you enjoy the show?"

"Yeah!" Liv shouted, a little too loudly and awkwardly for her taste. "Oh, umm, have you guys met? Josh Cameron, this is Colin Johnstone."

"Colin, is it?" Josh Cameron said. Liv thought she caught him sizing up Colin's date, but chose to pretend she hadn't. "You don't actually like this stuff, do you, mate?" He motioned in the direction of the stage and laughed. Liv's hunch had been correct. Josh Cameron did not like Shakespeare. *Marvelous.*

"Yes, it's Colin," Colin responded coldly, glancing at Liv. "And yes, I love 'this stuff.'" Liv shifted uncomfortably. Colin continued, "Liv, this is Lucy. Lucy, Liv." Liv shook hands with Lucy, curious about who the mystery date was.

A few seconds of awkward silence passed, then Josh Cameron broke in. "Well, this has been fun. Olivia, are you ready?" Liv nodded, and he turned to address Colin and Lucy. "We're off to the 400 Bar—I'm thinking of doing a little impromptu performance tonight. We'll see, people may get lucky." He winked and flashed his dimples. "If you would like to join us, I guess I can *try* to . . ."

Colin broke in, "We have other plans. Thanks for the generous offer." Liv groaned quietly. This meeting was not going well. *Why,* she wondered, *were both guys acting so rude?*

"It was nice to meet you, Liv," Lucy said kindly. She nodded at Josh Cameron, then linked her hand around Colin's arm and led him out of the theater.

As Liv followed Josh Cameron out of the theater's front doors, she briefly debated asking him why he had been so rude to her friend. She also considered asking him if it would have been so difficult to try to enjoy the date she had planned. But she didn't ask. She just followed him silently through the after-theater crowd and into his waiting limo. She sat quietly in one corner of the car while Josh Cameron made several calls, figuring out which club was hot that night.

"The 400 Bar it is," he exclaimed eventually, flipping

his phone closed. "The club owner is totally into me trying out my new single tonight." His face was flushed, and he suddenly looked much more like a little kid than an international pop star.

"That's great," she said hollowly, sinking into her seat across from him. "What's the new single called?"

"It's a remix of 'You're So Vain,' the Carly Simon song. You know the one?" He hummed a few bars of the song. Liv certainly did know the one, and smiled at the irony of the song's title. It somehow seemed just perfect for Josh Cameron. "I'm trying to work it out before my Music Mix concert. It's nice to try it out for my peeps, you know?" He paused, tapping out another text message. "All right! We're here!" Josh Cameron pushed open his door and hopped out of the limo. He turned, checking to see that Liv was following him.

Inside the 400 Bar, the lights were low and the floors were grimy. It was the opposite of Meat by appearance standards, but the people were equally intimidating. Liv had still not gotten used to the VIP scene. She could feel everyone staring at her, and she felt like a complete clod. She had worn a thin sweater and chinos to the theater, and realized now how ridiculous she must look wearing Gap at a trendy bar.

Liv followed Josh through the crowd to a small bar

across the room. Josh Cameron rested his arm on the juke-box against the wall and waved to a half-dressed bartender pouring a beer. She sauntered over, planting a kiss firmly on Josh Cameron's mouth. He chuckled; Liv gawked.

"What's up, El?" he asked the bartender, flashing a quick smile at Liv, who was still dwelling on the strange and unexpected kiss.

"Hey, Joshie," she responded with a thick Irish accent. "We've been waiting for you. Tracy!" She called to a large, bald man on the other end of the bar. The man—Liv could only assume this was Tracy—moved toward them. Wordlessly, he slid the jukebox away from its place on the wall, revealing a door that had been hidden behind it. Liv stared as Tracy pulled a large ring of keys off his belt and slid one into the old-fashioned lock on the wooden door. With a whine, the door slid open.

Looking through the hidden door, Liv could only see feet and legs. The bottom half of the door opening was sealed up with concrete, and the top half opened onto the floor level of another room. It appeared that the room behind the door was about three feet higher than the room they were currently in, and they would need to shimmy through a tiny little opening if they were going to enter it. As Liv stared in confusion, Josh hoisted himself up and slid into the secret room.

Suddenly Liv's feet left the ground. Tracy had lifted and spun her toward the door's opening. Before she had a chance to react, she was sitting on the floor of the other room, and the secret door was closed behind her. Liv could hear the jukebox sliding back into its place against the wall. She was trapped.

Standing up, Liv scanned the hidden bar they had just entered. Gone were the grimy, soiled floors and dark, depressing lighting. This bar was snazzy and clean, complete with smooth tiled floors and shimmery lighting. A low bench ran around the perimeter of the room, but it was empty. Most of the people in the room were dancing or mingling around the bar, clustered in small groups. Each group had at least one person whom Liv recognized as some sort of celebrity—including Bethany Jameson and Christy Trimble, the starlets she had first met at Meat. Luckily, Cherie Jacobson was nowhere in sight.

Josh Cameron had disappeared, leaving Liv to fend for herself. It suddenly felt like she had turned up at her high school prom with her dress tucked into her underwear and no date.

Luckily, most people in the bar hadn't really noticed her, so she took a moment to wander around the room and check it out. She noticed that one wall was a panel of murky glass that looked over the bar they had originally entered.

Liv assumed that they were, once again, in some sort of VIP section, and the lower-level bar on the other side of the jukebox was the "regular" area of the club.

"Hello, you." Josh Cameron had sauntered up behind Liv while she was looking through the window at the crowds of people on the other side of the hidden door. "Pretty incredible, isn't it?" Liv turned around, and he planted a soft kiss on her lips. Nuzzling into her neck, he continued, "This club is great for trying out new songs because we can see how the crowd responds on the dance floor." He gestured to the windows.

Liv decided not to tell him how creepy she thought that sounded. *This is like Pop Star Big Brother or something.* Her discomfort seemed to melt away as she relaxed into his arms. Liv wasn't really into the VIP club scene, but she liked having Josh Cameron's attention shining upon her. Maybe she could get used to the scene—if it meant more people noticing Josh Cameron noticing *her*. He kissed her again and a stray curl brushed against Liv's cheek.

"Well, baby," he said, breaking the moment with a quick kiss on the cheek. "You have fun. I've got some people I need to talk to. . . ." With that, he worked his way back into the crowd and left Liv alone again.

For the next three hours Liv sat patiently in the corner of the room while Josh Cameron worked the club, meeting, greeting, and schmoozing. She had—awkwardly—tried to join him a few times, but he had mostly ignored her. So each time, after a few minutes of standing or dancing on the outside of a circle of celebrities, she retreated back to her spot on one of the benches overlooking the lower bar.

She had never felt more like a boring, out-of-place loser than she did that night. She self-consciously adjusted her sweater periodically, attempting to lower the neckline to give herself a slightly more stylish look, but it was useless. No matter what she did to physically fit in, she would just never click in this world.

Just as Liv began to drift off to sleep (her cushioned bench had been too tempting, and she was Bored Bored Bored), Liv spotted her "date" coming her way. She smiled weakly as he slid up next to her. *Finally.*

"You," Josh Cameron said, poking Liv's nose softly, "are such a sweetheart for understanding that I have people to talk to and things to take care of." He ran a hand through his hair. "You know, it's so much easier dating a regular girl than a celebrity. I mean, it's amazing that you don't really have your own stuff to take care of—that way, it's cool for you to just sit here and chill."

Liv stared at him. *Did I just hear that right? I "don't have my own stuff" to do? I can just "sit here and chill"?! Am I a lapdog or something?*

"And," Josh Cameron continued, his dimples deepening, "dating you will do wonders for my image after Cherie. I've really come out of this breakup looking like the normal one, haven't I?" He leaned over to kiss Liv, but she quickly stood up before he could get within six inches. She had—officially—had it.

"Josh," she began, "yes, I am just a 'regular girl,' and yes, I have been patient while you've ignored me all night. But normal people do have lives. And I do, contrary to your opinion, have plenty of things I would be *much* happier doing. So while you may think that dating me will be good for your image, I don't think that dating you will be good for me." She paused to take a breath. "I thank you for *gracing* me with your presence over the past few weeks, but now I have *very* important things I need to attend to. And *this* is just not worth my time. So good night."

And with that, she pushed through the crowd, knocked on the secret door, and slid through the hole and out of her VIP existence.

Sunglasses at Night

Josh Cameron had called Liv at work several times in the days following her Girl Power moment, but Liv resisted his charms. On their final date, she had realized she didn't like the person she was when she was with him, and she hated that she felt so powerless around him. Liv had avoided her gut instinct the first few times they had gone out, but now she realized the celeb lifestyle wasn't for her, anyway—she wanted to feel comfortable being herself. And while Josh Cameron claimed to love her honesty and "all-American, real girl" ways, she just couldn't get into being the novelty date.

The only bad thing about the breakup was that Liv had

plenty of time to dwell on her now obvious—and depressingly unreciprocated—crush on Colin. She thought constantly about their run-in at the theater, disgusted by how rude Josh Cameron had been to him.

Liv was dying to know who Colin's mystery date had been that night. She had been tempted to ask Rebecca, but figured that was probably not the nicest thing to do. Either Rebecca knew about Lucy and chose to ignore her, or Liv would be the bearer of really awkward news. In spite of her relationship with Rebecca, Liv felt sorry for her roommate—did she know about Lucy?

One night that week, after a particularly grueling day at work, Liv decided to stop off at Tully's for a cup of tea. She had spent her day running around town looking for a particular brand of snack bar. One of Music Mix's performers had brought his girlfriend to the set with him, and she was craving some special Australian snack bar that she missed from home . . . so Liv was sent out to fetch one for her. After checking every sandwich shop and market around Oxford Street, Liv had finally found the bar more than five hours later at an Australian sweater shop in Notting Hill. By the time she got back to the studio, the guest and his girl were gone. *A day well spent,* she mused.

She breezed into Tully's and was greeted warmly by the woman behind the counter. As she waited for her tea, the frustrations of her day quickly fading, Liv was startled by someone tapping on her shoulder. Turning, she was pleased to see Colin. She had run into him at Tully's a million times that summer—when she was on cappuccino runs for Green Room guests and he was satisfying Andrew Stone's soy latte addiction—but seeing him startled her, considering how much she'd been thinking about him that week. "Oh, hi," she said, noticing a flush creeping up her cheeks.

"Hi, Liv. All right?"

"Yeah, good. You?" *This is awkward,* Liv thought, cringing. *Why?* Before he could say anything more, she continued. "You know, I've been looking for you all week. I just wanted to apologize for my, um, date last weekend—he was a real jerk to you at *As You Like It*. I'm sorry."

"Liv, you don't need to apologize for him. Unless you were telling him what to say, it really wasn't your fault."

"Thanks. But it's my fault he was there, so I guess I feel somehow responsible." She paused. "So, ah, did you enjoy the play?"

"Yeah, it was great." Colin turned to collect his order from the counter. Liv noticed two cups, and glanced quickly around the room. She spotted Lucy, the girl from the play, gazing out the window at a table across the room. Colin's jacket was draped over the back of the chair next to hers. He continued, "We loved it."

Liv grimaced. There it was—"we." Liv knew it wasn't any of her business, but she was just dying to know how this girl fit into Colin's relationship with Rebecca. Liv suddenly felt oddly protective of her roommate, and didn't want to see her get hurt. She couldn't stop herself from blurting out, "So . . . how are things with you and Rebecca?"

Colin groaned. "Man, I knew you were going to ask me that." Liv nodded, watching Lucy out of the corner of her eye. "Rebecca and I are *not* together, if that's what you're implying."

Liv raised her eyebrows. "Really?"

"Definitely. Rebecca is very much not my type. But I do value her as a friend. I know that might sound crazy, but she's really very sweet, and there's something about her that just makes me laugh."

"Yeah, something about her makes me laugh too," Liv said sarcastically, setting her tea down on the nearest table. Colin hovered next to her table as Liv poured milk in her tea and stirred.

Colin continued, "The thing you should probably know is, in our first week in London, Rebecca really confided in me. She was worried she wasn't fitting in, and felt like she couldn't get along with you or Anna. She felt like an outsider, and I think she thought that spending time with me might give her credibility or something." He paused.

"I liked hanging out with her. It's not a pity thing—she's really funny, if you get past that petty, selfish exterior. I just don't know if she's that great with other girls, yeah?"

"Yeah," Liv agreed. "I think that might be a fair assessment." She didn't know why she was being so rude, but she couldn't stop herself. *It's not Rebecca's fault I missed my chance with Colin,* Liv mused. *I'm the only one to blame for that.*

Colin was still holding both cups of tea and had begun to fidget. He said quietly, "But I think she also sort of thought that if she and I spent time together, it might make you jealous." Colin paused. "But that's ridiculous, considering . . ."

"Considering what?" Liv asked, curious.

"Considering . . . other relationships." Colin looked down at his feet, then glanced at Lucy. "Right . . . ," he said, suddenly awkward. "Well, our tea is getting cold."

"Yeah, you should probably get back." Liv couldn't believe she'd been so wrong about Colin and Rebecca. "It was good to see you, Colin. Again, I'm sorry about the whole Josh Cameron thing last weekend."

"No problem," Colin said. "I'm sure he's a really great guy once you get to know him." And then he lifted one of the teacups in a little wave and strolled back to his table.

* * *

"Ah was talking to some of the producers from the events team, and they are just pos-ah-ti-uhv that I will win this little VJ for a Day contest." Rebecca delicately sipped her coffee, and studied Liv's reaction.

"That's great, Rebecca," Liv said blandly, for what felt like the thousandth time that night. "I'm really happy for you."

Earlier that evening Liv and Anna had decided they needed a girls' night out. Feeling generous, they had invited Rebecca to join them. Liv had thought a lot about what Colin had told her about Rebecca, and felt guilty that Rebecca hadn't made many friends in London. She really didn't want to be part of the reason someone was so unhappy, and she had vowed to try to give her roommate another chance.

About ten minutes after they left the office, Liv had regretted her generosity. Rebecca hadn't stopped talking, and most of their conversations for the past two hours had centered on Rebecca's brilliance. And, much to Liv's dismay, Rebecca refused to stop talking about the VJ for a Day contest. The good thing about Liv's breakup with Josh Cameron was that it had freed up plenty of time for her and Anna to focus on their audition material. They had finally formulated the beginning of a plan, and had been working almost nonstop to perfect it. Liv was confident that they would have a great segment ready in time for the auditions in a few weeks, but that didn't mean she was any more excited about listening to Rebecca's take on the auditions.

As Rebecca chattered on, bragging about her "fab-u-lous" ideas for her audition, Liv and Anna finished their drinks and stood up to leave. Rebecca didn't miss a beat. She continued to talk while sweeping My Rover into her arms (she had somehow gotten away with bringing Hell Dog to work for "show and teh-ull" that day).

Then she drained her coffee and dropped her Gucci sunglasses back into place on her perky little nose. Liv couldn't figure out why Rebecca was wearing sunglasses at night, but, considering Liv's own fashion expertise, figured she really wasn't the best person to criticize someone else's style.

The three flatmates made their way outside and headed for the tube at Piccadilly Circus. "Ah don't know if you know this, but I actually won the Junior Miss contest in Texas." Rebecca fixed Anna and Liv with a serious stare through her Guccis.

"I never would have guessed," Liv muttered to herself. Anna heard her and started giggling.

"They told me I was a natural onstage." Rebecca held My Rover up to her face and pushed her lips out to give him a kiss. She continued in a baby voice, addressing My Rover. "So I just *know* I'm going to be the very best VJ that Music Mix has ever seen. Look out England—Miss Texas is here!"

Rebecca smiled widely, revealing her perfect white teeth. Liv wondered if Rebecca put Vaseline on her teeth in real life, like they do in pageants. They were unnaturally shiny.

"You know, Li-uhv," Rebecca said sweetly, pausing as they passed the Piccadilly Circus fountain. "Maybe you could just help me with *my* audition. Work behind the scenes or something? Ah mean, I just don't want it to be uncomfortable for y'all when I win." Rebecca pulled a coin out of her clutch. "Lucky penny. Here's to my win!" she said, lowering her ridiculous sunglasses to wink as she tossed the coin over her shoulder into the fountain. Then she walked up the steps to the fountain base platform and started strutting around the edge.

As she listened to Rebecca ramble on, Liv considered the question she had been asking herself all night. *Was Colin right about Rebecca? Why would she come out with us unless she actually likes us better than she lets on?*

Liv was jolted out of her head by a high-pitched squeal. She turned back toward the fountain just in time to see Rebecca teetering madly, her high heel stuck in a crack in the concrete. Flailing her arms, Rebecca buckled sideways and landed right in the Piccadilly Circus fountain. Several groups of tourists, out for a late-night stroll, quickly grabbed their cameras and snapped pictures. "Ah'm okay!" Rebecca said, flashing her pearly whites just before her hair hit the water. "Ah've got My Rover and my Guccis—I'm okay!"

Liv watched, horrified, as Rebecca floundered in the fountain. She was trying to keep her sunglasses and My Rover in the air. As Liv moved to help her out of the fountain, she could see tears of humiliation welling up in Rebecca's eyes.

For once, Liv felt genuine empathy for her flatmate. *She is normal,* Liv thought. *She's desperate for attention and doesn't know how to treat people, but she's not immune to humiliation.* In that moment Liv suddenly realized that under Rebecca's thick veneer of I Love Myself-itis, she was just as self-conscious and awkward as anyone else. Rebecca just hadn't figured out a normal way of dealing with it.

She may be annoying and weird and talk about herself way too much, Liv thought, *but maybe she just needs people to be nice to her so she can realize she's safe being herself.* Looking at her soaked and tear-drenched flatmate floundering in the fountain, Liv vowed to give Rebecca another chance—for real, this time. Reaching out her hand to take My Rover from Rebecca's slippery, wet arm, Liv smiled. "Are you okay?" she asked, true concern ringing in her voice.

Rebecca looked up at Liv as a tear rolled down her face. "Ah'm fine. Thank you," she smiled. "Li-uhv, can you please dry My Rover's ears? He's prone to infection."

You Spin Me Round (Like a Record)

"Have you ever heard the theory that people and their pets look alike?" Liv was sitting in a small windowless room, surrounded by no fewer than twenty assorted dogs, cats, and one very loud parakeet.

Anna, who was squatting by her side, straightened the hood on a greyhound's zip-up sweater and nodded. "I have heard that."

"Don't you think Josh Cameron's dog looks just like him?" Liv giggled, gesturing to a black cocker spaniel that was lying on a cushy armchair in the corner of the room, surveying the rest of the dogs with pity. "The curls, the charming look, the snobby attitude—it's all there. Poor dog. I have to say, every time I look at that dog, I freak out just a little. It's frightening how similar they look."

Liv had totally gotten over Josh Cameron, but couldn't stop a hint of bitterness from creeping up—in part, because she had been assigned the worst possible task at that night's Josh Cameron concert. Over the past two weeks the only thing anyone at Music Mix had talked about was the approaching concert, and now that concert was finally here.

Lucky Liv had found herself assigned to the charming job of tending to Josh Cameron's dog and his backup dancers' pets during rehearsal and the concert. Which is why she was, at that moment, locked in the pet-bed room she herself had prepared a few weeks before—along with twenty unruly, high-attitude designer pets.

Anna had volunteered to accompany Liv to the concert to help out—she hadn't gotten an invite to the concert as part of the wardrobe team, and really wanted to see the show. Liv had asked Brown if she could bring backup, and he had—in a fit of kindness—agreed.

The two of them had been stuck in the pet room for the past two hours while Josh Cameron and his dancers rehearsed and relaxed in style. Liv and Anna's Animal House was not quite as plush—each of the dogs and cats had a squishy bed or pillow, but Liv and Anna were forced to sit on the floor. There were no human-size accommodations in sight.

As Liv prepared doggie dinners, Simon Brown poked his head into the circus and gestured to Liv. "You," he barked. "You're needed at the stage. It seems one of the dancers couldn't part with her pooch until the show started. I refuse to have that . . . *creature* . . . crawling out onstage during the show. So you will collect it from her and hustle back here. Go, Girl!"

Liv groaned. This chore would potentially involve her running into Josh Cameron, which she had been trying to avoid. So far she had succeeded—her Pet Land head-quarters had certainly been a good hiding place. But she supposed she couldn't avoid it all night, and she hustled off down the hall in search of the rogue pet.

In the darkened hallway Liv literally ran into Christy Trimble. Christy was widely known to be the fiercest celeb-rity on the pop circuit, and everyone tried to stay on her good side. Liv suspected her rather loud outburst at the 400 Bar hadn't left her in Christy's good graces.

"Olivia, isn't it?" Christy asked, surveying Liv's pet hair–covered jeans and T-shirt. "I've been hoping I would see you again."

Uh-oh.

Christy continued, "Your little 'exchange' with Josh Cameron at the 400 Bar a few weeks ago . . ." She made little quotes in the air with her perfectly manicured fingers, then broke into a smile. "Well done. I haven't seen anyone stand up to Josh like that before. I'm impressed."

"Oh," Liv said, flustered. "Uh, thanks. Really?"

"Really. That speech of yours was priceless. He needed that. And, despite what the gossip rags say, Cherie Jacobson is a good friend of mine. I filled her in on your little outburst, and she got a huge kick out of it. She thinks you're fabulous now, and wanted me to pass along her congratulations. You were a hit, girl.

"If you ever need anything, give me a call." Christy hastily scribbled out her cell phone number on a piece of paper and stuffed it into Liv's jeans pocket. "I mean it. Anything, anytime. I like you—you have spunk." With a wink, Christy turned and strutted down the hall.

Liv laughed in disbelief, and wandered over to the stage area. As she walked through the wings, Liv heard Rebecca before she saw her. Rebecca had been given the opportunity to introduce Josh Cameron to the audience—a reward from the producers on the events team, apparently—and she hadn't stopped gloating about it all week. Now Rebecca was standing just off to one side of the stage, swooshing her hair and rehearsing.

"Y'all, please welcome Josh Cameron!" Liv cringed when she heard Rebecca's drawl. As Liv poked her head around a curtain to see if the backup dancers were anywhere nearby,

Rebecca spotted her and motioned her to come over.

"Oh, Li-uhv," she gushed. "Ah just can't wait to do this. I'm ready!" Liv was a little frightened—Rebecca seemed a lot like a cheerleader. A psycho cheerleader. There was something unsettling about how much enthusiasm she seemed to have about doing this introduction.

"Are you nervous?" Liv asked, only mildly curious. If she had to get up onstage in front of thousands of people, she would be freaked out. Her performance on the catwalk at Runway had been hard enough. But Liv suspected Rebecca wouldn't show weakness, even if she were mortified.

"Not one teeny tiny little bit," Rebecca said. Liv thought she saw a hint of terror cross Rebecca's face, but it was immediately covered by another huge grin and a hair toss.

Just as Liv was about to excuse herself to continue her quest for the missing dog, the lights dimmed and the crowd started cheering. The concert was about to start.

"Oh gosh, Li-uhv," Rebecca said, grabbing Liv's arm tightly for support. "Please don't leave me. It's almost time." Liv studied Rebecca's face in the dim light. The self-composed Rebecca that had been next to her a second before was gone—she had been replaced by a panic-stricken, teary-eyed mess.

Liv could hear the band tuning behind the curtain

onstage. She and Rebecca were shooed to the side as the backup dancers filed past and into their places onstage. One dancer hastily dumped a pug (who was wearing a PUG REVOLUTION T-shirt) into Liv's arms as she passed. Just as Josh Cameron sauntered past them and up the stairs to the stage (without so much as a glance in Liv's direction), a producer approached Rebecca with a microphone and announced, "You're on. Go!"

Pug in hand, Liv turned to wish Rebecca good luck. That's when she realized something was desperately wrong. Rebecca had turned a nauseating shade of green. "Oh, Li-uhv," she whined. "Ah just can't do this. You go." Then she handed Liv the microphone and pleaded with her eyes.

"No way," Liv said, pushing the mic toward Rebecca. "This is what you've been waiting for!"

"Ah can't! Ah swear." Rebecca was quaking with fear. "Please go, Li-uhv."

Realizing there were very few options—someone had to introduce the jerk—Liv took the microphone and moved up the stairs to the stage. She had no idea what she was supposed to do, but figured she could wing it. She gently pulled aside a small section of the curtain. The pug—which was still under one arm—whined as the roar of the crowd crept around the edge of the curtain. *Gulp.*

Liv gingerly moved onto the stage. She was greeted

by thousands of screaming, applauding fans. Before she could freak herself out any further, Liv leaned into the microphone and shouted, "Hello, London!" Huge applause. "Music Mix is proud to present . . ." She lifted the pug into the air. ". . . Josh Cameron!"

The crowd roared. Liv had survived. Taking a deep breath, she moved behind the curtain. As she passed Josh Cameron on her way offstage, he smiled at her and gave her a little wink. Liv winked back—and realized he didn't intimidate her anymore. She finally felt like they were on the same level. Before jogging offstage, she turned and said calmly, "Good luck out there . . . Josh."

"So it turns out, our favorite roommate is mortified of public speaking," Liv said. She and Anna were sitting in a banquette at the concert's wrap party later that night. Gloria had convinced Brown to rent out a nearby club to congratulate the Music Mix crew on a job well done and to impress Josh Cameron and his dancers—Brown had agreed it was a good idea after the pop star had agreed to attend the party. Now most of the interns were packed onto the dance floor trying to get near him—Liv did not feel inspired to join them.

"I think tonight probably ruined her chances for the VJ for a Day audition," Anna said, stretching back into the booth. "If she really was planning to audition—I wonder if it was all just for show?"

"You're right," Liv said thoughtfully. "This may sound crazy, but do you think there's any way we could work *with* her? We *could* use her help with the makeup and hair. Right?"

"Aha," Anna said knowingly. "A plan."

"A plan." Now that Liv thought about it, asking Rebecca to join their VJ for a Day team was perfect—she had a lot of good ideas; she just needed to be reined in. Liv hoped their flatmate would agree to collaboration. After her humiliation at the concert earlier that evening, Liv suspected Rebecca would do anything to avoid public speaking again—and Liv knew she wouldn't easily give up a chance to win something. Liv and Anna could be her only chance.

"Liv?" Anna was looking across the dance floor at the club's front door. She pointed to two familiar figures who had just entered the party. "Is that Colin and Francesco?"

Liv glanced up. Her heart skipped a beat when she saw Colin's grin from afar. "Uh-huh."

"So," Anna said quietly. "What do you want to do?"

"I just can't believe how much I've screwed this up," Liv responded. As she did, she stood and waved Colin and Francesco over to their table. "I think I need to just try to talk to him again—at the very least, I can salvage the friendship, right? There's no need to avoid him. . . ."

Liv's stomach was in knots. She hadn't seen much of Colin since their last run-in at Tully's. He'd been really busy with work—and helping Rebecca with her VJ for a Day audition—and Liv had been spending most of her time with Anna working on their audition. Though she knew there was no hope for anything more than friendship with Colin, Liv wanted to try to preserve that. She couldn't stop thinking about how much fun they had had that summer—if she could just get her heart to stop thumping so hard every time he was nearby, she knew they could have a really great friendship.

As Colin and Francesco approached their table, Anna stood and grabbed Francesco's arm. "Francesco! *Buon giorno!* Come—dance with me!"

Not so subtle, Liv thought, cringing. But she shot her friend a grateful look, and—after a quick cheek-kiss from Francesco—turned to Colin. "Hey."

"Hello," Colin murmured, sliding into the booth beside her.

"How have you been?"

"So formal, Liv," Colin said, grinning. "It's not like you, yeah? But to answer your question, I've been good."

Liv relaxed. Clearly, this was the same old Colin. "Good.

Sorry. So did you enjoy the Josh Cameron concert? Somehow I ended up onstage, introducing him. Which was awkward," Liv broke off. Of course, she just *had* to bring up Josh Cameron. *Swell, Liv, swell.*

"Awkward because . . . he's your boyfriend, yeah?"

"Oh no, no. That's done. Over. It wasn't pretty." She shrugged.

"Over?" Colin said, tilting his head.

"Yeah, I broke things off after that night at *As You Like It*."

Did he not know that? Liv wondered, thinking back to their recent conversation at Tully's. "The thing is," she continued, her heart thumping as she realized she couldn't stop herself. "I guess I was looking for more than just a famous date—I think I'm better suited to someone who I can be myself with. But sometimes you figure that out a little too late . . . ," she broke off, and stared down at the table.

Colin sat there quietly, waiting for Liv to continue. She flushed as he stared at her in the club lights. "But you know what?" she said boldly, looking directly at him, "I think I missed my chance with the right guy."

"I'm not so sure about that," he said, frowning. "Liv, can I ask you something?" She nodded. "Do you remember the night we went to the Globe?"

"Of course," she answered. "It's the highlight of my summer so far."

Colin looked relieved. "Well, do you remember how you kept nodding at everything my uncle asked you?" Liv nodded, hearing Ginger's thick accent in her head. She impulsively grinned at the memory of Colin in his kilt.

"Well . . . ," he said, smiling slightly. "While we were there, Ginger asked you a lot of strange things that you kept nodding at. One of the things he asked was whether you 'fancied his nephew'—did you know that?" Colin looked at Liv, hopeful. She shook her head, but a slow smile spread across her face. He continued, "I, ah, I didn't want to bring it up then—you know, Josh and all—but . . . well, is there any chance that could be true?"

Liv began to nod, then paused. She wasn't sure where this conversation was going, but she needed to clear something up. "What about Lucy, the girl from the play? Aren't you together?"

"Me and Lucy? Hmm." Colin scratched his head. "Sure, we've been together about seventeen years." He broke into a huge smile. "Liv, Lucy is my little sister. She was in town visiting me from Stratford. She loves Shakespeare, so we decided to go to the show. She thought you were very nice, by the way. Josh Cameron—not so much."

"Oh," Liv said, suddenly completely at ease. "I see. So you're not . . . together, together."

"Not quite. Liv, I wanted to ask you out the first night I met you—but you were distracted with . . ." He gestured to Josh Cameron, who had begun to break-dance on the dance floor. "And then after our day in London, and the night at the Globe . . . but I just couldn't compete."

"Is it too late?" Liv wondered, not immediately realizing she'd said it aloud.

Colin shook his head and tiny little dimples popped up in his cheeks. He looked so adorable that Liv just couldn't stop herself. So she leaned her face toward his, and hoped that—for once—she wasn't saying or doing the wrong thing. As their lips touched, Liv could feel a smile tugging at the edges of Colin's mouth. She smiled back, thinking about how long it had taken to get it right.

As she relaxed into the kiss, Liv could have sworn she heard Anna and Francesco whooping from across the dance floor.

Dancing Queen

"Oh, Li-uhv, you look so pretty. Ah had no idea you could clean up so nicely." Rebecca smiled sweetly, then turned to address My Rover, who was sitting regally on a captain's chair in the corner of Music Mix's hair and makeup room. "Doesn't she just look adorable, baby? Yes, she does. Yesss sheee does!"

Liv rolled her eyes in the mirror. She understood after all that Rebecca really wasn't mean. She was just really, really weird. Colin was somehow able to find humor in her oddities, but Liv still had a way to go before she could actually be *entertained* by Rebecca. In the meantime, at least they were getting along.

Right after the Josh Cameron concert, Rebecca had

quickly and happily agreed to help Anna and Liv with hair, makeup, and "style" for their VJ for a Day audition. And now, three weeks later, with just minutes before they were on, she was fluffing and puffing Liv's hair to perfection.

Anna was ready to go on, and was standing outside the soundstage door, running through her lines one last time before their session kicked off. Everything—the music, script, props, and costumes—was all set. Now it would just come down to the execution, and whether they could pull it off was still to be seen.

There were a total of five auditions, and Liv and Anna had been selected to go last. They had been waiting and prepping for several hours in a tiny room just down the hall from the *Hits Parade* studio as the other intern teams wrapped their sessions. Almost every intern had formed a team with others, and the competition had gotten intense in the past week as the day of taping drew nearer. Though the auditions weren't live—the winner's segment would air on Music Mix that afternoon—all the auditions were being taped without do-overs in the *Hits Parade* studio.

For their audition, Liv and Anna had decided to stage a series of Make Me a Star segments, in which several "regular" people would be made over to look, dress, and act like celebrities. The makeovers would be done in real time, interspersed with the day's top Video Hits.

If everything went as planned, viewers would see people go from Frumpy to Fabulous in just under an hour. Ideally, the "drama" of waiting for the final result would keep people tuned in throughout the show. The outlandish disco gear Anna had found in old Music Mix wardrobe closets guaranteed that the production would be a visual success, if nothing else.

Naturally, Liv and Anna had decided to use ABBA's "Dancing Queen" as the backdrop to their audition. The "regular" people would be morphed into the band ABBA and, at the end of the show, would do a silly dance performance as the band.

True to her word, Christy Trimble had answered Liv's call for help, and had eagerly agreed to help them with the final dance—she had won Best Pop Video at the VMAs the past two years, and was known to be an exceptional choreographer. But she had agreed to help under one condition: Christy thought it would be "fabulously funny" if Josh Cameron were one of the makeover victims. Liv had agreed, assuming Josh would *never* go for it—after all, he was far from "regular." But when Christy called Josh and told him that this would be a good way for him to make himself seem approachable and "down-to-earth," he quickly agreed.

Liv and Anna were the two female makeover victims.

Anna would also be the main VJ, and Liv would handle all the behind-the-scenes, makeover-in-progress interviews. After much begging and pleading, Liv had finally managed to convince Colin to be the second guy in the band, rounding out their ensemble.

Now, with only a few seconds to go, Liv hoped Josh—or anyone else in the "band"—wouldn't flake out. As the two-minute warning bulb flashed, Liv scurried off in search of Anna. Showtime!

"I look like somcone's dad," Josh Cameron surveyed himself in the mirror while rubbing his short, tan beard. "Are you sure about this beard?"

Liv stifled a laugh, while Rebecca reassured him he looked "mah-vel-ous." They were about half an hour into the audition, and the cameras were in Josh's dressing room to check in on his "Frumpy to Fabulous" makeover status. As Liv stood waiting for the cameras to roll (Video Hit #8 was just about to end), she chose not to tell Josh how he really looked. Rather than normal and approachable, as Christy had promised him, Liv sort of thought Josh seemed a little pitiful and desperate for doing this. But he was oblivious.

"You look fabulous," she said, just as the cameras flipped on. "Now—smile, Mr. Cameron!"

* * *

"Liv," Anna whispered. "My butt cheeks are showing. Any suggestions?" Liv glanced across the set, giggling uncontrollably as Anna spun around and wiggled her butt. She was right—her short, white dress left little to the imagination. But the effect was perfect.

Anna and Liv were wearing matching white retro dresses, both of which were tied around the waist with a gold belt. Anna's hair had been covered with a long blond wig, and Liv's naturally curly brown hair was puffed into an aerobic-instructor do. Both girls had a gold headband tied across their foreheads, and were wearing moccasin-style boots that laced up their legs. Liv had to admit it— Rebecca was a makeup genius and Anna had perfected her wardrobe skills. They really did make a great team.

Liv stole a quick glance at Colin, who turned and flashed a toothy smile. Liv burst out laughing. A few weeks ago she never could have imagined Colin would agree to do something like this, but now he was a natural. He had mastered the dance (which frightened her just a little), and had happily zipped himself into the ugliest white jumpsuit she had ever seen. Rebecca had outfitted him in a flowing brown wig and a sporty headband. He looked like the ultimate porn star.

Anna came up behind Liv to check out Colin's ridiculous getup. "He's your soul mate," she whispered to Liv, laughing. "A loveable dork—with absolutely no inhibitions. I never would have guessed."

Liv turned and squeezed Anna's hands. "This is it," she said. "Only one more chance to make complete fools of ourselves. You are totally rocking—if they don't offer you a job after this, they're crazy!"

"Gaaaah! Don't say that. You're freaking me out!" Anna said, grinning.

"We," Liv said, squeezing Anna into a hug, "are going to rock. Now, as Brown would say . . . Go, Girl!" Then she pushed Anna out onto center stage as the producers signaled the end of Video Hit #2.

The lights splashed onto the stage, and Anna lifted the mic to her mouth and flashed a huge smile. "The moment we've been waiting for is finally here," she said into the camera, just as Francesco cued up "Dancing Queen" on the stereo in the background. "Today's top video?" she continued. "Nuh-uh—that will have to wait. First, the grand finale of our Make Me a Star makeovers. We've gone from frumpy . . . to fabulous! Ladies and gentlemen, please welcome . . . ABBA!"

The first notes of "Dancing Queen" came pouring out of the speakers as Anna ripped off the tracksuit she had thrown on to cover her outfit. Liv joined her in the center of the *Hits Parade* stage. Back-to-back, they held their microphones up and lip-synched in time to the music. *"You can dance, you can jive, having the time of your life . . ."*

As the second verse started, Colin and Josh popped out from opposite sides of the stage. Josh's outfit was exactly the same as Colin's, but instead of a wig, his naturally curly hair had been straightened into a helmetlike flop over his face. Liv could hear the producers and camera operators chuckling as Josh and Colin swayed out onto the stage. They moved and shook their hips in time to the music, fanning their hands out every time *"ooh ooh ooh"* came pouring out of the speakers.

At the end of the song, the foursome all slid to their knees, arms raised, and held their pose while Anna pointed to the camera and introduced Cherie Jacobson's new single as that day's top video. "I hope you've had as much fun as we have," she said, winking. "Live it up, Dancing Queens!"

One of the camera operators shouted, "That's a wrap!" Liv sighed a breath of relief. She and Anna cheered as Rebecca came running out from backstage. The three roommates danced around in a circle, hugging and laughing. *We did it,* Liv thought happily. *We actually did it.*

Later that afternoon everyone gathered at O'Leary's, an Irish pub around the corner from the Music Mix offices. The owner, a shrunken, stooped Irish fellow, had agreed to air that afternoon's *Hits Parade* segment on the bar's TV. Andrew Stone would be broadcasting the winner's segment as part of that day's show, and until the broadcast, they were left in suspense, waiting to see who won.

A few minutes before *Hits Parade* started, Simon Brown entered the bar and lazily made his way to an armchair in a corner of the room. Liv stole a glance at Anna, who had been working up the courage to talk to Brown all day. Anna's mom had called that morning, saying she could accept that her daughter needed to figure her life out—and together, they had resolved that if Anna got a job offer from Music Mix, she would stay in London for one more year before deciding her next step. Liv knew her roommate was making herself sick wondering whether things would work out. Liv crossed her fingers and glanced at Brown slumped in the corner.

Anna caught Liv's eye before slowly making her way across the room to where Brown was sitting alone with a cigarette and a beer (Liv could only assume he had a fat wad of Nicorette tucked in each cheek). Liv watched Anna approach him. Knowing Brown had the power to dramatically transform Anna's future, Liv considered the fact that she would need to figure out her own future pretty soon. Living in London had been the only thing she'd ever really known she wanted to do, and it had turned out to be a perfect choice.

Though Liv didn't know for sure what her next move would be, Anna had helped her realize that uncertainty could be okay. She just needed to think a lot more clearly and carefully about what she might want to do after graduation next year. She smiled at Colin, who had been watching her from across the bar. He moved over to her and pulled her in for a kiss.

"I can't believe you have to leave," he murmured in her ear. "Stay."

Liv wrapped her arms around Colin's neck. "Mmmm," she murmured as she snuggled into the crook of his neck and breathed in deeply—she loved that Colin smelled like a combination of fabric softener and soap. If she had known how comfortable that crook was, she definitely wouldn't have waited so long to get rid of Josh Cameron. She just wished she had more time to burrow into Colin's neck before she had to go back to the States.

"I really don't want to waste our time together thinking about me leaving," she said, leaning back and looking into his eyes. "And who knows what could happen? Maybe I'll be back next summer. . . . My mom left London to come to the States—what's keeping me from taking her place in England?"

"You would really come back?" Colin said, brushing a stray curl off her face with his finger.

"This summer sort of proved that anything can happen, didn't it?" She leaned forward and brushed his lips with hers. He pulled her in tighter.

"I hate to interrupt." Anna had materialized at Liv's side, smiling broadly. Liv and Colin broke apart, and Liv looked at her roommate expectantly. Anna continued, "Guess who's staying in London?"

"You got a job?!" Liv asked, her excitement bubbling up.

Anna nodded. "Apparently, Gloria was just offered a position as a VJ—so her job is open." Anna was beaming. "Brown said it's mine if I want it! I guess my supervisor in wardrobe talked to him a few days ago and recommended me. Brown said he was impressed that I approached him— that it proves how much I want it."

Liv was ecstatic. She quickly gathered Anna into a huge hug, just as Francesco danced over. Colin and Francesco exchanged a shrug and then wrapped Anna and Liv into a big four-person hug. Liv broke away just in time to see the *Hits Parade* logo pop up onto the TV in the corner. The show was about to start.

She reached for Anna's hand, and they held their breath, waiting to see who had won. Liv closed her eyes—she couldn't stand the suspense. She reminded herself that even if they hadn't won, their performance—and Anna's job offer—had been a truly perfect ending to a perfect summer.

Just as the first notes of "Dancing Queen" came floating out of the television set, Rebecca's high-pitched yell cut through the din of the bar—"Ah did it!" she screamed, lifting My Rover into the air. "Li-uhv, Anna, I won!"

Some things never change. But for Liv and Anna, so much had.

And Liv was having the time of her life.

Prom Crashers

For my parents,
who have always supported my adventures
and who taught me that a weird sense of humor
is not optional.

Acknowledgments

Thanks to Barb Soderberg (my wonderful, goofy mom), my cute and clever husband, Greg, and superauthor Robin Wasserman for all your help creating and plotting this story in a hurry. Good ideas, guys! Thanks for letting me steal them.

Ginormous thanks also to my editor, Michelle Nagler, whose suggestions, compliments, criticisms, and humor make me love writing—and writing for her, in particular!

Finally, thanks to Duluth, Minnesota—my hometown—and all the amazing people and places there that inspired a lot of these characters and experiences. Very little in this book is based on reality, but some of it sure comes close. But I'll keep those details to myself, thankyouverymuch.

One

Prom was in less than a month, and Emily Bronson still didn't have a date.

No matter how hard she tried, she just couldn't make herself *not* care. It was so unlike her. Homecoming rallies, student council, the one consistently clean table in the lunchroom . . . she didn't get hung up on any of that. But prom—prom was another story.

So Emily was busy doing what she'd done every night for the past several weeks: leaning against the counter at her after-school job, twisting her silky hair into tiny tangles, and daydreaming about—what else?—prom.

Emily worked at the Leaf Lounge, the tragically unhip "tea lounge" in the mall, almost every school night until nine—as well as weekends—which gave her more than enough time to daydream. The mall wasn't a superfunky boutique mall with trendy shoe shops and retro bags, either. It was just your run-of-the-mill, suburban mall with four Auntie Anne's pretzel outposts and an Abercrombie in both the east and west corridors. In a word, boring.

The Leaf Lounge—less a true "lounge" than the Gap was trendy—didn't have the urban-funk feel of a hip downtown hot spot. The beige and teal walls were adorned with shoulder-high shelving that boasted the complete collection of "Teas of the World" teapots. The Leaf Lounge's owner, Gary, was thrilled that his was one of the ten shops in the United States that sold those teapots. It was his claim to fame.

As such, Gary wanted all his employees to take great pride in their tea expertise. It was already bad enough that Emily had to work there. The thing that made it worse was being forced to wear a name tag that read:

EMILY, TEA CONNOISSEUR

HOW MAY I HELP YOU?

And she had to act like she cared. Emily had been awarded the distinction of "Tea Connoisseur" after completing a three-hour (mandatory) class in proper high tea preparation. The class had been held in the back room of the Leaf Lounge one Sunday morning before the mall opened, and was run by a woman named Meadow.

Meadow had shouted "pinkies on alert!" repeatedly through the session, which had elicited countless snickers from Emily's cousin and co-worker, Charlie. Needless to say, the knowledge Meadow had imparted had been used a total of zero times since the class—there wasn't a lot of demand for fancy high tea in a suburban mall. Their customer base was just *slightly* less classy.

"I divide, you choose," Frank, one of the Leaf Lounge's regulars, called to Emily across the coffee shop's formica countertop, breaking through her don't-have-a-date-for-prom obsessing. He was gesturing to a prepackaged muffin split down the middle on a plate in front of him. He was the only other person in the shop at that moment, and he seemed eager to chat. "Banana walnut, Emmy." Frank insisted on calling Emily "Emmy," and she had never made an effort to correct him. She thought the nickname was kind of cute. Emily slid half the muffin off Frank's napkin and popped a piece in her mouth.

"Tasty as ever," she declared. "Packaged preservatives. Thanks, Frank." Frank was one of the regulars who spent too many hours at the mall, and considered the Leaf Lounge's employees among his best friends. He came in every night around six and stayed for exactly fifteen minutes. He always ordered a prepackaged muffin and a cup of coffee and insisted his seventy-year-old waistline couldn't afford eating a full muffin. So he shared his snack with Emily, knowing it would buy him a few minutes of conversation.

"How's school, Emmy?" Frank smiled through a mouthful of gummed-up muffin. "Lots of gentleman callers?"

"Same old story, Frank." He asked the same question every night. Her answer was always the same. "Zero gentlemen and zero callers. In fact I don't even have a date for prom yet—got any friends you could set me up with?"

Frank beamed. "Back in my day, the boys would have been lined up around the block to sign your dance card. I bet they're all just too shy to ask."

"That's what I keep telling her." Charlie winked as he slid a tray of cookies across the counter. He had been hiding out in the back room for the past hour, smoking clove cigarettes and pretending to do dishes. "I keep offering to take her myself, but I guess I'm not good enough for her."

"Right—that's what it is." Emily nodded. "It couldn't possibly be that you're my cousin. That's not at all sad."

Frank studied Charlie carefully. "How about you, kiddo? You must be quite the lady-killer." Emily and Charlie exchanged a look. "You don't have a date yet?" To anyone under the age of fifty, it was glaringly obvious that

Charlie was 100 percent gay. But Frank was of a totally different generation, and the thought never crossed his mind.

"I do okay," Charlie finally responded seriously. "But no—no prom date yet. My fingers are crossed, though, that the girl of my dreams will turn up one of these days and steal my heart."

Emily shot him a look as she stacked cookies into the cookie jar next to the register. Charlie couldn't say anything without dripping sarcasm. It was part of the reason she loved him, and part of the reason she often lovingly loathed him.

Frank sighed, then tumbled gently off his stool. "It's been a pleasure, Emmy. Charles"—he winked at Charlie—"your time will come . . . with the ladies, I mean." He nodded and shuffled toward the door.

"Sweet guy. Totally clueless," Charlie muttered through clenched, smiling teeth. "So, what are we doing now?"

Emily closed the lid of the cookie jar and turned to Charlie. "Bored?"

"Completely and hopelessly. I can't stand this place for one more second. Entertain me."

"It is *so* not my issue that you're bored. Maybe you could serve a customer or two, and your shift wouldn't feel so long?" Emily pushed past her cousin and into the back storage room. Charlie followed her like a lost puppy. "Hey," she said, thinking about what Charlie had just told Frank about prom. "Aren't you going to prom with Marco?"

"Ah, Marco," Charlie sighed. "Don't I wish."

Emily shot him a confused look. "Am I missing something? Can't you get him to come up for prom?" Marco and Charlie had been dating for almost a year, but things were complicated by the fact that they had been long-distance almost since the day they had met—Marco lived in a suburb of Chicago. Emily could never keep up with the drama.

"He doesn't believe in prom," Charlie stated simply. "He thinks it's an antiquated social custom that should have died with the eighties." He shrugged. "Plus, I'll see him in June when we get to the villa." The words rolled off Charlie's tongue as if spending a summer at an Italian villa was totally normal.

Charlie and his parents spent six weeks every summer in Northern Italy, which is where he and Marco had met the year before. Their romance had been kick-started during four shared weeks in the Italian Alps. Emily could think of nothing more idyllic, and every ounce of her wished that (1) *she* got to spend the summer in the Italian Alps instead of her suburban backyard, and (2) Marco was straight so it could have been *her* fairy tale (in addition to the Italian setting, Marco was hot). But she was happy for her cousin— when she wasn't overcome with jealousy.

"You tell Marco," Emily teased, "that prom is a rite of passage that should be respected. Prom rocks." She furrowed her brow seriously. "Unless I don't find a date, and then prom sucks." She grabbed a big bag of coffee beans off one of the shelves and returned to the front of the store. Charlie was still trailing behind her, hands empty.

"I'm with you," Charlie agreed, hopping up to sit on the counter. "I'm hoping he'll call me one day and tell me he's fully into prom and on his way here, but I think it's a lost cause. I'll find someone to go with—I can't say I'm worried. So let's focus on you."

"Let's not," Emily declared. She set the bag of beans on the floor. "Much as I want to go to prom, I really do *not* want to be a pity case. I'll either go on my terms or I won't go at all. I am *not* going to get desperate."

Charlie's eyes widened. "Sheesh. Touché." He poured himself a mug of coffee, then immediately poured it down the drain. "God, I'm bored," he declared again. He repeated his pour-coffee-dump-coffee routine. "Let's talk about what you'll wear to prom when you find your date."

"Here's a thought." Emily grabbed the mug out of Charlie's hands and set it in the dishwater. She loved working with Charlie—he was a thousand times more normal than Edna, the close-talking day-shift manager—but she had come to realize he was virtually useless and actually created work instead of doing work.

Luckily they almost always shared the evening shift, when demand for tea and coffee was low. They were never very busy, and usually work was just a good excuse to stand around and gossip. "Maybe you could go in back and check inventory on leaves. We should probably fill the canisters out here and put in an order for the stuff we're low on." She wanted to change the subject away from prom, and knew Charlie would just keep bringing it up if she didn't get rid of him.

Charlie lifted his arms over his head and cheered. "I'm on it! I'll be in back if you need me." As he pushed through the swinging door, Emily watched him pull his iPod out of his pocket and spin through his playlists. She doubted he would even bother checking inventory—Charlie had come to realize that whatever he didn't do during the evening shift, the morning shift would take care of the next day.

Emily bent down to pour tea leaves into one of the huge glass canisters on the shelf beneath the front counter. When she stood up again, her breath caught in her throat as a living incarnation of Prince Charming strolled past the Leaf Lounge's open storefront. She stared in admiration at his profile, and held her breath when he stopped just outside the entrance to the lounge.

Let it be said that Emily usually didn't go for the quarterback look. But as Prince Charming walked through the doors and leaned against the counter, Emily gained a newfound appreciation for sandy blond hair, chiseled cheekbones, and long, lean muscles tucked under a black T-shirt. His body screamed strong, but his face murmured soft, sensitive, and oh-so-perfect.

It had only been five seconds, and Emily was already in love.

"How's the chai?" he asked, staring above Emily's head at the menu posted on the wall.

Emily twirled her long, shiny black hair around her finger, putting on her biggest flirt. Her hair was her greatest weapon, and she had every intention of using it. "Give it a try," she responded with a coy smile, realizing too late that she was being neither clever nor amusing.

But the hottie smiled back, flashing his teeth at her! (Okay, maybe it was just a really big smile that got all shiny in the neon lights of the menu—because, really, whose teeth actually flash?) "I'll take one."

Emily pulled a glass off the shelf. "For here, right?"

"To go," he answered, but Emily thought she saw him pause. "I have to get home. I'm supposed to compose a sonnet for AP English by tomorrow. Haven't started." He flushed.

Aha, she mused. *A smartie!* She replaced the glass and pulled a paper cup off the stack next to the register. "Oh. Well, good luck with that." Emily foamed the milk for his chai while digging for another line of conversation. She finally settled on, "Do you go to Humphrey? You don't look familiar." She knew he didn't go to her high school—and knew she hadn't been required to write a sonnet for her own AP English class—but asking about school was always safe.

"No, I don't go to Humphrey. I was checking out the tux shop—you know, prom."

"Oh," Emily looked down. *Of course he has a girlfriend,* she thought. *Why wouldn't he be going to prom?* "Right."

He rested his elbows on the countertop, leaning over the counter toward Emily. "I'm going with one of my sister's friends, which sounds pretty sad, I guess." Emily didn't think that sounded sad at all—it sounded like hope. "I was looking forward to it, since I've known her forever and it should be fun going with a friend, but she's sort of making me regret asking her." Emily frowned—she was torn between feeling ecstatic that he wasn't going to prom with the love of his life, and sort of disgusted he was dissing on his date.

The guy continued, laughing. The corners of his eyes got all crinkly, which Emily loved. "That came out wrong. The thing is, I didn't realize she would have all these rules about what I wear. She wants me to rent this tux she saw in a magazine that has some sort of lining that matches her dress color exactly. I guess I'm a little irritated, since this is the fifth tux shop I've been to that doesn't carry the style. I'm starting to run out of time."

"You know where you could check?" Emily said, stirring chai tea into the foam cup of hot, frothy milk. "There's this vintage shop downtown that has the weirdest mix of stuff. Formal wear, vintage hats, Victorian gowns—they have a sign on the door that says 'We've got what you're looking for and more,' or something like that. I bet they could order it, even if they don't have it in stock. They're pretty helpful. It's worth a look, right?"

"Thanks for the tip." He smiled. Emily thought she caught him checking her out. *Woo-hoo,* she thought happily. She twisted her hair and flipped it over one shoulder.

"I'll check it out," he said, nodding appreciatively. She wished he was talking about her, but knew he was referring to the store.

Emily set the cup of chai on the counter. "Whipped cream?"

"Please."

"I'm Emily, by the way."

"I know." Emily furrowed her brow. "Your name tag," he explained.

Emily squirted whipped cream on the drink—it sprayed out too quickly, and a big glob plopped off the hot drink and landed in a messy splat on the counter. She reddened. Prince Charming didn't seem to notice. He was staring at Emily in a very, very positive way. *Maybe I have hope of finding a prom date after all,* she mused. *We would look* fine together.

"I'm Ethan. Thanks for your help, Emily."

"No prob." She wiped a blob of whipped cream off the outside of the cup and handed it to Ethan. He was watching her face carefully as he grabbed the cup.

"I've never done this before, but . . ." Ethan looked down and took a quick sip of his chai. Emily waited for him to continue. "Do you think you'd want to go out sometime?"

Emily grinned, trying to reign in her excitement. Better not to seem too desperate. "Definitely. I'd love that. Why don't you give me your number?" Emily hadn't ever asked a guy for his number before, but decided it was a cool way to play it. It made her seem much less eager, and put her in charge of how this would go down.

"Oh—okay." Ethan seemed a little taken off guard. But he scribbled his number on a paper napkin and shoved it across the counter. "Promise you'll call?"

"I promise." Emily grinned and put on a flirty smile. "I guess if I don't, you'll get the hint." She laughed. Visions of her and Ethan walking arm in arm into her prom danced wildly through her head. She knew she was getting ahead of herself, but just couldn't help it.

Ethan smiled back. "I guess I will. Well, see you, Emily." Then he turned and retreated into the fluorescent lights of the mall. Emily was staring off after him, transfixed, when Charlie emerged from the back room.

He let out a long, low whistle, squinting to see Emily's Prince Charming as he pushed through the mall exit. "Nice one. Your team or mine?"

"Definitely mine." Emily broke her stare. She turned toward Charlie just as he grabbed a napkin (*the* napkin) off the counter and hastily wiped up the melting pile of whipped cream that had toppled off Ethan's chai latte a few minutes before. She grabbed his arm to stop him, but it was too late.

When Emily opened the napkin, searching desperately for ten clear digits, the phone number Ethan had just given her had melted into a big, creamy blue blob. Ethan would be getting the hint—just not the one Emily had intended.

Two

Like a good suburban teen, Emily spent Saturday mornings mowing the precisely rectangular lawn of her parents' split-level house. She got paid five dollars, but she probably would have done it for free. She liked the alone time.

It was the first truly warm spring day, and Emily was enjoying herself. She loved to crank up her iPod and sing along to Jack Johnson or Mason Jennings (her favorite local Minnesota artist) as she marched back and forth across the patch of grass. She could shut out the sounds of her boring suburban neighborhood and pretend she was somewhere—anywhere—else.

She had never quite belonged in Minnesota. It's not that

there was anything wrong with her home state, exactly—
she had just always known, deep down, that she would flee
to a land far, far away as soon as she had the opportunity.
She couldn't wait to escape.

Emily had set her sights on NYU in middle school
after getting hooked on reruns of *Felicity*, and had studied
like crazy to get her SAT scores high enough to ensure that
she would get in and get a scholarship. Sure enough, she
had gotten a thick, manila package several months ago,
welcoming her as a partially-subsidized member of NYU's
Class of 2011. She had another three months of living in her
parents' suburban prison before she fled the confines of the
Midwest for the fabulousness of New York.

She was counting the hours (2,168 when she last checked)
until she and her dad would set off in their Grand Caravan
down I-94 en route to New York. Until then, she was bored
bored bored. She and every other senior she knew had a major
case of senior slide, and Emily had spent the past two months
trying desperately to entertain herself into survival.

"Gooood morning, *mi amore!*" Charlie sauntered up
Emily's driveway, sliding his aviator sunglasses into place
over his eyes. Emily waved, flipping the switch on the
mower to off and bluntly kicking the back to release the
chunks of grass that were stuck behind the front left wheel.

"Can't I get one morning away from you?" Emily and

Charlie had finished their shift at the Leaf Lounge less than twelve hours before, and were both scheduled to be back at work that afternoon.

"You know you missed me, love." Charlie grinned and gave his cousin a squeeze. "What'd you make me for breakfast?"

"Make your own damn breakfast, you lazy piece of sh—shingle." Sidney, Charlie's best friend, jumped out the passenger side of Charlie's blue 1986 Volvo. "Hey, Em. Hope you don't mind me crashing here this afternoon." Sid slammed the car door closed, cursing loudly when the window slid open. She glared at Charlie. "Your parents are loaded, you lazy moron. Get a new freakin' car."

Charlie's car functioned, but just barely. When a door was closed on the Volvo, another one opened. And not in the metaphorical sense. Literally, closing one door on the car caused a chain reaction of another door popping open, or a window sliding down. The car was falling apart, but Charlie loved it, in part because it always got Sid so worked up. She had a raging temper and no patience, which kept Charlie amused.

"Rich parents do not a rich kid make." Charlie winked over the top rim of his glasses. "She's so crabby these days," he stage-whispered to Emily. "I don't even know why I bring her out in public. It's embarrassing."

Sid grimaced and pulled her guitar out of the Volvo's trunk. "You know what's embarrassing?" She settled in on Emily's lawn to tune her guitar. Sid was an amazing songwriter and singer and brought her guitar everywhere. Charlie said it was like they had a live soundtrack to accompany them wherever they went—he liked to call it *Charlie: The Musical*. After a beat, Sid continued, "Those aviators are one hundred percent 2005. I don't read *Vogue*, and even I know that," she snapped. "Catch up on your fashion, Charlie. *That's* embarrassing."

Charlie and Sidney were an interesting pair, to say the least. They always came as a team, and they always bickered. They were like an old married couple: They clearly loved each other, but constantly teased one another.

Unlike Emily, who was a senior at Humphrey High School in the middle of a converted cow field, Sid and Charlie both went to South High. South was a public school that looked like an Ivy League college smushed together with Julliard. Thanks to favorable zoning laws, South drew all the rich, downtown kids with arty, liberal parents and four years of college tuition socked away in savings bonds.

Charlie was the perfect poster child for South. Always groomed, always the lead in the school plays (though never the musicals—Charlie's singing would easily have made the telecast for the worst *American Idol* auditions), always quick with a witty one-liner and clever comment. And his parents—Emily's aunt and uncle—were rich beyond belief. But they had worked for their money, and believed that Charlie needed to learn to manage money himself.

Thus, he was forced to take a job at the Leaf Lounge.

Charlie hated working. But he hated going without even more. Charlie spent every penny he had on clothes, dinners out, and iTunes downloads, knowing his parents would have his back when he got to college.

Emily's parents had gone the opposite route. Her mom, Elizabeth—Charlie's mom's sister—became a high school English teacher after college and married the history teacher in the classroom next to hers.

And so it was that Emily was born into a modest life of literature and long walks rather than wine tastings (Charlie) or summers in Italian villas (also Charlie). Not to mention parents who thought it would be the epitome of cool to give their child a name one syllable away from the writer Emily Brontë.

Emily pulled the mower into the back corner of the garage and pushed her damp bangs off her forehead. Charlie and Sid were still bickering, but both had settled comfortably into plastic lounge chairs they positioned around Emily's little sister's Dora the Explorer plastic pool in the backyard.

"Lemonade would make my life *perfect*, Em." Charlie

touched his fingers to his lips and made a kissing motion. "*Che delicioso!* My spa away from home."

"You know your way around—*mi casa es su casa.*" Emily pulled her long black hair into a low knot at the nape of her neck and shoved a stick into the chunk of hair to keep it in place. "You're the one who decided to come way out to no-man's-land today. You know I hate hanging out at my place. So if we add things up, you owe me for letting you come over in the first place. I'll take my lemonade with ice, thanks."

Most weekends, Emily got a lift into the city to chill at Charlie's family's loft downtown. Then in the evenings, they'd relax at Jitters, a cozy downtown coffee shop, to listen to live music, or go to the local bowling alley, Urban Bowl. Nights usually ended at Burrito Jack's for chili con queso and chips.

But lately Charlie had decided that Emily's family's suburban life was quaint, and declared that it was a hoot to hang out at her house—even though his family's loft had direct skywalk access to a bar with darts and foosball. Really, there was no comparison.

Emily could think of nothing more boring than spending one extra minute at her house, but Charlie was the one with his own car . . . so he usually decided where they would hang out. Charlie almost always got his way. It's just the way their relationship worked. And he was currently on a "bland suburbs=rockin' good time" kick.

"While you're inside, grab me a Pop-Tart, will you?" Sid batted her long eyelashes at Charlie, who looked like he had no intention of going anywhere. She hummed and plucked a string on her guitar, singing, "Pop-Tarts, Pop-Tarts. Strawberry Pop-Tarts."

"You're already up, Em," Charlie whined. "Why don't you just run along and grab us some snacks and drinks?" Emily's cousin was persistent and equally lazy. Though Emily had no interest in waiting on him, she knew Charlie wouldn't stop begging for the next hour.

Just as she was about to head inside to grab a pitcher of lemonade to shut him up, she spotted Max, her neighbor and best friend since forever, trekking across the cul-de-sac. She lifted her arm to wave.

"Perfect timing, my friend," Charlie shouted in Max's direction. "I was just about to run inside to get us some lemonade—could you be a love and detour past the kitchen to grab something tasty to drink? Since you're already up, obviously. An object in motion likes to stay in motion, right?" He glanced around, seeking approval. "Inertia."

Emily rolled her eyes in Max's direction. He laughed, familiar with Charlie's requests. The four of them had been hanging out a lot in the past few months. Charlie and Sid had always been friends, as had Max and Emily. But it was only after going out as a group the previous New Year's Eve that they all started hanging out regularly as a foursome. They complemented one another well.

"You got it," Max responded. "Can I bring you a cooling eye mask or a personal masseuse to go with that, King Charlie?"

"Strawberry Pop-Tart, please!" Sid called as Max pushed open Emily's front door. "Thank you, Max. You're a *lurve.*"

Max and Emily had been friends since the day a five-year-old Emily had run around the neighborhood wearing only Scooby Doo underwear and baby powder, shouting, "I'm Snow White! I'm Snow White!" Her family had just moved to the block, and Emily's parents were less than impressed with her self-introduction to the neighborhood. People had learned a little more about Emily that day than anyone cared to remember.

After baby Emily's afternoon adventure, her parents had felt it necessary to make a more modest introduction to each of their neighbors later that evening. So they had strolled around the hood, Emily dressed in a green gingham dress, and shook hands with all the parents. Emily coyly stuck her tongue out at each kid who hid behind his or her parents' knees.

Most of the neighborhood kids had been well trained

and knew they ought not reciprocate the gesture. Only Max had been bold enough to stick his tongue out in return and blow a raspberry in her direction. It was this little joint rebellion that bonded them as instant friends.

"Voilà!" Max had returned from the kitchen with a Pop-Tart and a glass of lemonade on a plate that he had covered with an upside down mixing bowl. He presented the plate to Charlie, fancy restaurant-style. "Bon appétit!"

"That's what I call service," Charlie remarked, pulling the bowl off his plate and nodding his approval. "I like."

Max snorted. "And for the ladies—" He presented two plastic SpongeBob cups filled with lemonade that he held clumsily with two fingers of his other hand, and produced a second package of Pop-Tarts from his back pocket.

"What about you?" Emily asked as Max sat down on the ground with his feet resting in the inflatable pool. "You just schlepped all this stuff out here for my charming cousin and didn't get yourself anything?"

"Not thirsty," Max said simply, closing his eyes and tilting his face up toward the sun. "I'm trying the grapefruit diet for a day, so I'm already nice and hydrated." Emily laughed and rolled her eyes. Max was always doing weird things like "trying the grapefruit diet for a day" or entering the John Beargrease Sled Dog Marathon.

On the outside, Max was a completely normal suburban

guy—a cute, medium-tall teen with slightly too-long brown hair and Abercrombie style. But his friends knew he was an aspiring journalist, and that he always chased potential—and often bizarre—story ideas wholeheartedly. Emily could only imagine the grapefruit diet had something to do with a story pitch he was working on.

Charlie studied his Pop-Tart package and held it out at arm's length toward Sidney. "Sid—trade?"

She studied him suspiciously. "Why?"

"Mine's crushed."

"Please tell me you're kidding." Sid stared at Charlie in disbelief. "Who the he—heck crowned you prom king?"

One could always count on Sid to say it like it is. Charlie liked to push people's buttons, but Sid always let him know when he'd taken it one step too far.

"Speaking of prom," Charlie said, artfully changing the subject, "Marisa Sanchez is freaking."

"Who's Marisa Sanchez?" Max asked, only half interested. "And we care about prom why?"

Charlie gasped dramatically. "Marisa Sanchez is only *the* most sure-to-win prom queen candidate in the history of South High. But I heard a rumor"—he paused for effect—"that she was busted with a bottle of Jack at Lainie Callen's Roller Derby party last week, and got kicked off the prom committee."

Sid giggled. Sid *never* giggled. Though she was short and petite and perky-looking (you could almost go so far as to say she resembled a cheerleader—gasp), Sid was much more pit bull than poodle. Giggling just did not fit her image. "This is especially funny since Marisa Sanchez is the girl that busted me for smoking a Marlboro outside the gym doors instead of rah-rahing at last fall's homecoming pep rally." Sid sighed contentedly and strummed a melancholy chord on her guitar. "Karma, bi—bella, karma."

"Sidney, Sidney . . ." Charlie jokingly tsk-tsked at Sid and took a long sip of lemonade. "Your vow to stop swearing is *not* going so well." Sid was as skilled at swearing as she was at singing, and had decided two months earlier to abandon her potty mouth. Charlie thought it was hilarious, particularly when Sid *started* to swear, then switched her words at the last minute.

Sid rolled her eyes. "Did I swear?" She narrowed her eyes at Charlie. "No, I did not. In fact I called Marisa Sanchez, prom queen extraordinaire, *bella* . . . beautiful. I am a sweetheart."

"Speaking of prom—again," Emily said, attempting to head off another bickering session between Charlie and Sid, "I have a date."

Her three friends turned. The looks on their faces suggested disbelief.

"What?" she said, smiling mischievously. "You don't believe me?"

"We're with you constantly," Charlie said in response. "When would you have had time to get yourself a date that we wouldn't know about?"

"Let me clarify. I have a date, if I can *find* him again."

"You do or you don't have a date?" Max looked confused and a little ill. The grapefruit seemed to be messing with him.

"I met the guy last night at the mall. His name is Ethan."

"Cut!" Charlie yelled, clinking the ice cubes in his empty lemonade glass over his head like a maraca. "I was *there*, remember? You don't even have his number, if I'm not mistaken. My apologies for that."

Charlie had already apologized a million times for his goof the night before. After Emily had run out the mall doors after Ethan and searched the parking lot until she was sure he was nowhere to be found, she and Charlie couldn't help but laugh a little.

Emily lifted her hand. "Clarification. I *had* his number. But you're correct—I no longer have his number. Which means we have some plotting to do."

"Is this another Emily plan?" Max asked, leaning his head back into the grass. He waved his fingers in the air and chanted, "Go, Tigers! Yay!" He was referring to Emily's sophomore-year plot to try out for the cheerleading squad, even though she hated cheerleading. She just thought it would be funny. "Because honestly, your plans sort of scare me." Like he was one to talk.

"Ding, ding, ding!" Emily replied, clapping. "I have a plan."

She continued, "Here's what I know about this guy. One: He is going to prom because he was shopping for his tux. And PS, he's going with his sister's friend, not a girlfriend, and he was definitely flirting with me—so this isn't some delusional one-way street. Two: His name is Ethan. Three: He doesn't go to Humphrey." She paused, flicking a leaf that had floated over her foot in the wading pool. "So . . . we go where we know he will be! Let's find a way to get into all the other proms in the city and find this guy.

"Oh my God. It reminds me of *Wedding Crashers*," Charlie said, grinning. He had a major celebrity crush on Owen Wilson. Which wasn't surprising, considering the fact that Charlie was completely narcissistic and actually looked a little bit like Owen Wilson. It was like he had a crush on himself. "We are going to be *Prom* Crashers!" He looked thrilled.

"So does this mean you're in?" Emily asked hopefully.

Charlie nodded. "Absolutely."

Emily looked at the other two expectantly.

"What?" Sid asked. "You have Charlie. Why do you need me?"

Max grunted from his post on the ground. "What she said."

"You guys!" Emily stuck out her foot and rolled Max onto his side on the grass so he was facing her. "We have to do this together. One last fling before we all take off for college. The ultimate challenge. What do you say?"

"I say"—Sid chewed her Pop-Tart with her mouth open—"screw prom. I'm not going to my own—why would I want to go to someone else's?"

Charlie pushed his lip out in a pout. "I need you, Sid."

"Forget it," Emily retorted. "I'm not begging. But it's going to be a blast. That's all I'm saying. I know that *I* need something to get me through the rest of this year. I mean, this is the last month or whatever of our last year of high school. It would have been fun to go out in style, the four of us, you know?" She blew her bangs out of her face and crossed her arms over her chest. "Whatever. You guys can spend the next month studying by yourselves. Charlie and I are going to rock crashing proms. Harumph." She had a faint smile tugging at the corners of her mouth.

Sid shrugged and glanced at Max. "Fine. I'm in." She grinned meekly. "When you put it that way."

"Nuh-uh." Emily shook her finger. "Not like that. If

you're in, you're in. No halfhearted 'fine.'" She made quotes in the air.

Charlie snickered. "Tough guy. I like it."

"I'm in! I'm in!" Sid sarcastically cheered her arms in the air. "Better? I'll take anything to kill the time until we graduate. It sounds sort of fun." She shrugged. "Besides, you literally couldn't drag me to my own prom. So this is a good way to see what this prom crap is all about. Do I get to wear pink?"

"I'll do it on one condition," Max broke in, pushing himself up on his elbows on the ground. He was laughing at the image of Sid in pink.

"Yes?" Emily prompted. She was giddy with the hope that this might actually happen. She could think of no better way to celebrate prom season—and get a date—than with a crazy challenge.

Max looked at Emily sternly. "This is about the quest. I couldn't care less about finding this guy—it just sounds like a good time. You promise you won't get all serious and psychostalker?"

"Come on. . . . Who would be more into the adventure than me? This is totally about the quest." She looked innocent and laughed when Max continued to look at her sharply.

"Fine," he agreed. "But promise anyway. This is *not* just about the guy."

She nodded seriously. "I promise. Of course I *want* to find Ethan. But prom crashing is the perfect distraction to kill the time before we get out of this lame town. And if we succeed in our mission, I will have a superfoxy date. What could be better than that?"

Three

"We have nine targets." Charlie had spread paper beverage napkins across the counter at the Leaf Lounge. Each napkin had the name of one of the local high schools written on it. He and Emily were working the Wednesday night shift, and Charlie had spent most of it plotting their first move for Operation Prom Crashing.

Max, who was sitting on Frank's stool at the counter, had come to the mall partly to plan, partly to flesh out his latest story pitch (a feature about some local guy who carved bears out of cheese rind), and partly to catch the tail end of Sid's set.

Sid often played her guitar and sang in the evenings at the Leaf Lounge. Gary thought she gave the place a cool vibe, and Sid was happy to have the venue. She was trying to get her start somewhere, and while she realized the mall coffee shop wasn't the Knitting Factory in New York, at least it gave her practice playing in front of a live crowd.

As was often the case, though, the "crowd" was only two people strong—Max, of course, and Vern, a cashier from Dylan's, the mall department store, who had hustled over to hear her play during his break. Vern always came to Sid's sets—he fashioned himself her biggest fan. He was maybe her *only* nonfriend fan. Sid's ultimate goal was to spend her life touring the country to play small clubs in big cities. But the first step was to extend her reach beyond the mall's four walls and gain a slightly cooler fan base.

Her bluesy-rock sound was fabulous. She just needed her break.

As Sid struck the final chord for her last song, Vern broke into mad applause. Emily rolled her eyes. Sid dropped her guitar into its case and strolled over to the counter, with a brief nod in Vern's direction.

"Complimentary beverage?" Emily asked. "Great set."

"Coffee?" Sid grabbed one of the napkins off the counter and studied it. She didn't like to talk about her performances—she always said that the lack of audience was painfully depressing. "What's all this?"

"All this," Charlie explained, "is the beginning of a plan. Did everyone do their homework this week?"

The other three nodded. After agreeing to Emily's prom crashing plan the previous weekend, each of them had contacted everyone they knew, trying to get intelligence about all the other proms around the city so that they could formulate a plan. As they reported their findings, Charlie pulled out each school's napkin and scribbled out the date and location of its prom.

Emily studied the napkins and began to sort them into piles. "We have four weekends. Nine proms."

"We can count out our own schools," Max said, plucking the napkins with South and Humphrey written on them. "We know Ethan won't be there, right? Charlie, Sid, you checked South's directory for an Ethan?" Charlie nodded. "So that's only seven. Not bad."

Sid slapped her hand on the counter. "Totally doable."

"We have a big weekend ahead of us," Emily said, grinning. "Three this Saturday—Marshall, Park, and Memorial."

"Like, three days from now?" Max asked, sounding mildly concerned.

"Yup. You worried?" Emily poked him in the arm. He poked her back. Emily hoped he was eating real food again and not just grapefruit, otherwise he'd be really crabby for their first proms.

Charlie shuffled three of the napkins so that they were

lined up in front of him on the counter. "All right," he said, suddenly very businesslike. "What's our strategy for these first three? Do we just break in? Show up? How are we gonna do this?"

Emily chewed her lower lip thoughtfully. "Well, I guess we could just sneak in," she said finally. "Though that seems a little boring."

"And not possible at Memorial," Sid said, sipping her coffee. "The guy I know who goes there said security is really tight on the day of prom. The dance itself is held in Memorial's gym. They lock all the doors a few hours before prom starts to keep the unsavory types out. And it's a superstrict ticket system. I guess the parents all get paranoid for their precious babies' security."

"Okay." Emily nodded. "So sneaking in isn't an option at Memorial. Maybe we could plant someone on the inside before they lock the doors?"

Charlie clapped. "I like that!"

"The other two are both at the convention center," Max broke in. He had found the details about Marshall and Park's proms online. "So maybe we divide and conquer? Two of us go to Marshall and Park, the other two to Memorial?"

"Yeah," Emily said, "that would be good, except I'm

the only one who knows what Ethan looks like. The point of our mission, remember?"

Max rolled his eyes. "Ah, yes . . . the guy."

"Ethan," Emily corrected. "Plus, isn't this more fun if we all do it together? Max, what if you and I try to break into Marshall and Park, then meet up with Sid and Charlie at Memorial later? They could sneak into the school that afternoon and hang out, then let us in through an unguarded door when we get there?"

"Nice." Charlie waved the napkin with Memorial written on it. "My first conquest."

Sid raised her hand. "One other tiny issue," she said, waiting to get their attention. "I have nothing to wear."

"I can borrow my dad's tux," Max declared proudly. "It might be a little big and boxy, but it's free. If I'm not going to my own prom, I'm not paying to rent one." Max didn't have a date for prom. He and Emily had sort of joked about going together, but neither had actually bought tickets.

"I own a tux, so I'm good," Charlie said. "I feel tacky wearing the same shirt more than once, but I guess since it will be different crowds at each prom, I can break the rule."

Emily and Sid exchanged a look. "Since I'm not *officially* going to prom—yet—it might be a little tough to convince my parents to buy me a dress. I'd have to do too much explaining. How about you, Sid?"

"Nothing. And I'm not borrowing from my mom. Nuh-uh. No freakin' way. She wears shoulder pads."

"So we can either buy something or go with what we have. We'll obviously look out of place in jeans, which makes crashing a little more challenging. Don't we need to fit in to get in?"

Sid nodded. "I'm going to propose a third option, since I refuse to buy a prom dress." She jumped off her stool. "Max, can you cover for Em? Charlie doesn't do anything, and someone has to serve the customers while I steal Emily for two secs."

"Hey!" Charlie feigned anger, but knew he had no right to be defensive.

"I don't even know what a green tea latte is," Max responded. "But yeah, I can cover." He moved behind the counter as Emily slid past him and untied her apron.

"What's the plan?" she asked as Sid pulled her into the mall.

"You're about to see me do something *very* scary. If you laugh, I'll bite. I mean it." Emily promised to keep a straight face, and she followed Sid into the mall's department store.

Sid sauntered up to Vern, whose break had ended and now stood sorting hangers behind the counter in the young men's department. "Hey, Vern." Vern looked up, a huge smile spreading across his face as Sid leaned in toward him. "Thanks for coming to hear me play tonight."

"Oh, uh, no problem." Vern said, obviously taken aback by Sid approaching him.

"What'd you think of the set?"

"Good," Vern replied, lowering his voice. It cracked slightly under the pressure. "You were great."

"Thanks, babe." Sid smiled suggestively. "I love that you always come to my shows. It means a lot to me."

Vern flushed and nodded. "Yeah, well, your singing means a lot to me. You look so confident up there."

Emily's head flipped back and forth like she was watching a tennis match as Sid expertly charmed and wooed Vern. She was highly impressed with—and surprised by—Sid's flirting skills.

"So," Sid said, elbows resting on the counter in front of Vern. "I have a teeny-tiny favor to ask. Do you think you could help me out? It would mean the *world* to me."

Vern stuttered. "Oh, ah, sure. What's up?"

Sid was twisting her shortish, caramel-colored hair between two fingers. A dyed-red streaky piece fell across her left eye. Vern stared at it, entranced. "The thing is, Emily and I are both going to prom. Together, as friends, of course—I don't believe in prom dates. It's so stifling." She glanced at Emily. "Anyway, neither of us has anything to wear. And I'm saving up for a new guitar." Sid broke off momentarily. "You will come hear me play it, right?"

Vern nodded, mouth slightly agape.

"Do you think there's any chance you might let us *borrow* dresses from Dylan's? We would clean them and return them as soon as we're done." Sid leaned in closer for her last line. "No one would need to know."

Emily stared, transfixed. She could only imagine how Vern was feeling at that moment.

"Um." Vern looked around to make sure no other clerks were within earshot. "It would be our little secret?"

"Our little secret," Sid confirmed, nodding.

"I guess it couldn't hurt anyone, right?" Vern's face cracked a smile. "Follow me."

Sid grabbed Emily's hand and gave it a squeeze as the two of them followed Vern through a set of double doors marked EMPLOYEES ONLY. When they reached the back room, Vern turned to face them with a huge grin. "Take your pick. I'll guard the doors. Do you think you can find something?"

Emily and Sid stared around at the racks and shelves of dresses hanging, folded, and boxed up, ready to be moved out to the floor. They both nodded, and Vern retreated, leaving them alone with their personal dress collection.

"I feel so sleazy," Sid groaned.

"Sidney Cristina Martinez, you are a flirt. A good one."

"If you blab, just kill me first. I'm not proud."

Emily laughed. "I promise not to tell." She flipped through a rack of dresses, searching for the size tens. There were only tiny sizes on the rack. Emily had always wondered who fit into the size zeros and twos—she was tall and lanky, with broad shoulders she had developed during her years as a competitive swimmer, and couldn't remember *ever* being a zero.

"Do you see any twos?" Sid asked, flipping through a rack across the room.

Emily groaned inwardly. "Yeah, over here." *So size twos do exist,* she thought. Sid was short and compact and absolutely adorable—until she opened her mouth. Then she was a size twenty-four.

Sid pulled off her T-shirt, revealing her black sports bra, and slid a Pepto-Bismol-pink A-line dress over her head. She gagged loudly before pulling the dress back over her head. "Prom sucks." She stood half-naked, selecting another dress to try on.

"Why are you so antiprom?" Emily asked, considering a magenta dress hanging on the rack in front of her.

"Why are you so not?" Sid retorted with a smile. "Seriously, what is it about prom that makes you so blubbery?"

Emily raised an eyebrow. "Blubbery? That's a flattering choice of words." Sid shrugged. "I don't know. . . . I guess

I've always had this romantic image of prom night, with flowers and pictures and kissing and dancing. There's just something sweet about it all."

"Oh, come on," Sid blurted out. "It's a totally old-fashioned custom that needs to die."

"You sound like Marco." Emily thought back to her conversation with Charlie a few days earlier. She knew her cousin believed in prom almost as much as she did—so it was weird that both his boyfriend and his best friend were so antiestablishment on the prom front. "You have to admit that getting dressed up and swooped off into a limo with a total hottie sounds fun."

"Sure." Sid poked her head through the loose neck of a strapless orange gown. "If you're getting picked up by your hot best friends and going to prom for a laugh. You can get me on board for that—but prom for real? Nope." She laughed at the orange dress—which made her look like a Caribbean cocktail come to life—and quickly unzipped it. "Speaking of friends and prom . . . I've always sort of wanted to ask you this." She threw the orange gown back on a hanger. "Why haven't you and Max ever . . . you know . . ." She winked. "Isn't this your big chance with him? You have seven proms to make it official."

Emily grimaced. People always asked if she and Max were hooking up. They had been friends forever, but it had never felt right. "I don't know. I guess we're just better friends. There's never been an attraction like that."

"Have either of you ever even *dated* anyone else? Maybe there's secret lust just sitting there, undiscovered."

Emily shook her head. "No secret lust. And yeah, I've dated people. Just no one decent. Slobbery-tongue Dan was my low period."

"What about Max? Does he have a hot history?" Sid pulled a sleeveless amethyst gown over her head.

"No, Max has been single forever. But that doesn't mean anything."

"Uh-huh. What do you think?" Sid asked, referring to the dress. The deep blue and sleek fabric complimented her medium-brown skin perfectly, and the cut made her look like a superstar.

Emily gave her a thumbs-up. "Perfect. You look like a tiny little model."

"Hey, bi—butterscotch! Tiny, I'll take. Little, no way. I'm tough. You having any luck over there?" Sid strolled over toward Emily's racks, her slouchy jeans sticking out the bottom of her dress. She pulled an emerald green cocktail dress off the rack and stood on her toes to slide it, still on its hanger, over Emily's head.

"So?" Emily prompted.

"Cute. But you can do better." Sid selected a rich pink

shimmery satin gown from a box on the floor. "Take off your shirt," she instructed.

Emily slid her coffee-stained shirt over her head and pulled the dress on in its place. The material draped seductively over her chest and clung to her slim hips, making her look half her original size. Sid whistled.

"You look like a pink Oscar statue. Hot." She studied Emily's figure wrapped into the pink material and growled. "Really hot."

"So this is the one?" Suddenly prom felt more real to Emily than ever before. She could see Ethan's smile, could feel his arms wrapped around her on the dance floor. She imagined their good-night kiss.

"That's it. When we find Ethan, he's going to be drooling."

Emily grinned and squeezed Sid into a hug. "That's the point, isn't it?"

Sid and Emily strolled happily back to the Leaf Lounge, dresses tucked under their arms in Dylan's bags. As they approached the shop's entrance, Neil, the clerk at the jewelry kiosk in the middle of the mall's corridor, called out to Emily. Sid hustled past, back into the Leaf Lounge, leaving Emily to fend for herself.

"Hey, Neil." Neil had asked Emily out once a week since she had started at the Leaf Lounge the year before. His parents owned the kiosk, so he worked most nights. He had greasy flaked hair, a rude attitude, and undeterred confidence. Neil was not her type. At all. Ever. "How's it going?"

"Good, good." Neil ran his fingers through his hair, releasing a storm cloud of flakes. "What'cha got there?" He pointed to her bag.

"Oh. Prom dress."

Neil stared. "Who's the lucky guy?"

"It's a long story, actually." Emily suddenly realized something. "What school do you go to, again?" She already knew the answer.

"Marshall." He narrowed his eyes. "Why?"

"No reason. Isn't your prom this weekend? Who are you taking?" Emily mentally crossed her fingers. This was a long shot, but she was suddenly realizing she may have an in at her very first prom.

Neil blushed. "I . . . ah . . . I'm not going." He looked sad and a little vulnerable.

"Why not?" Emily feigned surprise. She moved in closer to Neil, groaning inwardly. *Sacrifices, sacrifices,* she thought.

"Couldn't find the right girl."

"That's crazy!" Emily blurted out, feeling only slightly guilty. *I am a terrible person.* "Do you *want* to go?"

Neil's face brightened. He was beginning to catch on. "Hey! You should go with me."

"I don't even go to your school," Emily said, not caring in the least.

"That's perfect!" Neil exclaimed. Emily realized she would be arm candy—no one would know who she was, and it would make Neil look like he was some sort of stud outside school walls, since she could only imagine he wasn't the coolest guy at Marshall. *But you never know,* she mused. Neil looked giddy. "I mean, it doesn't matter if you don't go to Marshall. It would be fun. Whaddaya say?"

"Yeah, okay. Can I get your number?" This would be a perfect arrangement—she could give Neil girl credibility with his friends; he would be her in at prom number one.

Neil grinned in a way that made Emily feel a little oozy. "Sure, babe."

"Neil." Emily leaned over the counter. "Do not call me babe. We're not there yet."

He flushed. "Got it." Neil scribbled his number on a piece of Dress Yourself in Diamante stationery. "Should I pick you up at seven?"

"Oh." She didn't want Neil to know where she lived, nor did she want her parents to find out about this. The image of Neil pulling up in her driveway and shaking hands with Mr. and Mrs. Bronson while Emily paraded down the stairs in her prom dress made her want to gag.

She'd have to get ready at Charlie's and make up some excuse for why she was going out. Prom pictures with Neil were not suitable for the family photo album. "Why don't we just meet here?"

"At the mall?"

"Yeah." Emily nodded. "I'll meet you right here at seven. That's enough time, right?"

"There's never enough time for Neil."

"Right." Emily gritted her teeth, then smiled. "I'll see you Saturday. I'm looking forward to it."

Later that night when Emily got home, she flipped on the computer in her family room. She had a paper due in Honors English the next day and had six scenes left to read in *King Lear* before she had any hope of pulling something legible together.

But the last thing she felt like doing was reading the final pages. She would much rather catch up on Gawker Stalker scoop, and her NYU acceptance letter gave her the security of knowing she could coast for the next few weeks.

As she surfed through the day's celebri-gossip an IM popped up in the lower-left corner of her computer screen.

```
M: Hey.
```

Emily smiled. Max lived next door but always IMed. He was constantly online finding unusual story ideas. In addition to the grapefruit diet and cheese-rind-bear-carving stories, he was also developing a story about yurts—whatever yurts were.

E: hey back.

M: How was the rest of work?

E: so exciting. how's yr story?

M: I'm learning how to make turducken.

E: ??

M: It's a chicken that's cooked in a duck that's cooked in a turkey. Crazy!!

E: i'm a better person for knowing that. tx.

M: What r u up to?

E: wasting time. u?

M: Avoiding my Lear paper.

E: clearly. *sigh*

M: Movie?

E: k. here or there?

M: There in a sec.

Emily smiled and flipped off the computer. She headed toward the kitchen to get a bag of chips. Emily and Max had had at least one movie night a week for as long as she could remember. Max was a freelance movie reviewer for a local online arts website. He was using the movie reviewing to get an in with the editors so that he could work on features and profiles. But he'd been writing reviews for a year and, despite a ton of pitches, had yet to land a feature— though he did get to screen some really bad films. Emily loved to join him and make fun of the worst ones.

She had been thinking a lot lately about what she was going to do next year without their regular movie nights to look forward to. They'd hung out almost every day since third grade. Even when both Emily and Max had been grounded for setting up a bug dissection lab in Max's kitchen—and used Max's mom's good silver and china as tools—they had still "chatted" through their secret flashlight communication system. (Both hid flashlights under their mattresses and devised an illogical Morse code to communicate, just in case aliens had taken over their neighborhood.)

Now that college was drawing nearer, Emily wasn't sure what she was going to do when Max was in Appleton, Wisconsin, and she was all the way out in New York. Max poked his head around the corner and peered into the family room. "There you are. Your sister said you weren't home."

"As far as she's concerned, I'm not." Emily's little sister, Abby, was an eight-year-old "accident" that was now just a pain in her butt. Emily often came home from work and quietly tiptoed into the house without greeting anyone. She needed a few minutes of peace before the questions (from her sister) and advice (from her mom) started.

Lately her mom had been on a nonstop prom kick. She hadn't yet accepted the fact that her little girl might not be going. So she left magazines on the coffee table with dog-eared pages showcasing dresses she thought would look good on Emily. Emily didn't know what her mom would do when she found out that she had (a) selected a dress without her mom's guidance (that, PS, she didn't even buy) and (b) decided to go to every prom in the city *except* her own. She hoped to keep her crashing scheme a secret from her family as long as possible.

"I brought *Never Been Kissed*." Max beamed.

Emily smiled. "Perfect." As she nestled into the couch next to her best friend, giggling at the opening scene of the movie, she couldn't keep Sid's question from niggling in the back of her mind. *That's crazy,* she thought, dismissing the idea of her and Max together. This *is perfect.*

Four

The next afternoon, Emily waited for Max at her locker after school. Earlier that day he had stuck a note written on a chewing gum wrapper through her locker door, asking her to wait for him after chemistry class. She had the afternoon off work and knew Max would offer up some distraction to kill the time, so she happily obliged. Max appeared at her locker a few minutes after the last bell with two pairs of roller skates tucked under his arm.

"Uh-oh," Emily nodded toward the roller skates. "What's up?"

Max grinned mischievously. "I need your help."

"I figured as much. What's the plan?"

"New story idea," Max declared. "I'm going to write a

piece on the benefits of roller skates. I think they're about to make a comeback. I want to figure out how easy it is to get around on eight wheels."

Emily looked at him, her face blank. "You're serious? What happened to the cheese rind story? And the grapefruit diet stuff? And the turduck—thing?"

"I'm on to new pastures," Max said happily. "Those stories were going nowhere. *This*"—he held a pair of the skates out to Emily—"is going to be a good one."

She grabbed the skates and slammed her locker closed. "You'll drive, right? I was going to take the bus home."

Max nodded. "I'll drive as far as downtown. But then we can only go places we can get to on foot-wheels."

"Okay," Emily agreed. "I'll go on one condition." She twisted her hair into a knot and fastened it with a pencil from her backpack. "As long as we're going downtown . . ."

She paused and Max broke in. "Don't pretend to be difficult. I know you're going to go with me—you always do, and that's why I like you. And you know I'm going to agree to your condition, so what's the use of pretending to play hard to get, Emily B.?"

Emily laughed. "All true." She linked arms with Max as they strode out to the parking lot. "Here's my condition: I want to stop by that little vintage-type shop. You know, the one by the ice cream place? I told Ethan he should check it out, and I want to see if he's been there yet. Maybe we can find out his last name."

"Em, I will agree to your condition"—Max unlocked the car—"provided we can get there on skates."

She grinned. "I feel confident the shop is eight-wheel accessible." They hopped in Max's car, chatting about their day and their upcoming plans for their first prom crash. When they got downtown, Max parked his car at a meter and they fastened their skates. Emily rolled away from the car. "I haven't done this since I was about eight years old."

"Exactly!" Max cried. "But it's a very respectable form of transportation. I think our afternoon will be much more fun on skates."

Emily laughed. Max was a total goofball, and when they were together, he always came up with the weirdest things for them to do. But his ideas only took him so far—Max didn't always have the nerve to go through with his crazy ideas if Emily wasn't around. He needed her nearby to give him the courage to go for it. "Are you ready?" she asked.

They skated down the sidewalk, ignoring the looks they were getting from the businesspeople walking past. Emily stumbled a few times, but Max helped keep her upright. He grabbed her arm as they rolled past a local modern art museum and pulled her into the doorway.

"Should we go in?" he asked, a smile tugging at the corner of his lips. "Quick pit stop?"

"Why not?" Emily shrugged, slightly relieved to get away from the obvious stares of the people on the street. "Will it help your story?" Since she was dragging him to the vintage shop, she figured she owed him a few minutes.

Max nodded seriously. "Most definitely. This is a great example of one of the cool places your wheels can take you. So many people think museums, galleries, what have you, take too long to fully enjoy." He lifted a leg, balancing on one skate. "With roller skates, you can get through the whole museum in, like, ten minutes."

They smiled politely at the guy manning the front desk, who barely even noticed their skates. Student admission was free, so they both flashed their high school IDs and rolled into the first room in the gallery. Emily wheeled sideways behind Max, forming her legs into an awkward plié. She stuck her arms out to her sides to balance and took in all the art passing by in front of her.

After they wheeled through the whole gallery—which had in fact taken less than ten minutes—Max led her back outside. "Where now?"

"Vintage shop," Emily declared. "As agreed."

Max followed as Emily skated down the sidewalk. "What

are the odds I'll sell a story someday?" he asked suddenly. "Fifty-fifty? Eighty-twenty?"

"One hundred–zero. Or the other way around—whichever means the odds are for you. You're a great writer. You maybe just need to find your audience. Your stories are a little more niche than editors are accustomed to. For example, how relevant is roller skating in an art gallery?" She wasn't telling Max something he didn't already know. He was aware that his story ideas were out there, but continued to go after the subjects that made him laugh.

"Yeah, okay." Max nodded. "Is this the place?" He gestured to a wooden door set back from the sidewalk.

Emily pulled the door open and started down a narrow set of stairs on her skates. "This is it. Are you coming?" She turned back to Max, who stood at the top of the stairs.

"Yeah," he said slowly, eyeing the steep stairs. "I think I'll just hang out here. Keep an eye on things."

She laughed. "Uh-huh." He really was a chicken. All talk, no do. "I'll be right back." Downstairs, the little shop smelled like a combination of cinnamon and closet. There was a stick of incense burning on the counter, obviously there to mask the smell of old, musty clothes. "Hi," she greeted the clerk, who was a middle-aged guy wearing a fedora.

"What can I do for you?"

Emily rolled gingerly through the packed racks of

clothing, approaching the counter. "Strange question," she started.

The guy cut her off. "I doubt it. Try me."

"So I met this guy . . ." She told an abbreviated version of how she'd met Ethan, lost his number, and how she was now trying to find him again. "Anyway, he was looking for a tux for prom, and it was sort of a rare style, so I suggested he check here."

The clerk whistled. "Thanks for the referral. I can give you an extra punch on your loyalty card if you want."

"Oh, you know what, that's okay." Emily looked at him curiously. He thought she had told that story for praise? Yikes. "I was actually wondering if you remember a guy coming in and asking about a tux? I'm sort of hoping you might remember his last name."

"Yeah." The clerk nodded.

"Yeah?" Emily asked hopefully.

"There was some guy in here yesterday afternoon— about this time, maybe. He asked about a tux. Pretty hot, right?" *Ewww,* Emily thought. The clerk was old enough to be Ethan's dad.

Emily ignored the question. "So he was here? Yesterday?" Her heart sank. Had she come one day earlier, she might have caught him. Talk about meant-to-be.

"Yeah, yesterday. But I didn't get his name. We didn't

have the tux, so he left." The clerk extracted a new stick of incense from a small bag under the counter. "Swoosh—off like the wind."

"Oh." Emily's disappointment was obvious. "Well, thanks anyway." She started back to the stairs.

"If it helps," the clerk called after her, "he was wearing a sweatshirt with an *M* on it."

"*M*?" Emily perked up. "Like, *M* for Marshall or Memorial?"—two of the schools' proms they were planning to crash.

"Maybe." He looked strained, as though the process of digging into his memory was a full day's workout. "I do know it said Minnesota on the back."

She sunk again. "So probably more like *M* for Minnesota? Like, University of Minnesota?"

"Yeah, that's what it was."

"Not helpful," Emily muttered, and climbed slowly back up the stairs to meet Max.

"Where have you been, Emily? Why do you have roller skates, Emily?" Emily had walked in to her house less than ten seconds earlier, and her sister had already managed to squeeze in approximately eight hundred questions. "Do I look pretty, Emily?"

Emily ignored all of her sister's questions, choosing

instead to ask one of her own. "Where did you get that dress, Abby?" Her little sister was drowning in a sea-foam green lace gown with puffy, pleated sleeves. The dress fell past her ankles and had slid off one of her shoulders. Her hair was combed into two small ponytails over each of her ears. Emily grinned, despite her annoyance at the question barrage. Abby looked really cute.

"Do you like it?" Abby twirled. "Do I look like mom?" She hopped in place, making the dress slip farther off her shoulder. She tripped on the bottom of the dress and fell to the floor in a fit of giggles.

"Oh, Emily, you're home." Emily's mom came into the front hall from the kitchen. She helped Abby up off the floor and slipped the dress back onto her younger daughter's shoulder. "I found my old prom dress! I thought maybe you girls could try it on, just for a laugh. Doesn't Abby look cute?"

Emily groaned. The next four weeks were going to be really long. "Mom," she warned. "You promised to stop nagging me about prom."

"Oh, honey, don't be so dramatic," her mom chided. "It's just for fun."

"No, Mom, it's not just for fun. You're trying to get me in a prom state of mind so that you can do all your voodoo prom magic on me and try to get me to sit down and look through catalogs with you. I still don't have a date . . . which means I don't want to talk about it and I don't want to shop for a dress."

Abby stared up at Emily, then slipped her mom's dress up and over her head. Under the dress, she was wearing a T-shirt and It's Happy Bunny boxer shorts that said "You'd be cooler if you were me." "Want to try it on, Emily?" she offered. "Don't you think you'd be pretty in Mom's dress? Don't you just love prom?"

"Argh!" Emily kicked off her shoes and walked toward the family room. "I haven't even been home for five minutes, and I'm getting attacked by Mother Prom and her little Promling. Can you guys please, please, just give me a few minutes of peace?" She sighed dramatically. "Besides, that is the ugliest dress on the face of the Earth."

Her mom laughed in the hallway. "We love you, Emily. Don't worry about the dress—sea-foam green really isn't your color anyway. We'll find you the perfect prom dress. Maybe navy?" Emily ignored her and shut the door to the family room. The computer was on, and she logged onto IM, hoping Max was around. He was online, as always.

```
E: my mom's making me nuts.
M: Candied walnuts?? I like candied walnuts.
E: ha. she's giving me massive prom pressure.
```

M: Did u tell her about the crashing?

E: um. no.

M: Should I suggest she go 2 the mall on Sat night 2 snap some pics of u and Neil?

E: !!!!!! u better not!

M: R u ok?

E: yeah. a little annoyed. but i know she's just really into prom.

M: So r u.

E: which is why i don't want her 2 remind me every 4 secs that i don't have a date.

M: U will have a date. Soon enough.

E: i hope so. ready 4 sat?

M: Yup. My tux is pressed, my hair's been washed. I'm good 2 go.

E: great. clean hair's a plus.

M: Agreed. . . . r u gonna be ok?

E: yeah. have a good night, k, max?

M: U 2. Prom #1 here we come!

Five

Emily clutched the bottom of her dress in her fist, fabric pulled taut over the back of her thighs. She knew that when she released the ball of shimmery pink satin, it would be wrinkled and sweaty. She didn't care.

It was the first Saturday of prom season, and she was wiped. So far, crashing proms wasn't easy—particularly since Emily was attempting to attend her first two proms in the same building at exactly the same time.

She had just left date number one—Neil—right outside the doors of Marshall's prom, excusing herself to go to the bathroom. In reality, she was running off to prom number two.

It had taken *way* longer than Emily had expected to

get from the mall to Neil's prom. They had met up with a bunch of Neil's guy friends for a romantic preprom meal at Taco Bell, then the whole group went back to someone's house for pictures.

Emily had stood to the side as the parents—who were all gathered together at one house—took picture after picture of the guys hamming it up and trying to look manly. Except for a few choice "babe" remarks, they mostly ignored her. She chalked it up to their insecurity.

It felt like hours later when they finally piled into a big van and got a ride to the convention center from one of the dads. Emily had promised to meet Max at eight thirty outside Park's prom, and as they pulled into the parking lot of the convention center, she felt like it was already midnight. She felt bad for thinking it, but spending time with Neil and his friends made time drag more slowly than a really bad civics class. Emily was pretty sure she was late.

As soon as they stepped inside the convention center, Emily excused herself—agreeing to meet Neil outside the Marshall prom doors in fifteen minutes—and ran through the halls of the city convention center to find Max. She was a little scared Max would think she had already been there and would leave or try to get in himself. Patience wasn't one of his strengths.

Emily slowed to a walk as she came around the corner

into the main hall of the convention center. The entrance to Park's prom was at the top of a long escalator. She rode up, searching for Max in the crowd gathered near the main doors. She couldn't find him, but Emily was instantly aware of the ticket takers guarding the only entrance to the ballroom. She and Max would need to be creative if they had any hope of getting in.

Across the hall, Emily noticed a guy who looked vaguely familiar. *Uh-oh,* she thought, ducking her head. It was one of the guys from the Foot Locker in the mall—he knew she didn't go to Park. Slipping behind a pillar, Emily gave herself a second to breathe.

"Can I help you?" A perky-voiced brunette appeared in Emily's periphery. The bouncy hair and flushed cherub cheeks belonged to a short, well-endowed girl who was squeezed into a sequined silver dress. It looked like the dress was holding all her body parts in, and if someone snipped the back, everything would pop out. "Everything okay back here?"

"Yeah," Emily said, smiling back. "Okay."

"Are you looking for someone?" There was a glint of something—suspicion, recognition, kindness?—in her eyes. "Because I can help you. I'm Ally, by the way." She laughed. "But you knew that."

Emily nodded. She needed to get out of there. It seemed

like Max hadn't yet arrived, and she needed to get back to Neil. "Uh—," she stuttered. "Time?" she asked meekly. It was as though she suddenly couldn't form full sentences.

"What time is it?" Ally expanded the question for Emily. "Eight thirty. Time to vote for prom queen!"

"Uh-huh." Emily slipped past Ally and made a hasty retreat back down the escalator. She was right on time, and it looked like Max was late. She would have to come back again in a few minutes and just hope Max would wait nicely until she got back. Neil would surely think something strange was going on if she wasn't back soon.

As promised, Neil was standing just outside the Marshall prom doors waiting. She felt a twinge of guilt for double-dating behind his back. But the guilt melted away as soon as she stepped inside the doors to the prom and took one lap around the perimeter with Neil. The prom was scary, to say the least. And Neil? Not charming.

There were only eighty people at the event, and not a single one even remotely resembled her hot crush. Everyone was grinding on the dance floor, and the sweat from the perfumed bodies mingled with the smell of catered pork egg rolls to create a funky, floral mist in the air.

Emily wanted to vomit.

Neil paraded Emily around the small, cramped ballroom, stopping periodically to greet one or another of his acquaintances. While he and his friends high-fived and swapped postprom party plans, Emily looked around the room for Ethan.

He was definitely nowhere in sight.

Emily was itching to escape, eager to meet up with Max. But Neil had a firm grip on her arm, and she knew she couldn't use the bathroom excuse again this soon. She spotted a punch table across the dance floor and vowed to drink as many cups as were necessary to make it obvious to everyone that she really *ought* to go to the bathroom. "Hey, Neil," she said, tugging the arm of his tux. "Do you want a glass of punch?"

Neil smirked and said, "Sure." He looked around at his friends, then continued, "But don't you think we should get to know each other a little better first?" He laughed, slapping hands with one of his friends. Emily ignored the innuendo—she wasn't sure how his comment was even remotely relevant or appropriate to the question.

"Okay, Neil." She strolled across the room and filled two big glasses full of punch. She quickly took another look around for Ethan, then returned to Neil and his friends. She caught the tail end of their conversation as she returned to the outside of their circle.

"Emily's hot, isn't she?" one of Neil's friends was asking. Emily blushed—compliments were always appreciated, even from this crowd.

Neil's back was turned, so he couldn't see Emily approaching when he said, "Oh, yeah. I'm in there." Then he turned to gesture to Emily. When he saw her standing behind him, he grabbed his glass out of her hand, put it on a table, and led her to the dance floor.

She quickly downed her glass of punch and followed Neil's lead. After a few deliberately not-too-close slow dances, she grabbed another drink.

"Thirsty?" Neil asked, wagging his eyebrows.

Emily smiled thinly and nodded. "Mm-hmm."

"I know how to quench your thirst." Neil laughed at his grotesque line as he turned toward another group of friends. Emily gagged and rolled her eyes before following him. She got to his side just in time to hear her prom date announcing, "Neil's the man. This chick is totally into me!" while not-so-subtly pointing to Emily. She pretended not to hear.

She was playing dumb. It was her survival strategy.

Four cups of punch later, Emily finally managed to escape Neil's sweaty embrace, and she ran from the Great Lakes Ballroom to Hall A (with a bathroom break on the way), where Park's prom was already in full swing.

When she arrived, Max was standing with his back facing her, looking mighty fine in his dad's tails.

"Hey, you." Emily huffed. She was out of breath and suspected she was emanating the stench of egg rolls.

Max turned. "You look nice. Cute corsage."

Emily glanced down. She had managed to forget she was wearing the corsage Neil had given her. It was a bouquet of brightly dyed carnations, and itched her wrist like crazy. When Max pointed to it, she scratched at the raw skin on her wrist and peeled the cheap elastic and flowers from her arm. She tossed it into a nearby garbage can and reminded herself to come up with an excuse for its disappearance when she returned to Neil.

"Have you been here long?" she asked. She carefully studied the couples entering and leaving the hall, formulating a plan. "I came earlier, but you weren't here yet. Then I couldn't get away."

"Maybe half an hour. No biggie."

Emily spotted a group of several couples drunkenly making their way up the escalator toward the hall. She linked arms with Max and approached the group as they boisterously piled off the escalator. Emily plastered a smile on her face and approached one of the girls in the group, draping her in a huge hug.

"Heeeeey!" she said, giggling. "You look soooooo cute!"

The girl gave Emily a weird look. Emily continued. "Did you guys go to Monaco's for dinner? Yum."

Emily had now attracted the attention of another girl in the group. Luckily this girl was piss drunk and easily fooled. She pushed past her date and the first girl and slurred, "Nuh-uh. We went to Kelly's." She leaned in to Emily, whispering conspiratorially. "*So* good. But I maybe had a teensy eensy bit too much champagne in the limo. Shhhhhh." She stumbled, then righted herself again. "You're in my history class, right?"

"Yeah," Emily responded. "What's your name again?"

Drunk girl linked arms with Emily and Max. "Claudia!" Emily and Max blended into the middle of the group of Claudia and her drunken buddies—none of whom, except Claudia, had really noticed Emily or Max—and weaved past the teachers into the prom.

They were in.

Inside, it was insanity. Since prom had already been cooking for more than an hour, the dance floor was packed. The Black Eyed Peas were pumping from the speakers onstage, and there were several girls on the dance floor whose already too-short and too-tight skirts were now riding dangerously close to the butt-cheek line. A line of desperate-looking guys stood nearby, gawking and smiling at one another.

Emily held Max's arm tightly. She could feel him shaking

with laughter through the sleeve of his tux. She nudged him in the ribs to remind him that they needed to get their job done before pissing anyone off.

Glancing around the ballroom, Emily immediately gathered that the Park prom theme was Under the Sea. Streamers and crepe paper had been hung over the ceiling tiles, creating the illusion of waves and water. The streamers covered the air-conditioning vents, trapping the cool air behind crystal blue waves. As a result, under the sea felt a lot like a sauna.

There were tiny fish hanging from all the chairs, and clusters of shells were spread over the tablecloths. The buffet table was encased in a giant mermaid tail; a chocolate fountain erupted from the center. It looked like the mermaid was hemorrhaging mud.

Most of the tables had been pushed to the edge of the room. Emily and Max weaved in and out of them, making their way around the room. "I don't see Ethan," Emily said, squinting for a better view of the dance floor. She had glasses but refused to wear them. Her mom had gotten the frames on clearance at Dylan's, and they looked like something an evening news anchor would wear.

"What are you going to do when you find this guy?" Max asked, pulling off his jacket. His wavy hair had begun to curl in the humidity of the room, and his cheeks were flushed. "Do you just saunter up to him and say, 'Hey, I'm stalking you'?"

Emily hadn't really thought about that. She had only thought through the process of getting into the proms, but hadn't come up with a good explanation of why she was there. "Dunno. I guess I'll just have to figure that out when I find him. I'm hoping the circumstance lends itself to a reasonable explanation."

"Right," Max said. He didn't look convinced. "Care to dance?"

Emily grinned. "But of course." She led Max onto the turquoise-tiled dance floor. They squeezed into an open space next to a couple who seemed to be searching for lost treasure in each others' throats and another couple who was bickering about whether the girl's dress was "technically" green or teal. The guy seemed overly concerned.

"Bizarrely enough, I'm having fun," Max said as they started slow dancing. "You?"

"Other schools' proms are cheesy," Emily said honestly. "But yeah. It's good to get away from Neil, for sure."

"How's it going with him? No Ethan sightings, I assume?"

Emily shook her head. "No." She laughed and leaned back to look at Max. "But I enjoyed many delicious egg rolls and *a lot* of punch."

They danced silently for a few minutes—watching clusters

of girls sing along to Christina Aguilera, hugging and swaying in time to the music—before Max said, "Do you remember how every time I used to spend the night at your house, we would sneak out of your basement and into my parents' kitchen to get cake?"

She nodded. "Your mom makes a mean cake."

"I *know*. I could really go for a piece of that cake right now." Max sighed. "This prom crashing thing sort of makes me feel the same way I did those nights—it's that 'we could get caught, and it's exciting' feeling. But the stakes are higher, and this time you're wearing an almost-stolen dress." He shook his head before cracking a smile. "Emily, you used to be such a nice girl. What happened?"

She smiled back. "I'm still a nice girl. And because I'm such a nice girl, I guess I should get back to Neil." Emily leaned back and rolled her eyes. "But the breath! The hair! The lame one-liners! I don't think I can go back there. No, Max, no! Don't make me go!" She raised her arm to her forehead, Scarlett O'Hara style. With the pretty gown, she was feeling almost damsel-in-distress-like.

"What if you didn't go back?" Max said, eyebrows raised. "I mean, you've already collected your corsage. You've sampled the buffet. You've conquered the prom. Would it be so awful if you just left Neil to fend for himself? Is there any reason to go back?"

Emily considered his suggestion. Max was right. Neil had his friends, and she'd completed her mission. Neil definitely wasn't "in there." So going back was just delaying the inevitable. She would eventually need to ditch Neil to get to the third prom of the night, where Sid and Charlie were waiting for them.

"I guess I could leave him there."

"That's the spirit!" Max pumped his arm in the air. They had danced over to the edge of the dance floor, and when the song ended, they broke apart. "We should probably get to Memorial's prom sometime soon anyway." He checked his watch. "It's a little after ten."

Suddenly the short, silver-gowned brunette Emily had met earlier approached them. She now wore a crown and a sash that read "Prom Queen." A trail of small, wimpy-looking girls fanned out behind her. The prom committee, Emily presumed.

Prom Queen cleared her throat and spoke. "I don't know you. And I know *everyone*."

Emily stared blankly, buying herself time to organize a response. Now that the votes were counted, it seemed Prom Queen wasn't quite as eager to make friends.

Prom Queen lifted her overplucked eyebrows. "Hmm? Who are you?" She jammed her hands into her hips. "You need to leave." Several teachers turned to stare. Prom Queen had drawn a crowd. Emily and Max needed to get out of there—now.

"You know," Emily said, directing her response to Max and pointedly ignoring Prom Queen. Her voice had taken on a combination British-Swedish-German accent. "I am very sad right now."

Max caught on. He nodded his head and said, "Yah, yah."

Prom Queen continued to stare them down.

Emily shook her head and pouted. "We have been at your school for almost one whole year, and I have come to realize . . . no one ever notices the foreign exchange students." And, turning on her heels, Emily stormed away with Max in tow.

Two proms down, seven to go. And still no Ethan.

Six

At the same time across town, Sid stood alone, swaying with the music. She couldn't stop her fingers from snapping to the beat, but she could plaster a scowl on her face, daring anyone to ask her to dance. *You can get me to prom, but you can't make me dance,* she vowed.

She glanced around the room, searching the crowded dance floor for her best friend and obvious prom addict, Charlie. She spotted him surrounded by a group of girls, all of whom were clapping and hooting, cheering him on. Charlie had broken out his signature break dancing moves, and was busy impressing the prom crowd gathered in Memorial High's gymnasium.

You would never guess that an hour ago none of these

people had seen Charlie before in their life. You would think Charlie was the most popular guy at Memorial High.

Sid's dress was starting to bind under her armpits. She had been wearing it since one o'clock that afternoon, and could honestly say she had never worn a dress for this many hours straight in her entire life.

She was miserable.

Checking her cell phone, Sid was relieved to see a text message envelope flashing on her screen. It had come in just two minutes before:

On our way. See you in ten. Em.

Sid smiled for the first time all night. Their plan was working.

Charlie had picked Sid up that afternoon in his ratty old Volvo. In the car, she had smeared on some glittery eye shadow for comic effect. Sid preferred to go au naturel—with the exception of her hair streak, which she had adjusted in honor of prom to match the deep blue of her dress. She had smudged a stick of lip stain across her full lips, tilting the rearview mirror toward the passenger seat to make sure she'd colored in the lines. Charlie had protested, pulling the mirror back. Sid swore at him and slouched in her seat. If she was expected to play prom crasher, she wanted to look the part. That was *at least* half the fun.

When they had arrived at Memorial High hours ago, Charlie pulled his Volvo into a spot under a dying pine tree in the parking lot. The two of them sat silently in the car for a few minutes, watching the track team running sprints behind the school. They could hear the marching band rehearsing for their spring concert on the football field in the center of the asphalt track. The trombones were out of tune.

"Ready?" Charlie asked, turning to Sid with a giant grin. He was literally bouncing in his seat. "We're on."

"I'm ready," Sid answered, significantly more subdued. She pulled her dress up and tugged it to the side—she'd only been wearing it half an hour, and already it was riding funny. "You know what gets me down when I see a band like that practicing?" Sid pointed to the marching band on the field as she locked her car door. One member of the drum line was chasing another around with a sweaty pair of running shorts that he had presumably taken from one of the track team members. Sid didn't want to know what the track guy was now wearing.

"There are some hotties, but their gorgeousness is wasted because they're all band freaks?" Charlie had a tendency toward prejudgment, and assumed all band members were losers. He himself was a drama geek, so go figure.

"Not what I was thinking," Sid answered. "What gets me down is the fact that that guy"—she pointed to the drum guy holding the sweaty shorts; the guy was now sniffing them— "probably has a real band he plays with, and actually gets gigs, not just the completely lame mall tea shop."

"Do you want to be in that guy's band?" Charlie's lip was in a sneer. He buttoned the top button of his tux jacket and pulled at the lapel to straighten it. "Do you want to be like that guy?"

"No, dumbass, I just want a real gig sometime. How many times do I have to send out my CDs and get rejected before someone other than 'Teas of the World' Gary hires me?"

Charlie shrugged. "Your genius has yet to be realized. You're going to be huge. If I didn't believe that, I wouldn't hang out with you. Simple as that." He pulled out two pairs of huge, dark sunglasses. "Wear these."

Sid studied him. "Oh, come on."

"For me."

She pulled the sunglasses onto her small, button nose. "Do I look fabulous?"

Charlie grinned and nodded vigorously. "Like the star that you are." They walked toward the back of the school, just up the hill from the track. The plan was that Charlie and Sid would try to sneak into Memorial High that after-noon while the doors were unlocked for track practice.

They had received this suggestion from one of the McDonald's employees at the mall, who was a junior at Memorial. He told them the school goes into lockdown mode a few hours before prom, so their only hope of getting into the prom was to actually be in the school before prom started. So while Emily and Max attended proms number one and two, Sid and Charlie were assigned the task of sneaking into Memorial High.

A tall, lean guy in short shorts breezed past them as they neared the back door of the school. He did a double take when he saw their prom wear, then offered them a high five as he jogged past. Charlie raised his arm to reciprocate as Sid scurried forward, catching the door track boy had just exited from with her foot.

"Nice one," Charlie said, watching the runner retreat to the field.

"Must you check everyone out?" Sid teased, grinning.

"That is so not what I meant," Charlie insisted. "I was talking about you—good catch on the door." He squeezed Sid around the middle.

She shimmied out of his grip and opened the door farther. "After you."

They both glanced around. There was no one near the back door of the school, and the track was far enough away that people couldn't really tell from that distance that they didn't belong. Quickly and quietly, they slid through the open door and into the darkened school.

Charlie whistled. "Cute smell."

"It smells like crap." Sid plugged her nose with her fingers. "This school is nasty."

The back door of the school had led them into a dark hallway that dead-ended at the gymnasium doors. The locker rooms were on either side of the hallway, their doors propped open. Charlie pulled off his sunglasses and moved toward the gym. "Just one quick peek at how the decorations are coming," he said, motioning for Sid to join him. Memorial's prom was being held in the gym that night, so they knew the prom committee and parents would be decorating all afternoon.

They crept down the hall, studying the posters that lined the wall: CARMEN CAN! VOTE MENDOZA!; PETER FOR PREZ!; VOTE ONCE, VOTE TWICE, VOTE VINCE FOR VICE!; CHRIS FOR PROM KING!

"People actually campaign for prom king?" Charlie mused, chuckling. "That's just sad."

"Admit it—you would totally do the same if it wasn't completely classless. Being prom king is your dream come true, no?"

Charlie shrugged. "I can't say it wouldn't feel fantastic. But I would never campaign. I would expect my Midwestern good looks and superhot style to speak for themselves." Charlie ran his fingers through his blond hair and straightened his tux again.

They were just steps away from the gym when they heard voices approaching. "In here," Sid hissed, pulling Charlie into an unlocked room. They both pressed their ears against the inside of the door, listening to the passersby.

". . . it will be worth it," Voice One was saying.

"But you don't even like her, dude," Voice Two responded.

"If I get laid, what do I care? If I pretend to be into her . . ." They couldn't hear the next line. But finally the voice boomed out, ". . . we look too hot together to not win. And when she gets that crown, she'll be like putty in my arms. Wham, bam, thank you ma'am." Voice One laughed. He sounded like a major creep.

"Chris, dude, that's harsh," Voice Two said, then laughed. Charlie and Sid could hear the slap of a high five.

Charlie turned to Sid, mouth agape. "That's the prick who's campaigning for prom king—Chris. Sounds like a good guy."

"A major jerk, more like." Sid stated the obvious.

"I'd like to see that guy taken down," Charlie mused. "A prick like that doesn't deserve prom king." He looked thoughtful. "Hmmm . . ."

"Charlie, I'm worried about the look on your face." Sid lifted her eyebrows. "What are you planning?"

"No worries, my friend," Charlie responded. "It's all good. So, what have we here?" Charlie moved beyond the door and into the room they were using as a hideout.

"Looks like the teachers' lounge."

"That it does." Charlie flopped down on the couch in the center of the room. It smelled like old hotdogs and bad breath. He quickly stood up again. "Comfy."

"Wanna just hang out in here?" Sid settled into a ratty old chair in the corner of the room. The answer key for a math exam was perched on the arm of the chair. She cast it aside, turning sideways in the chair to rest her legs over the arm.

They had found their way in. Now they just had to wait and avoid being noticed.

Going unnoticed was not one of Charlie's assets. He had a tendency to solicit attention, then milk it for all it was worth. So now, seven hours after sneaking into Memorial High and two hours into the prom, Sid stood at the edge of the gymnasium watching her best friend surrounded by his circle of new best friends.

Charlie danced and swayed, teaching the girls' basketball team (who had all arrived at prom together, dressed in identical teal dresses) how to mambo. They thought he was a god.

Not so much their boyfriends, who all stood against the folded bleachers, glowering. They were whispering to one another, and Sid was pretty sure Charlie was about to be the target of a hostile takeover. The boyfriends wanted their prom dates back.

Sid checked her watch—five minutes had passed since she got the text from Emily, so she and Max should be arriving at their meeting point in just a few minutes. Sid glanced at Charlie and decided to execute the rendezvous alone. She would give Charlie a few more minutes in the spotlight before pulling him from the mission. Emily only needed a few minutes to look for Ethan, then they could sneak out before Charlie was mauled by angry jocks.

Sid slipped out the side door of the gym, avoiding notice by any of the teacher aides. She turned a corner and hustled to the door she and Charlie had come in earlier that afternoon. She pressed the bar on the door, releasing the lock, and peeked outside. She could see Emily and Max strolling across the parking lot toward the school.

"Hey, hot stuffs!" she called, whistling at them as they walked up the hill.

Max waved. Sid pushed the door the rest of the way open. Max and Emily slipped in and Sid pulled it closed behind them. "Tiny issue," Sid announced. "You better look for Ethan quickly, because I think our cover is about to be compromised."

"What happened?" Emily asked.

"Go have a look," Sid answered cryptically.

Max and Emily followed Sid to the gym, where all three slid in through the side door. Sid had realized early in the night that all the teacher aides were congregating by the main gym entrance off the front lobby of the school, and one of the side entrances (next to the athletic director's office) was completely unguarded.

Walking into the gym, the first thing Emily noticed was a huge faux-wooden pirate ship that couples paraded over to enter and exit the prom. The boat was almost ten feet tall, and was decorated with twinkling Christmas tree lights that spelled out PIRATES OF THE CARIBBEAN. She could only imagine that Orlando Bloom would be highly disappointed if he saw this sorry representation of the film.

The second thing Emily noticed was the huge mob of people in the center of the waxy dance floor. The mob seemed to be chanting something in unison, and she sort of thought it sounded like "Charlie! Charlie! Charlie!"

She moved toward the mob and realized that it was in fact what they were chanting. Her cousin was propped up on the shoulders of a bunch of girls in teal dresses, who were spinning him around the dance floor. Emily glanced over her shoulder at Sid.

"I warned you," Sid said, shrugging.

Max and Sid stood on the edge of the dance floor, keeping an eye on Charlie while Emily made a few rounds through the gym.

The gym was crowded and dim, making it hard to see faces clearly. At one point Emily thought she spotted Ethan, but as soon as the guy in question turned, she realized it was definitely not him. Emily weaved through groups of people, smiling whenever anyone looked at her curiously. Her heart sank every time she passed another Ethan-less group. Yes, it was only prom number three, but she still couldn't help but feel disappointed. She wanted to see him again.

After a few minutes of fruitless searching, she returned to Max and Sid, who were now fighting each other with plastic swords they had found on the punch table.

"Ladies and gentlemen!" An adult voice called out over a squawky mic, squealing over the din of the dance floor. "Ladies! Gentlemen! Your attention please!" A mousy woman was standing atop the pirate ship, waving her arms madly in the air. She was wearing an off-the-shoulder dress that looked dangerously close to ripping.

Parent volunteers should *not* dress up to chaperone the prom. It was wrong on so many levels.

"Folks, listen up!" mousy, off-the-shoulder mom screeched through her mic. "It's time to crown our prom king and queen!"

The noise in the gym quickly quieted down. The DJ lowered the music to a soft hum. One of the basketball girls' dates entered Charlie's circle and wrapped his arms around the waist of one of the tallest girls in the circle. "Chriiiis," she squealed, pushing him away.

Chris—the prom king candidate whose sexist comments had been haunting Sid all afternoon—was a huge, beefy sort of guy. He looked like an overripe tomato now that his face was flushed with the embarrassment of being shrugged off by his date. He chuckled to mask the awkward moment, then more loosely draped an arm over his date's shoulder. She pointedly ignored him, but didn't push him away.

Charlie's face was flushed and shiny from dancing. He hugged all the teal girls before heading across the gym floor to join his friends near the punch table. Emily and Max greeted him, then all four stood on the side of the gym, listening to the parent chaperone drone on and on about what a great four years it had been, blah, blah, blah, and how she was so proud of everyone for their accomplishments. She looked like she was primed for a good, long cry.

"Now the moment you've all been waiting for," she

said happily. "The crowning of this year's prom queen and king!" She motioned to one of the teacher aides, who was wearing a pirate hat. The teacher aide stepped forward and held up a cardboard circle with a red arrow stuck to it.

"What the hell?" Sid muttered to Emily under her breath.

"As always," the teacher aide shouted over the crowd, "the votes will be tabulated by our patented applause meter."

"Oh, come on," Emily murmured back. "This has to be a joke."

Max was shaking with laughter. "Too good to be true," he concluded.

The parent chaperone tapped her mic with three loud thumps to quiet the crowd. "Kids. Keep it down." She held up a clipboard. "Nominations have been collected all evening by Frances, your favorite cafeteria manager. Thank you, Frances." Mousy mom nodded to a maybe-man-maybe-woman near the door. She or he nodded back. "The nominations for this year's prom queen are: Shiloh, Jordan, and Britney C."

Three of the teal girls, including Chris's date, squealed and bounced with glee.

"By a show of applause, who would like to see Shiloh crowned?" A handful of people cheered and clapped. The teacher holding the applause meter moved the arrow to the center of the dial. A perky blond girl bowed her head and smiled.

"Jordan?" The room exploded with applause and hoots. The applause meter was adjusted so the arrow was almost all the way at the other side of the dial. Chris grabbed his slender, willowy date and planted a kiss on her mouth. She pushed him off.

"And Britney?" A slightly less exuberant roar came from the crowd, including a few of the boyfriends who were leaning against the bleachers. The arrow was moved to the middle of the dial.

"Jordan, congratulations!" The mom squealed with delight as Jordan ran toward Charlie.

Charlie gave her a huge hug and shouted, "You go, girl! Get your crown!" Jordan walked toward the pirate ship and climbed the plank. She was handed a crown and a bouquet of lilies.

"Congratulations, Jordan," mousy mom repeated earnestly. "And now, we'll find out who will be your king. The nominations for this year's prom king are"—she consulted her clipboard—"Shawn, Chris, and Charlie!"

Charlie looked around the room. Chris was shaking hands with another guy, but there didn't seem to be a third guy in the room. "Is that me?" he turned to Emily, grinning.

Emily shrugged. "Sort of looks that way, doesn't it?"

The teal girls all ran toward Charlie and surrounded him with hugs and cheers.

Chris did *not* look happy.

"Can I hear a round of applause for those of you who want to see Shawn crowned as your king?" A group of abnormally tall guys cheered and whooped—*Shawn must be a basketball player,* Emily surmised.

"And Chris?" All the guys slumped along the bleachers shouted and stomped. Chris bowed.

"Charlie?" The teal girls screamed and shouted and raised their fists in the air. So did half the other people in the room. The cardboard applause meter said it all— Charlie was the new Memorial High Prom King.

Charlie jogged toward the pirate ship, waving and grinning ear to ear. He collected his plastic and rhinestone crown, and gave Jordan a quick hug. The two of them promenaded across the pirate ship together, waving at the crowd below. Everyone was cheering as "You're Beautiful" began to play in the background. Charlie and Jordan descended to the gym floor and mamboed through their inaugural dance.

It wasn't until Charlie dipped his queen at the end of the song that he noticed the posse of large, imposing jocks (led by Chris) approaching the dance floor.

Luckily Sid noticed the pack at the same time and was able to quickly alert Emily and Max. The three of them ran together toward the dance floor, grabbing Charlie by the arms, then ran as fast as they could around the pirate ship, through the halls, and out the school's back door. They didn't stop running until they got to Charlie's Volvo in the parking lot.

"Get in," Emily panted. "We can come back for Max's car!"

All four jumped in the Volvo and erupted in a fit of laughter. As Charlie drove out of the lot, they could see Chris and his gang emerging from the school's front doors. Charlie pulled his crown off his head and waved it out the window at Chris. "I'll take care of the crown! You take care of your girl!" he called, then replaced it on his head and sped off toward the freeway.

Charlie was still wearing the crown later that night in a corner booth at Burrito Jack's. "My greatest goal in life has been accomplished," he declared, rubbing his thumb over the crown's rhinestones. "I am the prom king!"

"It's not even your own school," Sid said, dunking a chip in salsa. "Does that count?"

"Of course it counts," Emily answered for her cousin. "I say it's worth double *because* it's not your school."

"Agreed," Max said, pouring a packet of sugar into his glass of water.

Charlie sighed and leaned back into the puffy booth. "I wish Marco could have been there to see me tonight." Charlie was smiling, but Emily could tell he really missed his boyfriend. "Man, I would have loved to see the look on his face. Me as prom king? He'll never believe it."

Sid was first to respond. "He'll believe it," she said simply. She was drawing little dragons on the paper tablecloth with a purple crayon. She looked up from her art to say, "He does know you, right? It's not as if this is so unexpected."

"But it wasn't even my own prom." He turned to Sid. "What if I win prom king at South and he's not even there?"

"Is it desirable to win?" Sid scoffed. She drew horns on her creation.

"Uh." Charlie widened his eyes. "Yeah. Why are you and Marco both so negative about prom? Because my best friend and my boyfriend are both ditching me, I'm stuck going to our prom with Natasha Fine." He paused. Charlie had earlier that week agreed to go to South's prom with one of his drama club leading ladies. "Admittedly, Natasha Fine dresses well and is really fun, but still . . . not Marco."

"Charlie," Emily interrupted, "does Marco know you want him to go? Have you asked him?" She reached across the table to draw a green flame coming out of Sid's dragon's mouth.

"Not as such."

"Then it's your own damn fault," Sid retorted.

"Too late now, isn't it?" Charlie responded snippily. "I'm going with Natasha, and we will look *fine*." He faux-pouted. "Marco's payback will be my detailed phone account of each and every prom. Every last, cheesy detail. He will learn to *love* prom."

Through her teeth, Sid jokingly muttered, "And my payback is that I get to go to prom over and over and over again with you people."

Max had been mostly silent since they had left Memorial, but broke in suddenly. "You know, tonight gave me an idea."

The other three looked at him, waiting.

"We have four proms left to crash, plus our own, right?" Emily nodded yes. "How would you guys feel about me chronicling our prom crashing for an article? I think I could definitely sell this somewhere. I'll make you all sound much prettier and funnier than you actually are, of course."

"Oh, thanks," Emily said sarcastically, leaning against her best friend. "But seriously, go for it. It could be a good story. Oddly enough, prom crashing is more normal than your usual pieces, so maybe it stands a chance." Sid nodded her agreement.

Charlie grinned. "Will you include the part about me winning prom king?" he asked. "Because I did! I won prom king!"

Sid rolled her eyes, leaning her head on the table. "I get the feeling we might be hearing about this *forever*."

"So after tonight, we have four proms to go," Emily said. She had a feeling things would be getting a lot more complicated—their first night of crashing had been relatively easy.

"Are you still excited about finding this guy?" Sid asked.

"Mmm-hmm. If it's possible, I think I'm actually more excited about my own prom now that I've been to these other bizarre proms."

"You know"—Max grinned, wiggling his eyebrows— "I'm still willing to be your backup date for our prom."

Emily and Max had agreed years ago to go together if neither of them could find a real date. But Emily always thought going to prom just for the sake of going to prom was a little depressing. She really wanted her nice, long good-night kiss from a sexy tuxedoed date. Max just wasn't going to give her that.

"Um, yeah." Emily nodded slowly. "I think I'll keep holding out for the real thing."

Max shrugged. "Fine. The offer's out there. . . ."

Sid and Charlie exchanged a look.

"What?" Emily demanded. Sid just stared back at her.

"That just came out a little harsh, maybe," Max responded, clearly a little hurt. "I'm not *that* bad."

"You know what I mean, right?" Emily looked at him, concerned. She hadn't meant for her comment to be construed as rude or insulting—just honest.

"Of course. No hurt feelings." Max took a sip of his sugary water and smiled. "You know I don't want to go to prom anyway, so whatever."

"For sure?" Emily inquired again. Now she was worried. He was acting like they hadn't talked about this a million times. She *knew* how Max felt about prom.

"For sure," Max echoed. But suddenly Emily wasn't so sure she believed him.

Seven

"Big news! F—Flaming good news!" Sid came barreling into the Leaf Lounge the next Tuesday night while Emily was sitting at the counter, sharing a muffin with Frank. He had bought a chocolate-chunk muffin, making Emily happier than ever when he offered—as always—to share it.

"She's a little cutie, isn't she?" Frank asked Emily under his breath while Sid scooted a stool up to the counter.

"Don't let her hear you say that," Emily warned. "She's not big on little compliments."

"What am I not big on?" Sid asked. "Where's Charlie?"

"In back." Emily ignored her first question. "What's up?"

Charlie poked his head around the door of the back room,

iPod buds in his ears. "Sidney! My knight in shining armor!" He had been "sorting inventory" for the past two hours, and came flying out of the back room now, declaring that he "needed a break." Said break conveniently coincided with Sid's arrival.

Sid leaned over the counter to grab a clean mug from the dish rack. She filled it with coffee from the thermos next to the register. "Help yourself," Emily said. "Really."

Frank chuckled to himself, murmuring, "What a cutie. Such moxie."

Sid pointedly ignored Frank, then blurted out, "I got a gig!"

"What's a gig?" Frank asked Emily. "A horse?" He turned to Sid. "You got a horse?"

Emily shook her head at Frank and held a finger to her lips. "Where? When are you playing? I assume we can come, right?"

"That's the crazy part. It's this Saturday!" She drum-rolled her hands on the countertop. "At the Ridley Prep prom after-party!"

Ridley Prep was one of the smallest schools in the area, with only about forty seniors. So far, the only thing Emily knew about the Ridley prom was that the highlight of the night was always the after-party. Everyone went to the same party, and it was usually held at a downtown hot spot. Ridley Prep was known around town for its ultracool hipster reputation, and Emily and Charlie had been trying to figure out the best way in.

Charlie climbed up on the counter and leaned over to give Sid a big hug. "That's so great, babe!"

Frank stood up from his stool, patting Sid on the shoulder. "Good luck with your 'gig.'" He chuckled, making quotes in the air. "Gig," he muttered as he strolled out the front door.

"Wow, Sid, that's incredible," Emily said. "How did they find you?"

"The president of their student council heard my music on MySpace. He IMed me a few days ago, I sent him a CD, and I guess he must have liked it. They have a couple of bands lined up, and I'm second to go on."

"Can we come? Please please please please please!" Charlie hopped down from the counter.

"I was thinking I do sort of need stagehands, right?" Sid asked, winking. "I could use some help with setup, sound checks, that sort of thing. I think we can figure out a way to get you guys in. So prom number five is taken care of."

"That's fantastic." Emily smiled happily. "You have your first real, live, non–Leaf Lounge gig. I'm so impressed."

"Thanks." Sid raked her fingers through her short, choppy hair. "Aw, shucks, now you're embarrassing me."

A customer came through the front of the coffee shop. Charlie quickly grabbed a dish towel and pretended to be drying mugs. He looked at Emily, nodding his head in the direction of the customer at the front counter. She sighed and moved forward to take the person's order.

After preparing a large latte, she turned back to the side counter where Sid was sitting. Charlie was squatting in a corner under the counter, hiding. "You will do anything and everything to get out of work, won't you?" She pushed him gently, causing him to lose his balance and topple onto the nasty floor.

He flicked a dishtowel at her butt, then stood up to say, "So if we have an in at prom number five, we just need to figure out number four and we'll be all set for this weekend. My tux is clean, I'm in good health, it's all good. Now we just need to get into Jefferson."

"That's the problem—we have to get into Jefferson." Thomas Jefferson's prom was to be held that Friday night at the Legends Ballroom, and Jefferson's school events were famously well guarded. Emily knew they wouldn't be able to sneak in. Joey Frank, a movie star who was originally from one of the nearby suburbs, was a senior at Thomas Jefferson (though most of his course work was done via independent study from L.A.). Apparently he had invited his current costar, Simone Rocha, to be his prom date.

Everyone was desperate to get into the school's prom to catch a glimpse of the Hollywood couple in action.

Thomas Jefferson had scheduled their prom for Friday night, rather than Saturday, to better accommodate Joey's filming schedule. (He was due back in L.A. on Saturday afternoon for reshoots.) Which meant Emily and her friends could focus on one prom each night that weekend—if they could get into Friday night's event.

"What if we try the sneak-in-before-prom thing again?" Charlie suggested.

Emily shook her head. "Not gonna happen. The Legends Ballroom opens when the caterers and staff arrive for the event. There's no side entrance—we'll be way too obvious."

"I could try to have one of those crazy *Charlie's Angels* masks made that would turn me into Joey Frank. I'm sure they won't fault Joey for 'forgetting' his ticket."

"Yeah, no problem, Charlie," Emily responded. "I'm sure those are easy to come by. We could try to rappel in— hook up a wire that would string us down from the roof and through a window? That would be fun."

Charlie laughed. "Oh, and that's so much more reasonable than one of those masks?"

Sid suddenly knocked her palm against the counter. "I have an idea."

Charlie and Emily stared at her, waiting.

"Remember my cousin Sam?" Sid turned to Charlie expectantly.

"Floss-in-public Sam?"

"Yes, Charlie, Sam is the cousin who flossed his teeth while you were in the car. I know it was gross—get over it. Anyway, Sam's friend Jeremy has asked me out, like, a hundred times. And I think he goes to Thomas Jefferson. I would *maybe* be willing to try to get an invite to his prom. But there would be a condition, obviously."

Emily nodded. "Of course. What is it?" Sid's upcoming gig had made her overly generous. The old Sid would never have volunteered to ask out someone she'd already rejected. That was *not* her style.

"You would have to double with me, Em. If I can get us dates, are you in?"

"Of course."

"Let me see what I can do."

Emily spent half her lunch period the next day staring at Gina Morgenthal's table in the cafeteria. Gina Morgenthal had been one of Emily's best friends from fourth through eighth grade, but as soon as they'd hit high school, Gina had gone all loud and cheerleadery, and they hadn't really spoken since. Emily was still slightly fascinated by her, though, and had always wondered what had happened to break them apart.

It wasn't like Emily was totally out of the in crowd. But she knew she didn't fit into Gina's new world, with its wedged sandals and—if she were being honest—hoochy shirts.

That day, Gina had laid eleven *Seventeen* magazine spreads out on her lunch table, with a selection of prom dresses for her friends to admire and comment on. They were all actually sighing over a lavender satin slip dress.

"Jealous?" Max asked from across the table. He had a bite of pizza in his mouth, a piece of which slipped out when he spoke. He plucked the piece of crust off his shirt and popped it onto his tray. He smiled, which made little dimples appear in his cheeks. His smiles were contagious.

"Jealous about what?" she asked, grabbing his pizza from his plate and taking a bite off the side he hadn't eaten off yet. Her salad tasted like yard waste, and she had left it untouched on the edge of the table since three minutes into their lunch period.

"Prom. Our prom." Max gestured to Gina and her friends, huddled around the magazine clippings across the room.

"No. Why should I be?" A defensive tone crept into her

voice. "I have two weekends of proms to crash before our prom—so there's still a chance I might find my date."

Max raised his hands in a surrender motion. "Sheesh. I was just asking because you've been staring at Gina Morgenthal's virtual prom dress buffet for the last ten minutes. It just seems like you're a little . . . well, jealous."

Emily groaned, relaxing her forehead onto her fists on the table. "I don't know why I'm staring. Yeah, I guess you're right. I'm a little bummed about prom. I guess I always thought I'd be dating someone who would pick me up in a limo and meet my parents and take pictures, and we'd dance and laugh and maybe kiss next to the buffet table."

"A kiss next to the buffet table?" Max asked, dimples appearing again. "Sounds romantic."

"You know what I mean. I just thought things would be different."

Max reached across the table and set the rest of his pizza on Emily's tray. "Will cold mystery-meat pizza help?"

Emily lifted her head and faux-pouted. "Yes, I think it will. Thank you." She took a bite out of the slice of pizza, but set it down again as Lauren Ellstrom—student council president and certified hottie—walked past their table. She watched Max's gaze shift from her pizza to Lauren's approaching boobs. Emily was embarrassed for him. It was fully obvious.

Just as Emily opened her mouth to comment on his less-than-subtle staring, Lauren stopped short, just steps from their table. "Hey, Max," Lauren cooed. Emily was the one staring now. *When did my best friend become friends with* Lauren?

"Hey, Lauren." Max flushed red. "Thanks again for last week."

"No problemo, babe. Thank you for asking me. It was fun hanging out with you."

"You too," Max smiled, dimpling again. Emily got a sick feeling in her stomach. *Lauren?*

"Hey," Lauren said, leaning in toward Max, "do you have a date for prom yet?"

"Prom? No." Max was acting goofy. Emily wanted to slap him.

"Reeeeally?" Lauren smiled broadly. "Good to know." She smiled at both Emily and Max, then retreated to her own table.

Emily turned to Max, who was fiddling with a crumble of pizza crust on his tray. "What was that all about?"

"Lauren?" Max asked, still fiddling. "Nothing. She just helped me with a story idea. It was fun. She's cool."

Emily nodded. But watching Max smile as he pushed crumbs around his tray, she couldn't stop a jealous, possessive sort of feeling from creeping from her stomach into her throat. She had never had to deal with Max dating, or even being interested in anyone—and she wasn't sure she was ready to start. She didn't like to share.

The sound of her ring tone broke through her jealousy, relieving her of having to think about why she was feeling the way she was feeling. She grabbed her phone out of her pocket. A text message was flashing on her screen. It was from Sid:

> We're in at Jefferson. You're going with a guy named Danny. Call me asap, there's a catch.

* * *

"Hey, it's Emily Bronson." Silence hung on the other side of the phone. During a superquick call between sixth and seventh period, Sid had given Emily the name and number of her Friday prom date, and told her she should make nice and call him. But now Emily was thinking maybe Sid had given her the wrong number. Emily kept talking. "Your prom date? Sidney Martinez's friend?"

"Greetings, Emily Bronson." Silence.

Okaaaay, Emily thought, raising her eyebrows. Out loud she said, "How are you, Danny?"

"Well, Emily Bronson. I'm doing well." More silence.

"Greeeeat. So, I just wanted to call and figure out our plan for Friday. I was thinking we would just maybe meet up at the ballroom?"

"Think again, Emily Bronson." *Okay, freak,* Emily thought. *You're starting to creep me out.*

"No?" she asked. "Do you need me to pick you up?"

"In a sense," Danny said, getting weirder by the minute. If this guy didn't know Sid's cousin, she would swear he was psycho. Thank God they were doubling. "You'll need to come to my house to get ready and have our portraits done."

"Oh, pictures," Emily said, groaning.

"No, Emily Bronson." Danny's diction was frighteningly crisp. "Portraits, not pictures."

"Uh-huh, yeah." Emily wasn't sure this date was going to be worth it. She wrapped up the conversation as quickly as she could, getting Danny's address and agreeing to meet him at his house at six on Friday. "By the way, I'm wearing pink." Emily figured she should throw him a bone. Danny didn't sound like they type of guy who would be great at picking out a corsage.

"We'll see about that, Emily Bronson," Danny said, then Emily heard a click. Their conversation was over.

Eight

Emily's suspicions were confirmed when she turned up at Danny's house that Friday night. She had made a mistake agreeing to this date. The first warning sign was the bust of Shakespeare sitting on one of the branches of the apple tree in Danny's front yard.

The second was the garden gnome collection. Garden gnomes had always freaked her out.

The third warning sign—the one that came with whistles and bells and sirens—came when she knocked on the door and met Danny live and in person. She should have run screaming as soon as she'd met her date, but she politely stuck around. She figured she couldn't really leave before Sid got there—she wouldn't leave her friend to go it alone. And she *did* want to get into Jefferson's prom. It could be Ethan's school.

If nothing else, based on Danny's first impression, this stood to be the most amusing crashing target yet. Sid was right—there was definitely a "catch."

The catch was that Danny intended to go to prom dressed in a white wig and tails. For real. Not as a joke. He looked just like a teenage George Washington.

In their first five minutes together, Emily learned that Danny was the president of Thomas Jefferson's drama club and, because he apparently took his thespian reputation very seriously, felt the need to show up at prom in full costume.

Emily was mortified.

But even though things seemed bad when she met Danny and saw his outfit—and realized she would be going to prom with *that* guy, the one everyone else would be whispering about—things quickly spiraled into much worse. Danny expected his date—Emily—to coordinate her look with his. He had rented a matching costume for her.

The tag on the rental bag said "Victorian Lady." She wanted to crawl under one of the garden gnomes in the yard and hide. It was that bad.

Sid arrived, date in tow, at Danny's house while Emily was in Danny's upstairs bathroom changing. Emily had protested and fought and refused to put on the costume, but Danny's heart was set on going to prom as one half of a thespian couple. He told Emily that if she refused the "Victorian Lady" costume, she could forget about going to the prom. He then crossed his arms and tapped his foot.

She was left very little choice.

When Emily came gliding down the stairs in all her Victorian glory, Danny's parents whistled. Sid, who stood just to the side of the front door, choked back a laugh.

"Nice . . . ," she sputtered out. Emily cut her off with a loud cough.

"You," Danny declared as Emily pulled up her skirts around her ankles to descend the last few steps, "look *regal*."

"Great," Emily muttered. "Can we just go now?"

"Portraits! Portraits!" Danny's mom cried, pulling her camera off the front hall table.

"Yeah, Emily." Sid smiled politely. "Don't forget about pictures. We all want to remember this night."

"I'm not so worried," Emily said, smiling back at her friend. "I think this night may dig itself into my memory book *somehow*."

Sorry, Sid mouthed as Emily was pulled into Danny's living room for pictures.

Emily shook her head in response and shrugged. Out loud she said, "I can handle it."

334

She obligingly trudged to the front of the fireplace, where Danny had assembled an old wooden chair and a musket. He motioned for her to sit, while he stood behind her, one hand on her shoulder, the other holding the musket. She pursed her lips, posing in the most "regal" style she could muster. Danny beamed behind her.

Emily knew the subdued snickering was coming from Sid, who stood in the door of the living room next to her shy—but otherwise normal—date, Jeremy. Emily gave herself up to the moment, posing and preening in her costume to the best of her ability. Soon the photos were over, and Danny, whose boundless energy was somewhat startling, flounced over to the window.

Danny pulled a curtain aside and glanced outside. He turned back to address Emily, Sid and her date, and his parents. His face was flushed. "It's here!"

"What's here?" Emily asked, praying that his answer would be "An alien ship to take me away." Danny ignored her question and led them all outside. At the end of Danny's long driveway, parked between two garden gnomes, was a horse-drawn carriage.

"Everybody in!" he cried. "Action!"

Looking at each other, Sid and Emily couldn't stop themselves from cracking up. Emily shook with laughter, her chest pressing against confines of her corset. Sid hopped onto the seat next to Emily's and shouted, "Giiiiiiddy-up!"

As they trotted away from Danny's parents' house, Emily whispered to Sidney the question she'd been turning over in her mind: "What do I do if Ethan *is* at this prom?"

Sid linked arms with Emily and whispered back, "Let's just hope it doesn't come to that. Because honestly, it might be best if you *don't* reintroduce yourself while wearing a corset."

By the time the horse-drawn carriage delivered them to the front door of the Legends Ballroom—a long, chilly forty-five minutes after leaving Danny's house—Emily had numbed to the idea that she might run into Ethan in full costume.

If possible, she wouldn't let it happen. But if she did spot him, she would simply avoid him while somehow finding out his last name. Then she could track him down later.

Emily was a do-something-daring-and-unexpected kind of girl, like streaking through a cow field on a cold, snowy night in nothing but winter boots; or breaking into the condemned Elk Park Elementary school just for the thrill of it; or crashing proms to find a guy. But wearing a Victorian gown to a prom with three hundred attendees was definitely taking things one step further. This wasn't adventurous . . . it was just plain embarrassing.

She stepped out of the carriage after Danny and followed her date into the building amid stares and whispers. Danny puffed up his chest, adjusted his white wig, and pulled his tickets and school ID from his wallet. Clearly Danny was pretty comfortable in his own skin. He wasn't even reacting to the stares. Emily couldn't help but admire his unwavering self-confidence.

After passing security—which included a metal detector (Danny had to hand over his cane) and a swift pat down (it took two female guards to lift all of Emily's skirts to check for contraband)—Danny swept the door of the ballroom open for Emily, leading her into the crowded prom.

She and Sid were in.

The first thing Emily saw when she stepped into the room was the movie star and his date. Joey and Simone were crouched at a table near the dance floor, surrounded by teachers and parents. The students at Thomas Jefferson were mostly leaving them alone, but the same couldn't be said for the parents, who were all smiling at them and leaning in to hear Joey and Simone's conversation. Joey gestured to one of his friends, who shimmied across the dance floor to greet him. Joey whispered a few quick words in his friend's ear, then the friend shouted to some unseen person across the room, "Hey, Morris, how's that beer bong?"

All the parents and teachers quickly hurried off in the

direction of the supposed infraction. Joey gave his buddy a quick high five to thank him for getting rid of the chaperone huddle.

Danny, who had noticed Emily staring at Joey, scoffed. "That guy's a total fake," he declared, not even remotely concerned about who might hear him.

"Pardon?" Emily said, trying to stay in character. She had developed a character accent and language during their carriage ride to the ballroom. As she had told Sid, it helped make the bizarre situation a little more amusing for her.

"That guy—Joey." Danny gestured to Danny and Simone. "He's a terrible actor. He didn't even make the chorus in our sophomore year musical. He can't sing, dance, or act. He just looks pretty."

"I don't think he's that bad." Emily shrugged. "I really liked *The Hunt*."

"Of course you did. Every girl loves Joey Frank." Danny rolled his eyes. "I assume you want an introduction?"

"To Joey?"

Danny nodded. "Isn't that the reason you wanted to come to my prom? I'm not stupid, you know. I know you just wanted an in so you could meet 'the movie star.'" He made finger quotes and waved casually in Danny's directly. "Come on, I'll introduce you."

"No," Emily said, shaking her head. "I'm not at all interested in meeting Joey."

"Ohhhh," Danny said, nodding slowly. "You're obsessed with Simone, huh? That's cool. I don't know her, though."

"Danny, I'm not interested in meeting either of them."

"Then why are you here?"

Emily considered for a moment, and realized it wouldn't hurt if she let Danny in on their plan. He actually seemed pretty cool now that she was getting used to him, and if he was okay with the fact that she had, presumably, just come as his date to meet Joey Frank, how mad could he be that she had a different mission? "I'm here to find a guy," she said finally. She glanced across the room and saw Sid and Jeremy chatting at a table on the edge of the dance floor. Sid looked relatively content.

Danny laughed. "Don't tell me you're a serial promist." He laughed harder. "Do you use proms as, like, an alternative to online dating or something?"

"No! It's not like that!" Now Emily was laughing as she tried to defend herself. She filled Danny in on how she had met Ethan, and the prom crashing mission.

"So how many proms have you been to?" he asked when she had finished.

"This is number four."

"Four? You've been to four proms?" Danny whistled. "I'm impressed. How many do you have left?"

"After tonight, we have three left to crash."

"Wow. I wish I'd known this was the reason you wanted to come to prom with me," Danny said. "I probably would have scaled back the costume stuff."

Emily groaned. "Seriously? Did you make me dress like this just to punish me for using you to get to Joey and Simone?"

"A little," Danny confessed. "I've always wanted to come to prom in costume, though, so it worked out pretty well for me. It's always fun to surprise and shock people—everyone's so uptight at this school, I shake it up by doing things differently. But I guess I did put a little extra act on just to see how bad you wanted to be here. You passed the test." He smiled sheepishly.

"I guess I did." Emily looked down at her gown and grinned again. "You know what, Danny? I'm glad I came—even the ridiculous costume isn't so bad. You're right about people being uptight—everyone was totally staring when we got here."

He nodded. "You think I didn't notice? I've gotten used to it. Sometimes you just have to do things your way, and realize that not everyone is going to approve. That's sort of my motto. It's helped me survive the past four years—you think it's easy being the weird guy?"

"No, I can't imagine it is. But you seem to be pretty comfortable with who you are."

"Now," Danny agreed. "But when I was a freshman and sophomore, I definitely cared a lot more." He broke off. "Wait a second—what's the name of this guy you're looking for? We have a mission to complete tonight, right?"

"You'll help?" Emily asked. "His name is Ethan."

"Of course I'll help. Now, let's see . . . Ethan . . ." Danny looked around. "You know what? There's one guy named Ethan at Thomas Jefferson—a senior." He started to lead Emily around the room. Weaving through tables of couples, Emily could feel eyes turning to look at her and Danny as they passed. The staring didn't bother her nearly as much as she would have expected. But then again, it wasn't her school, and they weren't her classmates. Emily really admired Danny's confidence.

A few minutes of meandering—and many, many curious looks—later, Danny stopped suddenly, subtly pointing toward a full table of couples. "There. Is that him?"

Emily squinted. She moved closer so she could see more clearly. The one guy with his back to them . . .

"Is it him?" she whispered to no one in particular. It was possible. Her memory was fuzzy, but the tousled hair, the lean, strong muscles . . . yes, *definitely* possible. She stepped to the side of the table to get a better look at his face, and as she did, the guy leaned in and kissed his date tenderly on the neck. Her stomach sank.

Suddenly the guy turned and looked at her. He was smiling, and a mouth full of braces glinted up at her. Her stomach leaped, realizing that it wasn't Ethan. She was torn between relief (that kiss!) and disappointment (would she ever find him?!). Turning back to Danny, she shook her head.

"No?" he asked, looking as disappointed as Emily felt.

"No," she repeated. "But that's okay. There are other proms." Emily and Danny walked toward Sid and Jeremy, who were still sitting and chatting.

Sid looked up as they approached. "Hey, Em." She smiled. Emily could tell Sid was having a decent time, despite her distaste for prom. "Any luck?" she asked quietly.

"He's not here," Emily replied. "Are you having a good time?"

Sid shrugged. "It's not as bad as it could be." She looked at Jeremy, who was chatting with Danny. "He's nice."

"Yeah," Emily agreed. "So is Danny. I think tonight may not be a total bust," she declared. Suddenly Emily wanted to dance more than anything. She had never danced in skirts and a bustle before.

Fighting against her protestations, Emily dragged Sid

off her chair and pulled her toward the dance floor. She beckoned to Danny and Jeremy, and they followed.

Hearing Danny's words echoing through her head, Emily let everyone's stares pass right through her. *After all,* she reasoned, *what fun is dressing in costume if I don't make the most of it?* Caught up in their own semi-Victorian world on the dance floor, the four of them were among the last to leave.

Nine

E: u there?

M: Maybe.

E: can I get a ride 2 charlies?

M: Yeah. How was prom w. Danny?

E: supernice guy, surreal prom.

M: Details?

E: in the car. can we leave soon? my sister
is driving me insane.

M: ??

E: she and mom are discussing their "perfect
prom night." i do not lie.

M: Nice. I assume this conversation is for
your benefit?

E: probably a safe guess. meet u in your
front yard in 10?

M: Righty-o.

* * *

"Her costume wasn't bad." Sid laughed. She plucked an E string on her guitar, giving it a final twist into tune.

"You honestly wore a corset to prom?" Max had already asked Emily this question three times, and gotten the same answer three times.

Emily nodded her head again, taking a swig of her root beer. "That I did."

Max, Emily, and Charlie were all sitting on amps in the back room of Think, a low-lit club in the Warehouse District downtown. The postprom party for Ridley Prep was about to get under way, and they were helping Sid prepare for her set. As Sid tuned and sound-checked, pretending not to be nervous, Emily entertained the others with the details of their prom the night before. From the preprom portraits to the dance itself, she spared no details.

"And," Emily said, "I'm happy to report that Ethan was *not* at the Thomas Jefferson prom. So the costume didn't really hurt anyone. It was actually a blast."

"A successful prom number four!" Charlie declared. "I can't believe I didn't get to go."

"Trust me, you didn't miss much." Sid was leaning over

her guitar, strumming a few chords. She looked up briefly and caught Emily's eye. "Okay, it was pretty fun."

Charlie pointed at her and declared, "You're totally getting into it!"

Sid cracked a smile. "Well, it's better than studying."

"Right?" Emily said, not expecting any kind of answer. "This has definitely been fun. But there are only two more proms to crash after tonight! If Ethan doesn't go to Ridley Prep—which we'll find out tonight—then we have one more weekend of crashing. And the hardest target is up next."

"What's next?" Max asked, swirling his soda around his cup to create a mini liquid tornado. "And are you sure you want to keep doing this? Is this guy really worth it?"

Charlie scoffed. "Are you suggesting we stop now?!" He slapped Max on the head. "Are you crazy? This is just getting good."

"Do you guys want out?" Emily asked. She was totally addicted to the thrill of their mission now, and hadn't realized Max might be having doubts. She was almost happy they hadn't found her crush at one of the first proms, because then they wouldn't have had an excuse to keep crashing more proms. She continued, "Because I can crash the rest of the proms alone." She crossed her arms. "Not that that would be any fun at all." Emily scooted over to her cousin's amp and squeezed in next to him, laying her head on his shoulder. "At least I know I have Charlie to keep me company, right, cuz? It's the boat prom next. . . ."

"You bet!" Charlie declared, wrapping his arm around Emily. "I *love* crashing proms. I can think of no better cure for senior slide than a challenging and dramatic mission. We're like Tom Cruise in *Mission: Impossible*, but before he went all crazy and was still just a slightly too-old action star." Emily hugged him back.

Sid looked up from her guitar. "Are you kidding? I *was* sort of enjoying myself until you compared us to Tom Cruise. Now I'm just offended." She shook her head. "But I have to admit—after last night, I'm totally hooked. I am *so* in for the rest of the proms."

Both Charlie and Emily looked at Max expectantly. He shrugged. "What? It's prom. They're all the same."

"Really?" Emily asked, surprised and more than a little disappointed. "You're not having fun?"

Max held his hands up in a surrender motion. "I was just saying!" he said, then cracked into his dimpled smile. "But yes, I'm having fun. And definitely still in. Besides, there's a story to be sold after all of this, remember?"

"Good! We're all in!" Emily beamed. "How is your story going, Max? Do you need anything from us?"

Charlie ran his fingers through his hair and offered, "Let

me know if you need a physical character description of me for the article. I'd like to make sure you describe me as dapper and striking."

Max shook his head. "That was the plan, Charlie. Just keep your charming personalities and stories coming, and I should be all set. The story's good so far."

"Great," Emily declared, then shifted into planning mode. "So next Friday and Saturday night, we have the last two prom crashes. First up is Northwestern's boat prom on Friday night, followed by East on Saturday. If we can get into Northwestern, we're genius."

"Is it that guarded?" Max asked.

"This is going to be our toughest target," Emily explained, leaning forward. The first prom after-party attendees had begun to stream into the front of Think, and the music had been turned up to compete with the crowd. She raised her voice and continued, "We all know Northwestern is the richest school in the city. We also know that they rent out the Queen Mary yacht every year for their prom. I guess things usually get cooking while they're still docked at the pier on Lake Windham—the whole school piles onboard for their four-course meal, live band, the works. From what I've heard, the school principal personally greets every person boarding the boat. Then the boat takes off—sans principal—and it's just drunken debauchery."

"Debauchery is a great word, Em," Charlie interrupted.

"Thank you." She smiled.

Max interrupted her at this point. "I got a little info from one of the writers at *Buzz*." *Buzz* was the online paper that Max wrote reviews for. "Since almost all of the city's VIPs'—that's very important politicians'—kids go to Northwestern, most of the silliness on the boat is pretty much overlooked by the cops. The bigwigs don't want bad press, so they beg their buddies in the local precincts to turn a blind eye." Max shifted on his amp, getting into his story. "Rumor has it that at least half the school gets puke-up-your-dinner drunk, and things get completely out of control. Most years they have to dock early for fear of someone falling overboard."

"Good info, my man," Charlie nodded appreciatively. "So the question is, how are we going to get on that boat?"

Sid looked up from her guitar. "Someone needs to get a job on the Queen Mary. We need an insider."

They all turned and looked at her. Max slapped his knee. "That's genius!" he said.

"Thank you," Sid responded. "Now, can the three of you all please get the hell out of here? I need to finish getting ready, and you are terrible roadies. I'm much better off on my own."

Charlie stood up. "Touché!"

Emily stood up and passed Sid's pick—which Emily had been rubbing for luck—back to her. "This is it! Are you ready? You sure you don't need anything from us?"

"I'm all good." Sid ran her fingers through her rumpled hair. "Enjoy the show, all right? And don't tell me if it sucks."

"It will be fantastic!" Emily called over her shoulder as she, Max, and Charlie all slipped out the side stage door and into the main room of the club.

The club was crowded. The room itself was nearly barren, with a small stage carved into one wall. There were two bars running along two other walls of the club, and a few tall tables were set up throughout the room for people to stand around. But the majority of the space in the club had been cleared for dancing, which everyone was already doing.

Most people had changed out of their prom attire into low-slung jeans or more casual dresses. A few male stragglers had left their tuxes on, but loosened their bowties or tied them around their dates' necks. Emily, Max, and Charlie blended into the crowd well. They had packed their prom wear in the car just in case, but the jeans and—in Charlie's case—chinos they were wearing were more than appropriate.

As Emily led the others around the club, searching for

Ethan, Charlie cut through the noise to ask, "What does this guy look like again?"

"Hot," she answered seriously. "And yummy."

"That's really helpful," Max said, grabbing a plastic cup with an unidentified dark soda in it off the bar counter. "What color hair does hot and yummy have? And can you not refer to him as 'yummy'? It freaks me out. I picture a pizza or something."

Emily reached out to give Max a little swat in the chest, but he grabbed her arm and pulled her in toward him to prevent the attack. He wrapped her arm behind her back, trapping her in what she was pretty sure she remembered from childhood as a "half nelson." He held her tight against his chest, until she squirmed around to get in his face and fight back.

Their noses were millimeters apart when she turned. Emily's stomach leaped as Max's face settled in close to hers. They'd had this same type of battle a million times since childhood, but she'd never felt anything but a friendly connection, no matter how physically close they got. Until now.

She pulled back, breaking the connection. Max's face cracked into a smile when he said, "What's up, Em? You scared of me? You've never given up *that* easily before."

"No, I just got a little dizzy or something," Emily stammered, shaking her head in confusion. "But you know, it's prom. I'm supposed to act ladylike, not get into brawls with my boorish friends." She pursed her lips and took a dainty swig of her soda.

Charlie, who had been leaning against the bar scanning the crowd for interesting people to talk about, suddenly let out a holler. Sid had just stepped onto the stage and was settling in on a stool. Her guitar was loosely slung around her neck, and her hair was rumpled and messy. She looked like a rock star.

"Yee haw!" Emily yelled, cupping her hands around her mouth as Sid strummed out her first chord. A few Ridley Prep students turned toward at Emily, exchanging looks when they didn't recognize her, Max, or Charlie as one of their own. She smiled at them and raised her hand in a wave, mouthing *hi*. "What?" she asked Max, who was staring at her like she was crazy. "If you act like you fit in, no one notices you. Isn't Charlie and the prom king spectacle the perfect example of that?"

"That's right," Charlie said, staring straight ahead at Sid onstage. "I am the Memorial High Prom King."

After Sid finished her third song and started a mellow ballad, Charlie turned to Emily with a distracted expression on his face. "Remember the other night when you asked me if I've asked Marco to prom?"

"Yeah. Did you bring it up with him?"

"When we were talking last night, I mentioned how much I'm looking forward to prom, and how disappointed I am that he's not going to be here for it. And he just laughed at me."

"Seriously? That doesn't sound like him."

"I think he thought I was joking. But the thing is, I've actually been thinking about it a lot. I don't want to go with Natasha—I'm gay; I want to go with my boyfriend." He paused. "Emily, am I with the wrong guy?"

She turned to look at him. His expression was serious. "You don't really think that, do you?"

"I don't know, Em. I feel like he should know how much prom means to me, and come."

"But unless you tell him, it's not fair to expect that he just *get* that."

Charlie was watching Sid play onstage, but his mind was elsewhere. After a beat, he continued. "I guess I need to figure out how to have the conversation with him. I know it's too late for prom—I'm not ditching Natasha at this point, that would just be mean—but I guess Marco and I have to get a little better at telling each other where things stand." He turned to Emily.

She nodded slowly. "Even I didn't know how much prom meant to you, so I'm not surprised Marco's not getting it."

"*I* didn't know how much prom meant to me until last week." He grinned. "I always thought it was a little bit of a joke. I guarantee this is going to sound lame, but winning prom king at Memorial was seriously one of my highlights of high school. It got me all kicked up about prom."

"Yeah," Emily agreed. "I know what you mean." She smiled and gave Charlie a quick squeeze just as Sid wrapped her last song.

When Sid stood up to leave the stage, everyone cheered and whistled. Her bluesy-rock style had fit in perfectly with the vibe of the Ridley Prep crowd. She stepped off the stage and made her way through the crowd toward her friends at the back of the small club. Her guitar was still strapped around her neck. "So?" she prompted.

Charlie stepped forward first, planting two huge kisses on her forehead. "You!" He held her away from him, studying her face in the club lights. "You were amazing! I mean it. I'm so happy for you."

"You're acting like my grandma after my first communion," Sid said, sneering. "Was it that bad?" She actually looked a little nervous.

"Are you kidding me? I'm so proud to call you my best friend right now. Like I've said three million times before, you're going to be a huge star."

"It was great," Emily seconded. Max nodded and gave Sid a high five.

She looked relieved. "You really thought it was good? Sh—shmack, I was nervous as hell up there."

As they stood recounting all the brilliant moments in Sid's performance, a guy in a Skittles T-shirt and jeans sauntered up to their foursome. He looked familiar, but Emily couldn't place him.

Sid obviously knew the guy, because she stepped forward and said, "Hey, James."

"Hey," James responded slowly, nodding. "Good set."

Sid's face morphed into a smile. "Thanks." She turned to Emily, Charlie, and Max. "Do you guys know James? He's the lead singer of 1492. James, these are my friends— Emily, Charlie, Max."

"Ohhh," Emily said, nodding. *So* that's *where I know him from.* 1492 was one of the most popular local bands, and one of Sid's all-time favorites. Their popularity had spread beyond Minnesota's borders, and they were often on tour. But at least half the year they stuck close to home and played a regular Tuesday-night gig at one of the coolest bars in the area, French's.

Sid grinned at James again. "I didn't realize you were . . . shoot! Are you guys playing tonight?" She looked like she could burst, she was so happy.

"Yeah," James said. His voice sounded like molasses: deep, dark, and soulful. "We're headlining, I guess." He smiled slowly, twisting the lower corner of his T-shirt into a spiral. "Do you have a regular gig somewhere?" he asked Sid. "I'd love to come hear you play."

"No, not yet. I'm working on it." She shot Charlie a look that said, *Do not mention the Leaf Lounge.*

"We're looking for someone to open a couple of our shows at French's this month—would you be into that?"

"That'd be amazing." Sid's eyes opened wide, uncomprehending what had just happened. "Are you messing with me?"

James laughed—it was more of a chortle. "No, I'm not messing with you. Swing by next Tuesday around nine, and we'll get you hooked up. I'll introduce you to the rest of the band and French's owner, Jimmy. I'm sure it'll be cool, but I like to make sure everyone's happy with our opening band. Cool?"

"Cool," Sid said. "See you Tuesday. Thanks, James."

Charlie waited until James was a few feet away before turning to Sid and declaring, "When they produce your *E! True Hollywood Story*, the moment we just witnessed is going to be that part in the show just before a commercial break when the narrator starts getting all excited and says,

'Things were about to change for Sidney Cristina Martinez.' You are going to *open* for 1492!"

"No way," Sid said, shaking her head. "This is *so* not happening."

By the time 1492 hit the stage later that night, Sid had finally begun to believe that what had happened with James was real. She stood sandwiched between Emily, Charlie, and Max, all four of them bouncing gently in time to the music.

As they all sang along to 1492's song "Promises," Emily put her arms around Sid from behind, resting her chin on the top of her friend's head. Charlie and Max each put an arm around the two girls. They hadn't found Ethan, but none of them could deny that this had been the best prom yet.

When Emily got home that night, her mom was waiting up in the family room, reading. Emily poked her head in the door to say good night and make a hasty retreat.

"Come here, honey," her mom said.

Emily stuck one leg into the doorway, hoping that was enough to make her mom feel like she was making an effort. "Why are you still up?"

"I couldn't sleep. When are we going prom dress shopping?" Her mom sat up a little straighter on the couch, pulling her robe closed over her bare legs. "I saw Miriam

Arnold at the gym today, and she said Kristi is going with that nice boy you used to see—Dan, isn't it?"

"Yeah, Dan." Emily wasn't sure where this conversation was going, but so far didn't like the tone in her mom's voice. It sounded like comparisons would be coming next, and questions about Emily's love life.

As a teacher at her daughter's high school, Emily's mom was privy to far more information than she should be. For example, she knew Emily had not yet bought her prom tickets, even though they'd been on sale for more than a week. She also knew Emily didn't have a date, but chose to ignore this apparently irrelevant piece of the puzzle.

"Well, she told me that Kristi and her friends are going to the Lighthouse for dinner." Her mom paused, studying Emily in the lamplight. Emily crossed her fingers—it looked like her mom had just gotten distracted. "Where were you tonight? You look sweaty."

Emily swiped her arm across her forehead. "I was out with Charlie, remember? We went to one of Sid's gigs." *Not lying,* she reminded herself. *We were at one of Sid's gigs.* "It was gross there—hot—I should take a shower. Good night."

She gave her mom a quick kiss, then headed up the stairs to the shower. Emily knew she'd left her mom hanging on the prom conversation. She considered trekking back downstairs to tell her mom about their prom crashing, but once again decided it was a bad idea. Mom would positively die if she knew Emily had been going to proms without giving her a chance to take pictures to commemorate the nights. Not to mention that it was a lot more fun to keep their inappropriate—and bordering on illegal—little escapades to herself. No need to drag the parents into things. There were a lot worse things she could be doing—and wasn't.

There was another reason that she kept climbing the stairs—though Emily barely admitted it to herself. She already felt crappy enough about the fact that she didn't have a date for her own prom. If her mom knew she was on a mission to find the perfect date (a move that, to an outsider, might seem a little desperate), her mom might leap forward and try to fix things for her.

Emily couldn't face the pressure cooker.

As she grabbed her robe and headed toward the bathroom, Emily felt sure she was making the right choice. She needed to deal with this on her own and couldn't manage her mom's expectations on top of her own prom disappointment. She just hoped they would find Ethan the next weekend, or she was going to need to face up to the reality that her prom fantasy wasn't coming true.

Ten

Charlie's head popped out of the top of a stretch white limo. "Let's move!"

Emily waved from her post outside the front entrance of the mall, where she was waiting for her "dates" to pick her up. Her face lit up when she spotted Charlie's head coming around the corner—she hadn't realized he would be picking her up in a limo, but somehow it wasn't all that surprising. "You look happy. What's with the ride?"

"You like? It's my little treat. We deserve to go to one of these proms in style." Charlie tapped his hands on top of the roof of the car. "Hop in."

The limo driver opened the back door for Emily, and she slid onto the leather seat next to Sid, who had her feet resting on the seat across from her. Max saluted her from his spot in the back of the limo. The interior had green and pink lights running through the door paneling. There was a bottle of bubbly submerged in a tub of ice in one of the wall panels. Charlie had a glass poured for himself next to an already-burning clove cigarette perched in the ashtray.

When the driver closed the door behind Emily, Charlie descended from the sunroof and flopped back onto the long seat next to Sid's feet. He squeezed his cigarette between two fingers and took a long drag. Emily grabbed the cigarette from him and stubbed it out. His smoking disgusted her, and Charlie knew it. He didn't smoke that often, but always seemed to light up more around Emily—Charlie liked to push her buttons.

"I am *exhausted*," he declared, lifting his feet onto the seat and leaning back on his elbows.

Emily frowned. "Are you really going to complain? One of us smells like burned coffee right now, and I'm going to guess that's not you since—oh, *that's right*—you got out of work today." Charlie had been scheduled for the Leaf Lounge's after-school shift with Emily but had only been there for about an hour. Emily had agreed it was a good idea for one of them to skip out of work to finalize their plan for that night's prom with Max. Charlie had immediately volunteered to leave. When Gary had come in to take over for the evening shift, Emily had made up some excuse about Charlie getting sick. Then she scooted out of the coffee shop and into the mall's public bathroom to change into her dress before he could ask any questions. "But you're forgiven, on account of this limo."

"Thank you." Charlie exhaled a long, deep breath. "Just so you know, it's not as easy as it might seem to coordinate a four-way prom date. *That's* why I'm so exhausted." He glanced at Sid, whose eyes were closed. "Sid refused to get dressed. Let's just say, I had to take drastic steps to make things happen." Sid kept her eyes closed and smiled in response.

The four of them were on their way to Northwestern's boat prom, where Max would don a waiter's uniform (maroon boat shoes and an all-cotton, machine-washable "tux" with a maroon Queen Mary logo emblazoned on the back) and sneak them into the boat through the service galley. After Sid's brilliant suggestion that one of them get a job on the Queen Mary so they would have an insider working the event, Max had remembered that one of the guys on his dad's curling team was a Queen Mary captain.

It hadn't taken much for Max to convince his dad to help him get a summer job working as a crew member. His parents had been nagging him for months to make some spending money before college in the fall, and the

Queen Mary was a perfectly reputable option. Max's dad had pulled through, and Max was now gainfully employed.

As one might have expected, none of the long-standing Queen Mary employees wanted to work the pukefest high school prom with zero tip potential. So that Friday night— the night of Northwestern's boat prom—would be Max's maiden voyage as a busboy. The boat's management had hurried him onto the payroll specifically for this event— Northwestern's prom was *that* bad. Max's first shift started at eight, just in time for the hors d'oeuvres.

Max appraised Emily from the backseat of the limo and said, "You look nice. Have I seen that dress before?"

"Funny." Emily had worn her prom dress a total of three and a half times—the half was her date with Danny. "You might think the novelty of the dress would have worn off by now, but it hasn't. By the way, Max, the maroon boat shoes? Nice."

"You do look nice in pink, Emily. Your mom always says you should wear it more often." Charlie smirked. He loved to tease Emily about her mom and her nagging ways, particularly since Emily's mom was his aunt, and she treated Charlie like some sort of wonder child. Emily often got the impression she was her parents' third favorite child, behind Abby and Charlie. She really couldn't wait to get out of Minnesota and into her own life in New York.

Emily ignored her cousin's comment and popped her head out the top of the limo. She let her hair blow free in the wind, putting her arms up to catch the air as it circled around her.

When they stopped at a traffic light, Charlie popped out next to her, wearing his Memorial High Prom King crown. The car that was stopped at the light next to them honked. A high-school-age guy in the driver's seat waved— he was wearing a tux. "Seriously?" Emily asked, gesturing to Charlie's crown.

"Why not? It's my badge of honor, and I'm proud to wear it." He turned toward the car that had honked and waved back. "Think that guy's going the same place we are? We already have a friend." Charlie smiled at the driver, who was still waving. "A really, really eager friend."

Emily hoped everyone at Northwestern was as nice and dopey as the guy in the car next to them. They had a big challenge ahead of them, and if they had bitchy students to deal with, it would make their mission that much more complicated. As the limo pulled away from the light, Sid and Max both squeezed out of the sunroof to join them. All four friends lifted their arms and waved at the pedestrians walking past. Emily grinned—though it wasn't her romantic prom fantasy, this version of prom night certainly came close to perfect.

The limo pulled into a circular drive that was packed with other limos and dress- and tux-clad teens. Emily, Sid, Charlie, and Max all slid back into the limo's interior. Sid watched people through the limo's darkened windows, while Charlie adjusted his tie. Checking his watch, Max announced, "Five minutes until my shift. Are we ready?"

Emily twisted her hair into a low knot, which she secured with a few pins. "Come here," Charlie gestured, holding his glass of bubbly loosely in his hand.

"What's wrong?" Emily patted her head nervously. "Is my hair a disaster?"

"Sheesh, chill. It looks great." Charlie pulled a tiny blossom from a small vase in the wall of the limo. He pinned it into Emily's hair, just behind her left ear. "Now it's perfect."

Emily smiled at her cousin. "Thank you. I don't know why I'm so nervous. I guess since there are only two proms left, the chance of finding Ethan tonight is that much higher." She adjusted her dress, fiddling with a wrinkle that had formed over her thigh.

"That's why we need to get in there." Charlie poked his head out the roof of the limo, then popped back down again. "You ready, Em?"

"We're on." Emily's stomach made a nervous little flip. "Let's move."

The driver opened the door of the limo for them. Max

jumped out, followed by a surly-looking Sid. Charlie quickly directed the driver to wait until they returned to the dock later that night. Then he held his hand out for his cousin. "Take my arm," he instructed.

Emily did as she was told, and they followed Max and Sidney toward the dock. The other prom attendees were boarding the enormous tour yacht via a ramp that led onto the fore deck. There were tables piled high with appetizers and mocktails, none of which had yet been touched. Most of the prom crowd was still mingling on the dock, comparing outfits and preparty stories.

Max stopped at a small gift shop that sold souvenirs and tickets for the Queen Mary and other dinner boats. The gift shop was also the office and home base for the boats' employees—Max stepped inside the shop to punch in for his shift. When he returned to the dock, he handed Sid, Emily, and Charlie each a white chef's smock to put on over their formal wear. "Everyone ready to work?" Max winked.

The other three followed Max past the prom revelers and moved farther down the dock toward the aft deck. Max greeted a few of the Queen Mary waiters who were standing near a second ramp that was being used to load catering gear into the boat's galley. Other tux-clad employees bustled past the foursome, who had stopped a few feet short of the ramp.

Max glanced at the other employees, all of whom were too uninterested and/or busy to notice the newcomers. No one seemed to care that Charlie, Emily, and Sid were wearing formal wear under their smocks—as long as they were helping, it seemed they were invisible.

On Max's cue, Emily grabbed a steaming platter of dumplings off a rolling cart on the dock. Charlie followed suit, turning up his nose at his permanently stained uniform and groaning under the weight of the hot plate he was carrying. Sid lifted a small crate of freshly washed plates off the dock.

They stepped one at a time onto the long, wobbly ramp and paraded into the boat's galley. Inside the galley, Emily set down her dumplings and pulled off her uniform to reveal her dress again. She straightened the perma-wrinkle over her thigh, slid out the galley door, up a few short stairs, and onto the expansive yacht's deck. Charlie and Sid were steps behind her. Max waved to them from down in the galley, then returned to work.

Their plan had worked. They were in.

Moving to the front of the boat, Emily, Charlie, and Sid slipped into the crowd easily. There were several groups of people gathered near the buffet table, and many more parading onto the boat. Charlie scanned the crowd. "I don't see anyone who fits your description of Mr. Yummy."

"Me either." Emily twisted her hair nervously. "But I do see a lot of flasks out and in use. Max was right about this prom—there will be a lot of drunk people on this boat tonight."

Sid nodded to a guy on the other side of the deck. "That guy's already down for the count." Emily looked in the direction Sid had gestured. There was a tall, out-of-shape guy sitting on one of the benches, resting his forehead on his knees.

"It's only eight!" Emily giggled. "Looks like he's not gettin' lucky tonight." The drunk guy's date was standing at his side, one hand clutched around her cell phone, the other patting one of his shoulders. She looked pissed and embarrassed.

The three friends chatted and strolled around the main deck while the rest of Northwestern's students piled on board. Soon the boat pulled away from the dock and set sail into the inky black night. The Queen Mary was crowded and loud, and Emily was starting to feel a little seasick and smushed. She wanted to escape, but was stuck in the middle of Lake Windham.

While appetizers were passed, Emily weaved her way through the main deck alone but didn't see Ethan anywhere. Many people had moved into the well-lit and festive covered area on the main deck, where dinner was being served. A few lone couples stood on the outer deck, giggling and kissing in the moonlight. Charlie and Sid had followed a few of Charlie's new friends into the dining room, where Emily could see them laughing through the windows.

The appetizers had been cleared from the front deck and the tables had been folded up for storage. The front of the boat was now decorated with tiny, glowing lights that blew gently in the breeze.

Emily breathed in the clean, cool night air. She held on to the railing circling the deck and strolled back toward the rear of the boat. A circular staircase led her upward to a smaller, unpopulated deck overlooking the main level of the boat.

"Hey, you." Max's voice cut through the stillness of the night, surprising Emily.

She turned, seeing her best friend perched on an overturned plastic crate in one corner of the back deck, looking out over the lake. He was surrounded by dirty appetizer dishes piled high with food. "Hey," she replied.

"No Ethan, huh?"

"Seems that way." She moved toward Max's dish outpost, leaning back on a railing. "Charlie and Sid are having a good time."

"You're not?"

"Not really," she said, blowing her long bangs out of her eyes. "Can I help?" Emily offered.

Max held a dirty plate out to her. "Scrape, then stack." Emily nodded and pushed the food off one of the dirty plates into a big garbage bin propped up next to the railing. "You don't need to help though."

"I know." She grabbed another plate, carefully keeping it away from her borrowed dress. "This is really disgusting."

"No kidding. You'll notice I'm on my own out here." Max grimaced and scraped. "New guy."

"The job suits you," Emily teased.

"This is making me appreciate the college career ahead of me. I don't think I'm cut out for dish duty the rest of my life." He paused and looked up at Emily. "But I'm going to miss this."

Emily turned to him. Her stomach knotted like it had at the Ridley Prep post-prom the weekend before. "Me too." She set her now-empty plate in the plastic dishwasher tray Max was stacking plates in. "These last few weeks have been really fun. I'm going to miss you guys. You especially . . . and Wisconsin is really far from New York."

"Nine hundred eighty-four miles to Appleton from Manhattan." Max cocked his head to the side and smirked. "MapQuest. I'm preparing for my Emily withdrawal. I thought you were dying to get out of here. Haven't you been counting the days?"

"Yeah," Emily admitted. "But I sort of forget that when

I leave *here*, I'm also leaving you and Charlie and Sid. And painful as it is to admit it, I think I'm going to miss my little sister a tiny bit."

"Don't worry about that," Max said seriously. "I bought you a clock that has her voice recorded on it. Every hour, on the hour, Abby will announce: 'It's one o'clock! Do you miss me, Emily? It's two o'clock, do you want a snack, Emily?'"

Emily laughed. "I assume you're kidding, but I wouldn't put something like that past you. Man, Max, I'm gonna be a mess without you next year. Who's going to keep me up to date on the news of the weird?"

"I think you'll find plenty of bizarre stuff in Manhattan. I'm going to seem normal comparatively. Besides, Charlie is what, like an hour away?"

"Is Yale that close to New York?" Emily shuddered. "I didn't really think about that. That's a little too close for comfort."

Max laughed. "You'd probably be lonely way out there by yourself. But if anyone can handle New York, it's you."

"Yeah," Emily agreed. "I'll be all right."

"Oh, hey," Max interrupted, grinning in the moonlight. "I sold my prom crashers story!"

Emily grinned back. "Really? Max, that's fantastic. To *Buzz*?"

"Yep. It's going online Sunday. I'm in edits now. I have to write up the rest of the proms before I turn in my final draft. They definitely want me to use the stuff from tonight and tomorrow night—our last prom—before I finish up. But you're going to be famous. As 'Emmy,' though, not Emily. They made me change names."

"I would hope. I can't believe you didn't tell me about this. It really is going to be hard next year. I see you every day now, and still I feel like I'm missing things."

Max laughed. "I just found out yesterday."

"So? This is just a sneak peek of what next year's going to be like. Do you promise to IM with me every day?"

"Maybe," he teased. When Emily threatened to drop a plate of discarded food in his lap, he laughed. "Yeah, yeah, I promise!"

"Good." Emily set down her plate and leaned against the railing, looking out into the dark lake. After a few minutes of silence she murmured, "It's really pretty here. I sometimes forget."

Max nodded. "It's not bad." He scraped silently, studying Emily in the dim spotlight illuminating the back deck of the boat. After a few moments, he asked quietly, "Why aren't you having fun tonight?"

She turned, sighing. "This whole prom thing is starting to really get to me." She tucked a stray piece of hair behind her ear when the wind blew it loose. "I know it's just a dance, but I guess I always thought prom would really be *something* for me, you know? Romance and flowers and, well, the whole thing. . . . I thought I had maybe found that when I met Ethan a few weeks ago. But now things are starting to feel a little . . ." She broke off.

"Hopeless?" Max offered, not-so-helpfully.

"Yeah." Emily winced. "Thanks."

"I don't think it's hopeless. And I don't think it's unreasonable that you're looking for all that. You wouldn't be Emily if you just went to prom the way everyone else goes to prom. This prom crashing thing—that's how the Emily Bronson *I* know and love would want to do prom. It makes it an adventure. It seems to me that you *have* gotten your prom thing out of your system. Would you give up all this"—he gestured around at the boat—"for just a regular, ordinary prom? Would a good date with pretty white teeth really fulfill your every fantasy?" Max was gesturing wildly by the end of his little speech, and inadvertently flung a fork off the edge of the boat. "Oops."

Emily laughed and leaned forward to give Max a hug. He reached up from his seat on the crate, his arms stretching around her waist. The hug was clumsy, but warm and comfortable. Max's arms wrapped around Emily's waist and he pulled her in close. When he did, she felt the same suspicious spark in her chest and pulled back—this was getting ridiculous. She shivered in the cool breeze, rubbing her arms to keep them warm.

Max stood up from his crate and moved closer to Emily. "Are you cold?" he asked, concerned.

"I'm fine." But she wasn't fine. She wasn't sure if it was the slow prom song playing in the background or the lake setting (though scraping food remains wasn't particularly romantic) or her companion himself, but Emily was once again feeling an awkward electricity around Max.

"You're not fine," Max said. "You're cold. Come here." He moved forward, bundling her in his arms. Emily relaxed into his shoulder, only slightly aware of Max's dirty uniform. She tucked her arms in against his chest and her ear brushed his.

Her whole body was tensed up with the delicious feeling of what might happen. She leaned back and met Max's eyes in the moonlight, and they both smiled. Emily was surprised to discover how natural—and yet totally new—their connection felt. Max pulled her back in toward him, tipping his face toward hers.

Just then, Emily heard Charlie's yell from the lower deck. She pulled out of Max's arms and leaned over the railing to look for her cousin. Charlie spotted her and yelled again. "Em! We have to go. Now!"

"Now?" Emily asked, a smile tugging the corners of her lips. "We're on a boat, Charlie." Max leaned over the railing next to her and waved at Charlie and Sid.

"Hey, Max," Charlie said, grinning mischievously.

A loud, booming grunt came from the front deck of the boat, then a guy yelled, "Where is that dude? I'm gonna kill him!"

"Trust him," Sid announced in a loud whisper. "We need to get out of here. Em, are you in or out?"

Without thinking, Max quickly unhinged one of the lifeboats hanging next to him and lowered it to the water. "Go," he told Emily. "Take the spiral staircase down. There's a ladder just there." He pointed over the rail at a white wooden ladder hanging from the lower deck into the water. "There are oars in the boat. I'll explain to the captain somehow—luckily it's one of the college guys driving the boat tonight, so he should be cool about it."

Emily was confused. So confused. What had just almost happened? She didn't think she was imagining it—but had she and Max maybe just almost kissed? It was so unexpected and strange and thrilling, all at once.

Charlie was gesturing wildly from the lower deck and had begun to climb down the ladder and into the lifeboat bobbing gently in the water below. Sid was already in. Emily could see lights from the lakeshore just a few hundred yards away. She knew if they got into the lifeboat, they would be on dry land in just a few minutes if they rowed hard— though the rowing would, of course, be up to her and Sid. Surely Charlie's little getaway plan didn't allow for any exertion on his part.

The spiral staircase was wet, and Emily felt her shoes slip. She pulled them off and crossed the deck to the ladder. In less than thirty seconds, they were all three safely aboard the lifeboat and Max had untied the ropes from the Queen Mary. They were free.

Laughing maniacally, Charlie leaned back into the bench in the lifeboat. Emily pulled the oars out and dipped them in the water. Sid was hunched over laughing in the front of the boat. *"What* did you do?"

Charlie was too hysterical to talk and just pointed. An almost naked guy was standing on the front deck of the boat, staring after them, waving his fist in the air and swearing.

Emily's eyes widened. But it wasn't because of Charlie or the naked guy or the fact that they were stuck in a lifeboat in the middle of Lake Windham.

She was staring at the deck of the boat, where a crowd of Northwestern students had gathered to watch their lifeboat drift away and chuckle at their naked classmate. There, in the middle of the crowd, yummy as a slice of

Max's mom's cake, stood Ethan, just as gorgeous as Emily remembered him.

"Emily?" Ethan had seen her, too. He was shouting over the noise of the crowd to be heard.

Emily nodded. Lifting an oar, she shouted, "Hi, Ethan," as waves carried the lifeboat away and the yacht blurred into twinkling lights in the distance.

Eleven

Emily yawned and slurped a mouthful of milky coffee. It had been twelve hours since they'd left Northwestern's prom on a lifeboat, and she'd slept four of them. Now she was slumped behind the counter at the Leaf Lounge, downing coffee and waiting for the first morning regulars to arrive.

She, Charlie, and Sid had gotten to shore quickly the night before. They had tied the boat to a post on the dock and climbed into their waiting limo. Emily still couldn't understand the full story of what had happened that made them have to abandon ship so quickly—Charlie started gagging on his laughter every time he tried to tell the story, and Sid just kept shaking her head and said Charlie needed to tell it.

But Charlie had spluttered out enough for Emily to know that the big naked guy had, for some unidentifiable reason, removed his tux to puke up his preprom drinks in the ship's toilet, at which point Charlie had apparently led a little gang of other drunk people to grab the guy's clothes from outside the bathroom door as a fun prank.

Charlie had stowed them in one of the ship's life jacket containers, and the guy had emerged from the bathroom in boxers, socks, and a raging prehangover. He had sobered up slightly during his pukefest, and was embarrassed and angry about his missing clothes. Charlie's laughter hadn't helped to calm him down.

Apparently a bunch of the guy's friends had threatened to throw Charlie overboard as payback, which is when he had yelled to Emily, interrupting her and Max's almost moment.

She felt her thoughts once again drifting back to the strangely electric hug from the night before. She pushed them to the side of her mind, recognizing that years of friendship don't change overnight. She would never risk losing Max as a friend to pursue any feelings that might be there. Things would be so awkward between them if she were wrong and she said something to Max—he would think she'd gone crazy.

And anyway, she had now (sort of) found Ethan. There was still a little glimmer of hope that she would get to go to her own prom as one half of a developing couple. He went to Northwestern. Now she just needed to track him down on Facebook or MySpace or something.

The key was making that seek-and-find seem as un-stalkeresque as possible. He obviously remembered her—but had he been interested enough during their first meeting to think it was normal that she had gone to so much effort to track him down? It was doubtful that he would appreciate the humor of prom crashing as much as Max, Charlie, and Sid. In fact there was a pretty good chance he'd think she was sort of psycho.

Emily was staring off into space, resting her lips on the mug of her coffee cup. She hadn't noticed anyone come into the coffee shop, so she started a bit when a deep male voice roused her from her daydreaming. "Hi."

She looked up, pushing her bangs from her eyes. "Hi," she repeated quietly. Ethan stood on the other side of the counter. He was hotter and tastier-looking than ever. And he had come to find her! "How are you?"

"I'm okay." A smile played at the edge of Ethan's

mouth. He had something to say to her, but was measuring his words carefully.

Emily smiled. "Another chai?" she asked. She really hoped he wasn't there for chai. *Oh,* she thought suddenly. *What if he is?*

"I guess I got the hint," Ethan said suddenly and awkwardly. He was smiling, but looked a little uncomfortable. "I'm still waiting for that call you promised."

Emily stared back at him. He was waiting for her call! "It's a long story," she said. "But let's just say that I definitely *did not* mean to give you the impression that I did. I *definitely* wanted to call you." She paused. "Give me your cell," she blurted out suddenly. Ethan obliged, and Emily punched her number into his phone. "Now you have my number, and it's on you to call me."

"Well, maybe I don't want to call you," Ethan said. Emily frowned—had she totally misread the signals? Ethan continued, "Maybe I'd rather just make plans right now. Honestly, I don't really trust you to follow up." He grinned mischievously. "What time are you off work?"

Nice, she thought. *A take-charge guy.* "Three."

"Can I come by and pick you up?"

Emily's stomach fluttered. "Sure."

"Good." Ethan grinned. "See you then." When he got

to the door, he turned back. "Do I seem like a stalker for coming here to ask you out?" he asked.

Emily laughed. "Just a little bit." She raised her hand and held her thumb and forefinger close together. "Honestly, though, I can think of a lot crazier things you could have done."

But we'll save that conversation for another time, she mused, smiling at the memory of the past few weeks. *I just hope he can appreciate a good story.*

"I hope you like this place." Ethan pushed aside a branch, guiding Emily along a rocky path.

Emily tilted her chin up, inhaling the scent of the pine needle canopy above her. "How far are we going?" she asked. She studied Ethan's calf muscles as they propelled him forward on the path in front of her. She was enjoying the view, and wasn't eager to stop walking yet.

"Just a little bit farther. Are you hungry?" Ethan turned to look at Emily, concerned.

"I will be. But I can wait." She smiled. "Thanks for asking."

Ethan grinned back at her again, the corners of his mouth crinkling. "Good. I have a ton of food. I don't want to eat alone, so you better be hungry." Emily took this as a good sign, since she had never been one of those girls that didn't like to eat. She *loved* food. Ethan had a backpack slung casually over one shoulder that was stuffed with tasty treats. Emily could see a dark chocolate bar peeking out of the slightly open compartment. Her mouth watered.

They had been making small talk since Ethan had picked her up from the Leaf Lounge a half hour earlier. They chatted about the usual subjects—school, family—and she couldn't believe it when he told her he would be going to Columbia University in New York City that fall. They would be only a hundred blocks apart. While they talked, Ethan drove to a little hiking trail that crawled along a brook just a few miles from the mall. It was a gorgeous trail—she couldn't believe she hadn't known it was there.

Emily had no idea how exhilarating a date could be. Strange and awkward sorta-dates she knew all about. The few losers she'd "dated" had been friends of friends before she had made the mistake of taking things to the next level. She'd never actually been out—on a bona fide date!—with a guy she was really into.

Except Ethan. So she really didn't want to mess this up.

"I hope you don't mind me asking you this. . . . Why were you on a lifeboat on Lake Windham last night? Were you at my prom?" Ethan kept walking, staring straight forward. "Do I want to know?"

"Well," Emily started, smirking to herself, "that's an interesting story."

Ethan suddenly stopped at a grove of trees that formed a sort of canopy over a clearing on the ground. The grass was soft and fluffy, and the river gurgled and splashed nearby. "We're here," he said, pulling the backpack off his shoulder and tossing it on the ground.

"It's gorgeous," Emily murmured.

"So what's the story?"

"What?" Emily asked, settling into a cross-legged position on the ground in the middle of the grassy knoll. "Oh! The prom thing." She smiled self-consciously as Ethan looked at her from his seat next to her on the grass. Then she reluctantly started from the beginning and told him everything.

She realized it was better to go for full disclosure and let him make his decision about her based on the truth. So she told him about how his number had been smudged away, told the story about Neil and Danny and the crazy costume, and finally about Max getting a job on the Queen Mary so they would have an in at Northwestern. As she talked, she noticed Ethan's eyes widening in disbelief. When she got to the end of the story—Lake Windham—he whistled. "So you were just looking for me?" He cocked an eyebrow.

"No!" Emily covered her eyes with her hands. "Well,

initially, yes. But ultimately, my friends and I were just sort of looking for something fun to do. Proms were a good challenge. And who doesn't love going to prom?"

"Gotcha. So I was secondary to the bigger mission?" Ethan grinned. "An innocent bystander?"

Emily groaned through a smile. "This is all coming out wrong." She lay her chin on her knees, which were bent up toward her face.

"I'm teasing you," Ethan said, grabbing one of Emily's knees. She looked up when he touched her. "I think it sounds like a lot of fun. It's flattering that I inspired something so cool."

His hand lingered on her knee a few seconds longer than it needed to, and Emily shivered despite the warm day.

Intentional? she wondered. *Flirting?* She could only hope.

"So you don't think we're crazy?" she asked, hiding part of her face behind her knees. "I guess I would if I were in your shoes. You have to know my friends to get them."

"They sound cool," he said, pulling the chocolate bar out of his backpack. "I hope I get to meet them." He broke open the chocolate bar wrapper and offered her a piece. "I have some sandwiches and stuff, too. But I'd rather start with dessert. You mind?"

Emily shook her head happily. "Nope." She grabbed the chocolate. "So now that I've told you about prom crashing, it's your turn. What's something crazy you've done?"

"Honestly . . ." Ethan chewed his chocolate as he spoke. "Not much. I've been pretty focused on soccer and getting good grades, so I haven't really done anything too wild. We toilet-papered a guy's house once for soccer, but we got caught. So that was maybe crazy, but not so fun."

"That doesn't count. Come on," Emily pushed. "There must be something."

Ethan suddenly stood up. "I just thought of something. Follow me." He left his backpack sitting on the patch of grass and led Emily a few yards farther down the trail. Moments later they came to an old wooden bridge that carried the wooded path up and over a deep, wide portion of the river. "I've been swimming here a hundred times."

"It's tempting," Emily interrupted. *What does he have in mind?*

"But I've never jumped." Ethan smiled at Emily, pulling off his shirt. His broad chest was a golden brown—obviously a regular "skins" player on his soccer team—and lean and muscular. He was wearing only green athletic shorts, and Emily was definitely impressed. "My buddies and I come here a lot, and everyone else always jumps off the bridge into the water. I always avoid it and climb in from the shore down below. What do you say?"

Emily leaned over the edge of the bridge. The water was

at least twenty feet below them. Her heart began to race, a little out of fear, a little out of anticipation. "I'm in," she said, smiling broadly. "Are you sure?"

"I'm not gonna lie—I'm afraid of heights." Ethan rubbed his arms. "But I'm pumped." He clapped his hands and whooped, making Emily laugh. Ethan was goofy—in a good way.

"You're doing this for me?" she asked, lifting an eyebrow.

"Hey, you crashed proms for me. That has to take courage. I need to even things up, right?"

Emily nodded. "I'll go if you will." She was glad she was wearing her cute, red boy shorts under her jeans that day. They were just as covering as a bathing suit and a little sexy-cute to boot. She thanked her lucky stars that she'd worn the black tank top instead of her white one to work—wet and white would have left very little to the imagination.

She peeled off her jeans and hoped Ethan's fear had paralyzed his eyesight. She wasn't sure she was prepared for the full-body once-over. He politely averted his eyes.

Together they moved toward the edge of the bridge, and each of them sat on the wooden platform. "On the count of three?" Ethan suggested.

"One," Emily started. They dangled their legs off the edge of the bridge.

"Two," Ethan grabbed her hand.

"Three!" they shouted together. Then they both scooted forward and off the edge of the bridge. Emily could feel Ethan's hand tighten around hers as they fell forward. The force of the water broke their hands apart, but Ethan sought hers again as their bodies popped through the surface of the water. When they emerged from the murky river, they were both laughing and sputtering water. Emily adjusted her tank top to make sure nothing had fallen out.

"That was great!" Emily exclaimed, pulling herself up onto a big rock on shore that was warm from the sun. "You really haven't done that before?"

Ethan grinned. "Okay, maybe that's not quite true." His eyes were alive with laughter. "But I wanted to make sure you'd go in with me." Emily swatted him playfully as he climbed onto the rock next to her.

"You *have* jumped before?"

He nodded. "But it's never been that fun."

"You totally had me going. I thought I was helping you overcome this great, momentous fear." Emily shook her head. "I feel so used."

"I can't apologize. It was worth it. You looked so cute scooting off the edge of the bridge." Emily reddened at the compliment. "Am I in trouble?"

"Yes," she declared. "Now you owe me." She was flirting, and knew it was working.

Ethan maneuvered on the rock so he was right next to Emily, almost touching her legs with his. His hand was at his side, and his fingers lightly touched her thigh as he shifted position. Emily watched them and moved her own hand to her side to meet his fingers. Her heart was racing.

"Does this make up for it?" Ethan asked, then turned her face toward his and lifted her chin so her lips touched his. His mouth was wet from the river, and his eyelashes were beaded with water. Emily closed her eyes, soaking in the heat of the sun, the warmth of the rock beneath her, and the strength of Ethan's hand, clutching hers. The kiss was short, timid.

"Mmmm," Emily murmured as she pulled back just slightly. "That makes up for it." She smiled, relaxing into a second kiss. Ethan adjusted on the rock so he was facing Emily. She sat cross-legged, leaning in toward him. His legs were spread into a crooked *V*, wrapped around her in a leg hug.

They sat like that for a long time, kissing and laughing and teasing each another. They chatted easily about a million things—their friends, families, college—and only separated for a few minutes when Ethan ran up the hill to grab their clothes and bring food back to the rock.

When the sky began to get dark and a chill crept into the air, they were still talking. Ethan pulled a blanket out of his backpack and spread half of it on the rock beneath them. He snuggled her in so that her back rested against his chest, his legs still wrapped around her. Ethan pulled the rest of the blanket in close to their bodies, tucking them in under the stars.

She felt protected, refreshed, and exhilarated. Ethan was amazing, and she couldn't think of a better first date. She lay her head back, resting it on his shoulder and staring up at the sky.

"Can I ask you something?" she whispered, tilting her neck so she could see his face.

"Mmm-hmm," he murmured back.

"This might sound silly, but . . ." Emily paused. She was suddenly a little nervous. "Would you go to my prom with me?"

Ethan laughed, squeezing his arms around her stomach. "Were you scared to ask me that?" She nodded vigorously, laughing with him. "Of course I will."

"Really? It's next weekend." Emily turned her body so she was facing him.

"Yeah, definitely. It will be fun."

"Fab." Emily beamed. Ethan hugged her close and she smiled contentedly. Suddenly she felt a niggling of paranoia. "Oh no," she said, sitting up suddenly. "What time is it?"

He pulled his watch out of the backpack. "Eight fifteen." Ethan pulled her back toward him. "Does it matter?"

"Yes!" Emily cried out, sounding more panicked than she would have liked. "I'm supposed to be at our last prom at eight. I promised Max I'd be there. He needs this for his story."

Ethan looked confused. "Story?"

"I'll explain it in the car. Can you drive me to the Maritime Hotel?" She stood up, hastily stuffing the remnants of their picnic into Ethan's backpack. She pulled her cell phone out of her pocket. No service. "He's going to be pissed." She knew it was crappy and self-centered of her to stand up her friends because she was on a date. They would probably understand, but she wanted to help Max see his story through to the end, and worried she may have messed things up by being late.

Ethan folded the blanket and stuffed it in his backpack. "Okay," he said, tossing the pack over his shoulder. "Let's go." He grinned at her in the moonlight. "I've had a great time, Emily." He pushed her bangs away from her face and kissed her forehead. "Thanks for finding me."

"Me too," she responded truthfully. Then she climbed back up the steep bank to the main path and out toward Ethan's car.

Twelve

Half an hour later, Ethan pulled his car into the circular driveway of the Maritime Hotel. Max was standing outside the hotel's revolving door, tuxedoed and alone. Emily could tell from the look on his face that he was irritated.

Emily stepped out of the car in her jeans and tank top and approached him. "Hey," she said, heart pounding. She hadn't prepared herself for seeing him again after their almost-moment the night before. She felt awkward with him, especially knowing Ethan was in his car behind her. "I'm really sorry I'm late."

"You know what?" Max said, barely looking at her. "It's no big deal. We already went in—just snuck in a side door and checked things out. I got what I needed for the story."

"You went in without me?"

"We waited for an hour—it was pretty obvious you weren't coming."

"Max, I'm sorry." As she said it, she noticed Charlie's car pulling up to the front of the hotel from the parking lot.

"Seriously," Max said blandly, "don't worry about it. I figured I'd wait a few more minutes, just in case you showed up. Charlie and Sid went to get the car. Is that the guy? He was on the boat last night?"

Emily turned to look at Ethan, who was watching them from the driver's seat of his car. "Yeah, that's Ethan."

"Hey," Max called to Ethan, waving halfheartedly at him. Ethan waved back.

Charlie pulled his car up to the front of the hotel, then poked his head out the window to chide, "Well, well, lookie who decided to show up."

Emily flushed. "I'm sorry," she said again. "I didn't realize I was this late."

"Well," Charlie said, "you are. And now Sid and I are late for our prom. In case you've forgotten that one as well, South's prom is tonight. Luckily, Natasha's driving with a group of girls, so we're meeting there. So your lateness didn't totally screw up her night as well."

Emily groaned. She had almost derailed Max's article, and now she'd made Charlie late for his own prom. "Can I make it up to you?" she offered.

Charlie grinned. "That's the spirit!" he said. "Come with us to South's prom. Crash it."

"You're on," Emily agreed. She leaned into the window to address Sid. "Sid, are you going to your prom? When did that happen?"

"I'm playing!" she declared.

Charlie clarified. "Now that she's the opening band for 1492, Marisa Sanchez and the prom committee are all into Sid. They called her this morning *begging* her to play a set."

"Then I'm definitely in. Any chance to hear my favorite singer-songwriter play. Okay if I bring Ethan?"

"Yeah." Charlie shrugged. "Max, you're in, right?" Max was standing behind Emily on the sidewalk. He was quiet. *Maybe,* Emily thought, *it's my imagination, but something seems off.*

"No, I don't think so," he responded. "I have to finish writing my story."

"You have to come," Emily declared. Though she wasn't sure if that was really what she felt. She didn't know if she was prepared to be with him and Ethan at the same time.

Charlie whined, "Yeah, Max, come on. It's the perfect ending to your article."

"Um, okay," he agreed blandly. He opened the back door

on Charlie's Volvo and stepped in. "I'll go. I don't have much choice, since you were supposed to give me a ride home."

Emily was now standing alone on the sidewalk, uncomfortable when she realized she wouldn't be riding with her friends, as usual. Emily's dress was in Charlie's car—she had been leaving it in there after most of the proms so that her mom wouldn't get suspicious—and she pulled it out of the trunk now, holding the shimmery fabric in her arms. Charlie gestured to Ethan. "See if he has anything to wear. Then you guys can follow us there."

She nodded and returned to Ethan's car. He rolled down the window and she leaned in. "Hey," she breathed. "Do you have any interest in coming to my cousin's prom with us?" Emily sort of expected him to say no. So far, he was a little too good to be true.

"Absolutely," he answered quickly. "And this is your lucky day," he continued. "My tux is in the trunk." In a move that could only be classified as lucky, Ethan had put his tux in his car that morning, intending to return it to the rental place that afternoon. But his date with Emily had run over and he hadn't had a chance.

"Great," she said. "Then we're good to go."

Twenty minutes later, Emily and Ethan pulled up at South's prom. Charlie, Sid, and Max had already gone into the ballroom. Emily and Ethan had stopped along the way so that they could change into their formal wear in a gas station restroom. As they approached the door to the dance, Ethan turned to Emily and declared, "This is exciting," then leaned over to give her a kiss. Her lips burned.

Inside, they had no trouble getting into prom. No one was guarding the doors, and people were coming and going freely. Ethan looked a little disappointed.

Emily quickly spotted Max, who was standing by himself against one wall of the ballroom. She led Ethan toward her best friend, realizing again how uncomfortable she felt about having her two guys alone together. Had Max felt their connection the night before too? Was he feeling as uncomfortable around Emily as she was with him?

Once introductions were out of the way, the three of them stood silently for a few minutes, taking in everything around them. Emily was acutely aware of her position, standing between her hot new crush, Ethan, and best-friend-with-potential-spark, Max. Ethan had his hand resting lightly in the curve of her back.

After a few minutes of desperate searching, Emily finally noticed Charlie and his date, Natasha, across the room. She waved madly to get his attention. He left Natasha with her friends and came sashaying over. "This must be the yummy guy you've been talking about," Charlie declared, ignoring Emily and giving Ethan the once-over.

Ethan reached his hand out toward Charlie. "Ethan." He pretended he hadn't heard Charlie's comment. "You must be Charlie."

"When does Sid go on?" Emily asked Charlie.

"Yo!" Sid broke through the noise of the prom by shouting at them from across the room.

Ethan turned to Emily. "Sidney?" he guessed. She nodded.

"I am flipping nervous," Sid declared, storming over to them. She looked at Ethan suspiciously.

Emily smiled at Sid. "Nerves really do bring out the best in you, Sid. This is Ethan, prom guy."

"Oh, right." Sid sized him up. "Good to finally meet you. Hey, what happened after we left your prom last night?"

Emily clutched Ethan's hand at her side. She caught Max sneaking a peek as their fingers intertwined. He averted his gaze.

Ethan laughed. "Brian finally found his tux, but ended up puking on it later. So he probably would have been better off without it. You sort of did the guy a favor by taking it in the first place. He stunk at the after-prom party."

"Once again," Charlie declared proudly, "a successful

prom crash on all accounts." He broke off, pointing to the stage area, where a DJ was playing eighties classics. One of Charlie's drama club cronies—the guy responsible for lighting—was beckoning Sid to the stage.

"I guess this is it . . . ," she said. She clapped her hands twice. "No amount of adrenaline can get you through the nerves of playing in front of your whole school. This is just messed up," she said, then turned to Charlie. "Enjoy the rest of your night, Charles." She winked cryptically, then strode off toward the stage.

"What did that mean?" Emily asked Charlie.

Charlie stared after her. "No clue." He waved at Natasha, who was dancing with a bunch of their friends. Natasha had tied the hem of her ankle length black slip dress into a knot near her knees to free her legs for dancing. She looked bohemian and chic, twirling and spinning in time to the music.

"Are you and Natasha having a good time?" Emily asked. When she did, Ethan released her hand and put his palm in the small of her back again. Her skin tingled where his hand connected with her body, then the tingle expanded outward like a firecracker. She turned to smile at him, eager to be alone again.

Charlie nodded. "Yeah, I'm having fun. I don't necessarily think she cares that we're here together—she just wanted to go to prom. Which is good, I suppose, since I'm hanging out with you guys." He grinned.

Suddenly a static-filled shout broke through the room. Members of the prom committee were standing onstage, and one of the girls had shouted into the microphone to get everyone's attention. People covered their ears and turned toward the stage. "Sorry," she said with a shrug. "Okay, everybody, we have an amazing surprise for you all tonight. First, we're going to announce this year's prom king and queen, and then"—she paused, relishing in the suspense— "Our very own Sidney Marquez—" Emily winced . . . that wasn't even Sid's last name. Ouch. One of the other girls onstage whispered something to the girl with the mic. Mic girl continued, "Sorry, Sidney Martinez, is going to play a few songs to finish our year in style! Our very own South High music celebrity!"

Everyone clapped, and Charlie laughed. He leaned over to Emily, Ethan, and Max. "It's funny to see Sid at such a school-spirit-heavy event. This is just so out of character for her." Emily laughed and nodded, but Max just stood silently, staring forward. "She must be dying backstage." Charlie chuckled.

"So first"—mic girl waved an envelope over her head— "on behalf of the junior year prom committee, I'm delighted to announce this year's prom king and queen!" The DJ turned on a CD with cheesy drumroll music. "This year's prom queen is . . . oh, this comes as no surprise to anyone . . . Marisa Sanchez!"

A pretty brunette in the middle of the room feigned surprise and waved her hands in front of her face. The whole room was cheering and clapping, and Marisa managed to muster up a few tears of happiness. She made her way toward the stage to collect her crown.

"And now," mic girl announced, "we'll reveal Marisa's king! Drumroll please. . . . This year's South High Prom King is . . . Charlie Delano!"

Charlie jumped a little next to Emily. He turned to Emily, his face a mask of pure disbelief. A huge smile spread across his face as everyone in the room cheered. He raised his arms over his head and took a low, deep bow. Then he moved forward to collect his *second* prom king crown of the year.

As Charlie hastily made his way through the crowded ballroom and toward the stage, Emily felt a little tap on her shoulder. She turned, and there was Marco, Charlie's boyfriend, standing right behind her. "Hey!" she cried, giving him a hug. "What are you doing here? Does Charlie know you're here?"

"No," Marco responded. "It's a surprise. I hit traffic coming out of Chicago, so I'm a little late. I just got here.

You look great!" He grinned at Emily. They hadn't seen each other in a few months. "Where is he?"

Emily pointed to the stage, where Charlie was just ascending the steps to claim his crown. Charlie lifted his hands in the air and whooped as the crown was placed on his head. "You're dating the prom king. How does it feel?"

"Again?" Marco smiled, referring to the Memorial High prom. "I wanted to be here for him. He called me earlier this week and told me how much this prom meant to him and how sad he was that I wouldn't be here. I had no idea it meant that much to him. I've never heard Charlie be so earnest. So I e-mailed Sid and got the details. She knew I was coming, but I asked her to keep it a surprise."

"It will definitely be that," Emily said. "Hey, Marco, this is Ethan. *My* prom date." She blushed a little as she said it. Ethan shook hands with Marco and nodded knowingly. "And you remember Max, right?" Emily said, moving in closer to Ethan to make a space for Marco between her and Max.

Marco moved forward and said, "Yeah. Hey, Max. How've you been?" Max just nodded. Charlie was now leading Marisa down the stage steps toward the dance floor for their inaugural dance. Sid walked onto the stage, her guitar slung over her shoulder. She sat on a stool centerstage and started to play one of Emily's favorite songs, "Hello You."

Sid sang while Charlie and Marisa danced together.

Everyone had formed a big circle around the king and queen and were cheering and taking pictures. Marco excused himself and moved away from Emily, Max, and Ethan so that he was standing on the outer perimeter of the dance floor, watching Charlie from a distance. About halfway through the song, Marisa's boyfriend made his way onto the dance floor and cut in. Charlie hugged Marisa, then moved away toward the edge of the circle. The rest of the prom committee and their dates swarmed onto the dance floor and joined Marisa and her boyfriend.

Like a scene out of a movie, Charlie suddenly looked up and noticed Marco, who was now standing twenty feet away, right in Charlie's line of sight. Charlie's face broke into a huge smile. Marco moved forward, and Charlie pulled his boyfriend into a giant hug.

Ethan, who had been watching Charlie and Marco's reunion, turned to Emily and murmured, "Care to dance, gorgeous?"

"Absolutely," she declared. She looked at Max, who was standing alone next to them. "Do you mind if we dance?"

Max ran his hands through his hair. "Feel free." He gave Emily a strange, uncomfortable look that caused her stomach to flip nervously. "Actually," he said, "I'm going to take off. I have a story to finish. Tell Charlie I called a cab." And with that, he spun on his heels and walked away.

Thirteen

"Hey, Em." Max sauntered up to Emily the next Tuesday night, with Charlie in tow. Emily and Ethan were meeting the two guys to watch Sid's first gig at French's. Emily's stomach leaped at the familiar sound of her best friend's voice. She was scared to see him. *Ridiculous,* she chided herself. *This is* Max!

But Emily knew why she was uncomfortable—she hadn't *truly* spoken to Max since their almost-moment four days earlier. They had never gone this long with awkwardness between them. They had exchanged a few lame bits of chatter on Saturday night, but she hadn't had a chance to really *talk* to him.

She was still haunted by the feelings she'd had on the

boat Friday night and didn't know what to make of it. She kept trying to ignore the sensation she had felt that night, but there was something tap-tapping away in the back of her mind that just wouldn't let it go. And she had no idea if Max had felt it too.

"Hey, guys." She greeted Max and Charlie as naturally as possible. But her palm was sweaty in Ethan's hand. "Are you excited for tonight?"

Charlie beamed. "Definitely. Sid is *so* nervous." He looked giddy.

"Did Marco leave?" she asked. Emily hadn't really spoken to Charlie since Saturday night either, since she'd spent almost every spare moment with Ethan.

"Uh-huh," Charlie said, his face turning somber. "I miss him already."

"Did you guys stick around at prom for a while?" Emily asked. She and Ethan had only stayed at South's prom for a few more songs, then left to grab a bite to eat. Ethan had dropped her off at home close to midnight, and left her with a scrumptious, exhilarating good-night kiss. Thankfully everyone in her family was asleep when she got there—she was able to sneak in and hang her prom dress deep in her closet before anyone saw it and started asking questions.

Charlie nodded. "We stayed until almost the end. It's

a prom king's duty." He grinned. "Then we hit the after-party at Marisa's house. I think Marco had fun. He seems to be more proprom now."

"Are you going to our prom after-party?" Max asked Emily suddenly, out of the blue. "Lauren is having an after-party at her house. I think I'm going."

Emily turned to stare at her best friend. *Lauren Ellstrom?* "Oh," she said, not sure what to say. She hadn't realized Max was going to prom, and she wondered who he was going with. How could so much happen in four days?

She realized she was being completely self-centered, but Emily didn't want Max to go to prom—she wanted to live out her own prom fantasy, but didn't want Max to have his. Totally hypocritical. "We're not sure yet what we're going to do." She looked at Ethan.

"Right," Max said distractedly. "Well, have fun." Ethan clutched Emily's hand in his, oblivious to her discomfort. Max went back to silence.

Charlie grabbed Emily's arm and pulled at her sleeve. "Can I talk to you for a sec?" he asked quietly.

She told Ethan that she'd be back in a minute, and followed Charlie toward a corner of the club. "What's up?" she asked.

"What happened between you and Max? You're acting like you hardly know each other." Charlie looked back at

Ethan and Max across the room, who were standing a few feet apart without speaking.

"I don't know!" Emily exclaimed. "This is going to sound ridiculous, but I think something might have almost happened between us at Northwestern's prom—right before you showed up. It was really, really surreal."

Charlie gasped. "Like happened, happened?"

"Maybe?" Emily pushed her bangs away from her face. "I seriously don't know. But it's been weird between us ever since. I think he was really pissed at me for being late to East's prom, and now it seems like he's avoiding me, and I guess I'm sort of avoiding him because of the whole boat thing, and Ethan's fabulous and hot and perfect for me, and *I don't know!*" She sighed. "Oh, Charlie, have I massively screwed up?"

He gave her a hug. "Oh, sweetie, no. We'll figure it out." He waved at Ethan, who was shooting Emily a slightly desperate look from across the room. "What do you want to do?" he asked. "Could there be something between you and Max?"

"I might be imagining the whole thing. But I might not. Either way, I can't really get into this relationship with Ethan if I'm messing things up with my best friend, can I? I mean, Max means the world to me."

"I hate to ask this, since I sound like your mom,

but"—Charlie paused—"what do you think is right? Aren't you really into Ethan?"

"Yes!"

"And what about Max?"

"I don't know. We've never gone down that road before, so I can't say for sure. I guess it's possible—there was an unfamiliar spark."

Charlie studied both guys from across the room. "You can't really go wrong with either one," he teased.

"So helpful." Emily grimaced. "I guess my biggest fear is that Ethan won't fit in with you guys. Or what if I'm imagining my chemistry with him—though I don't think I am—and I give up on Max, and then in a couple of weeks I'm left with no boyfriend and a best friend who hates me. I really need to know what Max is feeling right now. Or I need a sign that Ethan's the right guy—or that Max is."

Sid suddenly stepped onstage, guitar in hand, and the lights in the club dimmed. Charlie grabbed Emily's arm and yelled over the sound of the music, "It will work out. I promise." He pulled her back through the crowd toward the two guys waiting for them on the other side of the club.

Emily returned to Ethan's side, and he pulled her in close. Max watched them snuggle up together, then strode across the room to buy a soda. Charlie and Emily both watched him go, then shared a look.

This is bad, Emily mused silently. *And it's just going to get worse at prom.*

After the show, Emily and Ethan split off from the others. Emily had spent most of Sid's show thinking about the awkwardness between her and Max, and had finally come to a resolution about what she needed to do.

When they got to his car, Ethan pulled Emily toward him in the shadowy parking lot and ran his fingers along her cheek. She let him kiss her only briefly, then pulled away. "Can we go somewhere and talk?" she asked, walking around to her side of the car.

"Sure," Ethan said, unlocking the doors. "Everything okay?"

"I don't know," Emily responded. It was the truth. During Sid's show, Emily had realized that she needed to pursue whatever might be happening with Max. Though she felt like things with Ethan were going perfectly, she knew she could never fully enjoy their relationship if she thought it had potentially ruined things with her best friend. So she leaned back in her seat, took a deep breath, and said, "Listen, Ethan . . ."

He sighed. "You're kidding me, right?"

Am I that obvious? Emily wondered. He seemed to know where she was going, which certainly would make it easier to say. It wouldn't make it any easier for her to feel good about the decision, though. She continued, "I am having so much fun with you, but . . ."

He had started the car, but sat with the engine idling. "But?"

"But," Emily went on, "there's some stuff I need to deal with right now. I don't know how long it's going to take, or what I'm going to resolve, but I just need a little while to figure things out. I don't think it's fair to you or to me to keep hanging out." A knot crept up into her throat. She felt like sobbing as she said, "I don't think I can go to prom with you."

"So that's it?" he asked, turning toward her.

"I guess so," Emily said. "Things just don't feel right. Not right now." She knew it sounded lame, but she didn't know how else to put it. She couldn't tell him she didn't like him—that was a lie. And she couldn't say things were going nowhere—she didn't know if that was true either. She just knew something didn't feel right with her life, and she needed to try to fix it.

Ethan stared straight ahead when he repeated, "Not right now?" He turned to look at her in the darkened car. "Does that mean there's still a chance someday?"

She met his eyes in the moonlight and knew she couldn't answer his question definitively one way or the other. "I don't know. I hope so? But I know that it's not fair to hold on to you right now, and I don't expect you to wait around. I'm sorry. You have no idea how hard this is for me."

Ethan pulled out of the parking lot silently, and they rode in silence all the way to her house. Emily's hands were folded in her lap. She opened her mouth a few times to say something, but couldn't think of the right words. "I'm really sorry," she managed finally.

They pulled into the darkness outside Emily's house. Ethan hadn't parked his car in the driveway, and Emily couldn't see his expression in the darkened car. "I understand," he said, turning to look at her. "I'm sorry too. I'm really happy with you, Emily."

She choked back tears and managed to squeak out, "Me too," before she opened her door and left Ethan alone. "Good-bye, Ethan." It wasn't until she was alone in her room, tucked under her covers with her prom dress laid out on the bed next to her, that Emily let herself cry.

A few nights later Emily sat alone in her bedroom again. She was picking her fingernails nervously. She felt sick.

Ethan had just called. She had offered him no further explanation, other than telling him again that she was sorry about everything and that she just couldn't commit right now. He had been understanding and kind about it, but said he was really disappointed, which had made the conversation that much harder. Emily was heartbroken; she wished they had met at a better time.

Emily had discussed the situation with Charlie and Sid at the Leaf Lounge the night before, and they had both agreed that she'd made the right decision. When Emily complained about losing Ethan, Sid had declared that Emily "needed to get over herself. Sh—crap happens." And that's how Emily felt now—like *crap*.

The phone was back in its cradle and Emily felt alone and miserable—Ethan was gone. Her dad's laptop was open on her bed in front of her, with the home page of *Buzz* on screen. Max's prom crashing article had been published on the website a few days earlier, and Emily had finally had a chance to read it for the first time. It was really funny—he had captured all the nuances of their weeks of crashing perfectly. He had cast Charlie, Emily, and Sid in a hilarious light, and his style was spot-on for the tone of the website. The only thing missing from the article was her and Max's maybe-almost-could-have-been-a-kiss. She wasn't surprised it wasn't in there.

Emily was so proud of Max and wanted nothing more than to tell him how excited she was for him. She knew

she couldn't ignore this big achievement just because
they were apparently avoiding one another. She pulled
up her Instant Messenger.

E: max?

E: r you home?

Nothing. He wasn't there. Nor was he home when she
called his house. She would try to find him at school the
next day, but there was an assembly during their lunch
period, so it was unlikely they would have any time to talk.

Sighing, she flopped off her bed and walked to her window. She had a perfect view of Max's room from her own.
Emily still had the flashlight she had used as a kid to send
him messages out her bedroom window, and she pulled it
out from under her mattress now. She flicked it on—the
light still worked.

She flipped it off and stowed it under her mattress
again. Max's shade was closed, and his yard was empty.
Emily couldn't believe that just a few awkward moments
had put a kink in their friendship after all these years. She
and Max had never even considered dating, and she wondered if maybe this was some big misunderstanding.

Until they had an honest conversation, she would just
have to hope that things would go back to normal—or

something better than normal. They would have to talk to each other eventually, and when they did, Emily could see if she had been alone in feeling the spark between them on the boat.

But no matter what happened with Max, one thing was certain: Emily was going to be alone for prom.

Fourteen

"I'm not going."

Emily had told her mom that she wasn't going to prom six different ways, but her mom was still convinced maybe she would change her mind. "You'll look so pretty in navy."

"*Mom.* I'm. Not. Going. End of story."

"Maybe lavender would set off your dark hair better."

"Prom's tonight." Emily threw her hands in the air. "It's too late."

"Why aren't you going with Max?" Her mom asked the question innocently. But Emily wanted to scream and shout and tell her she was horrible for asking such a loaded question.

Why aren't I going with Max? she fretted as she stomped

up the stairs to her room. She had obviously been debating this very question for the past few days, and couldn't come up with an answer she was happy with—other than the fact that he was going with someone else, of course.

"Are you okay, Emily?" Abby's pigtailed head poked around the door of Emily's room, breaking her out of her head.

"Yeah. Fine."

"Do you want me to go to prom with you?" Abby looked so sincere that Emily knew she hadn't asked the question to be malicious or to make Emily feel totally lame. Abby just wanted Emily to be happy.

"Come here," Emily beckoned, and her sister happily trotted into the room and curled up next to Emily on her bed. "Thank you for offering to be my prom date."

Abby grinned and snuggled into her sister's arm. "You're welcome."

"You know what?" Emily closed her eyes. "I've been really stupid for the past couple of months."

"Stupid how?"

"I guess I thought that prom with my best friend would somehow be less perfect than prom with a knight in shining armor, who would buy me a pretty rose corsage and kiss me at the end of the night. And now that misguided fantasy made me lose my best friend."

"Do you like roses?" Abby was missing the point, but Emily was relieved. Her sister didn't need to worry about stuff like this yet. She'd get her share of it someday.

"Yeah, roses are pretty. But Max would have probably brought me a daisy corsage or something silly and frivolous, just to be different." Emily paused. "And I would have loved it." She sighed, and Abby snuggled in deeper. "But you know what?" She asked that question blankly, quietly, more to herself than to her sister. "Prom with Ethan would have been perfect too. He would have more than definitely kissed me next to the buffet table and made all my prom fantasies come true."

Abby craned her neck around to study Emily's face. "Is there a buffet at prom? Do they have mini hot dogs?"

"But if I'd gone with Ethan . . ." Emily ignored her sister's question and continued her musings. Abby was like a free therapy session. Her questions were unrelated to the point of the conversation, but there was something soothing about having her there. It was making Emily think about things in a way she normally wouldn't. ". . . I would always wonder if the connection between me and Max was real or imagined."

As she said it, Emily knew she had to find out more. Her friendship with Max was built on too much to have it ruined by the uncertainty of not knowing what *might* have happened. That's why she'd broken up with Ethan, after all. It's the reason she'd given up her chance for a perfect prom. She couldn't face looking back at prom as the night that caused her friendship with Max to end. No amount of romance was worth that.

So if she was doing the right thing, how was everything still so totally wrong?

"What am I doing?" Emily asked no one in particular.

"You were going to get me a snack?" Charlie offered helpfully.

"Why am I missing my own prom?"

"Because you broke up with your yummy new boy-friend, didn't want to go with me, and completely screwed things up with your backup-date-slash-best-friend-slash-maybe-future-loooover." Charlie smiled. "Does that answer the question?"

Emily groaned. She was curled up on the couch in her family room, with Charlie's feet partially blocking her view of the TV (she didn't mind—she wasn't watching anyway). *Pretty in Pink* was on, in honor of the fact that Emily had screwed up her prom night and now wanted to watch Molly Ringwald get all dolled up and live out her happy ending.

Charlie had offered to take Emily to prom, but she refused to be the girl who went with her cousin. She really believed that might be worse than not going at all.

"You could have gone with me," Sid chimed in. She was stretched out on the floor, facedown.

"I should have," Emily smiled. "At least I would have gotten points for going with a rock star. I could have said I knew you when."

Sid blushed. She still hadn't gotten used to the fact that she was now a *real* rock star. After her gig at French's earlier that week, 1492 had been so impressed with her performance and the crowd's reaction that they had offered her a spot touring with their band when they hit the road in a couple of months. "Aw, shucks," she said. "You make it sound like I've already turned into a diva. Give me time, lurves, give me time." She looked up and grinned. Her now-green hair streak flopped over one eye.

"I'm going to go put on my dress," Emily announced suddenly. "I can pretend I'm going to a John Hughes prom with Andrew McCarthy."

"Oh, Em," Charlie sighed. "Don't do it. That's just sad."

Emily laughed. "No, really, I think it will help. Yes, it *sounds* sad, but *I* believe that wearing my dress will make me feel *better*." Charlie and Sid looked at each other with wide eyes.

"Girl, you're nuts." Sid's voice was muffled by the carpet.

Emily laughed and bounded up the stairs to her room

and closed the door. Her parents had gone out for the night—taking Abby with them—so she knew she would probably be left alone. But she shut the door just in case. She wanted a few minutes to herself.

Opening her closet, Emily pulled her prom dress from the back corner and laid it out on her bed. She sat next to it, staring out across her backyard through the window— fireflies flickered periodically in the dusky sky, like mini Christmas tree lights.

After a few minutes of staring without really seeing, Emily realized a light besides the one coming from her own bedroom was shining into her backyard as well. Max's bedroom light was on. Emily checked her alarm clock. Prom had started an hour ago, so he shouldn't still be home.

Then Emily noticed someone moving in Max's room, and she recognized her best friend's striped oxford. *Why isn't he at prom?* she wondered. Suddenly Max turned and looked out the window. He spotted Emily looking at him from her window. They stared at each other without movement for a few moments.

Emily backed away from her window, turning off her light. She had an idea. Reaching under her mattress, she grabbed the flashlight she had discovered a few days earlier and shined it at Max's window. A few seconds later Max's light flicked off and he flashlighted her back. Emily smiled in her darkened room.

She needed to talk to him immediately. She couldn't handle one more second of not knowing what was going on between them. Leaving her flashlight in the on position, propped up on her windowsill facing Max's room, she turned and jogged back down the stairs.

As she thumped out the front door, Emily could hear Charlie calling after her. She heard footsteps following her but didn't care. She just needed to talk to Max. She ran around the corner of her house and into Max's backyard. There was an old oak tree that Emily had climbed a million times—just not for a few years. She awkwardly ascended it now, carefully avoiding the thin, brittle branch halfway up the tree.

Charlie and Sid were beneath her now, calling out in hushed yells. "What are you doing?" Charlie asked. "Em, come down."

Emily shook her head, though she knew Charlie couldn't see her in the dim light. "I have to talk to Max," she replied, huffing from the effort of climbing the tree. "Don't worry—I've done this a million times." She reached Max's room and tap-tap-tapped on the window from her perch in the tree.

Max's bedroom light flashed on, illuminating Emily in

the tree. She was sure she looked ridiculous. "What the . . ."
Max was just as surprised to see Emily as Emily was to realize
she'd just climbed the tree.

"Hey," she panted. "How are you?"

"Okay." He crossed his arms over his chest. "What are
you doing here? Shouldn't you be at prom?"

"Shouldn't you?"

"No." Max looked down. "I don't have a date."

"I thought you were going with Lauren Ellstrom?"

"I never said that."

"You did. We were talking about the prom after-party,
and you said you were going with Lauren."

"No." Max shook his head. "I said I was going to
Lauren's after-party. But I never said anything about going
to prom with Lauren."

"But you . . ." Emily stopped. This was going
nowhere. "Max, listen." She paused. She still hadn't really
thought out how she was going to approach this awkward
subject. "I'm really sorry about being late to meet you
last weekend."

"That's okay," he replied. "The story got written."

Emily was sidetracked for a second. "I know! It was so
good—I read it, and am so impressed."

"Thanks." He looked at her expectantly.

"But, um—okay, listen." Emily settled into a more

comfortable position in the branch of the tree. "I've been feeling really weird lately about something. I don't know how to bring this up, but I sort of feel like we have to talk about it or I'm just never going to know if I was imagining something or—"

Max cut her off. "I was a little freaked about what almost happened on the boat too."

"You were?!" She wondered if she should be worried about his choice of words—"freaked" wasn't exactly reassuring. She continued. "Did you feel like there was almost a moment?"

"Yeah," Max answered sheepishly. "But then Charlie showed up and you found Ethan and everything got . . ."

"Weird." They said it at the same time, then laughed.

Emily spoke first. "I broke things off with Ethan." Her heart pitter-pattered when she said that.

"He seemed like a good guy."

"Yeah," Emily agreed. "He is. But what I had with him isn't as important as what I have with you."

There was a pause. Max was looking at her in the moonlight. *Is he going to kiss me?* she wondered. Her heart thumped in her chest.

And then Max started laughing. Not just a little laugh, either. It was a big, from-the-gut, almost-falling-out-the-window guffaw. Emily had just bared her soul—if she was using romance writer language—and Max was *laughing*.

She stared at him for a moment, then she too started laughing. Tears pooled in the corners of her eyes, and the branch she sat on was shaking.

Max's dimples deepened. "It's so great to hear you say that. . . . I'm sorry, I don't mean to laugh."

"No, I get it," she said, matching his smile. "This feels better, doesn't it?" Emily asked. She knew Max was feeling exactly the same way she was. There was absolutely nothing romantic between them. There never would be.

"Much," Max confessed. "Don't get me wrong—there was some sort of spark the other night, and maybe there's been some funky spark sparking around for the past month—but I think we were both just caught up in a bizarre, promesque mood." Some friendships were meant to be just that—friendships—and hers and Max's was one of those. He reached out and touched her hand. "We're much better off as best friends, aren't we?"

Emily nodded. "Agreed." Then she leaned forward on her branch to give him a hug. It was awkward, considering that she was balanced somewhat precariously in the oak tree, but it still felt good. "But you know what?" she said, suddenly remembering her prom dress draped across her bed next door. "I wouldn't want to go to prom with anyone but you. We really should have planned to go together."

"I offered," Max declared. "You shot me down!"

"I know, I know." Emily groaned. "Okay, I'll admit that I would have really liked to have my romantic prom fantasy come true. But now I'm thinking a little excitement and intrigue on prom night is way more fun than a lot of romance."

"I agree."

"And could Ethan—however yummy he is—live up to the standards you, Charlie, and Sid have set for prom? I think not. Kissing by the buffet table just doesn't compare to the excitement of prom crashing." She paused and looked down at Charlie and Sid, who were still standing, looking up at her, from the base of the tree. "So," she said, loud enough for the other two to hear, "who wants to go to Humphrey's prom?"

"Em," Max said slowly. "None of us have tickets, remember?"

"Ah," Emily said. "That hasn't stopped us before, has it?"

Max's dimples deepened again. Charlie started clapping from his post on the ground. "One more target?" he asked excitedly.

Emily grinned. "That's what I'm thinking."

Emily heard her parents' car pull into the driveway just as she emerged from her room in her perfect pink prom dress a few minutes later. By the time she got to the top of the stairs, Abby was clapping with Charlie and Sid in the front hall as Emily's mom snapped pictures of her eldest daughter descending the stairs. Her mom was so caught up in the excitement of it all that she didn't seem to notice that Emily had a prom dress she knew nothing about and had never seen before. Emily was sure the questions would come later.

When Max walked through the Bronsons' front door decked out in his tux a few minutes later, Emily's mom couldn't stop herself from tearing up. With the camera following his every move, Max happily wrapped his arm around Emily's waist and together they posed for pictures with huge grins on their faces. Emily's mom only let them go when she was certain she had at least one shot that would be good enough for the Bronson family Christmas newsletter.

It was after ten o' clock by the time they finally arrived at Humphrey's prom. They had swung by Charlie and Sid's houses to pick up their formal wear, then all of them put last-minute finishing touches on their hair and outfits in the car outside the convention center. Charlie was still trying to tie his bow tie as they rode the escalator up to the ballroom that had been the site of Max and Emily's first prom together—Park High—just four weeks earlier. Emily couldn't believe how much had happened since.

"Hello, Emily." Mrs. Fenton, Humphrey's composition teacher, greeted her at the door of the ballroom. She was checking people in and collecting their tickets. "Max, how are you?"

"Hi, Mrs. Fenton," Emily responded politely.

"How's your mom?" Mrs. Fenton gave Emily a knowing smile. It was the same smile all the teachers gave her. The one that said, *I know a lot more about you than you would ever guess, because your mom talks about your private life in the teachers' lounge, but I'm going to pretend I don't know that you still grind your teeth in the night, et cetera.* Emily hated that smile. "She must be so excited about you going to prom."

What she didn't say is, *I know she was worried about how you were a huge loser who didn't get a date for prom, so isn't this exciting that things worked out for you?* At least, that's what Emily was imagining she was thinking in her head.

"My mom is fine. She got lots of pictures." Emily smiled back. "Have a good night, Mrs. Fenton. Enjoy prom!" She started to walk through the door, with Charlie, Max, and Sid trailing close on her heels.

They were steps away from safety when Mrs. Fenton called out. "Oh, Emily!" Emily turned back, a nervous smile plastered on her mouth. "I need to take your tickets."

"Oh," Emily said, thinking quickly. "We turned them

in earlier tonight when we first got here. We just stepped outside for a quick breath of fresh air. But we're back now!" She sounded way too chipper.

"That's impossible," Mrs. Fenton said. "We have a lockdown policy, so if you leave, you leave for good. No readmittance. You understand, right, dear?" Mrs. Fenton suddenly looked like a mean old lady.

"Of course." Emily sugarcoated her response. She could tell Charlie and Max were both laughing silently behind her. "Well, good night then."

They turned and rode the escalator back down to the lower level of the convention center. Rejected.

"Plan B?" Charlie jumped off the last step of the escalator.

"Looks that way," Max responded. "Very suave, Em. Nice attempt."

Emily shrugged. "It was worth a shot, right? Now I guess we have to get in the hard way."

"Breaking and entering?" Sid asked hopefully. "I noticed a side door that looked pretty unguarded up there."

They all agreed and moved to the east entrance of the convention center. They climbed a set of stairs to the ballroom level. There was a catering service door that led into the kitchen. Sid stood cover as the other three slid along a wall and ducked through the door, then she followed.

The kitchen was steamy and loud, with waiters and bus-boys bustling through the crowded mazelike countertops. The four of them weaved through the kitchen, following a team of waiters carrying trays of passed hors d'oeuvres out into the ballroom. The door swung open to reveal Humphrey's prom in full swing.

"Easy peasy!" Charlie declared, moving into the ball-room while straightening his jacket. "Let's get down!"

Charlie and Max grabbed Sid—despite her protests—and pulled her onto the dance floor. Emily was dispatched to grab sodas.

She noticed a few of her old swimming friends across the room and waved. They waved back, and Emily realized why her own prom meant more to her than the other proms they'd crashed. The whole room was full of friends. These were the people she had spent the past four years with—and some she'd known as long as thirteen years, if you counted those who'd gone to the same elementary school.

She really *was* going to miss the comforts and familiar-ity of home next year. Suddenly nostalgic, she looked back at the dance floor to find Max, Charlie, and Sid. Charlie and Sid were rocking out in the middle of the dance floor, while Max chatted with Lauren Ellstrom nearby. He looked really happy—Emily was happy *for* him.

Waiting for her sodas at the bar, Emily looked around

the ballroom at all the couples and friends dancing and laughing in their dresses and tuxes. Even though her prom had a familiar, friendly feel, Emily still felt something was missing. She'd had a riot crashing proms with her friends— it had been the perfect ending to high school, and the perfect cure for senior slide. She knew she would have always regretted it if she'd gone to her prom with Ethan and jeopardized her and Max's friendship . . . but she missed Ethan horribly. He'd been so perfect for her.

She hustled over to the dance floor and joined her friends. The song that had been playing ended, and the DJ kicked off the next song—Green Day's "Good Riddance (Time of Your Life)"—with a dedication. "This next song goes out to Emily . . . who finally made it to the right prom."

Charlie gasped and both Max and Sid looked at Emily. "I didn't dedicate this song to you!" Charlie declared.

"Not me," Max shrugged.

Sid sighed. "Are you kidding?"

Charlie lowered his voice to a hushed whisper. "Who knows about us?"

They all looked around, searching for the person who had uncovered their plot. Emily's stomach fluttered nervously— she was totally busted. It was their last prom, and she'd been caught by someone.

The lights on the dance floor dimmed, and a figure stepped out from behind the DJ booth and onto the dance floor. Emily turned just as Max, Charlie, and Sid all noticed that the person was winding through the crowded dance floor toward them.

Emily's breath caught in her throat—it was Ethan. "Good dedication?" he asked, trying to hide a smile. But his eyes gave him away—Emily could tell he was about to laugh. "You look nervous."

"Was that your dedication? How did you . . . ? What are you . . . ?" Emily stuttered. "Are you a DJ?"

Ethan laughed. "No, I'm not a DJ. But my cousin is—with a little help from him, I was able to crash your prom. I owed you, right?" He looked unbelievably proud.

Max nudged Sid and Charlie, suggesting that maybe they should take off and give Emily and Ethan some alone time. Both Sid and Charlie nudged him back and stayed put. They wanted to know where this was going.

"Oh," Emily said lamely.

Ethan looked suddenly uncomfortable and glanced around, as if searching for someone. "You're here with someone, aren't you?"

"What?" Emily asked. When she realized he was asking if she had a date, she laughed. "Oh! No." Then she saw Charlie, Sid, and Max all grinning at her goofily from a polite distance away. "Well, actually, I'm with my friends. But they're great dates, and they're willing to share, if that's what you're asking."

"I wanted to see you, Emily." Ethan suddenly turned serious. "When we had our conversation earlier this week, I didn't know what to say. But the more I thought about it, the more I realized how wrong you were. We're good together. We need to give this thing a shot. I'm hoping you might be ready now."

Emily smiled and twirled her hair. "So you crashed my prom to find me?"

"I figured it was the only way to show you I meant it. I was hoping you'd show up. I assumed you wouldn't miss it."

"You were right," she agreed. "And you're right about us, too. Thank you for giving me time to figure things out."

Ethan held out his hand. "Dance with me?"

Charlie, Sid, and Max all whistled. They were totally unsubtle, but Emily would have expected no less. Ethan bowed in response, earning him an extra cheer from Charlie.

She let him pull her close and rested her chin on Ethan's shoulder. They had drifted to one side of the dance floor, away from the crowds of other dancers.

As the song ended, Ethan pulled back slightly and turned Emily's face toward his. She smiled at him, and he kissed her. Emily let the rest of the room blur out of focus—she could only see Ethan and a tray of tiny sand-wiches over his left shoulder.

Melting into his next kiss, Emily sighed happily. She was being kissed next to the buffet table at prom. Some dreams do come true.

Drive Me Crazy

For Henry and Ruby.
May you always be surrounded
by love, laughter, and tasty treats.

Acknowledgments

This book wouldn't exist without my sparkly new editor, Anica, who has marvelous suggestions and anecdotes that make writing much more fun.

And, as always, thanks to Greg—who gives me very clever plot ideas, and who washes the dishes while I write.

Prologue

Love, Wisconsin

The first kiss tasted like toasted marshmallows, the sweet and sticky flavor of a summer bonfire. His mouth was soft and warm from days spent outside in the sun at the lake. As they kissed, his hand traced a line up her spine, twisting her insides into spirals. She melted into him and thought about their summer together, weeks of flirting and teasing that had finally progressed to a real kiss on their last night together.

He pulled back and looked at her, his piercing green eyes cutting through the dark night. A smile tugged at the corners of his mouth. It was the same look he'd given her all summer—but this time it was different, because now she knew where things stood. They had kissed. There was a new kind of bond between them, the kind of connection she'd seen played out in movies and the "Your Stories" section of her favorite magazine. She sighed, as she knew she should, and he leaned in for another taste. When he pulled away, she felt her lips hang on, sticky with marshmallow.

But in one tiny second the moment of bliss turned to a scene of horror. His hands gripped her arms and his eyes snapped open. His look was no longer teasing; it was terrified. "Kate, my lip is stuck in your retainer."

One

New Jersey

Gasp! Kate Rogers's mouth snapped closed and her eyes popped open, suddenly awake. A tiny trail of drool had begun to escape from her mouth, and she swept the back of her hand across her chin to dry it.

It was the last day of school, so study hall was essentially empty. The few people who had bothered to show up for last period were stealthily sending text messages or paging through magazines while Mrs. Coyle pretended not to notice. Kate was there only because she'd feel guilty if she skipped . . . even on the last day of school, when she had nothing to study.

Kate glanced around the room to try to figure out who'd seen her napping. As usual Curtis Chin was watching her from his table across the room. Curtis was a very nonthreatening type of creepy. Kate shot him a look, and he eagerly waved at her. Kate was glad Curtis was graduating. She had lucked into study hall with him every semester since ninth grade, and his apparent attraction to her hadn't faded.

Curtis's crush wasn't flattering, since he also harbored an unrequited crush on Kate's best friend Alexis Goldstein, and had gone so far as to send snail mail *letters* with his drawings of fairies and dragons to her other best friend, Sierra West. Sierra had graciously thanked Curtis for his kindness and artistry, and had gently explained that he wasn't her type; Alexis had just growled at him to "get lost, freak."

A quick peek at her watch told Kate there were only six minutes left in her junior year of high school. She pulled a magazine out of her bag and flipped through it absentmindedly, thinking about the dream she'd just had. The marshmallow kiss, the feeling of Lucas's hand tracing its way up her spine, the look in his eyes.

This wasn't the first time Kate had fallen asleep in study hall, and it definitely wasn't the first time she'd had that dream. The scene was always the same, an exact replaying of the moment she and Lucas had shared at the end of last summer. In real life, the kiss had been perfect, but the ending was a different version of awful each time she relived the moment in her dreams. Once, Lucas had pulled away in a dream because Kate's dad had been standing next to them singing "Itsy Bitsy Spider." Another dream had ended with Alexis and Sierra both watching their kiss from a judging table, holding up scorecards. (She'd gotten a 4.4 out of 10.)

This time she wasn't sure what the deal was. . . . Kate hadn't worn a retainer during the day since eighth grade. (She still wore it while she slept, which is something only Alexis and Sierra knew about.) She imagined these freak-out dream endings were just her nerves acting up, wondering what would happen between her and Lucas this summer. They had ended things with such a magical moment at the end of last summer, and had been exchanging flirtatious e-mails and IMs all year. She couldn't wait to see him in person in less than a week!

The bell rang, signaling an end to study hall, eleventh grade, and Kate's years with Curtis Chin. Kate smiled thinly at Curtis as she passed him on her way out the door, then breathed a sigh of relief that he was out of her life for good.

Now that the school year was through, she was just days away from reigniting the fire that had started to simmer last summer. As they had every year for the past ten years, Kate and her family and friends would be spending the next month and a half at the Cattail Cottages Resort in Love,

Wisconsin (pronounced Loave, Wis-*can*-sin, which amused Kate tremendously). This year Kate would finally live out her dream of spending the summer kissing and whispering under the big pine tree, and she couldn't wait.

Kate grabbed her bag out of her locker and slammed the empty metal cavern shut with a hollow *thwack*. She had left only a small piece of notepaper tucked into the far back corner, with a tiny "hello, you, from kate" scribbled on it. Kate did this every year—a message-in-a-bottle-style greeting to whoever moved into her locker the following fall.

Kate was a true romantic, and liked to think that the future inhabitant of her locker would find her note and track her down, and he would end up being the love of her life. This romantic scenario hadn't yet played out (in fact, this past year Curtis Chin had moved into Kate's old locker, and the secret note had only fueled the fire of his crush), but she left a little greeting again this year anyway, just in case.

Someday her prince would come.

"Kat!" Alexis hugged her from behind and pushed her toward the front doors. "We're seniors, Kat! Yaaaaaaah!" Alexis pumped her fist in the air, her long almost-black hair swinging out behind her.

Alexis had called Kate "Kat" since fourth grade, after Kate had hastily climbed up—and even more quickly gotten stuck in—a tree, and the fire department had had to come and help her down with their big ladder. Just as the nickname had started to fade, in the middle of fifth grade Kate had scratched Justin Thornton when he'd called Sierra "chubster" on the playground. Justin had sported a cat-scratch-like mark for about a week, and Kate's nickname had stuck with Alexis ever since.

"Woo-hoo!" Kate cried, hopping off the last two steps toward the front lawn of campus. She and Alexis skipped outside with the rest of the student body, everyone cele-brating their summer freedom. It was a muggy New Jersey spring afternoon, and people had rolled up their jeans and sleeves to enjoy the sunshine.

Kate and Alexis sprawled out on the school's lawn to wait for Sierra, who was probably bidding each and every teacher a personal farewell. Sierra did those sorts of things, which is certainly why she was so successful at everything she did. Sierra had just won student council president for the upcoming school year, and she was pretty obvi-ously going to get valedictorian next year as well. She'd been given the honorary faculty prize in this year's awards assembly, earning her a thousand-dollar college scholarship, compliments of the local business association.

In spite of her good-girl seemingly perfect exterior, Alexis and Kate loved her anyway. They knew the real Sierra, and she was a lot more fun and interesting than her campaign posters would suggest. "Hey, bitches." Sierra had slid up behind her two friends on the lawn and whispered this in their ears. Ms. Mohan passed them at that moment and flashed a wave of hello. "Have a fantastic summer, Ms. Mohan!" Sierra said as she waved, dripping candy sweetness from her sugary smile. Then she turned to her friends and said, "Let's get this party started!"

Kate grinned. "Eighteen hours until the girls' road trip hits I-80!" she announced, pulling Sierra's slides off her slender feet for her. Then she unsnapped her bag and pulled a list out of the interior pocket. "I think we're just about ready. Are our road trip tunes set?" she asked.

"Check," Alexis declared, tapping her iPod inside the back pocket of her jeans. "My road trip playlist is so hard core that you will puke before we get through every song. And I'm making us listen to it until we hit Ohio, just for fun."

"Snacks?" Kate asked. Her stomach rumbled at the thought.

"Swedish Fish and Diet Cherry Coke!" Sierra clapped. Sierra was a total snack fiend, which you would never guess from her looks. Her "chubster" nickname was long forgotten. . . . She was now as long and willowy as a professional ballet dancer. Her dark skin glowed from within, as though she only ate spinach salad and water. Kate, on the other hand, was average height, "curvy" (Kate called herself "stocky," which was far from the truth), and subject to skin disturbances every time she approached a french fry or processed sugar.

Kate studied her road trip prep list, growing more excited. For the first time ever, this summer the girls' parents were letting them drive themselves to Love, and they had been planning their road trip for weeks. "And I have the entertainment covered," she concluded. "Quizzes from the last six months of four different magazines, maps, travel and accommodation guides—"

"Ooh," Alexis cut in sarcastically. "Fun!"

"Bite me," Kate cheerfully shot back, then continued. "—And a detailed map of every possible amusement park along the way, including one that has one of those freaky fortune-telling machines."

Sierra waved at a few girls from her AP history class, then turned back to Kate and Alexis. "I am so excited about this trip, y'all." Sierra had lived in Birmingham, Alabama, until third grade, and tiny little bits of the South still popped up in her vocabulary every now and again.

"Me too," Kate agreed. "My two best friends, the open road, a cute boy waiting for me at the end . . ." Not to mention that the road trip across country with her two best friends meant that she didn't have to sit in the back row of her parents' minivan with her little sister for the almost twenty-four-hour drive to the lake house. And Lucas's warm, tan, scrumptious body was the pot of gold at the end of the road! "I had my dream in study hall again," she said, lying back on the grass and looking up at the big oak tree hanging over them. "This time Lucas's lip got caught in my retainer." She cringed at the thought of Lucas's perfectly smooth, scrumptious lip tangled in her mouth gear. Eek.

"By the time you finally get some, you're going to be so freaked out that you won't remember how to kiss," Alexis said, and rolled her eyes. "You'll see him in a week, Kate. We have almost a week of girl time ahead of us—please tell me that the whole trip won't be consumed with romantic speculation about your upcoming summer o' love."

Kate smiled at her. "In fact," she said smugly, "I had planned to talk about Lucas every single moment of each of those days, if you don't mind."

Alexis hopped up onto her knees and leaned over Kate, her scrawny 104-pound frame silhouetted by the sun above her. "I do mind. I think we're all pretty clear about exactly what happened last summer—your 'magical' kiss"—Alexis wiggled her fingers in the air—"and it's obvious exactly what needs to happen this summer. I have made it clear that you just need to jump him when we get to the lake, and everyone will live happily ever after."

"Okay, okay," Sierra cut in. "Alexis, you must be patient. Kate is preparing for her romantic rendezvous with her summer crush, and it's our job to be supportive and talk her through it." She smiled at Kate. "We know Kate wants the big moment to be perfect, and I'm willing to help with that. On the other hand . . ." She furrowed her eyebrows. "The Lucas talk better stop by the time we get to Pennsylvania, or there will be no Swedish Fish for you. Enough is enough!"

Kate frowned at both of them. But in all fairness she knew she'd been yammering on and on about Lucas for almost eleven months. She was ready to get some action, and wanted to stop talking about it just as much as her friends wanted her to. But Kate also wanted to make sure that everything was perfectly planned out, so her reunion with her hot soon-to-be-boyfriend would be as magical as their farewell night together the previous summer.

Lucas and Kate had been building a serious flirtation for almost three years—ever since Lucas's family had started renting a summer cabin at Cattail Cottages—so their first kiss had been a major milestone. Their online flirtations all year suggested he was as ready as she was to take things to the next level as soon as they were together again. Lucas and his family were flying in his dad's private plane from Winnipeg, Canada, in two days, and were scheduled to be in Love a few days before Kate, Alexis, and Sierra rolled in. Just enough time for him to build up the appropriate level of longing for the moment Kate would arrive.

"I don't know how you've waited a full year to get some," Alexis declared, settling into a cross-legged position on the grass. "I'm dying, and I saw Kevin when he was home for spring break." She blew her long bangs away from her eyes. "I don't think our one-day stop is going to be enough time to catch up, if you know what I mean." She giggled mischievously.

Sierra looked at Kate, her eyebrows raised dramatically. Kate laughed, then said, "We get it, Lex." One of the benefits of the girls driving separately from their parents was that they could stop to visit Alexis's boyfriend, Kevin, at the University of Michigan en route. He had just finished his first year of college and was planning to stay in Ann Arbor for a summer internship. Alexis had decided to surprise him with a quick visit.

"I packed my boob shirt," Alexis announced proudly, just as Mr. Prince, their English teacher, walked past. He covered his ears and cringed. "Sorry, Mr. Prince. Have a good summer!"

"Nice, Alexis," Kate chided. She abruptly changed the subject away from Kevin. Sierra and Kate thought Alexis's boyfriend was a creep. Sierra could hold her tongue, but Kate preferred to avoid the subject since she rarely had anything nice to say and often blurted out something she would later regret. "Sierra, is your mom staying the whole month?"

The Rogers, West, and Goldstein families spent the summer together at Cattail Cottages Resort. Greg Rogers, Cynthia West, and Sara Goldstein worked as professors together at the university in their town, and for the past eleven years each had taken at least a month off after classes ended to relax and read academic papers by the lakeshore in Wisconsin.

Alexis's family had found the resort—she and her cousin Adam's family had started going there together when they were babies—and had convinced the West and Rogers families to join them one summer when there was availability in the neighboring cabins. It had become a tradition, and now every year the whole crew caravanned from New Jersey to Wisconsin as soon as school let out.

This summer the university had finished finals a week earlier than the high school, so the Rogers and West families had decided to leave for the lake a little early, after agreeing that the girls could drive out on their own. Alexis's parents weren't leaving until next week . . . most likely so someone's parents were still around to keep an eye on things until the girls' road trip motored off to the west.

"My mom is playing it by ear," Sierra responded quietly. "She's not sure how long she's staying. I think she has a lot going on in the lab this summer, but I'm sure she's a little freaked about committing to a whole month with my dad."

"Are they still in the test phase?" Kate asked. Sierra's parents had been separated off and on for the past year, and had only just recently returned to "half-on."

"Yes," Sierra muttered. "Their new therapist is big on 'demonstrating your feelings,' which means they're constantly kissing and hugging and rubbing each other's hands. It's completely disgusting, and Sasha and I are both concerned that a summer cooped up with them in a tiny little cabin in the middle of nowhere could be brutal."

Alexis chuckled. "Perhaps they'll consider your feelings before demonstrating theirs when it's just the four of you in two small rooms."

Suddenly a soccer ball landed in the middle of the three girls, leaving a muddy print on Kate's road trip prep list. "Yo, pass that back!" A guy with dark, shaggy hair snapped his fingers. All three girls just looked at him. "Hello? Toss me my ball."

"Adam, you kicked it at us. Walk over here and get it yourself." Kate lay on her back in the grass, idly watching the clouds. Adam was Alexis's cousin, and Kate had known him for years. Not only were Adam and his two brothers over at Alexis's house most weekends, but Adam's family also rented one of the cottages at Cattail Resort every summer.

When they were younger, Kate and Adam had actually sort of been friends—especially during their time at the lake. Their idea of fun almost always overlapped, and he used to be downright hilarious. But as the years had passed, his humor had turned to arrogance, and what used to be fun just came across as rude and inappropriate the older they got.

The end of Kate's patience came in sixth grade, when Adam spread a rumor around their new middle school about Alexis sleeping with a whole collection of Barbie dolls every night. (Which was only a little bit true. . . . It was just Malibu Barbie and a Ken doll, but the specifics were irrelevant.) Alexis was tortured for the first three weeks of school, and most people called her Baby G for the rest of the school year. She hadn't been able to shake the nickname until she'd started dating—and kissing—Kyle Stevenson, the captain of the football team, and he'd forced people to shut up already.

Kate hated Adam for ruining her friend's reputation (if only temporarily), but also because Adam was a prick with a serious sense of self-righteousness, and a bossy, argumentative streak that bothered her immensely.

Out of the corner of her eye Kate watched Adam lift his eyebrows and move toward them to get his ball. "Okay, Kate, if you want to be a bitch about it, that's the way we can play it." When Adam reached the edge of their circle, he didn't stop moving. He stepped on Kate's stomach and walked over her. He grabbed his ball, turned, and lifted his foot to step on her again.

Kate sat up, grateful for her Abs of Steel workout video, and nimbly grabbed Adam's ball out of his hands. Ignoring the muddiness, she shoved the ball inside her shirt and declared, "*This* is the way we can play it, Adam." She held her arms across her stomach and shoved her bag into her lap to hide the ball. She knew she was being childish, but her adrenaline had kicked into high gear. She *hated* Adam and was sick of the way he always did whatever he wanted to. "Now, run back to your friends and find a new game. We're through with you here."

Alexis and Sierra exchanged a look. They knew Kate was stubborn, but they both knew Adam was just as much so. This war could go on for hours. With a tiny little smirk Alexis leaned back to watch the drama unfold. Sierra looked mildly uncomfortable but was clearly enjoying the scene.

"I see," Adam said, crossing his arms over his chest. "So you're telling me that you like my ball inside your shirt? You'd like to keep it there?"

"All I said," Kate spat back at him, ignoring his totally lame attempt at sexual humor, "is that you can run along now." She held her hand up like a stop sign and yawned. "You're boring me." Kate was mortified at the way she was acting. She sounded like a third grader . . . or like Adam. He totally brought out the worst in her.

"Well, this should make things a little more interesting for you," Adam said. He grinned, bent down, and pulled Kate's bag out of her lap. In the single moment it took for this to happen, Kate lost her concentration. So when Adam's hand reached up her shirt and pulled the ball out, she just sat there staring. "I hope that was fun for you," Adam said. "Since *that* was one sexy move, and probably the only action you'll get this summer." With a wink and a snap of his fingers he trotted off to rejoin his buddies, leaving Kate, Alexis, and Sierra staring after him.

Kate felt her skin burn where he had touched her. Her heart was racing, and the anger bubbled up inside. Had it been anyone other than Adam, she would have been blushing. Because as far as Kate was concerned, there was nothing sexier than a good, well-fought fight.

Two

On the Road to Pennsylvania

The next morning Kate stood outside her house with her duffel bag by her side. She'd been packed for weeks and couldn't stand the wait for even one more moment. Alexis had planned to pick Sierra up at her house. Then they would head to Kate's before motoring off to the west in Alexis's little green Ford.

Kate stood in her driveway, growing agitated for no reason at all. She had come outside more than ten minutes before her friends were supposed to get there, and couldn't blame them for the fact that she was still waiting. She reached into her bag to grab her cell phone to check the time, and realized it wasn't there.

Crap. She'd left it plugged in overnight, and had forgotten to grab it from the kitchen counter before she'd locked up. She pulled out her keys and let herself back in. The phone was right where she'd left it the night before.

She had six new text messages and a voice mail. Before she could look at her messages, she heard Alexis's horn sigh in her driveway. The horn sounded like a dying cow sucking its last breath, and Kate chuckled as she slipped her phone into her pocket and hurried out the door.

Sierra waved to her from the front seat, and Alexis leaned her head out the open driver's side window. "I'm driving first shift so I can control the tunes, yo."

"You can drive every shift, babe. I will man the navigation." Kate swung her bag into the trunk and moved around to the back door. She stopped short when she realized the backseat wasn't empty. "What are you doing here?"

Sprawled across the backseat, one foot lounging into Kate's space, was Adam. He was drinking a bottled Frappuccino, and a little bit spilled as he shifted to make room for her next to him. Kate leaned into the window to glare at Alexis. "What is he doing here?" The panic was evident in her voice.

"Dude, why didn't you call me back?" Alexis swiveled in her seat. "I called you last night, and texted you, like, eight million times."

"I didn't get the messages." Kate was staring at Adam suspiciously. His precious soccer ball sat in his lap, taunting her. Her skin crawled at the memory of what had happened the previous afternoon. "Does anyone want to tell me what's going on?"

Adam put on a fake smile and—in a ridiculous Valley girl accent—said, "Like, I'm coming with you!" He clapped. "Road trip with the girls!" His face turned expressionless. "Yes, that's right, Kate. You and I will enjoy the magic of each other's company for the next"—he looked at the clock on the dash of the car—"one hundred twenty-six and a half hours in this car—approximately."

Kate shot a desperate look at Alexis, who glanced in the rearview mirror, and then said, "Adam has a scholarship interview at the University of Michigan. He has to be there on Monday afternoon, and Aunt Michelle can't leave Jersey until Sunday. My parents knew we were planning to stop to see Kevin in Ann Arbor anyway, so they made me bring him with us. They insisted he didn't need to take the skanky bus when we were going to the exact same place."

Sierra leaned her head out the window. "Come on, Kate, just get in." Kate scowled at her before reluctantly sliding into the open spot next to Adam.

"I may have come across as genuine a few moments ago, when I jumped for joy about this road trip." Adam adjusted his position so he was taking up as much of the backseat as was humanly possible. "But let me tell you that I'm looking forward to crashing your road trip just slightly less than you ladies are looking forward to having me here. But fate aligned and brought us all together, so I think we should make the most of it."

Alexis rolled her eyes and signaled to turn onto the interstate. They were on their way. All four of them. As Kate turned to look out the back window to watch their hometown shrink into the distance, Adam said, "So, who wants to play truth or dare?"

When they stopped at a gas station in the middle of Pennsylvania for toilets and treats four hours later, Kate was convinced that she had died and gone to hell. Absolutely everything she had envisioned for their girls' road trip had soured into a giant disappointment.

Alexis was snippy (she refused to wear her glasses, and straining to see highway signs had given her a headache); Sierra was distant and quiet (Kate knew her parents' split was bugging her, but Kate couldn't talk to her about it with Adam lurking around); and Adam was rude, sarcastic, and condescending (translation: asshole). As far as Kate was concerned, the start of their highly anticipated road trip had been four of the worst hours of her life. She'd spent most of them folded into her corner of the car, trying to put as much distance as possible between her body and Adam's.

"Only one toilet works, so we'll have to flip to see who gets to test the waters." Adam was swinging a giant rubber fish with a key attached to it. He had been sent inside the gas station to find out where the loo was located. "I, personally, am relieved that I stand to pee."

"I'll go first." Kate rolled her eyes at Adam and grabbed the limp fish from his hand. "I brought seat covers."

"Of course you did." Sierra laughed. "I'm coming with you."

"Me too." Alexis grabbed Kate's hand. "See ya, Adam. Girls pee with partners."

When they were safely out of earshot, Alexis blurted out, "What's with you, Kat?"

"What do you mean?" Kate pulled out a tissue to open the door to the bathroom. The knob was grimy, and pieces of the tissue stuck to the metal when she twisted her hand away.

"I mean, why are you being so abrasive to Adam? What's your deal with him?" Alexis held the door open, and Sierra and Kate followed her into the restroom. The smell of cigarettes and sanitizer was overpowering. The size of the room made the disgusting toilet cowering in one corner look miniature. There was a machine on the wall dispensing Purple Passion condoms, and next to that was a wooden sign that said: WOMEN ARE LIKE FISH: THE BIGGER, THE BETTER.

"My deal is he bugs me. He's rude, arrogant, and is ruining our road trip."

Sierra held her hand out for a seat protector, which Kate proudly pulled from her bag. "Ladies, turn away. I'll go first." Sierra laid the thin piece of paper over the toilet seat and groaned when it soaked up little wet puddles that had been camouflaged on the black seat. "This is disgusting—I'm squatting."

Alexis and Kate turned to face the condom machine to give Sierra some privacy. Alexis nudged Kate's foot with her own. "So you're saying that you are already convinced you're going to have a crap time on this trip, just because Adam is here?"

"Do you feel like things are off to a great start?"

"No, but I think that's because—" Alexis cut off as Sierra flushed the toilet with her foot.

Sierra piped up from behind them. "Because you're being a brat, Kate. Do you need to be so argumentative? I mean, he asked if anyone was hungry this morning, and you told him you'd rather starve than share his bag of pretzels. That's just sort of mean. I know he's not your favorite person, but maybe you could give him a chance, and see if things could be a little more . . ."

"Fun for everyone?" Alexis finished.

"So now it's my fault that our *girls'* road trip is ruined?" Kate couldn't decide if she wanted to scream or cry. How could her friends not see her side? "You're saying that since I think Adam is annoying, I'm the one ruining the trip?"

Alexis moved toward the toilet for her turn. "God, this is gross. No, Kat, that's not what we're saying. I guess I'm just wondering why he bothers you so much. You're not usually like this, and he's not *that* unbearable."

"You know I've hated him since middle school. And now he's always just such a prick that I can't really get past it. Lex, I can see why you deal with him—he's family. But, Sierra, doesn't he get under your skin?"

"Come on, Kate." Sierra washed her hands in the filthy sink, lifting her long, slender leg up to turn the faucet off with her flip-flop when she'd finished. "You know I don't let him bother me. He actually sort of cracks me up, if you want to know the truth."

"Dude, how did you do that?" Alexis was referring to Sierra's leg-faucet trick. "Kat, maybe you're just being a little bit dramatic? I've forgiven Adam for the Barbie doll rumor. . . . You should too."

"I'll do my best to be civil," Kate said as she moved to take her turn at the toilet. "But I can't promise anything. I don't like when people mess with my friends, which he did, and you guys are just going to have to deal with that. I'll try to get over it, but unless he starts to act less like the asshole that I'm certain he is, then this car ride will be a little hostile."

"Kat: the defender of my reputation!" Alexis laughed, turning a quarter into the Purple Passion machine. "How effective can a twenty-five-cent condom be? This place freaks me out." She pulled the lavender package out of the dispenser and set it on top of the machine. "Free protected sex, courtesy of Alexis Goldstein. Some creep will find this later and it will make his day."

"So generous, Lex. I'm glad you're looking out for the people of Wherever-we-are, Pennsylvania," Kate said, and then giggled as she washed her hands. When she'd finished, she gestured to Sierra to bring her leg over to turn off the faucet with her foot again. Sierra happily obliged. Then the three girls hustled out of the bathroom to give Adam his turn.

When he emerged from the bathroom thirty seconds later, Adam was waving something in his hand as he strolled back to the car. "Check it out!" he called, grinning widely. "Purple Passion!"

Kate, Alexis, and Sierra looked at one another and all burst out laughing. For the first time all day Kate felt like there could still be hope for their road trip after all.

* * *

Late that afternoon, somewhere on the other side of Pennsylvania, the girls decided it was time to call it a day. The sun would be going down soon, and they had passed a sign that said there was a campground a few exits up the highway. They had a tent, and were excited to use it. Most of the motels they'd passed that they were able to afford were far creepier than a tent, anyway, and camping was much more fun.

Adam had volunteered for a shift as navigator and was holding the atlas upside down—just to be funny—and calling out random directions every time they passed an exit. Kate was driving, and found Adam's map humor to be about as amusing as Mr. Tannen's famously painful history class. But Sierra's constant giggling was egging him on, and Alexis periodically chimed in by loudly reading the billboards they passed. Kate felt like the only outsider, which made Adam seem even more annoying.

"Seriously, Adam, can you please just pay attention and figure out where we're going?" Kate slammed her hand on the steering wheel, startling Alexis out of her zoned-out state in the backseat.

Adam laughed. "Geez, Kate, chill. Take the next exit, and then trust me. . . . I'll get us there."

"I'm sure," Kate grumbled, then stuffed a handful of

Swedish Fish into her mouth to keep from saying what she wanted to say.

Adam leaned across the front seat and studied the dashboard. "Hey, daredevil, you're really risking it driving fifty-five in a sixty."

"Adam . . . ," Alexis warned sleepily from the backseat. Things hadn't gotten a lot friendlier between Adam and Kate over the course of the day, and Alexis and Sierra had started to mediate. Adam had started to push Kate's buttons just for the fun of it. He seemed to get a thrill from pissing her off.

Adam grinned. "This exit, please."

Kate signaled to exit, and followed Adam's direction to take a left off the exit ramp. They drove for nearly ten minutes down a narrow, empty road in silence. The only sound was a periodic shuffling of paper when Adam adjusted the map. "How much farther?" Kate asked eventually. "I'm starting to get a little freaked out. This sort of feels like the setup for a horror movie."

"I think the map might be outdated," Adam responded. "We should have been there by now."

"Give me the map," Kate demanded. She slammed her foot on the brake and pulled to the side of the road. She glanced at the atlas and said, "We should have gone right off the exit ramp. We're going in the wrong direction." She shoved the map at Adam, put the car back into gear, and pulled a U-turn.

Ten minutes later they pulled into the campground, which was less than a mile off the interstate the *other* way. As they drove through the park searching for a spot to call home for the night, neither Kate nor Adam said a word.

Three

Pennsylvania

"Since you can't find your way around a map, I'm quite certain you'll struggle to figure out how to put a tent together," Kate said, and then smirked.

Alone with Adam, Kate was free to vent all of her frustrations toward him without her friends getting uncomfortable. Sierra and Alexis had set off in search of dinner food, and had left Kate and Adam to set up the tent. Kate wanted to do it herself, but Adam had insisted he needed to stay to help. As if.

"Well, now," Adam muttered under his breath, but loud enough for Kate to hear. "Those are fighting words."

Kate fixed him with an evil look and muttered right

back, "What did you expect, loving glances and doting compliments?"

"Hey," Adam shot back, "you don't need to be snobby about it. We're going to be together twenty-four-seven for the next few days, so maybe you could try to be just the tiniest bit civil, instead of an evil bitch from hell?"

"That doesn't even deserve a response," Kate retorted. "Are you going to help me put this tent together, or would you just like to sit on that log over there and enjoy a cool soda while I show you how to be useful?"

"You are feisty, aren't you?" The look on Adam's face suggested he was sort of enjoying their banter. "So you're saying you need a gentleman's help?"

"That would be great," Kate stated calmly. "I'd love to have a gentleman's help. Unfortunately, I have to use you instead. Can you please contribute for approximately thirty seconds?"

"Yeah," Adam said, surrendering. "Of course I'll help. It would have been easier if you'd asked nicely. Possibly a 'pretty please'?"

Kate wanted to scream. Adam clearly thrived on pissing her off. Opting to ignore him, she pulled the pieces of the tent out of their nylon bag and started laying them on the ground in straight, orderly piles. Long stakes, short stakes, sections of tent fabric. Once everything was out of the bag,

Kate stepped back to survey the project. Three neat stacks of tent parts, all straight and organized.

Adam was watching her with an amused smile. "All set?"

"Yes, thank you." She looked at him suspiciously. "Why are you looking at me like that?"

"Would it bother you if I, say, did this?" Adam reached his leg out and pushed one of the tent stakes with the toe of his shoe. The stake was now lying at a ninety degree angle to the other stakes and looked completely out of order.

Kate reached her shoe out and pushed it back into place, neatly next to the others.

"It does bother you, doesn't it?" Adam chuckled.

"No," Kate insisted. She didn't want to let Adam know that disorder bothered her immensely. "You bother me."

Adam started laughing harder now. "That's becoming clear."

Kate pulled the tent's assembly instructions out of the bag and squatted down to start to put the pieces of the tent together. "Step one . . . ," she muttered, grabbing a couple of pieces off the ground.

"Why are you doing it like that?" Adam asked, squatting down next to her. "These pieces go here." He pushed two long poles together. "See? Like that."

"You're supposed to put this part together first." Kate pulled the pole apart and adjusted it slightly. The way

Adam had put them together would maybe have worked, but it wasn't the way it was supposed to be done. *She* had the instruction booklet . . . not him. "*Then* you can push these two poles together."

"Oh, I see." Adam nodded. "So even though the end result is exactly the same, the way you've done it is right, because you're incredibly bossy and stubborn and want to be difficult?"

"Or maybe it's because I have the instruction booklet and don't want you to assemble a tent that's going to fall apart on us during the night? Fine, I'll just let you put all of these poles together. Let me know when they're done. Don't screw it up."

Kate stormed off and grabbed their tarp out of the trunk. She laid it down on a flat part of the campsite that looked like a good place to set up the tent. It was right next to the campfire pit, which seemed like it would help keep the tent nice and toasty if the air cooled off overnight. She could feel Adam watching her as he put the pieces of tubing together. "Do you have something else to say?"

He held his hands up in front of him defensively. "Nope. By all means, keep doing what you're doing."

"What's wrong with the way I'm doing it?"

Adam surveyed the tarp and glanced around the rest of the campsite. "I guess I was just thinking we could put the tent up back there," he said, and gestured to a tall stand of pine trees that had a gorgeous, soft-looking grassy space in the center. "But if you want to sleep right next to the fire and hope the wind doesn't blow the fire onto the tent and burn us all up in the night, by all means . . ."

Huffily, Kate grabbed the tarp and pulled it across the campsite to the stand of pine trees. Adam had made his point, and she decided it was easier not to argue with him. Maybe if she ignored him, he'd just go away.

After a few glorious minutes of silence while they each worked independently, Adam had all of the tent poles assembled and Kate had the tarp laid out. She had put rocks on each corner of the tarp to keep it in place. Adam brought the long poles over, and Kate dragged the pieces of tent fabric.

"So next," Kate said, pulling the instruction booklet out of her pocket, "we put these little stakes into the ground to hold the corners of the tent in place."

Adam paused, then said simply, "Okay."

"Do you have a different idea?" Kate could tell he was questioning her logic. It was the way he'd said "okay" with a totally non-okay tone.

"I think we need to put the long poles through the channels before we secure the corners—that way we know how big the tent will actually be."

Kate was boiling with frustration. Adam was *so* bossy and couldn't stop acting like a tent know-it-all. In truth she had never actually *been* in a tent before, but there was no way she was going to admit that. Instead she said simply, "I have the instruction booklet, Adam. So let's do it the way it's supposed to be done." She hated the way he brought out this side of her. She knew she was being completely confrontational and argumentative, but the way he criticized her every move was infuriating.

After a few false starts the center of the tent eventually lifted into the air. It wobbled slightly in the evening breeze, but stayed upright. "That looks about right," Kate declared, stepping back to admire her work.

"Nicely done," Adam complimented. She realized he was being genuine, and swelled with pride. "Let's get our gear inside," Adam instructed. "It's getting dark, and we should get things ready before Lex and Sierra get back with dinner."

"Don't we need to finish securing the tent first?" she asked, studying the instruction manual.

Adam shook his head. "No, we can do that afterward. As long as it's up, we're fine pulling our gear inside." Kate shrugged and tossed the instruction manual outside the door of the tent. She'd let Adam have his way this time, since things seemed to be going okay. *No thanks to him.*

They walked together back to the car. Kate popped open the trunk and pulled her big duffel bag out. "Do you want me to get that for you?" Adam offered.

"I can handle it," Kate snapped back. *Now he's trying to be helpful?* she mused. When they got back to the tent, Kate climbed in with her bag and Alexis's sleeping bag. Once she'd finished arranging Alexis's spot in the center of the tent—next to Adam, who was on the far wall—she unzipped her big bag and started to pull out her pillow.

She had just lifted her pillow to fluff it when suddenly the center of the tent made a snapping sound and the whole thing came billowing down around them. "Ayeeee!" Kate shrieked, buried in the mounds of tent fabric.

"You okay?" Adam cried from somewhere nearby, under the fallen fabric.

"I'm buried alive!" Kate declared, then burst out laughing. Adam cracked up too, and they both started flailing around in the tent trying to find an escape route.

"Stay still and I'll try to get it back up again. There's no sense in both of us risking our lives to dig out of here," Adam joked. A few moments later he was standing in the center of the tent fabric with the posts back in place. Kate applauded from her seat on the ground. Adam shrugged. "I guess you were right. . . . We should have secured it a little better before we started to get our stuff inside."

Thank you, Kate mused silently. *Ha, ha! I was right!* Out loud she said, "No biggie. If you hold it up for a sec, I'll get the final stakes in place and we should be back in business." She went outside the tent and quickly read through the rest of the instructions. After she placed the stakes, she was confident that everything was in order. She ducked back inside the tent and started to get her bedding out.

"Did you bring a *duvet?*" Adam was rolling his thin sleeping bag out on the floor on the other side of the tent, but had stopped to watch what Kate was doing. "Please tell me that's a duvet."

"It is. Why is that funny?" *Here we go again.* Kate had started to consider that maybe Adam wasn't as intolerable as she had thought, but now she suspected things were about to sour again.

"Princess, we're in a tent. You don't bring a duvet to go camping." Adam was cracking himself up. "Did you bring your hair dryer and tanning oils as well? Do you need me to pick up your mattress from the front desk? Shall we call for room service?" Adam held his hand up to his ear like a phone and spoke in a fussy accent. "Yes, yes, I'll take the lemon verbena hand massage and a salmon salad, thank you."

Kate narrowed her eyes at him but kept her mouth shut. It wasn't worth engaging with him further. Once she had her sleeping space in order, she turned to Adam and blurted out, "Can you get out of here? I need to change into my pajamas."

"Are you going to bed? What about dinner?"

"I'm not hungry."

"Don't you need to brush your teeth or anything?"

"Is that any of your business?" Kate wanted him to scram. She just wanted to change and go through her night-time routine in silence and privacy. She hadn't even thought about how they would get ready for bed and change and all the other things you just *do* in front of your girlfriends but that seem especially private and embarrassing when there's a guy nearby. She noticed that her retainer case had fallen out of her pajama pants pocket, and she quickly shoved it deep inside her pillowcase away from Adam's prying eyes.

"Brushing your teeth is not my business," Adam responded, just sitting there, completely disrespectful of her wish that he leave her alone. "But it will be my business when you're breathing dragon breath all over the car tomorrow."

"Ugh, you're such a pig!" Kate cried out.

Adam grinned, the way he always did when Kate started getting loud and angry. "Sorry."

"If you're really sorry, you'll get the hell out of this tent immediately. I just want to go to sleep, and I want to do that without you staring at me like some sort of creep. Tell Lex and Sierra good night. I'm sure I'll be up first in the morning, so I can drive first shift."

Kate zipped the tent shut after Adam crawled out, closing the door on her terrible day. It couldn't be over soon enough.

Four

Ohio

By noon the next day everyone was in a foul mood and ready to stop for lunch. They'd been driving since before eight that morning, and they were all tired and at one another's throats.

Alexis and Sierra had apparently gotten lost on their way to find a grocery store the night before, and hadn't gotten back to the campground until almost eleven. Adam had sat up waiting for them next to a crackling fire—Kate had been able to hear his banjo strumming quietly as she'd tried to fall asleep. As annoying as Adam was, he had a beautiful voice, and his singing had helped her drift off into slumber. Of course, the thought of seeing Lucas in a few days had kept her tossing and turning. Her imagination was running wild and kept her up far longer than she would have liked.

"Lucas texted me this morning and said we should go to this huge amusement park that's about thirty miles off the next exit, if anyone's up for it," Kate offered hopefully. They were a full day and a half into their trip, and so far, they weren't having a lot of fun. A roller coaster could put a smile on anyone's face, she figured.

"Well." Adam slapped his knee. "If *Lucas* suggests we all go there, then by all means we should!"

"What does that mean?" Kate whipped around from her front seat to glare at Adam in the back. Adam and Lucas knew each other from summers at the lake, but they'd never really been friends. Lucas hung out with his brothers and a couple other guys whose families owned cabins near the Cattail Cottages Resort. Adam had always been buddy-buddy with the guys who worked at the resort during the summer. Totally different crowds.

"I think an amusement park sounds fun," Sierra cut in.

Alexis nodded her agreement. "Let's do it. We're ahead of schedule, anyway, so we have some time to kill. Adam's interview isn't until tomorrow afternoon, and we're only a few hours' drive away from Ann Arbor."

"But Kevin awaits you in Michigan, Alexis. Don't you want to keep on truckin'?" Adam pulled a twine of licorice from the bag that was resting between Kate and Sierra. "Thanks."

"Kevin is at some sort of orientation training session thing this weekend. He's not getting back until late tonight, and I want to make sure he's there. So no rush. Tomorrow's good." Something in her voice sounded strained, and Kate made a mental note to ask her what was going on later. Later, when they could get rid of Adam.

Half an hour and no further conversation later, they pulled into the amusement park parking lot. "Fifteen dollars for parking?" Kate exclaimed. "That's insane." She was tight on cash for the road trip, and couldn't stomach spending that much to park. They still had to pay the entrance fee!

"I can cover it," Alexis said quickly, and Kate knew it wasn't worth further discussion. Alexis was in a different financial position from Kate, and it was stupid to pretend otherwise. Kate didn't have a lot of money to spare, unlike Alexis, whose family seemed to be made of money. Alexis got to pick a car for her sixteenth birthday; Kate got dinner out at the steak and sushi place near her house.

The difference in financial status sometimes caused tension in their friendship, but usually Alexis was pretty good about not treating Kate like a charity case. Kate was pretty frugal all year long, since she gave up the chance to get a summer job in order to spend every June and July at the lake. During the school year they usually just hung out at someone's house, and it helped avoid uncomfortable money situations.

As Sierra eased Alexis's car through the line toward the parking lot booth, Adam announced, out of the blue, "I just realized I forgot a shirt for my interview. Why don't I just drop you off here, and I'll hit that mall we passed a few miles up the road. Pick you up in a few hours?"

Kate couldn't hide her enthusiasm at the idea of getting a few hours alone with her girlfriends. "Sounds great." *Dumbass*, she thought. *What kind of loser forgets his shirt for such an important interview?*

"You're going to the mall instead of a roller coaster?" Alexis chided. "Pick us up by that big elephant over there, okay?" She pointed to a giant green elephant near the entrance to the park. "Say, four o'clock?"

"Right." Adam saluted at Alexis. The girls hopped out of the car, and Adam jumped into the driver's seat. He did a quick U-turn and sped off, as though he couldn't get out of there fast enough.

"He seems to be having a lovely time on our road trip," Sierra joked as Adam drove off.

"Hmm," Alexis mused. "Maybe not so much. But *we*

didn't invite him to ride across the country with us, so I'm not too worried about it." She pulled several twenty-dollar bills out of her wallet and hastily paid the entrance fee for all three of them. "My treat. . . . Please accept this as my apology for us getting stuck with my cousin on our road trip."

Kate smiled appreciatively. *Count on Alexis to find a way to pay without making me feel like a total mooch.* "Thanks. You don't have to do that, though."

"It's the least I can do. But he's not all bad, is he?" Alexis looked at her friends hopefully, clearly feeling guilty about their trip going awry.

Sierra replied, "Not at all. Adam cracks me up."

At exactly the same time Kate declared, "Ugh. He's so annoying!"

Alexis laughed. "Two very different opinions."

"I'm sorry," Kate said, and she meant it. She didn't mean to complain about Adam, but he was just so obnoxious and rude. She continued, "He wasn't even willing to read the instruction booklet about how to put the tent together last night, so it collapsed on top of us. And he totally mocked my duvet, which was just childish. It's not *that* funny that I brought a duvet, is it? Just because he has a ratty old sleeping bag, somehow he's, like, Captain Camping, granted full liberty to criticize the way I packed for a road trip or something?" Kate stopped for a breath, and both of her friends cracked up laughing.

"Why is that funny?" Kate asked, starting to laugh herself. "Okay, so he irritates the hell out of me. I guess you get it? Plus, what an idiot. . . . Who forgets to pack their shirt for a scholarship interview? It's the whole point of him being here."

"He's afraid of heights," Alexis said, shrugging. "I think he used the shirt as a less-embarrassing excuse to avoid the roller coasters."

Sierra laughed. "He couldn't get out of here fast enough. I was wondering what was going on. Aww . . . It's Adam's sweet, vulnerable side. Poor guy."

Just then Kate's phone beeped, signaling a new text message. From Lucas.

"Ooh!" Alexis declared. "Is that from Prince Charming, who will greet you at the end of the road with a big fat smoochy kiss?" She grabbed Kate's phone and flipped it open, reading the message aloud: "'Just got to Love. How long till you get here? It's not as fun without you.' Aww! He's so sweet." She rolled her eyes and tossed the phone back to Kate, who reread the message and melted a little.

"Okay. Now I want to skip the rest of the road trip and just get there already," Kate confessed.

"Hey, now!" Sierra scolded. "Y'all need to remember

that this summer is just as much about the road to Love as it is about Love itself. This is *our* adventure."

Alexis lifted her eyebrows. "With all that Love in there, you sound like Kate, Sierra."

"What's wrong with being a romantic?" Kate protested.

"All right, all right," Sierra mediated, as she often did when both Kate and Alexis started to show their stubborn streaks. "Do you guys want to get a picture?" They were just inside the entrance to the park, and people were stopping in little groups to have their pictures taken as a souvenir of their trip to the amusement park.

"Oh, yeah!" Alexis grabbed both of her friends around their waists and grinned at the greasy guy behind the camera. The photographer complimented Alexis on her smile, which cracked them all up. Kate looked at Sierra, and they both stuck their tongues out at the same time.

The photographer checked his work and gave them a thumbs-up. "Perfect!" he cried, then kissed his fingertips at them.

"Icky," Sierra observed quietly. They made their way over to the printing station, where all the recent pictures were displayed on a big screen. Their picture wasn't posted yet, so they scanned the other pictures that had been taken. There was a funny shot of a bunch of white-haired old ladies, all making faces at the camera. One of the ladies was doubled-up with laughter because another was tickling her side as the photographer captured the shot. "That's priceless," Sierra declared, pointing at the photo.

"Of course, I peed my pants a little when she tickled me," said a voice behind them. One of the old ladies from the picture was standing behind Sierra. She chuckled, then pointed at the picture screen. "Now, that's a cute one. You girls look like you're having fun."

The picture of Alexis, Sierra, and Kate had just been posted on the screen. Sierra and Kate were grinning at each other with their tongues out, but their bodies were only half in the picture. Apparently, the photographer had been a little too excited about Alexis's smile. It was a great shot nonetheless. "Yeah," Kate agreed. "We *are* having fun."

"Good," the lady responded, then rubbed Kate's shoulder. "Girlfriends are the spice of life. Even when they torture your weak bladder." She chuckled, then sashayed off with the picture of her and her friends, waving the photo in the air for them all to see.

Kate watched as the group of old ladies giggled about the picture and teased one another about the way they looked. As she stared at them walking off into the amusement park, having a great time, Alexis dangled a photo key chain in front of her face. "I bought one!" she announced. "We'll share it."

* * *

An hour later they had gone on the big roller coaster three times. Every time they got in line, they found themselves behind the same group of old ladies. They'd discovered the women were on a bus tour around the Midwest. There were forty of them in total, and they were louder than a high school volleyball team on their way to an away game. Kate, Alexis, and Sierra could hardly talk while they waited in line, since the tour bus gang was so chatty.

Kate felt the buzz of a text message in her pocket during their third ride on the roller coaster. After they piled out, she pulled her phone out and checked it. Lucas again.

"What did he say?" Sierra prodded.

"He just said he's getting ready for the barbecue, and wishes we were there tonight." Kate blushed, thrilled that Lucas seemed to be on exactly the same wavelength that she was on about their summer together. She was glad she had the road trip to hang out with Alexis and Sierra, since she was getting the impression that Lucas wanted her all to himself when she got there.

Alexis rolled her eyes, prompting Kate to ask, "What's your deal, Lex?"

"You're so delusional about your so-called relationship with Lucas."

"What is that supposed to mean?"

"It means, you're bound to be disappointed." Alexis said this harshly, clearly intending to hurt Kate's feelings. "I wish you would just live in the present and not fantasize about some perfect relationship with a fantasy guy you barely even hooked up with a year ago."

"Lex," Sierra warned, "don't bring your own relationship issues into Kate's romance."

Alexis narrowed her eyes at her friends. Then tears sprung to her eyes, and she quickly turned away from them. Kate reached out to grab her arm, and Alexis pulled away. "What's going on?" Kate asked gently. "Lex, are you okay?"

"I'm just being stupid," Alexis grumbled bitterly. "Let's get cotton candy, okay?"

Sierra laughed. "Air-spun sugar is not going to distract us. We *need* to know what's eating you."

"Fine," Alexis relented. "But I still want cotton candy."

Kate bought a bag of blue, purple, and pink cotton candy, and they all settled on a bench overlooking the water ride. It was oppressively hot, and the periodic splash of the water at the bottom of the track was refreshing.

Alexis dipped her hand into the bag of sugar and said, "I guess I'm just angry at Kevin for not coming home at all this summer. I'm at the lake for the first part of summer anyway, but then I'm stuck in Jersey without a boyfriend the entire month of August. I feel like he should want to be with me, but he's doing this whole internship thing instead." Alexis paused to let a piece of cotton candy melt on her tongue. She rolled her tank top up at the bottom, exposing her flat stomach to get some sun. "I know it sounds selfish, and I guess I should have known this was coming, but I'm not sure I'm ready to deal with whatever it is we have to deal with now that he's all into his college life and I'm, well, not."

"Lex, that's not selfish," Kate said seriously. "It's fine to want to see your boyfriend. You're soul mates, right? So it's important to spend time together."

Alexis laughed loudly. "Soul mates? I don't know about that. It's more like we hook up and have a good time."

"Come on," Kate insisted. "There has to be more to it than that. You're in a *relationship*. If he's not giving you the attention and respect you deserve, you need to find someone who will. You owe it to yourself." Kate knew Kevin would never treat Alexis the way a boyfriend should. He was a jerk with his own agenda, and she wished Alexis could see that. But she also wanted to be supportive of Alexis's choices.

Sierra had been sitting quietly, biting off bits of blue cotton candy. Finally she broke in, "You two have to realize that you're looking for totally different things with relationships." She let the sugar melt on her tongue, then continued. "Kate, you're looking for storybook romance and a guy who treats you like the leading lady in a romance movie. Lex, you're looking for, um . . ."

"Are you trying to politely say that Kate is a hopeless romantic and I'm just hopeless?" Alexis offered this suggestion jokingly, but Sierra clearly felt bad.

"No! I'm just saying that Kate's fantasy of what it is to be a girlfriend is very different from your reality."

Alexis shrugged. "Yeah, I guess. And you know what? If things don't work out with Kevin, I'll find another guy. I always do." Then she smiled brightly, prompting Kate and Sierra to both crack up laughing. "Now, who's up for another ride?"

Five

Ohio

The interstate stretched out in front of them, semis whizzing by with a loud *fwump* every few minutes. Kate had taken over in the driver's seat when Adam had picked them up at the amusement park, and Adam had insisted that he should sit in the navigation seat to prove that he wasn't an idiot with the map. Kate had relented, but only after both Alexis and Sierra had begged to take the backseat so they could nap.

Now her best friends were soundly asleep, awash in slanted early-evening sunlight, and Kate was stuck with only Adam to keep her company. In an unfortunate case of bad luck, the AC in Alexis's car had decided to take a siesta of its own shortly after they'd left the amusement park, so all the windows in the car were down. The temperature had crept up to near ninety, so they were all sweating and miserable. But at least the open windows provided enough noise that she and Adam didn't really need to have a conversation. They sort of had to yell over the noise of the wind and the highway to hear each other.

Adam was playing basketball with a tiny suction cup net and foam ball he had bought at the mall that afternoon. He had the net affixed to the dashboard, and was throwing the ball from a semi-reclined position in the front passenger seat. He was about 0 and 60, since the wind whooshing through the car was blowing most of his shots off track. Kate was mildly amused, watching him struggle to land a single shot. But Adam didn't seem fazed by his lack of skills. . . . He just kept trying, clearly enjoying the little game he'd devised for himself.

Finally his shot went straight into the net, and Adam lifted his arms into the air. "That was hot. Snap!"

"Snap?" Kate mocked loudly. A truck whizzed by, its giant tires roaring next to their window. "Seriously? Snap."

"What?" Adam asked, leaning toward Kate so she could hear him. "I can't say 'snap'?"

"You can. If you want to sound like a freak."

"Why is 'snap' freaky?"

"It's not. It's just out of place on you." Kate thought for a second. "It's a little like you saying something's hot, unless it's a direct comment about a girl. And since you just called *yourself* hot, I guess you're oh-and-two in the normal department."

"Hold on," Adam said, and fiddled with the glove compartment, opening and closing the latch, making his net flip up and down. "You think I'm abnormal?"

Kate shrugged. She could see Alexis stir in the backseat, but she stayed asleep. "I think you're sort of a jerk, but I guess that's still considered normal, right?"

"Oh, that's nice," Adam replied. "So I'm a jerk, and you're a real delight? A lovely girl with absolutely no inner bitch, right?"

"Did I say that?" Adam was totally right, and she was willing to admit it. "I have plenty of inner bitch. And you're adept at bringing her out to play."

"Well, aren't I a lucky guy?" Adam said sarcastically. "A special part of you is reserved just for me? That's awfully romantic."

Kate looked over at him, disgusted. "I'm not trying to be romantic, so if you're getting romance vibes from me, your intuition is in serious need of repair."

Adam flopped back in his seat, grinning. "Aren't you glad I'm on this road trip?"

"No."

"Admit it," Adam encouraged. "I amuse you."

"Um, no."

"Then I'll keep trying," Adam said seriously. "It might take time, but I'll crack through." Kate ignored him. It was easy to do.

They sat without talking. Adam studied the road atlas while Kate memorized highway signs advertising IHOP and gas stations. "I'm dying," Kate declared suddenly. The sun had gone down, but still there was no relief from the heat. Kate's hair was in two braids going down either side of her neck, and little beads of sweat were traveling down her exposed skin. "No AC is torture."

"Take this exit," Adam announced, grinning mischievously. Kate looked at him quizzically. "Just take it. There's a pretty big town near this exit. Let's go swimming."

"Where?"

"We need to find a country club," Adam answered. "They have the best pools."

"How are we going to get into a country club? They're members only."

Adam grinned mischievously. "You're so focused on the rules all the time, Kate. You're missing out on all the fun in life. We'll figure out a way in."

* * *

"Where are we?" Sierra mumbled sleepily from the backseat about twenty minutes later. "How long did I sleep?"

They had just pulled into the parking lot at a super-ritzy country club that Adam had located on Alexis's iPhone. He'd stolen it out of her purse while she slept, Googled "country clubs" in the area they were driving through, and successfully navigated to a wealthy-looking town about fifteen miles off the interstate. Kate couldn't deny the fact that she was impressed.

"Oy," Alexis groaned crabbily. "I'm hot."

"Kate and I have masterminded a very clever plan to remedy that," Adam bragged. "Who wants to go swimming?"

"Nuh-uh," Alexis said, and shook her head. "These roadside motel pools are nast. I wouldn't put my foot in, even if I already had a toe fungus."

Adam tsk-tsked at her. "You are such a snob, Lex. What would you say if I told you we were going swimming at a country club?"

"And how are you going to swing that?"

"Like this." Adam hopped out of the car and walked toward the gate that led into the club. It was just after nine, and the sign said the country club had closed at eight. They all followed Adam as he moved alongside the fence that divided the interior of the club from the parking lot, and down into a little marshy area that took them back out along the main road.

Silently they walked along the road for about a hundred yards. There were no cars, and it was getting dark, so Kate started getting freaked out. They could go missing, and no one would even know where to find them. "I don't think this is a great idea," Kate said finally. "You don't even know where you're going, Adam."

In response Adam just held a finger to his lips and cut back in from the road, leading them through a thick patch of trees. The branches and pine needles bit into Kate's arms, and just when she thought she could go no farther, the trees opened up onto a grassy golf course. Off to their left they could see the big clubhouse, its exterior lamps lighting up the night sky. They walked up the fairway together.

"If I were a betting guy, I'd put money on the pool being in there," Adam said as they got close to the club-house. He was pointing to a rectangular area that was closed in with wide-plank wooden fencing. The top of a lifeguard chair was poking up over the top of one section of the fence.

Kate pulled her flip-flops off her feet and carried them as they walked toward the pool. Her feet were sore from their day at the amusement park, and the cool grass felt amazing. Her whole body was sticky and hot, and she was momentarily tempted to lie on the grass to cool off.

As they approached the pool, Kate's hopes fell. She could see no obvious way to get inside the fence. Alexis slid down on the grass to rest while Adam scoped out the perimeter. Sierra and Kate both watched nervously for any signs of authority. Neither of them was particularly good at breaking the rules, and—to Kate at least—all of this felt a little risky.

"The gate is locked," Adam declared.

Kate stared at him, dumbfounded. "Did you think it would be open?" she asked. "That was your plan?" She was no expert at sneaking in, but even she could have told him the gate would be locked.

"*No*, that wasn't my *plan*. But I figured it couldn't hurt to check." He fixed Kate with a frustrated look, then his face broke into a goofy grin.

Why does he stare at me like that? Kate wondered. *It's like he's trying to annoy me and knows his stupid grinning makes me want to slap him.* But the way Adam made Kate's blood boil was invigorating, and she had to admit that she sort of enjoyed sparring with him.

There was a golf cart parked next to the fence. Adam climbed onto the hood. He lifted one leg up onto the roof of the cart and hoisted his other up onto the top of the fence. He dangled there for a minute, then flipped his other foot effortlessly over the edge and lowered himself down so only his fingers were in view over the top of the fence.

Kate, Sierra, and Alexis watched from the ground, listening for a deadly thud on the other side. Adam's whoop of success told them he had landed in one piece. Finally Sierra vocalized the thing they were all thinking: "How are *we* supposed to get over?"

"Sierra, you could make it . . . but there's no way I'm tall enough," said Alexis.

"Quit your nay-saying, Cousin," Adam said, as his head poked over the top of the fence. "We're all going swimming." He lifted a lifeguard's rescue ladder over his head and twisted it in midair to lower it down on their side of the fence. "Thanks be to lifeguards. Who wants to go first?"

Kate bravely stepped forward to the ladder. Her foot touched the bottom rung, and she got a shiver of excitement. She'd never really broken the rules before, and she was in the process of breaking and entering. She realized it was the most harmless kind of trespassing, but still . . . they could get caught!

Another foot, then another, and suddenly she was at the top. Adam was smiling at her, and when he grabbed her arm, she felt incredibly safe. He held her hand to help her over the top of the fence, then guided her hips as she settled her feet onto the ladder he was standing upon on the other side of the fence.

Kate tensed up. There was something in his touch that was so reckless, yet so gentle, that she shivered in the hot night. It was a momentary thing, but Kate was shaken by it nonetheless. Adam usually made her boil with frustration, but this time the feeling was different. When she hopped off the last rung of the ladder on the pool deck, Adam lifted his hand to give her five.

"Nice effort, princess! Good to see you're able to have a little fun, even though we don't have an instruction manual." Then he winked, and climbed back up the ladder to help Sierra over.

Kate instantly hated him again. She couldn't believe she'd started to warm up to him just because he'd helped her over a freakin' fence! As though he was some sort of Prince Charming, coming to rescue her. *Whatever.* They didn't need him to have fun, and they didn't need his help to break into the pool. They could totally have done this without him. *Just because he wrapped his hands around my hips, I don't need to be all charmed by him,* Kate reminded herself.

"I'm so glad Adam is here," Sierra said breathlessly when she stepped off the ladder. "This is exciting!"

Kate pretended she hadn't heard her, because she didn't want to acknowledge that Sierra was right. They would, of course, have been having fun, but they probably wouldn't have been sneaking into a country club pool to cool off.

Adam did bring a level of excitement to their trip that she wasn't sure they would have achieved without him.

Kate surveyed the pool area. There were two separate swimming spots: one that was shallow for little kids to wade in, and another that was deep and dark and refreshing-looking. There were padded lounge chairs all around the edge of the pool, and little cabanas in each of the corners. A concession stand stood next to the entrance gate and was stocked with sodas (behind locked refrigerator doors) and boxes of candy bars.

As soon as Alexis had been safely shepherded down the lifeguard's ladder, Adam grabbed the ladder he had propped on the exterior of the fence and secured it back on its stand alongside the interior wall. No one would ever know it had been moved. Then he plunged, fully clothed, into the deepest part of the big pool. He pulled off his wet shirt and whipped it onto the pool deck, narrowly missing Kate. She, Alexis, and Sierra sat together on the edge of the pool, dangling their feet in the water.

"Ohhhh." Alexis sighed. "This feels amazing. I'm going in." Then, with her tiny little shorts and T-shirt still on, she lowered herself down into the pool and dog-paddled around before finally submerging to swim the rest of the width of the pool underwater.

Sierra was next. She pulled her skirt off (it was from

Anthropologie, and probably wouldn't have fared well in chlorine) and wore just the bike shorts she had on underneath and her tank top. She eased herself into the water and dipped under.

"You're all alone out there," Adam said to Kate, paddling over to her on the edge of the pool. "After all the hard work of busting in, don't you want to swim?" She did, but she didn't have bike shorts on like Sierra, and she wasn't wearing short shorts like Alexis. Ridiculously, she was wearing jeans—which helped explain why she had been so hot all day. If it had been just her girlfriends, she'd have happily gone in the water in just her skivvies, but with him there—not so much.

"I do, but . . ." Kate didn't really want to tell Adam why she hadn't yet joined them in the pool. He'd already made fun of her for being such a priss, and she didn't really feel like ruining the evening by fighting with him again. But if he started teasing her, she knew she'd be pissed, and that would be the end of the fight-free period.

"But what? You don't want to come in naked, eh?" Adam was smirking again, which started Kate's blood boiling. "Oh, don't get feisty. I'm just teasing you. I bet you look great naked."

Before Kate could get mad, Adam splashed her, which cooled her off tremendously. Then he grabbed his wet T-shirt off the pool deck and set it next to her on the edge of the pool. "Wear this," he suggested. "It will be like a dress on you. Then you can come in and play with the rest of us."

"Okay," Kate agreed. She slipped inside one of the cabanas and pulled her hot jeans and tank top off. Adam's shirt was soaked and chilly, but it felt great against her toasty skin. The T-shirt hung down to Kate's midthigh—perfect. She ran out of the cabana and jumped straight into the pool. "Ayeee!" The water was colder than she'd thought it would be, and it felt amazing.

They bobbed around in the pool for a long time. Kate and Sierra easily beat Alexis and Adam at a game of chicken, knocking Alexis off Adam's shoulders in about five seconds flat. Alexis and Sierra settled into padded lounge chairs on the side of the pool, watching Adam and Kate do flips into the water. Kate had mastered the art of flips during their summers at the lake. Her little sister had taught Kate all her figure skating jumps and spins. Kate couldn't stay upright on skates to save her life, but she could execute all the moves perfectly when she did them off the dock.

Just as Adam hit the water with a loud *thwack*—his triple spin had gone awry and had turned into a basic cannonball—Sierra's cell phone rang. Sierra shushed them all and flipped her phone open to answer it.

"Hey, Mom," she said innocently. "Yeah, we're having

a great time. We just got to our hotel for the night. . . . No, it's pretty nice. It has a pool." She smiled at the others, holding her finger to her lips while her mom talked on the other end of the phone. "No, Mom, don't do that. . . . It will get easier. . . . Please. I'll be there in a few days." She paused again, and they all sat silently, listening to Sierra's end of the conversation. "Can you just try? For Sasha. . . . Okay, I'll see you in a couple days. . . . I love you, too. Say hi to Daddy."

She closed the phone, and exhaled a huge sigh. "Everything okay?" Kate asked.

"Yeah," Sierra mumbled. "My mom is threatening to go back to Jersey."

"Things aren't going so well with her and your dad?" Alexis guessed.

Sierra fidgeted with her phone, clearly uncomfortable and on edge. "I think it's getting better. But my mom isn't really willing to try. She gets herself in a huff every time they have any kind of little disagreement. I just want her to try to get along with him. I feel like she's keeping things from getting better between them."

They all waited for her to continue. Sierra leaned her head back against the chair, eyes closed. Kate climbed out of the pool to move closer to her friend. She sat on the pool deck at the end of Sierra's chair, dripping wet. Sierra finally murmured, "I mean, she's always looking for some excuse to be mad. She expects me to smooth things over between them, and when I'm not there, it all falls apart. I'm glad they have this time to themselves to try to figure things out without me. My sister's too little to really notice everything that's going on. . . . I can't be in the middle." She cut off, her voice cracking. "I just can't." Her eyes remained closed, but it was obvious that if she opened them, she would start to cry.

Alexis and Kate looked at each other, unsure of what to do or say. Kate finally said, "Sierra, you can't deal with their issues for them. . . . It's not your fault." Alexis chewed her lip and remained silent—she didn't like to deal with emotional issues. Kate reached out to hold Sierra's hand.

Finally the silence was broken by Adam. "My folks went through something similar a few years ago." He spoke quietly. "My brothers and I were always caught in the middle, and it felt like crap."

Sierra opened her eyes to look at Adam. "Really?"

"We used to hide under the stairs while they were fighting. No one wanted to be around them after a fight, since we either became targets for criticism or had to deal with my mom moping around, which just sucked." He hoisted himself out of the pool. "We used to escape to Lex's house whenever we could, just to get away. But then something must have clicked, because after about a year things started to get better. Every day a little bit more of the tension would ease up. Now it's cool again. This will sound crass, but I have to say it: They'll either work it out, or they'll end it. Something will change."

"Yeah," Sierra agreed. "I guess that's true." She nodded. "I've gone through the trial separation, then the reconciliation, then the real separation, and now whatever this is. . . . I guess it can't get a whole lot worse than this. I just want them to get to a place where it's not a mystery every day. The uncertainty makes me crazy."

Adam was nodding, as though he knew exactly how she felt. Kate hadn't known any of this about Adam, and watching him relate to Sierra so compassionately made her start to see another side of him. "It will get better," he told Sierra again. "The bickering might not end the way you'd like it to, but it *will* end."

Sierra smiled at him gratefully, then said, "You know what? There's really no point in me worrying about this here. For once I can't do anything about it, so let's just enjoy ourselves. Here we are, uninvited guests at this gorgeous pool, and I'm moaning about my parents' issues. Kate, can you teach me a double flip?"

Kate nodded, happy to see her friend in a better place. She knew Sierra was still dwelling on her conversation with her mom, but felt like the best thing they could do was help her forget about everything for a while. So they all practiced backflips and spins and cannonballs, enjoying the privacy and relaxation of the pool. At one point Adam raided the concession stand, grabbing candy bars for each of them. When he handed Kate her favorite—a 3 Musketeers—she jokingly shot him a scolding look. He grinned, then pulled four soaking-wet dollar bills out of his pocket and left them under the counter as payment for their snack.

It was near eleven when they finally decided they'd better get moving to find a place to crash for the night. Kate slipped back into the cabana to trade Adam's wet T-shirt for her jeans and tank top, and they all sat on the chairs to dry off for a few minutes.

Suddenly a loud voice boomed out, "Who's in there?"

Kate and Sierra screamed, startled and scared of getting caught. They all jumped up, and Sierra quickly pulled the lifeguard rescue ladder from its stand against the wall. Together she and Adam propped it up against the fence.

Adam scaled the ladder first, and flung his leg over the top to drop down to safety on the outside of the country club wall. The girls could hear a ring of keys rattling in the lock on the fence, and they hustled to follow Adam up and over the ladder. They had to jump from the top of the fence down into the grass on the other side of the wall, but Adam stood on the ground, ready to help catch each of them. Just as one of Kate's legs flung over the top of the fence, the door of the pool popped open and a security guard came barging in. He and Kate locked eyes for one brief moment before she flipped her other leg up and over and dropped to the ground.

As Kate scrambled to her feet on the safe side of the fence, she heard the guard call out, "You better hit the road, girls." All four of them went running, wet, happy, and a tiny bit freaked out, back to the safety of their car.

A few minutes later they were back on the road again.

Six

Michigan

"How do my boobs look?" Alexis adjusted her shirt so it was barely covering the top edges of her bra. Her tiny chest had been squished into a push-up bra that made her A cups look like a solid B–C, and every little bit was spilling out of the top of her shirt.

"Pretty impressive," Sierra replied. "If you're not careful, those suckers are going to take that last step right out of your shirt and walk to the party themselves."

Kate laughed. "She's right, Lex. Your boobs are pushed up about as far as they can be without actually removing them from your body. Great shirt. I'm sure Kevin will be glad to see them . . . uh, you."

"Funny," Alexis said dryly. "Geez, you guys. I'm so

nervous!" She giggled, then covered her mouth with her hand. "I don't know why I'm being such a ditz. You would think the nerves would disappear after two years together, but I swear . . . I'm panicking at the thought of seeing him."

Kate squeezed her friend's hand, but stayed silent. She was just as nervous as Alexis about this reunion with Kevin. A surprise visit to a total cad of a boyfriend just wasn't a good idea, and Kate was paranoid about what they were going to find. She really wanted to support Alexis's relationship but just couldn't. Much as she wanted to believe in true love, Kate had a hard time understanding Alexis's romance with Kevin. She just didn't get it—but watching Alexis prepare for her reunion all day had made Kate even more excited about the fact that they were only a day away from Love!

They had spent the night before at a seedy roadside motel very near the country club. It had been late when they'd left the pool, and Adam had wanted to sleep on a real mattress so he'd be rested for his interview the next day. The motel was only an hour from the university, so they had slept in and then had driven to Ann Arbor around lunchtime to check out the campus and check into their hotel. Since they'd gone cheap the previous night, they decided to splurge and stay at a hotel with an indoor corridor, rather than a place where you could drive up to your room door.

Alexis had called Kevin at work that morning, but hadn't told him they were in town. She was determined to surprise him. He had mentioned the fact that his fraternity was hosting a party that night. So the three girls were on their way there now, with Alexis's boobs leading the way. Adam had spent the afternoon at his interview, and was now having dinner with a student on the scholarship committee. He was planning to meet up with them later at the frat house.

"Kat, can you figure out where we're going?" Alexis had stopped and was scanning addresses for the right frat house. Lex had never been to visit Kevin before, and was struggling to reconcile the setting Kevin had described over the phone with the real-life college block they were wandering down now.

"It's right there, Alexis," Kate responded, pointing at the big brick building directly in front of them. "Are you ready?" Kate adjusted her own shirt, pulling uncomfortably at the stretchy, shimmery green material in the humid heat. She noticed Sierra was doing the same thing, and Kate smiled to herself.

Alexis had insisted upon outfitting them all for the party, which meant Kate and Sierra were both uncomfortably stuffed into shirts borrowed from Alexis's suitcase. Kate's was far tighter than she would usually wear, and she felt like she was squeezed inside a roll of duct tape. The electric blue strapless shirt Sierra was wearing was a few inches too short for her long frame, but pulling it down to cover her belly risked a full-frontal boob flash. Sierra squirmed to try to shrink herself to fit into it.

There was a mob of people on the porch outside the frat house, several of whom looked drunk already. As the three girls made their way up the steps toward the front door, a scrawny guy shouted out a second-floor window. "Caitlin!" He was waving at Sierra out the window, so she timidly waved back.

She crinkled her forehead at Alexis and Kate. "Who is that guy?"

They shrugged, and proceeded into the house. Inside, the living room—if you could call it that—was packed. It was humid and hot, and the music was so loud they couldn't hear their own voices. Alexis led them through the room, scanning for Kevin in the crowd. He was nowhere to be found on the main floor, but Alexis found herself stalked by potential suitors as she made her way through the kitchen and den. She was constantly cut off by guys who looked first at her chest, then at her face, and usually said something along the lines of, "Where have you been all my life?"

Alexis seemed flattered at first, but quickly bored of the

cheesy line. "Kevin chose *this* over *me* this summer?" she mused, flipping her hair over her shoulder. Sierra shrugged, clearly unimpressed by the party.

Kate's left butt cheek was squeezed as they made their way upstairs, but when she turned around to see who it was, all she saw was a guy and girl making out a few steps below her. Sierra's window friend appeared out of nowhere when they got to the second floor. He wrapped Sierra in a big hug and said, "I was hoping you'd come!"

"Babe, I think you're mistaking me for someone else," Sierra said gently, prying the guy's hands off her back.

"Get lost, loser," Alexis said with more force. When the guy just stood there staring, she said, "Seriously, freak. You don't know her."

"Lex," Kate cautioned. "Be nice. He's just confused."

"He's drunk," Alexis said. "So he's acting stupid. I don't want him to touch my friend and use booze as his excuse. It's vile."

The guy chuckled, then wandered off down the hall. He yelled back, "I'll find you later, Caitlin. We have catching up to do." He blew a kiss at Sierra, and they all burst out laughing. The guy laughed too, confident that he was in on the joke.

"Ick." Kate shuddered. "Creepy."

They peeked into each of the rooms on the second floor,

but found no sign of Kevin anywhere. A group was playing Twister in one room, and Alexis knocked one guy down when she shoved the door open. "Oops." She looked amused rather than apologetic. Continuing their climb up to the third floor, Alexis said, "What if he's not here yet?"

"Then we'll wait for him," Sierra promised. "We can dance and hang out. We're meeting Adam here, anyway, so we have time to kill."

The third floor was quieter than the lower levels, and each of the rooms they peeked into were either empty or had small clusters of people who were listening to music and chilling. The door at the far end of the hall was open, and they could hear John Mayer playing inside. Kate peeked in, and what she saw made her close the door quickly behind her. "Nothing in there," she said cheerfully, her voice squeaky and high.

Alexis whitened. "You're clearly lying, Kate. You always do that high voice thing when you're lying. Is Kevin in there?" She looked nervous.

As she should, Kate thought. Kevin was, in fact, inside— and he wasn't alone. "No," Kate lied, flashing a desperate look at Sierra. Her voice went up another octave and she sounded overly excited. "We should go back downstairs. I'm thirsty."

Alexis pushed past Kate and opened the door. Kate and

Sierra followed apprehensively. Kevin was sitting on a bean-bag chair, with a girl who looked eerily similar to Alexis perched squarely on his lap. The girl's head was resting on his shoulder, and his hand was cupped around her knee. They both looked up, and Kevin's face caught on faster than his hand did. The shock was evident in his expression, and finally he released his hand from the girl's knee. He pushed her off of himself and jumped up.

"Surprise," Alexis muttered, her eyes narrowing.

"Lex!" Kevin cried. "What are you doing here?"

"It's good to see you, too, asshole."

"Lex, she's not . . ." He looked at the girl who'd been on his lap and who was now standing there staring at Kevin with her hands on her hips. "We're just . . ." He lowered his voice to a whisper. "I can't get her away from me. She's totally nuts. I mean, psycho, and she thinks she has a chance with me."

Alexis smiled at Kevin. "Oh, isn't that an unfortunate problem. You're being so sweet to let her play out her little fantasy. *On. Your. Lap.*" Alexis was acting tough, but Kate knew her friend was hurt. On Kate's right Sierra crossed her arms and stepped up to show she had Alexis's back.

"Lex, don't act like that," Kevin pleaded. "I'm so glad you're here." He moved to hug her. "Why *are* you here?" Alexis shrugged him off.

"I came to see *you*, you lying, disgusting pig. Now I've seen you, and I don't need to again." Alexis turned and walked out of the room.

Kate and Sierra turned to follow her. Kevin grabbed Kate's arm as she stepped into the hall, and he said, "She's really mad, isn't she? Will you let me explain?"

Kate looked at him in disbelief. "Kevin, I think you got off pretty easy. You're a jerk—you always have been, and always will be—and she should have done a lot more than just walk out of here. I'm surprised you're not in physical pain. If you ever try to call her again, I'll find you and make sure that you regret treating Alexis like this. Got it?" She delivered this message with a big sugary smile, then hurried off to find her friends. Her blood was boiling and her hands were visibly shaking. Alexis didn't deserve to be treated like this, and—even though she had sort of seen it coming—Kate hadn't thought Kevin could be so completely disrespectful of their relationship.

If Lucas ever did that to me . . . , Kate thought somberly as they climbed back down the stairs. But she knew Lucas would *never* do that.

Back downstairs Alexis yelled through the noise, "I guess I can't say I'm surprised." She looked more angry than hurt. "When he told me he wasn't coming home at all this summer, I guess I sort of knew we were close to the end."

She shook her head. "I didn't really prepare myself to actually *see* him with someone else, so that really sucks. Man, this is so embarrassing." She chewed her lip.

"Lex." Kate reached out to pull her friend into a hug. "Lex, you guys have been together for two years. You don't have to be embarrassed about feeling sad."

Alexis blew her bangs away from her face and blinked a few times to compose herself. "No, he's an asshole, and I don't want to waste any more time on him by feeling crappy about our relationship fizzling out."

Kate couldn't stop herself from smiling. She and Alexis were such opposites—Kate couldn't help but think about how she would have felt if that *had* been her with Lucas. She knew that she and Alexis processed things differently. It would have taken Kate at least a year to recover; she suspected Lex would be mostly recovered by later that night. "If it makes you feel better," Kate yelled over the music, "I will remove his toenails one by one if he ever calls you or in any way hurts you again." Sierra nodded her agreement.

"Oh, Kat." Alexis smiled. "My hero. Grrrrrr . . . ," she growled. "If you girls don't mind, I see no reason to waste this Wonderbra. Excuse me." She air-kissed at them, then sauntered over to a hot guy who had been eyeing her from across the room. Sierra and Kate watched as Alexis expertly flirted with him, laughing and chatting as though nothing had happened that night to put her off her game.

"How does she *do* that?" Sierra wondered aloud.

Kate shrugged. "That's Lex, right?"

"I'm actually sort of jealous. How long did it take me to stop mourning my breakup with James last winter? Like, four months?"

"Something like that. You were miserable! I'm sure Lex is pretty broken up too, but she's so good at distracting herself." Kate pursed her lips, remembering Sierra's breakup with the guy she'd gone out with for a few months at the beginning of the year. "If it were me . . ."

"Let's not even go there," Sierra said, and shook her head. "I really have to pee," she declared. "Look, there's Adam." She pointed toward the front door, then said, "Will you be okay if I go look for a toilet?" Kate didn't say anything, but Sierra grinned and said, "Oh, of course you'll be okay. . . You and Adam will be just fine."

Kate called after Sierra, "Hey, what does that mean?" Sierra just smiled and headed off into the crowd. Kate waved at Adam—he looked so different with his hair all tidy and his shirt tucked in. He'd bought a blue and white striped button-down for the interview, and it still had some of the crisp creases from being folded into its package. Kate couldn't help but giggle when she saw how straight-laced he looked, considering his usual tousled hair and T-shirt style.

"How'd it go?" she shouted over the music.

Adam gave her a thumbs-up and looked around the crowded room. "Is Lex off with Kevin?"

"Um, no," Kate shouted back. She pointed toward the front door and said, "Let's go outside and I'll fill you in." They headed out onto the porch, which was emptier than it had been when they'd arrived. The keg had been set up down in the basement, and most people had migrated down there to be closer to it.

They sat on the front steps, and Kate recounted the events of Alexis and Kevin's reunion. She also told Adam that Alexis was now off exacting her revenge on Kevin with one of his frat brothers.

"Oof, that's brutal," Adam declared. "I've always hated Kevin, so good for her."

"Really? You hated Kevin?" Kate asked. She'd figured Adam hadn't ever really thought about it or cared about his cousin's relationship, but maybe he had.

"Didn't *you*? He never treated Alexis right." Adam grabbed a soda out of the cooler on the porch next to him. "Want one?"

"Oh, sure. Can I get a Cherry Coke?"

"Not a diet?" Adam asked.

"What's that supposed to mean?"

"Nothing. It's just that girls always take diet soda."

"I don't."

"I guess not. That's cool." Adam clicked his can against Kate's in a little toast. "You're cool, Kate."

Kate furrowed her forehead. *Is he being serious, or rude?* Kate couldn't read Adam, and it bugged her. "Why do you say that?"

"I like that you say what you want, and it's fun when you fight back." Adam tipped back his soda, offering no further explanation.

"It's fun when I fight back?"

"Sure. That's why I like hanging out with you—you're a challenge. Don't you get a rush when we fight?"

Is he serious? Kate wondered. "Not really," she answered, partially lying. "I don't understand why you have to be such a jerk all the time," she said truthfully.

Adam laughed. "Come on, now. I'm not a jerk. You just don't see my side of the argument. I can't be that bad. You liked me when we were kids."

"You're a total asshole now, though," Kate declared. "You turned evil in sixth grade, when you spread that rumor about Alexis sleeping with Barbie dolls. It took her months to live that down."

"*That's* why you hate me?" Adam asked. "Because I told people about my cousin's Barbie doll fascination?" He looked surprised, then amused. "That was a true story, you know."

"Whatever." Kate dismissed him with her hand. "It was a crappy thing to do, and I don't like when people don't treat my friends with respect."

Adam was grinning. "Seriously? Your grudge against me is that I spread a rumor about my cousin in *sixth* grade? Well, aren't you a loyal friend."

"Yeah, I am. And you're not such a great cousin. You took private information that you had only because you're family and turned it into a rumor, just to be mean to Alexis."

"Did you know . . . ," Adam started, then broke off.

Kate looked at him critically. "What? Did I know what?"

He took a swig of his soda and shook his head. "Nothing."

They sat in silence, watching people walk by the frat house. Every few minutes someone would come out the front door, looking for relief from the noise and heat inside the party. Kate heard some girls talking about the length of the line for the bathroom, so she guessed Sierra was stuck in it.

The heat of the evening was oppressive, and Kate stretched her hands up, searching for a breeze in the sticky air. When she lowered her arms, she propped them behind her on the porch so she could lean back to look up at the brilliant stars that seemed almost dull back in Jersey.

Adam followed suit, and as he placed his hands on the disintegrating wood of the porch, his hand unintentionally grazed hers. He left it where it was, his pinky finger overlapping with hers. His relaxed posture suggested the touch meant nothing, but Kate was singularly focused on his hand, and her entire body, from the tips of her ears to her purple-painted baby toe, was buzzing.

Finally Adam said quietly, "In the interest of full disclosure, I should mention that right before sixth grade Alexis told every single one of my friends that I wet the bed every time I slept over at her house. She also told them that her parents had bought a special plastic sheet with Teletubbies on it for the bed I slept on so that I wouldn't ruin the mattress." He smiled. "*That* is why I told people the very true story of Alexis and her Barbie dolls. Peeing the bed is not something to joke about. Man, I was *tortured* after she spread that story."

"Was it true?" Kate asked, laughing. Adam sat up, causing their fingers to pop apart.

"No, it wasn't true!" Adam feigned anger, but he was laughing, too. Suddenly he said, "We used to be friends, Kate."

"I know. Stuff happens, I guess."

"I always liked hanging out with you. Remember that summer when we canoed out to the island almost every day, just you and me? That was actually the summer I started to play the banjo too, if I remember correctly."

"Yeah," Kate answered, thinking back to one of their first summers in Love, when she and Adam had spent almost every afternoon together while everyone else went waterskiing. It was before the Barbie incident, and long before Lucas's family had started coming to Cattail Cottages Resort. "You were the only other person that didn't like to spend every second on the boat. My anti-waterskiing companion."

"I actually really like waterskiing. I'm no good at it, but it's still fun."

"Why didn't you go at all that summer?"

"Because . . ." Adam turned toward her. "Because then you would have been stuck all alone or gotten roped into riding around in the boat watching everyone else ski. Chilling out with just you was always a lot more fun anyway. You've always cracked me up, princess, and I liked hanging out with you. . . . Still do."

Just then Alexis and Sierra both came barreling out the front door. Alexis was wild-eyed, and Sierra was laughing hysterically. "Let's go!" Alexis called, running down the front steps. "We have to get away from Sierra's lover."

As they all took off down the sidewalk toward their car, they could hear a guy yelling, "Caitlin, don't go! Caitlin!"

"What did you do?" Kate asked, breathing heavily as they ran down the sidewalk.

"I didn't do anything!" Sierra declared. "Lex?"

Alexis laughed harder. When they were finally in the safety of their car, back on the road to the hotel, Alexis said, "I told the drunk guy that Sierra, or rather, Caitlin, was easily wooed by poetry. So the dumb guy stripped down to his underwear and started reading random Shakespearean sonnets to her from the landing between the first and second floors. It was freaking hilarious!"

"Poor guy." Sierra laughed. "I feel bad for him."

"He was drunk, Sierra! He'll have no recollection that he did that, until someone reminds him tomorrow. Maybe he'll realize he shouldn't act like such a fool next time."

"At least he'll never see us again," Kate offered. "Even though I'm sure he'd love to see you, Caitlin." They pulled into the parking lot of their hotel. As they walked into the lobby, Kate's phone rang. "Hey," she murmured into the phone, waiting for a response on the other end. "I'm excited to see you, too." She smiled to herself, but was fully aware that her friends were watching her. "Okay, g' night." When she hung up, the other three were waiting for her next to the front desk.

"Lover boy?" Alexis asked, raising an eyebrow.

"*Yes,*" Kate said. "I can't believe I'll see him in less than a day! I just keep visualizing that moment when we'll pull up at the resort and Lucas will come greet me with a kiss. Mmmm," Kate murmured, closing her eyes to picture the scene. When she opened them again, Adam was watching her closely. "What?" she asked. "Why are you looking at me like that?"

He didn't say anything, just shook his head.

"What?" she demanded. "Are you trying to find a way to kill my fantasy, just like your cousin?" Kate looked at him angrily, anticipating the rude comment he was sure to make. "Because you won't, and your criticism will just piss me off."

"No," Adam said simply. "I'm happy for you, Kate. I hope it all unfolds exactly as it should."

Kate stared at him and realized he was being genuine. "Thank you. That's a nice thing to say." They all headed off toward the elevator to go to their shared room, but as they passed the breakfast area off the lobby, someone singsonged, "Hello, girls!"

Inside the dining room were a bunch of white-haired women, smiling and waving. "Oh, hi!" Kate said, stepping into the room. "You were at the amusement park yesterday, right? What are you doing here?"

"This is the next stop on our tour," one of the women said. "Lovely Ann Arbor. We move on to Chicago tomorrow. Then we'll be making our way up into Wisconsin and the shores of the Great Lakes!"

Another woman shouted out, "If I have anything to say about it, we're staying in Chicago until this money in my pocket is gone! I have some shopping to do." All the other ladies laughed, despite the fact that her comment wasn't funny. Inside joke, apparently.

"Okay . . ." Alexis was obviously eager to get out of there. "Well, have a good trip. Really nice to see you again." She yawned and gestured toward the elevator.

As they were on their way out the door, one of the women said, "Do any of you kids play pinochle? Joyce went to bed, and Fern is missing her partner." A woman—presumably Fern—waved at them.

"Yeah, sure, I play. Are you willing to play with a guy, or is this ladies-only?" Adam asked, and stepped into the room.

Fern stood up and shimmied a little, then said to the other women in the room, "Ooh-hoo, girls. Look at my luck! Of course I'll play with a fellow. I've been on a bus tour with forty women for the last week and could use a little distraction!" She laughed, and Adam turned to look at Kate, who was struggling to keep from cracking up.

Adam wrapped his hand around Kate's forearm, then announced, "I'll only play if Kate agrees to stay and help me. What do you say, Kate?" Kate looked at Adam like he was crazy, then back at the roomful of women. They were all looking up at her hopefully, so she nodded.

Alexis and Sierra both giggled behind her before saying good luck and good night. Alexis whispered, "Sorry to ditch you, but . . . Well, I'm not sorry!" Then they hustled off down the hall toward the elevator. Kate knew Alexis and Sierra would settle into one of the beds while she and Adam were downstairs, meaning she would have to fight Adam for the roll-away.

As they made their way over to Fern's table, Kate whispered, "Why are you doing this to me?"

"It will be fun," Adam whispered back. "It's quality together time for you, me, and the Q-tip tour."

"Q-tip tour?"

"Sure," Adam said, and grinned. "When they're all sitting in the bus with their white hair peeking up over the windowsills, it looks like a bunch of Q-tips lined up in a row. So it's a Q-tip tour."

"Superfunny," Kate deadpanned. They sat at Fern's table and Adam picked up the hand of cards that had been dealt to him. For the next hour Kate watched as Adam charmed and flirted with the ladies on the Q-tip tour. She had to admit that she was impressed at how friendly and charming he could be.

But more than anything, Kate was surprised at how

much fun she was having. Not only were the women hilarious, but she was having a great time with Adam. It was as though they were back in the fifth grade again, having a great time hanging out—and getting along.

At one point, after proudly laying down the ace of hearts, Fern looked up at Kate and Adam. Adam was whispering something to Kate, and Fern said, "You two sure do make a charming couple." She pointed at Kate. "You're a lucky girl."

"Oh, no—," Kate said, starting to explain that they were very much not a couple.

Adam cut her off to say, "Thanks, Fern."

Before Kate could protest, the buzz of a text message in her pocket distracted her. She pulled out her cell and glanced at the screen.

The text was, of course, from Lucas, who had simply written: "Good night, sleep tight!" Kate took that as her cue to excuse herself from the game to head off to bed. The road trip had been fun, but she couldn't wait for tomorrow to come.

Seven

Wisconsin

"Ah, nothing says home like the smell of rotting fish carcasses." Adam rolled his window down as they passed the turtle pond that was just down the road from Cattail Cottages Resort. No one knew why it was known as the turtle pond, because in all the years they'd been coming to Love, the turtle pond had been nothing more than a boglike hole filled with mud that smelled like dead fish. Adam sniffed deeply, then coughed out, "You gotta love Love."

They had just run into Sierra's mom, who was out for a walk, and had dropped Sierra off to walk the few miles back to the resort with her. A few minutes later Alexis steered the car into the dirt parking lot at the end of the gravel road. They had been driving since very early that morning. They'd been eager to get there—Kate especially—so they'd just driven straight through with only a few quick bathroom breaks.

Alexis hopped out of the car and jogged over to the main house to grab a wagon they could use to pull their stuff from the car to their cabins. Lucas was nowhere nearby, so Kate started to unload the bags, eager to get to her cabin, where he'd surely be waiting.

Adam came up behind Kate and reached around her to get his arm into the trunk. "Can I help?" he murmured, gently pulling her hand off Alexis's huge suitcase. His hand stayed on hers for what felt like a few seconds longer than necessary, and while his skin touched hers, Kate's heart stood still. Her chest constricted, catching her breath between her ribs and holding it hostage there.

"Thanks," she muttered when finally he pulled his hand and the bag back out of the trunk. *I guess I'm extra sensitive now that I'm finally so close to Lucas*, she reasoned.

Adam smiled his dopey grin at her, and walked away from the car. She shook the flirty sensation off and grabbed her duffel bag out of the trunk. When they had everything loaded up in the giant wagon, the three of them headed off toward the cabins near the lake.

Their families always rented the same cottages, so

instinct led them each toward their usual summer homes. Kate's family was in cabin four, Alexis's was in two, and Adam's family rented cabin number seven, which was sort of off by itself around a curve on the lakeshore. Lucas's family rented one of the more distant cabins with greater privacy and better views of the lake. As they approached Kate's and Alexis's cabins, Adam grabbed his bag off the wagon and said, unceremoniously, "See you later. Thanks for the lift."

Kate and Alexis split up a moment later, agreeing to meet before the bonfire that night. For as long as they could remember, every night there was a group barbecue, followed by a bonfire where all the under-twenties hung out until the mosquitoes got too persistent for anyone to stay outside any longer. The trick, Kate had learned, was to sit in the line of the campfire smoke, and the mosquitoes stayed away. That was her plan for that night, when she wanted to stretch her first evening with Lucas out until the last possible moment.

Kate stepped inside her family's cabin, and was happy to see that nothing had changed from the summer before. There was a lumpy futon couch that divided the kitchen-ette from the living room. She and her sister fought every year over who got to sleep in the tiny second bedroom, and which of them was relegated to the futon in the common room. The "dining area" was defined by a warped card table that stood between the other side of the kitchenette and the bathroom. The table still had a small hole where Kate and Alexis had dropped a burning candle during a late-night giggle fest more than five years before.

As Kate surveyed her surroundings, the screen door burst open and her little sister, Gina, came charging in. "Oh." Gina stopped short when she saw Kate. "You're here. Mom! Kate's here!"

"Hey, G," Kate replied, and smiled at her sister. Gina was fourteen—and the boss of the family. Gina had been a competitive figure skater since she was four, and the whole family revolved around Gina's skating practices, competitions, and performances. Kate had never excelled at anything, so she just tried to stay out of the way while everyone planned around Gina. "When did you guys get here?"

"Two days ago," Gina replied, while applying a shiny lacquer to her lips. "You're on the futon."

Kate rolled her eyes. "Whatever." She would deal. It was easier to just relent than to fight with Gina, who would surely find a means to get her way. Kate planned to spend most of the summer with Lucas, anyway, so it's not like she'd be hanging out in her room reading books or anything.

"Have you seen Lucas yet?" Gina asked, innocently enough.

"No. We just got here," Kate responded as evenly as she could. "Why? Have you?"

Gina giggled. "He's cute, Kate. Cuter than last year. And he's been talking about you." Gina was a romantic, just like her sister, and she knew all about Kate's kiss from last summer. Even though Kate and her sister weren't all that close, Kate enjoyed talking to her about guys. Gina *got* guys.

"Really?" Kate's anticipation bubbled up inside, and she could hardly stop herself from running out of the cabin and straight into Lucas's arms.

"But he's out on the boat." Gina frowned dramatically. "He and some of the other guys went out waterskiing about an hour ago. If it's like yesterday, they probably won't be back until it gets dark. Well . . . see ya! I'll send Mom inside in a little bit to help you with your sunscreen. You need it, whitey." Gina spun and flounced back out the door to go back down to the dock.

They won't be back until dark? Kate mused. It seemed her Lucas reunion would have to wait . . . but Kate didn't know if she could stand the suspense.

Kate brushed her teeth for the third time in half an hour, carefully stretching the bristles to reach the way back teeth.

After she rinsed, she rolled her tongue in her mouth, checking for any residual Cheetos film. All clear.

She trotted back out to the living room and grabbed her jeans. The cool evening buzzing with abundant mosquitoes and sand flies made long pants a wise choice. Kate was pleased, since she'd always felt her legs had never looked quite right in shorts. She had one of those better-naked sorts of bodies. Long pants were okay, but there was something about the way shorts cut her thighs in two that just didn't work. She'd tried the long shorts style, but then her calves looked stumpy.

Kate was okay with her body, but struggled to find the right way to outfit it. She'd always wanted to be a skirt person, but her family didn't have the right income to support a multifaceted wardrobe for Kate *and* a skating career for Gina. Kate could wear the same jeans most days and no one noticed or cared. But she worried it would be pretty obvious if she started wearing the same decorative skirt every Tuesday and Thursday. So she just stuck with her basic style.

She spun around, studying her reflection in the big picture window at the front of the cabin. It was getting dark out, and the light inside caused the window to function more like a mirror. She knew that people rarely used the hidden path that ran past the cottage, so she didn't worry that anyone would see her checking herself out. She pulled her tank top on over her head, tugged it into place, and then promptly pulled it back off again. Too bland for her Lucas reunion.

A rejected green T-shirt, brown wrap top, and black halter later, Kate was still only half-dressed. A knock at the door startled her out of her clothing-induced frenzy. "Alexis, thank god," Kate declared when the door creaked open. (Kate had covered up with a dish towel.) "I can't find anything to wear."

Alexis brushed past Kate and started pawing through the mounds of shirts piled up on the floor. "Try this one," Alexis demanded, pulling off her own light blue cotton polo. Kate pulled Alexis's still-warm shirt over her own head. It was tight, but in the good way. "Yep." Alexis nodded. "That's the one."

"Really, Lex? You're sure?"

"Yup. I've been looking for a good excuse to steal your hot pink tank, and I think I just found it. Deal?"

"Deal. Did you see him out there when you passed the fire pit?"

"Who, Adam?" Alexis teased. Kate was annoyed at the joke. "Oh, *Lucas*? No, he's not there yet. The boat isn't at the dock, so they must still be out on the lake."

"Oh, well, that's okay." Kate pretended to be upbeat, but inside she was frustrated that Lucas hadn't been around all day to see her. He had known she was getting to Love today, and she had really hoped he would be waiting for her when she arrived. Obviously that was silly, since Lucas couldn't make his brothers and friends sit around waiting for him to go out waterskiing, but still . . .

Alexis could sense Kate's frustration and reached out to touch her arm. "It's not really okay," Alexis verified. "He should have been around when we got here. You've been waiting all year."

Just then the whir of the speedboat motor cut through the quiet evening, and they could hear guys' voices down on the dock. Sierra came bursting into Kate's cabin, out of breath. "Lucas is back!" Her dramatic flair made Alexis start laughing hysterically, while Kate paced in semi-freak-out mode. She'd been waiting so long for this moment, and it was finally here.

"So? Are you going to go grab him and make out?" Alexis nudged Kate toward the door. "Go on. Get your guy."

Kate stepped out onto the cabin's tiny front porch and made her way down the gravel path that led to the lake. She wanted her reunion with Lucas to be perfect and knew she had to be alone—so her friends hung back.

Her family's cabin was close to the resort's main beach and the docks, but the resort's barbecue area stood between her and the lake. There was a huge group gathered near the barbecues, eating hot dogs and bratwurst. Kate's parents stood chatting with Adam's. Sierra's parents cuddled together on a log bench, apparently getting along. Gina and Sierra's little sister, Sasha, were giggling about something while Jake, one of the guys who worked at the resort, was working on getting the bonfire going. A group of guys hung around near Jake, tossing sticks into the fire. Kate tried to step past everyone to hurry down to the lake. Just when she thought she was in the clear, Adam stepped out of the group of guys and grabbed her arm to stop her.

"Let go." Kate twisted away.

Adam looked startled. "Sorry," he snapped back. "I just wanted to say hey. I got used to seeing you all day."

"Oh." Kate chewed her lip, feeling guilty for being snippy. She could see some of the guys unloading their gear from the boat onto the dock, and Kate knew she needed to hurry if she was going to catch Lucas before he made his way up the hill to his family's cottage. "I have to go," she said bluntly.

She turned away from Adam, and stopped short when she came face-to-face with the one she'd been dreaming about all year: green eyes, sandy blond hair, chiseled cheekbones—a perfect specimen of summer boy. "Adam," she said, her smile cutting across her face. Then she realized what she'd said, and hastily corrected herself. "*Lucas*. Lucas . . . hi."

"Hi, Kate." Lucas was holding two wet life jackets. He handed them to Adam—who was standing right behind her—so he could pull Kate into a hug. "It's great to see you," he murmured into her ear.

All of Kate's senses were buzzing. Everything felt right as she pressed against him, his bare chest separated from hers by only a tiny bit of shirt fabric. The hug lasted only a few seconds, but in those moments she could feel his breath rising and falling. The droplets of lake water in his hair ran down his neck and onto Kate's cheek, which was pressed against his bare shoulder. The world around them faded away, and Kate could only feel the sensation of his body against hers.

"You look good. I missed your hot body," Lucas said as he pulled away, which made Kate happy about her shirt choice, even if the body comment was a little bit crass.

"Wow." Adam was still standing next to them, and he started clapping his hand against one of the life jackets. "That's romantic, man."

"What?" Lucas said, draping an arm around Kate's shoulder. She melted into the warmth of his embrace, looking forward to time alone with him later. Alone—and away from Adam.

"Nothing. Carry on, Prince Charming." He laughed obnoxiously, then passed the wet life jackets back to Lucas.

Kate spat out, "It's fitting that you would comment on someone else's charm, Adam." Then she grabbed Lucas's available arm and pulled him toward the fire pit. There was no way Adam was going to ruin the romantic reunion Kate had been planning all year. No way. Even though he was sort of right.

She noticed that Adam was still watching them when she settled in next to Lucas on an empty log bench near the bonfire. Kate closed her eyes, desperate to get Adam's face out of her mind. When she did, Lucas took it as his cue to pick things up where they'd left off last summer.

He leaned in and touched her cheek, his lips close to hers. Startled that things were playing out the way she'd imagined them, Kate's eyes snapped open, and the moment was lost. She closed them again, eager to recapture the moment, but nothing happened. When she cracked her lids open, Lucas was smiling at her and his face sparkled mischievously. "We have time," he whispered, his hand cradling the back of her neck. "Let's take this slow."

Kate nuzzled against him as the sun dipped lower in the sky. He wrapped his big zip-up sweatshirt around her, and the rest of the world just melted away.

Eight

In Love, Wisconsin

When Kate woke up the next morning, she was still wrapped in Lucas's sweatshirt, her body tucked up against one edge of the futon. She had forgotten to take his shirt off after the bonfire, and when she'd gotten back to her cabin, she'd decided to wear it to bed. She held it up to her face and breathed in Lucas's familiar scent.

"Are you smelling your boyfriend's sweatshirt?" Gina had just dragged herself into the living room, and was pouring a cup of coffee in the kitchenette right next to Kate's bed. Their parents had already snuck out for their morning walk, so the girls were alone in the cabin. "Had fun last night?"

"Are you drinking coffee?" Kate stuffed Lucas's sweatshirt under her and rolled onto her stomach, watching as

Gina sipped coffee while she made herself a bowl of instant oatmeal for breakfast. "Yeah, I had a good night."

"Was the big reunion as perfect as you'd imagined it?" Gina was using a mocking voice, but Kate knew she wanted the dirt.

"It was good," Kate admitted. "You were right—he is cuter than last year!"

"And sweet, too. He sent you home with a sweatshirt. A real gentleman. What are you guys going to do today?"

"Dunno." Kate stepped out of bed and sat at the folding table, watching Gina flutter around the kitchen. "We're meeting up this morning. I guess I should get dressed and head down to the dock."

"You could use a little color before he sees you in your suit," Gina said, and slurped up her last bite of oatmeal. "You look pasty."

Kate rolled her eyes. "Wow. Thanks, G."

"Make sure you shave your legs too. I can see the stubblies from here." She giggled, then traipsed off to the bedroom to change into her suit.

After scarfing down a couple of pieces of toast, Kate brushed her teeth. She hastily shaved her legs in the tiny bathroom pedestal sink, then slipped on her suit and sunscreen. The suit was a one-piece, but the cut of the legs was slightly more revealing than her previous years' suits. The pale blue color worked well with her hair, making it look close to blond, and when her hair was braided into two loose braids down either side of her neck—as it usually was—she was pretty confident she looked cute. She threw a pair of thin sweats on over her suit and made her way out to the dock.

Sierra was already at the lake, soaking in the sun with her sister. Sierra's sister, Sasha, was painfully shy, so when Kate showed up with her folding chair, Sasha went off to walk along the sandy shoreline alone.

"So? How was the kiss?" Sierra demanded as soon as they were alone. She had returned to her cabin early the night before, long before Kate and Lucas had called it a night.

Kate frowned. "No kiss yet. I'm sure he's waiting until we're alone. He's being a gentleman, right?"

"If that's how you see it," Sierra teased, lifting her eyebrows.

Just then Lucas and his brother arrived. "Morning, ladies!" Lucas called. "How was your sleep, Kate?"

Kate blushed, realizing this was the first time she'd seen Lucas in the daylight. His shirt was off again, and she wanted to jump up and rub her hands against his tan skin. It looked so warm and soft, and she knew it felt amazing when he pressed against her. But she knew she had to wait until later, when they could be alone for real. "I slept well," she answered calmly.

"You're coming out on the boat with us today, right, Kate?"

"Oh," Kate said, realizing that meant they would be spending their first day together on the boat with all the guys. "Sure, that sounds fun."

Sierra looked at her quizzically, knowing Kate had never liked waterskiing—it just wasn't her idea of fun. And Kate hated hanging out on the boat while everyone else was waterskiing. She always had. It made her feel like some sort of pitiful groupie, just sitting in the boat watching everyone else ski. Sierra also knew Kate had been hoping for some alone time with Lucas, and the boat wouldn't be the place they could get that.

"Cool," Lucas said. "Let me grab you a life jacket, and we can take off. Sierra, you want to come?"

"I'm happy here," Sierra answered.

"Your loss," Lucas's brother, Zack, said while hauling gear from the little storage cabin under the boat up to the main deck. "Lucas and I set up a killer course yesterday. You could see us in action."

"Whee, fun," Kate muttered under her breath, loud enough for only Sierra to hear. She grinned at her friend, then stood up to step into the boat. "Hopefully I'll be back soon. . . . Like, twenty minutes?"

"Don't count on it," Sierra teased.

Lucas revved the motor on the boat, signaling his readiness to leave. He held his hand out to Kate, and she stepped into the boat, fastening her life jacket. Lucas patted the seat that backed up against his. With her there, he could keep one of his hands on the wheel and another around her shoulder, which is exactly the scenario she would have set up if she had orchestrated the whole thing herself.

Kate beamed, excited that Lucas had invited her to join them, despite the fact that she never had enjoyed this exact activity. She felt special somehow, invited to be part of his day. It seemed like he wanted to integrate her into his summer, and she was willing to hang out on the boat with him if it meant they could talk and snuggle.

But about an hour later, after they'd picked up some of the other waterskiing crew from their cabins across the lake, Kate and Lucas had yet to exchange more than just a few words at a time. The roar of the boat was overwhelming, and there wasn't a lot of opportunity to talk. There had also been absolutely no cuddling, beyond an arm draped casually across the back of her seat. For the most part Lucas was engrossed in driving the boat and making sure they got people up on their skis and safely back into the boat. The other guys mostly ignored her.

The scene reminded her of one of those movies where the guys do very manly stuff, like fight gladiators and race cars, and the poor women are stuck sitting on the sidelines watching and cheering and eating cake or doing some other useless activity. But in Kate's scene the guys were all water-skiing and she was stuck watching and shivering and pre-tending to have fun from her seat in the boat. She felt like a total outsider. It wasn't fun to sit there like a limp fish just watching. She would much rather have been doing her own thing while Lucas was waterskiing, then have gotten some time alone with him later to catch up.

Right when she had resolved to tell him just that, Lucas turned around in his seat to say, "Have you ever skied? Want to try?"

"Um, yeah," Kate said, answering his first question. "I skied a few times when I was younger, but I seriously lack coordination. It's just not my thing."

"That's cool," he said, nodding and turning back to look at the open lake in front of him.

"So, um, what else do you like to do?" Kate had to shout this over the roar of the boat motor. The question embar-rassed her, but it had slipped out before she had been able to think about it. It sounded like she knew nothing about him, which wasn't true, but she realized they'd never really talked about anything outside their summer world.

She only vaguely knew about his life beyond Love from his e-mails and texts over the past year. She knew he played hockey, and she knew he'd been up for homecoming king (but hadn't won), and that he was going to be a freshman at Notre Dame in the fall, but other than that, he was sort of a mystery. She wanted to know simple things, such as what he liked to do for fun on a regular day.

"What?" Lucas yelled over the roar of the motor.

"Nothing," Kate said, happy to have the opportunity to retract her stupid question.

"You look good with your hair all wild like that," Lucas said, and grinned. He twisted a strand of hair that had been blown free from her braids around his finger. "It's nice having you on the boat with me. You sure you don't want to try waterskiing again?"

Kate shook her head. "I'll try just about anything else, but not that."

"Okay. I don't want you to get hurt or anything, anyway," Lucas said seriously. "You can just sit there and look gorgeous." He held her cheek in his palm and grinned.

Kate gritted her teeth when she realized he wasn't kidding. Now she felt even more useless, and felt like a total doormat of a girl to boot—what a waste of time. Just sit there and look pretty. Ugh.

It was sweet that he'd called her gorgeous, but she could take care of herself, and didn't need him to protect her. Now she was sort of tempted to go skiing, just to show him she could handle herself just fine in the water *and* look good afterward, thankyouverymuch.

But since she truly didn't *want* to water-ski, she decided it was far more respectable to go back to the dock and hang out with her friends while Lucas got the skiing out of his system. Then they could get some quality together time later—when they could really talk and build their relationship. So the next time he slowed the boat down to switch skiers in the water, Kate said, "Lucas, would you mind taking me back to the resort? Maybe we can hang out later?"

Lucas obliged, and steered the boat back toward the resort to drop Kate off. Now Sierra and Alexis were sitting on the dock, along with Adam and one of his brothers, Danny. Jake, who worked at the resort, was cleaning the canoes on shore and flirting with Alexis. It was pretty obvious that he was making headway—she had her head tipped back, laughing hilariously at something he had said.

When Lucas pulled the boat up to the dock, Jake strolled over to catch it and tie it up. "Hey, no worries, man," Lucas said. "We're going back out. You can leave us untied. I just needed to drop this beautiful girl off first."

Everyone on the dock was staring at Kate and Lucas as

he helped her out of the boat. She stood on the driver's seat to climb onto the dock, stumbling slightly when the boat rocked in the water. Lucas, who stood beneath her, held her hand to steady her. But just as she reached her leg out to step onto the dock, he grabbed her around the middle and pulled her back down so she was standing on the seat and he was standing beneath her on the floor of the boat.

He spun her around and his green eyes shone up at her in the midday sun. Still holding her around her middle, he eased her down toward him. Lucas wrapped his arms around her and she could feel the heat from his tan arms penetrating through her own cool skin. His face was close to hers, and his upper lip curled into a smile before bringing her in for a soft, sensual kiss. Her eyes closed, and the boat spun beneath her as the kiss pierced through her body. She melted into his arms, and felt the warmth of his lips against her own.

It was the kiss she'd been waiting a year for . . . and the wait had been worth it.

"My legs feel like they weigh about three tons," Kate huffed out between steps. That afternoon she and Sierra had decided to go running—but Kate had forgotten how much she disliked it. She preferred exercises that integrated naturally into her daily life—walking, biking, swimming in the lake. Sierra's long legs propelled her easily down the gravel road, but Kate felt like she was hauling a third grader on her back.

"You're doing great," Sierra cheered. "You'll feel great later—full of energy."

"I highly doubt that," Kate grumbled good-naturedly.

Sierra laughed, checking her watch. "We can head back whenever you want. I need to turn around pretty soon anyway. My mom wants us to have family dinner tonight."

"Ooh, family dinner. That sounds promising." Kate glanced at Sierra, who had been pretty silent about the state of her parents' reconciliation since they'd gotten to the lake.

"They're trying to make it work," Sierra acknowledged. "It looked like you and Lucas were trying to make it work this morning too," she teased.

The kiss with Lucas that morning had been sensational, there was no denying that. But as soon as the moment had ended, Kate had been embarrassed that Lucas had chosen the dock as the site of their first kiss of the summer. She had felt really exposed, and would much rather have been somewhere alone with him. Her parents could have seen them, which would have mortified her no end—not to mention the fact that her dad would *not* be cool with her hooking up with someone less than a day after she'd gotten there. He didn't know the backstory, and she was pretty certain he wouldn't approve even if he did.

But still, a kiss was a kiss, and it had felt amazing. "Yeah, the kiss was great."

"Great?" Sierra asked, clearly expecting something more from Kate. "Just great?"

"It was incredible, okay?" Kate slowed down to talk. "Can we walk now?"

Sierra stopped running and reached her arms over her head to stretch. "Why are you so much less enthusiastic about the kiss *after* it happened than you were before?"

"I don't know," Kate admitted. "I guess I was just a little embarrassed that our first kiss of the year was so public, you know?"

"Public? It's not like he kissed you on the JumboTron at Yankee Stadium. . . . We were the only ones who saw it."

"I know," Kate was sweating from their run. She hoped she would cool off a little before they got back to the resort. There was nothing less flattering than blotchy post-run skin.

"Was it a little awkward because Adam was there?" Sierra was clearly trying to sound casual.

"Why would that be awkward?" Kate asked defensively.

Sierra smiled knowingly. "It just seemed like you guys

were maybe starting to get along a little more at the end of the road trip. I guess I was just thinking—"

"Sierra!" Kate swatted at her friend. "That's crazy! Adam? You think I have a thing for Adam?"

"Not necessarily. Maybe it's the other way around? Maybe it's mutual?"

"Sierra! Stop."

"Okay, okay," Sierra said. "I just wanted to check, since it seemed like there was some chemistry. But maybe not."

"Seriously, you have to stop." Kate looked at Sierra sternly. "Adam and I fought the whole road trip."

"The fighting seemed a lot like flirting."

"Okay, enough." Kate stopped walking, since they were at the outskirts of the resort and she wanted to be done with this conversation before they were within earshot of anyone else. "I'm with Lucas. You know that. I've been waiting all winter to be with him again, and now we're here and it's going to be an amazing, romantic, perfect summer. I just need some time alone with him and it will all be incredible."

Sierra grinned. "Fine."

As they approached the cabins, they could hear Alexis's laughter from near the dock. They strolled down the hill to find their friend, and when they got past the cluster of trees, they found a lot more than they'd bargained for. Alexis and Jake were lying under the big oak tree next to the lake, making out as though no one could possibly spot them.

Sierra blushed a little, then called out, "Hey, take it inside!"

Alexis just rolled away from Jake and looked up at her friends from her spot on the ground. "Hey," she purred happily. "Kat, you've met Jake, right?"

Kate nodded, then looked enviously out toward the lake, searching for Lucas's boat. With her best friend's summer romance already in full swing—mere days after the breakup with Kevin—Kate wanted Lucas to hurry up and get back from waterskiing already. This summer she finally had her chance to have the romantic ending she'd been imagining ever since she'd met Lucas, and she was ready to get on with the fairy tale already.

Nine

Still in Love, Wisconsin

The ground was squishy between Kate's bare toes as she walked across the old football field. A storm had blown through Love the night before, washing out the evening bonfire at the resort. Kate had been stuck inside her cabin playing Yahtzee with her sister all night. Lucas and his family had gone to a friend's cabin across the lake for dinner, and the storm had forced them to stay sheltered there until late, which meant Kate and Lucas hadn't gotten the alone time she'd been looking forward to the whole day before.

Tonight, however, the air was fresh and the sky clear. The rain had washed away the humidity, so it was warm but not muggy. Kate clutched Lucas's callused hand at her side as they made their way toward the center stage at Love's

Blues Festival. The blues fest was Love's major annual celebration, and she and Lucas were going to the opening night's performances with a bunch of other kids who were staying at the resort.

Kate's shoes were off, and she was enjoying the feeling of the still-wet grass on her bare feet. The field was packed with people who had come from miles away to enjoy the weeklong festival. Kate, Lucas, Sierra, Alexis, Jake, Adam, and a few other friends from the resort had all piled into two minivans for the short drive into town. They'd parked near the ice cream shop and had walked four blocks to the other side of town and the run-down football field that held the makeshift performance stage.

"Let's sit over there," Lucas suggested, gesturing toward a rough patch of ground off to one side of the stage. He led the group across the field, holding Kate's hand tightly. After laying a blanket on the ground, Lucas pulled Kate down to sit in his lap. His hands wrapped around her waist, and his fingers tickled her bare skin between the top of her jeans and her tank top.

It was still hard for Kate to believe that she and Lucas were finally together. She'd had a crush on him for three summers, but it had always seemed like being with him would always be a fantasy rather than her reality. They'd been pretty flirty during bonfires at the end of last summer, but even then it had always been around a group, and nothing more than the one kiss had ever happened.

Kate's obsession with Lucas had initially developed because of how hot he was and—if she were being honest—how cool and unavailable he'd always seemed. She'd never imagined that they would ever move beyond the flirty stage, but their kiss at the end of last summer had changed all of that. It had been something much more than just a kiss, and Kate knew in that moment that there was potential for something much deeper.

But until their reunion a few days ago, they had never really been *together*, so it was still sort of surreal and a little unfamiliar to be with him, just hanging out as a couple. Kate had never been in a relationship before, but she'd envisioned what it would feel like her entire life. The holding hands, the sweet words whispered in her ear, the comfortable teasing between two people in love. When Kate was younger and her parents had taken her and Gina to this festival, they had watched young couples dancing and laughing and joking with friends, and she'd always been so envious. Now, finally, it was her turn, and she had the perfect boy at her side.

"Are you comfortable?" Lucas whispered in her ear, shifting his leg to help her settle in on his lap.

"Yes," Kate murmured back.

He wrapped his arms around her more snugly and pulled her in against his chest. Her heart raced—tucked against his neck, she could smell sunscreen mixed with a hint of his cologne. His body felt warm and soft against her, his arms strong and solid.

"Do you want a soda?" Adam was standing over them, pointing down at Kate. "Coke?"

Kate furrowed her brow and looked up at him, resentful of the fact that he'd crashed their moment. She knew it hadn't been intentional, though. "Um, sure, thanks."

"Lucas?"

"No, dude. I'm cool."

"You *are* cool," Adam said back, flashing a thumbs-up.

Lucas grinned, oblivious to Adam's cheeky tone. "Thanks, man. You're cool too." He held up his hand for a five. Adam responded with an unenthusiastic hand-slap, then set off with Alexis to buy sodas from the concession stand.

"Are you cold or anything?" Lucas said, rubbing Kate's arms. "Do you need my sweatshirt?"

Kate turned her head to look at his face in the darkening sky. "Lucas, it's, like, seventy degrees outside."

"So?" he said, holding her more tightly. "As your boyfriend, it's my job to make sure you're taken care of."

"Uh," Kate said, and furrowed her brow, mildly concerned about Lucas's definition of "boyfriend." (But he *had* called himself her *boyfriend*!) "I don't necessarily think that's true." She smiled at him, adjusting her position on his lap so she was still snuggled in close but better able to make eye contact.

"Oh you don't, do you?" Lucas tickled her.

"No, I don't." Kate pulled back slightly. She wanted to tell him she wasn't a damsel in distress, but realized she might come across as somewhat brusque. "It's just, I don't want you to think I'm totally helpless or anything. I'm not like that." She grinned. "I brought myself a sweater, just in case."

Lucas laughed, then whispered in her ear, "I didn't mean it like that, babe."

"Okay," Kate murmured back, then purred, "I certainly do appreciate your concern."

"Good." Lucas punctuated his response by tugging gently at her ear to turn her lips to his. She could feel him lick his lips in the instant before he leaned into her, and she could smell his spearmint gum. Her body hummed, buzzing with the anticipation of the kiss. His lips brushed hers, then pushed more persistently.

Things had just started to get interesting when Adam and Alexis returned. Adam tossed a bag of gummi worms to Sierra, who was sitting with the rest of the crew from the resort on another blanket a few feet away, then thrust a bottle of Coke toward Kate. Kate pulled back, frustrated once again by Adam's unique ability to appear everywhere he wasn't wanted exactly when he shouldn't. The road trip with the girls, her reunion with Lucas, and now, at their first real date. He had even been there for their first kiss of the summer—gross.

Adam sat down next to Lucas, placing Kate's soda on the ground between them. "Ooh-hoo, wet ass!" He hopped up and pulled a corner of Kate and Lucas's blanket over to protect his baggy jeans from the damp grass. His tug uprooted Kate from her perch on Lucas's lap, and she tumbled off.

"Hey, watch the language around my girl," Lucas scolded jokingly. "These ears are delicate." He put his hands over Kate's ears like earmuffs.

Kate readjusted herself, now sitting right next to her boyfriend rather than *on* him. The lap thing hadn't really been working on a number of different levels. Most important, this level of PDA was a little uncomfortable. But also, she wanted to be able to see him while they chatted. She loved to look into his sharp green eyes, and think about the fact that she was the only girl who could get this close to them.

Adam snickered. "I don't think Kate really needs your protection, buddy."

"Actually," Kate said haughtily, leaning around Lucas to

speak directly to Adam, "I love that Lucas is being so sweet. He treats me like a lady." She knew she sounded ridiculous saying this, and it wasn't fully true, but it pissed her off that Adam was acting like she was some sort of shrew or something.

She suddenly realized that maybe she *did* like her guy watching out for her. It wasn't as if she was a member of the X-Men, able to fight off her verbal attackers and cold weather with superhuman strength and a skintight rubber suit. She found it cute that Lucas was treating her like such a delicate flower—it was sort of a nice feeling. She figured he would soon realize how feisty she was, and this whole fairy-tale princess thing would end, but she didn't mind preserving it while it lasted. It's not like he had her locked up in a padded room or something.

"All I'm saying, Kate, is that you're pretty able to take care of yourself. If that's rude, then I'm sorry." Adam muttered the last sentence under his breath, but it was still audible.

Lucas straightened up, leaning toward Adam. "Dude, lay off." The guys were talking pretty quietly, but Kate saw Sierra get to her knees behind Adam and look over at her. Kate rolled her eyes, pretending everything was okay.

Just then the first band took the stage and the music poured over them, washing away Kate's discomfort from the little brawl that was simmering (because of her!) between Adam and Lucas. The twang of the banjo rang out across the stage as the singer took the mike. The vocalist was a surly-looking woman with a beer in one hand and a harmonica in the other. She belted out a few lyrics, and the crowd went wild.

Many people in the audience were dancing, and Alexis unabashedly joined in. She stood from her blanket and pulled Jake up to join her. Alexis reached her hand down to pull Sierra up, then came toward Kate. As Alexis approached, Kate could feel Lucas's arm seize her shoulder in something that resembled a vise grip.

Alexis leaned down to yell, "Come on, Kat!" Adam stood up to join them, but Kate stayed rooted to her spot on the blanket. She was being held down, and she looked at Lucas to figure out why he had such a strong hold on her. He was scowling at Alexis and the others, watching them suspiciously as they danced around like fools. Kate was fully jealous, and wanted to be with her friends, kicking back and having a good time.

"What do you say?" She put her mouth right up to Lucas's ear so he could hear her over the music. "Dance?"

"I wouldn't call it dancing," Lucas responded. "They're embarrassing themselves. You actually want to be a part of that?"

Kate frowned. "They're just having a good time. You don't even know anyone here. How is it embarrassing?"

"They look like losers. Besides, I can think of a better way to spend the night," he said coyly, pulling her legs over his and grabbing her into a tight hug. As the music played on, Kate melted into his embrace. She soon realized this was an easy choice . . . snuggle under the stars with her super-hot boyfriend who kissed like a rock star, or dance like a nut around a broken-down stage?

Out of the corner of her eye she could see Adam slapping wildly at his knee in time with the music. Sierra was doubled over with laughter, and Alexis had her head tipped back happily—but Kate was already long gone. As the music played on, she drifted further and further away from the football field and into her own private world with Lucas.

An hour or so later the first band stepped off the stage and everyone returned to the blankets to relax and cool down. Alexis was sweating, but somehow managed to make it look sexy instead of nasty. Jake pulled her, squirming, onto his lap and tipped her back for an overdramatic kiss. Kate turned away, embarrassed by their PDA and horrified that she'd been doing the same thing for the last hour.

Adam pulled out his banjo and strummed away, entertaining everyone in their near vicinity with his upbeat tune and goofy lyrics:

Well, the girl I love she's down on the dock.
I love this girl, but she don't love me back.
She treats me wrong, I love it bad, she's got
    her hold on me.
She says, Adam! You're an arrogant guy.
She says, Adam! You're a pain in the ass.
She treats me wrong, I love it bad, she's got
    her hold on me.
If she were my girl, I'd make her eggs.
If she were my girl, I'd make her smile.
But she treats me wrong, I love it bad, she's got
    her hold on me.

As Adam sang, Sierra sidled over, plunking down on the blanket with Kate and Lucas. Seconds later Alexis climbed off of Jake's lap and came over to sit with them as well. When Adam finished singing, he stood up and took a bow.

"So tell me, Lucas," Alexis said abruptly. "What do you usually do for fun?"

"For fun?"

Alexis nodded slowly, as though Lucas was stupid or something. "You know, with your friends?"

"We play a lot of hockey," Lucas said, and shrugged. "Hang out with the guys, stuff like that."

"Sounds fun." Alexis widened her eyes, clearly critical of Lucas's chosen pastimes. Kate was getting sick of Alexis's obvious disapproval of her boyfriend. She could be so snobby about this stuff sometimes.

Adam was sitting with them now too, and Lucas looked over and gestured to Adam's banjo. "You play the guitar, eh?"

"Yes, sir, I do—but this is a banjo." Adam grinned. "Are you a blues guy?"

"Not really," Lucas said. "I just came along tonight to hang out with my girl." He squeezed Kate's thigh. She tensed up. For some reason Lucas's hold on her was starting to feel sort of stifling.

But Alexis was watching Kate carefully, and Kate was sick of her friends judging her boyfriend. Why couldn't Alexis just be happy for her and not question Lucas's perfection? Kate smiled and leaned into Lucas, snuggling against his chest. She looked up at him and asked, "The show's good so far, don't you think?"

"It's okay," he muttered. "I've gotta get back pretty soon, though. The guys and I are going out early tomorrow, and I need to get some stuff ready down at the boat. Get some of the slalom skis in, grab a few wakeboards. Come with me?" This was more of a statement than a question, but Kate was game. Maybe some alone time, away from annoying Adam and judgmental Alexis, was exactly what they needed.

"Sure," she answered, nodding.

Lucas stood up quickly, clearly eager to go. "Grab the blanket, okay?" He picked up the cooler. "I'll take the heavy stuff." He winked, but Kate still bristled. Did he think she was a puppy?

Adam, Sierra, and Alexis were all watching Kate closely. She didn't usually take well to commands, and she knew they were waiting for her to say something that had a little bit of backbone. She didn't. Sierra picked at her fingernails, and Alexis offered them Jake's van keys to get back. But neither of them said anything more.

As Kate folded the blanket, Adam blurted out, "Gee, Kate, you must really be looking forward to trotting along behind him while he does his thing."

"What's that, dude?" Lucas clearly hadn't heard him, but Kate had. She silenced Adam with a look of pure evil, then grabbed Lucas's hand and walked away before her friends could do any more damage.

* * *

561

The moon was full when they returned to the resort. Kate followed Lucas down the wooded trail to the lake and his boat. She had finally shaken away the doubt that her friends had begun to plant in her mind at the blues fest, and had resolved to let Lucas take the lead. He clearly had a plan in mind, and she was a willing follower when there were kisses on the agenda.

He stepped into the boat first, then turned to help her in. The waves were echoing with *pat-pat* sounds on the edges of the dock, rocking the long fiberglass hull back and forth against the wood. Kate sat on the driver's seat while Lucas hauled skis from a storage container on the shore into the boat, then rearranged the life jackets and tow ropes in the side storage bins.

While he worked, Kate was distracted. Even though she and Lucas were finally alone in a gorgeous and romantic setting, she was having trouble concentrating on anything other than Adam. *Who does he think he is?* she wondered, wishing she could just shake his comments off. But as much as she wanted to, Kate couldn't stop caring about what Adam thought. He was like a termite, burrowing under her skin.

Finally Lucas's focus returned to Kate. He grabbed a few beach towels from the storage compartment under the front of the boat and laid them down across the open back area. She forced herself to concentrate on the scene at hand, preparing herself for what was to come.

Kate sat watching him. His arms looked extra chiseled in the shadow cast by the moonlight. "Come here." He gestured for her to join him on the floor of the boat. Then he set a firm cushion up as a backrest for her. She snuggled into the little nest he had created, silently begging him to touch her.

On cue, his right hand slipped into hers. His left reached around her, pressing against her lower back to pull her torso in toward him. She arched slightly from the motion, and her head tilted back. Expertly Lucas swept in and brushed his lips across her neck, sending a hot current rushing through her. His lips traced slowly up her neck, stopping to pull at her ear, then making their way toward her face.

When finally his mouth reached hers, she was ready. It made her insides feel just like they had during the kiss at the end of last summer and erased all thoughts of Adam from Kate's mind like a magic wand. The questions and doubts were long forgotten in the heat of the moment, and Lucas was the real-life version of her fairy tale Prince Charming once again.

Ten

In Love, Wisconsin

Sierra slid her long sarong off her legs and piled it onto the dock next to her. She sat down, and her left leg stretched across the width of the dock. She gracefully reached her toe out to touch the water. Kate, who was sitting right next to her, stretched her legs out as well and couldn't even reach the other side of the dock. Making a face, she pulled her legs up against her body and draped a towel across her knees. She leaned her head back against Alexis's lounge chair and let the sun warm her face.

"You look a little red." Kate cracked her eyes open—Sierra was leaning over her. Sierra pressed her thumb on Kate's shoulder and released it, testing for sunburn. "Yeah, you're red. Do you want me to grab the umbrella from my cabin?"

"I can get it," Kate offered. She'd been wearing SPF 30 every day since they'd arrived in Love, but still the sun had taken its toll on her bright white skin. "You're lucky you don't have to worry about sunburn, Sierra."

Sierra stood up, stretching her lean body. "Totally false," she said. "I get sunburned, but dark skin just doesn't show it as well. But I've been known to peel."

"Where is the umbrella?"

Sierra dipped her foot into the water, then said, "Um, I think it's in the living room, next to the futon." Kate set off up the hill, toward Sierra's family's cabin. When she returned a few minutes later, giant umbrella in hand, she was giggling.

"What's funny?" Sierra asked. Alexis peeked her eye open to look at Kate as well. She'd been napping most of the morning in her chair. She and Jake had been up until late the night before. In fact, Kate wasn't entirely sure Lex had ever made it to bed at all.

"I just fully walked in on your parents making out," Kate said. She was still giggling, but was also mildly horrified.

"See what I've been living with all summer? At least they're getting along, but it's disgusting! They're all over each other all the time."

"Ew," Kate said, turning up her upper lip. She inserted the

big sun umbrella into one of the holes on the dock and opened it, positioning it so she was shielded from the sun.

Alexis snorted, her eyes still closed. "Ew? You're not really one to talk, Kat."

"What?"

"You and Lucas were full-on making out in front of everyone a few nights ago at the blues fest. I thought you hated PDA."

"I do," Kate acknowledged. "I didn't realize he would want to spend the whole night making out. I figured the blues fest was a good chance for us to hang out and chill with everybody. Get to know each other, you know?"

"You know each other now," Alexis said, and chuckled. "Is he still the man of your dreams, Kitty Kat?"

"He's great."

Alexis perched herself up on her elbows, lifting her sunglasses off her eyes to look at Kate seriously. There was a heavy pause before Sierra finally said, "Really?"

"Yeah." Kate looked at them suspiciously. "Why?"

Sierra dragged her toe through the water, avoiding Kate's gaze. Alexis blurted out, "Because he doesn't necessarily seem right for you, sweetie."

The pit that had been growing in Kate's stomach dropped like a bowling ball, dragging the remains of her insides along with it. She felt like she was going to puke.

Her best friends, the people who knew her better than anyone else in the world, thought she was with the wrong guy. "Why?" she demanded.

"Kate," Sierra said soothingly, "don't take it the wrong way."

"Why can't you guys just be happy for me?" Kate said angrily. "He's totally sweet, and kissing him is the best feeling in the world. He makes me feel like a goddess, and he's excruciatingly hot. It's perfect, if you ask me." Alexis and Sierra both sat silently as Kate listed off Lucas's virtues. "And today I'm surprising him with a picnic out at the island, just the two of us."

Kate had spent all morning packing a picnic basket full of tasty treats, and as soon as Lucas came down to the dock, she was going to surprise him with a romantic outing. After their quasi-date at the blues fest a few nights before, the last few evenings had been spent around the bonfire with the whole resort crew. She and Lucas had snuck away a few times to make out, but they still hadn't really gotten any time to talk. He always found another way to spend their time together.

"So you really think he's going to give up waterskiing today to hang out with you on the island?" Alexis's doubtful tone frustrated Kate even further.

"Yeah," Kate retorted. "We talked about it last night.

We agreed to spend the afternoon together." When she saw her friends watching her with true concern on their faces, she softened a little. She realized that if she could share her doubts with anyone, it was with Lex and Sierra. "The thing is, I feel like I hardly know him still. All we ever do is hook up."

"That's all Jake and I do," Alexis said, and beamed proudly. "But that's all I want to do. Have you guys noticed how *stupid* Jake is? Geez. It's pretty much impossible to hold a full conversation with him."

Kate giggled. "Lex! That's terrible!"

"Seriously, though. He's not very bright."

"Okay, so that's what you're looking for this summer— but I want more than that."

"We know you do, Kat. That's why we're worried about what you're going to get with Lucas." Alexis perched her sunglasses up on her head, pushing her long bangs away from her face.

"All he ever does is water-ski," Sierra accurately pointed out. "He doesn't necessarily seem as interested in long afternoons talking and nights curled up together in a blanket under the stars as, say, *you* might be."

"I see where you're going with this, but you're wrong. Besides, after the blues fest we *did* sit in the boat curled up in a blanket under the stars. That counts!" Kate started to feel sort of desperate, realizing that she was trying to convince her best friends of her boyfriend's strong points— and she was having a hard time making her case. She had to admit that things weren't turning out exactly as she'd wanted them to.

Kate couldn't help but wonder if she'd had impossibly high expectations about the summer she'd been waiting for all year. "I'm not ready to call it a lost cause," she finally said. "And I need you guys to stop questioning it, okay?"

Jake waited until Kate was comfortably situated in the back of the canoe with her picnic basket at her feet, then gave the canoe a push to guide it into the lake. "Have fun!" he called, and Kate could have sworn he was laughing as she clumsily dipped her paddle into the lake.

Kate looked at the empty seat in front of her, where Lucas should have been, and sighed. Less than an hour after her conversation on the dock with Alexis and Sierra, Kate had set off in search of Lucas. Despite the fact that at the bonfire the night before, they had discussed spending the afternoon together, Lucas had apparently decided to go waterskiing at a neighboring lake instead. She found him loading his gear into his family's car around lunchtime, which meant Kate's planning and packing had been all for nothing.

She acted as though she didn't care, and told Lucas to have a good time. He kissed her quickly as he hopped into the car. As soon as he pulled away, Kate decided to head out to the island for a picnic anyway, refusing to let a guy spoil her plans. It would be good for her to get some time to sit and think about things on her own, and she didn't want to spend the afternoon with her friends looking at her with I-told-you-so looks on their faces. Dipping her paddle into the water again, she felt the canoe tilt dangerously low to one side, and she cursed under her breath.

After spending this many years at a lakeside resort, Kate should have been far more adept at paddling a canoe by herself. But when she tipped the wooden paddle into the water, she realized that she'd always sat in the front of the canoe and let someone else steer. Adam had been that guy when they were kids, and Kate hadn't done a lot of canoeing since.

She dug her paddle through the calm lake water and attempted a C-stroke to steer the boat toward her favorite island. It was only a few hundred feet offshore, but it looked a million miles away as Kate struggled to turn her boat in the right direction while moving forward at the same time.

The canoe spun in several circles before beginning to make progress away from shore and toward the island. Kate thrust her hand into the picnic basket at her feet and grabbed a handful of M&M's for sustenance. She needed the chocolate as fuel to make it the rest of the way to her destination. She was sufficiently embarrassed, as well, and was mildly relieved Lucas was out with the guys, since she knew she didn't look like the vixenlike water goddess she longed to be. She looked slightly more like a water bug, spiraling and spinning in frantic circles in the lake in her canoe.

After a few more large circles Kate finally straightened the boat out and paddled the rest of the way to the island with no further snafus. She was beaming with pride and self-confidence as she eased the front of the canoe up onto the little sandy shoreline and stepped out into the shallow water. After hauling her picnic basket up onshore, she grabbed the tip of the canoe and pulled the boat up onto dry land.

Not exactly the romantic picnic I had planned, she mused, pulling a woven blanket out of her basket. *Screw him,* she thought, suddenly angry at Lucas for dismissing their date and even angrier at herself for letting herself get so upset about it. She wasn't comfortable enough with Lucas yet to tell him how pissed she was, which frustrated her even further.

Kate shook the blanket and spread it on the ground under a tall pine tree. Needles had fallen off the tree and created a soft blanket on the ground. She lay down with the picnic basket at her side and closed her eyes, relaxing in the warm afternoon. She tucked her shirt into the underside of her bra, which allowed the warm breeze to float over her bare stomach.

"You look comfy."

Kate shot up, alarmed at the voice. She had been certain she was alone. There was no other boat onshore, and few people knew the island was a great place for a picnic. She had always believed this place was sort of her little secret. "You didn't look quite that relaxed in the canoe on your way over here."

"Adam," Kate groaned, yanking her shirt out of her bra and pulling it back down over her belly. She recognized the mocking, sarcastic voice even before he came into view from behind some bushes. "Just my luck."

"Hey, now." Adam looked hurt. "I'm just teasing."

Kate closed her eyes again and lay back on the blanket. "I know. It's been a crap day," she muttered. "I'm not really in the mood."

"There's always room for teasing, even in a bad day," Adam said, and grinned. "Right?"

"Your annoying comments? Not so appreciated today, okay?"

Adam sat, uninvited, and dipped his hand into Kate's

picnic basket. He pulled out the loaf of bread she had packed, ripped a chunk off the end, and stuffed it into his mouth. "Mmm."

"You're a pig," Kate declared. "This . . ." She sat up and gestured toward her basket. "Not your picnic." She realized she was being especially abrasive, but after being ditched by one guy that day, she wasn't in the mood to deal with another. And a part of her still saw this as Lucas's picnic. Watching Adam eat it was making things worse.

"Come on, Kate." Adam looked at her seriously. "Don't take it out on me. I don't know what happened, but I seriously doubt it's my fault."

"Fine. Eat whatever you want. No one else is going to." Kate's mood was quickly souring. She had gotten up that morning planning to spend the afternoon alone with Lucas, and now she was stuck alone on an island with Adam. *Great.*

Adam munched on his bread. "Do you want to talk about it?" He asked so simply, so genuinely, that she was tempted. It really seemed like he cared, but she knew he had an agenda. He was so bent on criticizing both her and Lucas, and she knew he was just fishing for something else to be rude about.

"Not really," she finally muttered. She knew Adam

would be full of arrogant I-told-you-so's if she 'fessed up to what was going on.

"Okay." Adam started to stand up.

Without thinking, Kate grabbed his arm. "Stay," she insisted. She didn't know why she wanted him there, but she suddenly didn't want to be alone.

"I was just going to grab my banjo. It's in my kayak on the other side of the island." Adam smiled. "I thought you might like some music."

She nodded. When he returned a few minutes later, she had scooted over on the blanket to give him room. Though she was lying down with her eyes closed, she could feel him watching her. "What?" she demanded.

When he didn't respond, she cracked her eyes open and peeked at him. The look on his face was strange, an expression she hadn't ever seen on him. He was squinting in the filtered sunlight, but his eyes were firmly locked on her face. When she realized she was looking back at him, he blinked and coughed a little.

"Do you want some chocolate?" Kate offered, just to say something. Before he could reply, Kate blurted out, "Can I be honest about something?"

"In my experience you've been honest about everything," Adam said.

"That's just me."

"I know."

Kate relaxed into their easy banter. "I've never been good with the filter."

"Really?"

Kate sat up and narrowed her eyes playfully. "Are you being sarcastic with me?"

"Who, me? Sarcastic?" Adam grinned and pulled his knees up against his chest.

"I just don't like wasting time figuring out what people are really thinking. It seems to make more sense to just say what you have on your mind and move on." Kate picked at a piece of fuzz that was sticking out of the blanket beneath her leg. "If people are honest about what they're thinking and feeling and whatever, everyone knows where everyone stands. You avoid that whole level of confusion that's introduced into situations when people say things they don't really mean and then get upset when things don't work out the way they're supposed to."

Kate stopped rambling and pulled at the fuzz. It had pulled loose from the blanket and she twisted it around her finger like a tiny sleeping bag. Adam watched her fingers do their work and said, "So you're trying to tell me you're always honest and straightforward?"

"You don't think that's true?" Kate could sense Adam's disagreement in the tone he was using.

"No, I don't."

"Why's that?" Kate flicked the fuzz off her finger and watched it drift down to the ground and settle onto the pine needles.

"I don't think you're being totally honest when you're with Lucas."

"Whatever." Kate shook her head. Leave it to Adam to bring Lucas into this.

"I mean it, Kate. I was with you day and night all the way across the country, and I watched how you act around your friends and I've seen the real you."

"Oh, so you know me better than anyone, do you?" Kate rolled her eyes. Adam felt it was appropriate to analyze her now? As if.

"I just don't think you act like you when Lucas is around. You're sort of . . ." Adam paused for a second, apparently searching for the right word. "Blah."

"Blah? You're an asshole." He hadn't searched for the right word *quite* long enough.

"Not blah! Not blah," Adam said, and laughed. "That came out wrong. It's just that you don't seem like *you* when he's around. You're less feisty or something."

Kate sort of got what he was saying, and realized he wasn't trying to be entirely rude. So she decided to let it go. "Why do you dislike Lucas so much?" Kate asked this without really expecting an answer. But she couldn't stop herself from asking.

Adam paused, and his face turned toward hers in the pinkish afternoon light. For a moment he said nothing. When he did finally speak, his voice was quiet and deliberate, as though he'd taken the time to think it through for once. "Because he got the girl I'm falling in love with—and he's not treating her the way I would."

Kate's breath caught in her throat. She sat quietly, absorbing what he'd just told her. Adam must have taken her silence and stillness as the right sign, because he leaned toward her on the blanket and reached his hand out to touch her face. Just as his fingers brushed her jawline, Kate jumped up off the blanket and ran toward her canoe.

"Kate!" he called. "I'm sorry. I . . ."

Kate's legs were propelling her forward, even as her heart begged her to go back to him. *This is crazy,* she thought, and jumped into the canoe. She pushed her boat back from shore, and tears immediately sprung to her eyes. She could feel them rolling down her face the whole time she paddled back toward the resort.

As she approached shore, she could see Lucas standing at the end of the dock, ready to catch her canoe. Her emotions were already in a tailspin, and now she was spinning out of control . . . because half of her wanted to throw herself into Lucas's arms, but the other half wanted to paddle back to the island and find out what would have happened if she had stayed with Adam.

But now it was too late for that, and she couldn't stop the tears from falling.

Eleven

In Love, Wisconsin

For a few days after the island incident Kate mostly just holed away.

There was a permanent dent in their cabin's futon that resembled a less shapely version of her butt. She blew through three novels, and her sunburn had totally faded by the time she emerged from her hiding spot.

Of course, she hadn't been inside the *whole* time. She had spent plenty of time with Alexis and Sierra—who still had no idea what had gone down between her and Adam on the island—and every night at the group bonfire, Lucas was by her side. But ultimately Kate's main goal was to avoid Adam. She didn't have anything to say to him, and didn't know how to look at him after what had happened.

More than anything, she couldn't explain her tears and had a hard time understanding why his eyes—the way they had locked on hers that day—were the first thing she saw when she closed her own.

The one time she had bumped into Adam around the resort, he had just acted like a slightly more distant version of himself. He didn't mention their day on the island, and it seemed like he was making a point of not coming to the bonfire in the evenings.

"Are you going to get your lazy butt off that futon and go outside today?" Gina asked, barreling into the cabin and fiddling with the tie on her halter top bikini. "Can you get this?" She nimbly sat down on the floor in front of the futon and thrust the ties of her swimsuit at Kate. "Hello?" She whipped her head around with an entitled look on her face, staring openmouthed at her sister. "What's wrong with you, anyway?"

"Nice, G," Kate said. "Your caring is so apparent." She tied her sister's bikini, then flopped back onto the futon.

Gina hopped up to sit next to her. "Seriously, Kate. You're a total bummer." She pouted dramatically. "Everything okay?"

"I'm fine," Kate said, convincing neither herself nor Gina.

"Is it Lucas?" Gina's eyes grew wide, preparing for the scandal.

"No."

Gina tilted her head, unconvinced. "It is."

"Seriously, Gina. It's not Lucas."

"Did you know Zack told Sasha he thinks I'm hot?" Gina giggled. "How cute would that be?"

"Lucas's brother?"

"Mm-hmm. We would be dating brothers!"

Kate scowled. "That's disgusting. Besides, G, all Zack does is water-ski all day. How does he have time for a girlfriend? Have you ever even spoken?"

"Oh, my God. Like you can talk! Lucas is, like, the leader of the ski crew. If it weren't for him, there's no way Zack would be out on the boat all day. Lucas is the one that's obsessed."

"And that's the problem," Kate muttered. Luckily, Gina was distracted by a bag of Doritos on the counter, and in her haste to open them and declare their deliciousness, she hadn't heard Kate's comment.

"The guys just got back from skiing," Gina announced, heading toward the door again. "Come down to the lake?"

"Fine." Kate shoved her book under the futon and changed into her suit. She grabbed a granola bar for the walk down the path, realizing she hadn't really eaten all day. *Nice,* she thought bitterly. *I'm totally losing it. What kind of idiot forgets to eat?*

Down at the dock she was relieved to see that Adam wasn't there. Kate's parents and their friends were loading into the pontoon boat for a cruise out on the lake. They went out most afternoons, spending the latter half of the day discussing thrilling research articles each had read, while drinking wine from a box. Kate waved at them, flashing a thumbs-up when her mom yelled out a reminder to put on sunscreen.

Kate hastily hid her granola bar in her towel after her mom turned to Gina with the comment that she shouldn't be snacking before eating lunch. (Gina had the whole family-size bag of Doritos on the beach with her.) Kate recognized that Gina's skating encouraged her to maintain a certain figure, but she felt angry realizing that her sister was going to have major food issues because of her mom's vigilant caloric observations. Luckily, Gina didn't seem bothered by their mom's nagging. She waved to acknowledge the comment but flashed her mom the middle finger from behind her bag of chips and then grabbed another handful.

At the boat dock Lucas and the ski crew were lounging around in the boat drinking sodas. A quick glance at the dock told Kate that neither Lex nor Sierra were around, so she sauntered over to the guys. Lucas came over to say hi, slipping his hand under her shirt to feel her exposed back.

Kate shivered and backed away, embarrassed to have him touching her like that in front of everyone down at the lake.

"Hey," he said, pulling her close again. "Come here."

She gestured to the pontoon boat, which was still only a few hundred yards away, and said, "My parents . . ."

"Oh," he said, pulling back. "Right." He looked back at the other guys on the boat, and chuckled when one of them made a rude gesture in their direction. Abruptly Lucas turned to Kate again and said, "What are you doing tonight?"

"Um, nothing much."

"Let's go out, eh?"

Kate's face instantly broke into a huge smile. "Yeah, that'd be fun."

"We can grab some pizza in town."

"Sure." Greasy pizza at Romano's wasn't exactly the most romantic date ever, but it would be her and Lucas, alone . . . on a real date!

"We should be back in by about five. Wanna meet me by the barbecue pit around five thirty?"

"Yes," Kate said happily. This was major progress. Okay, so it shouldn't be such a major event having her boyfriend ask her out on a real date, but considering the circumstances . . . it was. Baby steps. And this was just what she needed to forget Adam and reconnect with the guy who really mattered.

Zack turned the key in the boat's ignition, gunning the motor to send up a roar of engine noise. It was Lucas's signal that the guys were all ready to go back out on the water, so Kate sent him on his way, planning their evening in her mind.

The lip gloss Alexis had forced on Kate was called Cherry Bliss, but Kate was anything but blissful. She was nervously licking her lips every ten seconds, and had licked off and reapplied the gloss so many times that she was starting to feel a little ill. Sierra and Alexis had helped Kate put together a perfect date uniform, complete with some sort of bronzing powder between her boobs that Alexis had dabbed on against Kate's will.

Kate was waiting on the steps of her cabin's small front porch, trying to look casual and demure. But instead she could feel the heat of the late afternoon sun baking into her skin and was paranoid the bronzing goop would be carried down her chest in a river of sweat. She pulled at her tight black tank top and tipped her face forward to blow into the dark cave of her shirt. Just as she was feeling cooler and more confident, she looked up and saw Adam standing a few feet away. She released the top of her shirt, embarrassed.

"Anything good in there?" he asked, nodding toward her chest.

She ignored his question and the amped-up fluttering of her heart in her chest. "I'm waiting for Lucas," she declared.

"Hot date?"

"Actually, yes."

"Nice." Adam nodded, then paused. "You look pretty."

"Adam . . . ," she warned. This wasn't the time to do this. "I can't . . ."

"Don't freak out," Adam said quietly. "I'm not trying to make you uncomfortable. You look beautiful, and I just thought you might like to know that."

"I don't," Kate said, tears welling up deep inside. They were too far from the surface to make an appearance, but she could feel them bubbling up. Any more comments like that and she'd be in trouble. Besides, the combination of dormant tears, Cherry Bliss, and nerves was making her insides queasy. "Please don't say things like that to me."

Adam looked at her seriously, then said, "Okay. I get it. Honesty only sometimes, right?"

At that moment Lucas came sauntering up. In his green polo, jeans, and sun-bleached hair, he looked like a male model. His hair was still wet from the lake, and she could see comb marks running through it. "Hey, bro," he said to Adam, glancing from Kate to Adam and back again. "What's going on?"

"I'm ready," Kate declared. "Let's go."

Lucas draped his arm around her. "See ya, Adam." He tugged at Kate's shoulder, steering her in the direction of the parking lot. They walked silently, and the gravel crunched beneath their feet as they trudged along. Kate was still trying to shake the feeling that had rocked her when Adam had appeared a few minutes ago. She was finding it more difficult than she would have hoped.

During the short drive into town Kate remained distracted, and she was much more nervous than she had thought she'd be. Lucas spent the whole drive telling her about that afternoon's wakeboarding showdown. "Zack and I totally creamed the other guys!" he declared proudly, thumping the steering wheel.

Kate tried hard to muster up the right level of enthusiasm. "Wow," she replied. "That's really exciting." He rubbed her knee absentmindedly. Kate hated the fact that it just felt sort of irritating.

When they got to the pizza place, Kate followed Lucas inside. She was still looking forward to their date, but was also starting to realize that maybe they would never have anything to talk about. At least he was making an effort. A date was a date, and it was exactly what she'd been craving. "Should we sit up here by the window?" she suggested.

"Nah," he said, shaking his head. "Not big enough."

She furrowed her eyebrows. "They're booths." The two booths in the front window could easily hold four people and several pizzas. How much was he planning to order?

"We need a table for eight," Lucas informed the waitress. Then he turned back to Kate. "The guys should be here in a few minutes. Turbo is slow getting ready. He's like a chick."

"Turbo? The guys?" Kate's face fell.

Lucas nodded, as though it was obvious. "Zack, Turbo, Johnson . . . the ski crew."

"Uh-huh." Kate could feel the frustration fermenting inside her, morphing into something horrible. *Chill,* she cautioned herself. *He never said it was a date. You just misinterpreted.*

She ordered a soda and waited patiently. Sarcasm dripped from her voice when she said, "I'm really looking forward to tonight."

Lucas put his hand over hers. "Me too." He didn't seem to get it.

When the guys got there, Kate felt even more like an afterthought—some sort of fifth wheel, unable and unwilling to discuss the merits of that afternoon's wakeboarding adventure.

She was a spectator on her own date.

When finally the last of the pizza had been consumed—capped off with a prize-winning burp, courtesy of Harris Johnson—everyone decided to head back to the resort for the bonfire. Kate hadn't weighed in on this decision, but she was pretty willing to do just about anything that would get her out of this one-on-seven date.

As an extra treat—something to make her date with Lucas even more memorable—they took Turbo and Nick in their car on the way back to the resort. Turbo spent the drive mooning people out of the backseat passenger window. *Nothing says romance like a fat, naked ass*, Kate mused.

Apparently Kate was living in a choose-your-own-adventure fairy tale, only someone else was making all the choices for her, throwing her into the parts of the story that should have been edited out. As Lucas pulled the car into the lot at the resort, Kate resolved that she would stop letting her heart be thrown around like this. Enough was enough, and Kate was tired of pretending this was paradise.

When they got out of the car, the bonfire was already in full swing. Sierra and Sasha were sitting on a log bench with Gina, roasting marshmallows for s'mores. Alexis and Jake were sitting with some of the kids who worked at the resort, singing along as Adam played his banjo.

It was the first night since their afternoon at the island that Adam had come to the bonfire. Kate suspected he had come out that night because he'd assumed she would be out on her date with Lucas.

Looking at him, strumming his banjo and cracking everyone up, Kate was struck with a sudden sense of longing. She longed to know what might have happened had she stayed that day on the island. And she longed for the "debates"—okay, arguments—they'd had on their road trip. More than anything, she missed their friendship.

He drove her crazy . . . in a good way, it seemed.

"Hey, Kat!" Alexis spotted Kate first, beckoning her toward her spot near the fire. "Back from your date already?" she asked, quietly enough so she wasn't screaming it out to everyone, but still loud enough for the people nearest them to hear. Adam was watching closely, so Kate squatted down right next to Alexis, out of his line of sight.

"Not a date, as it turns out," she whispered.

Alexis whipped around to face her completely and blurted out, "Shut up."

"I'm serious," Kate whispered again. "Pizza with the guys."

"Oh, Kat . . . Are you pissed?"

"Not thrilled," Kate admitted. "But I guess I'm not surprised."

Sierra sauntered over, a s'more in hand. "Dessert?"

Kate nodded happily, grabbing the gooey treat from her friend. The marshmallow stuck to Kate's lips. Kate leaned up against the log Alexis was sitting on and listened to Adam play for everyone. Sierra settled in next to her, resting her head on Kate's shoulder.

While Adam sang, Kate's mind wandered. But no matter how far it wandered, she kept coming back to one thing—the memory of Adam's face looking down at hers that day on the island. His voice floated over her now, singing Cat Stevens (or Yusuf Islam or whatever his name was), and when she glanced up, he was looking at her with the same expression again. But this time she didn't run. She looked back at him, watching the firelight cast shadows across his arms, making him look almost mystical in the smoke-filled sky.

Then the wind shifted, blowing a line of smoke straight at Adam, forcing him to break their gaze and sending him into a hacking coughing fit.

Kate averted her eyes, then felt a pair of arms wrap around her from behind. Lucas was lifting her off the ground, fixing Adam with the same look he had earlier that night, before they'd left for their "date." Lucas pulled her around to face him, and tipped her chin up toward him for a kiss.

It was the exact same marshmallow kiss they had shared at the end of last summer, but this time when Kate closed her eyes, all she could see was Adam's face looking back at her.

Kate pulled back and pushed her arms against Lucas's chest to stop the kiss. When she turned, looking for Adam again, he was gone. Lucas was staring at her, clearly awaiting an explanation.

As Kate looked at him, then back at the spot where Adam had been sitting with his banjo just moments before, Kate wondered if it was too late to back up and get on a different path in her choose-your-own-adventure fairy tale. This one was all wrong.

Twelve

In Love, Wisconsin?

As often happened with true romantics, Kate's late-night confusion did not transform into daytime clarity.

She woke up superlate the next morning feeling absolutely awful. Her head ached, and her stomach felt ill. Whether it was from the mushrooms on the pizza or her emotional upheaval, she wasn't sure. But one thing was certain: She'd visualized her summer so clearly in her head, and nothing was going according to plan.

By afternoon she'd made herself insane thinking through her situation. It didn't help that it was a gloomy day and she was stuck inside. Of course, she'd heard the waterskiing boat motoring off early that morning. Only thunderstorms kept them off the lake, it seemed. Luckily, Gina had decided to join the guys in the boat that day, so she wasn't around to harass her sister.

The longer Kate sat staring at her open book, the more she realized she had completely lost perspective, and needed her friends to help sort things out. She threw her jeans on in place of her sweats, just in case, and rifled through the cupboards for a package of Oreos to bring along to Alexis's cabin.

Kate was fully aware that going to Alexis for romantic advice was about as reliable as picking the name of your future husband out of a hat—but at least Alexis was always honest, and introduced a little humor into situations. Sierra was as levelheaded and practical as anyone, so she'd surely have some solid suggestions.

Just as she was texting Sierra to ask that she meet up at Alexis's cabin, the door to Kate's cabin burst open and her two best friends came crashing in.

"Dish," Alexis declared bluntly, fixing Kate with a stern gaze.

Sierra threw a bag of Swedish Fish onto the futon and settled in next to it. "*Why* is Little Miss Romantic glooming and dooming in her cabin all by herself?"

"Hi, guys," Kate laughed. "I was just coming to find you."

"I'm sure," Alexis responded sarcastically. "You've been

holed up in this cabin all day. Annnnd, you were acting really weird last night at the bonfire."

Sierra nodded. "You took off without even saying good night. Not to mention the fact that the stars hadn't come out before you left. Our Kate never finishes her night before she can wish upon a star, right?"

"I'm not Pinocchio!"

"No, you're Snow White—waiting for your prince to come and sweep you away." Alexis snorted. "In the meantime, you're stuck with Grumpy and Dopey."

"As if that's going to happen," Kate muttered, grabbing an Oreo out of the bag. "You guys, I don't know what to do about Lucas."

"You mean, you don't know how to dump him?" Alexis grinned, bursting with pride.

"Hang on," Sierra cut in. "Which of us is Dopey? The other option is Grumpy?"

"They're the only two dwarves I can remember." Alexis shrugged.

Kate flopped back against the futon. "This is so not the point."

"You're right." Alexis settled into a cross-legged position on the floor and rested her chin in her hands. "We need to get back to the matter of you dumping your so-called prince."

Kate sighed dramatically. "Is that really what I'm supposed to do?" Hearing Alexis say it so certainly was depressing. Kate really did want to make things work with Lucas—she'd spent a whole year planning it out. "Why isn't it working?" she whined.

"He's kind of an ass," Sierra stated plainly. "To put it bluntly."

"You don't have anything to talk to him about," Alexis continued.

Sierra chimed in, "He brought friends on his date with you last night."

"And I saw Turbo's naked tushie," Kate said, and giggled. "Such a romantic way to end our date."

"You didn't tell us that!" Sierra covered her mouth with her hand. "Gross!"

"Listen, Kat," Alexis said, and fixed Kate with a firm gaze. "In all seriousness, if you're looking for romance and a Mr. Right that's going to treat you like Cinderella at the ball, you're looking down the wrong rabbit hole, so to speak."

"Enough with the Disney metaphors!" Kate cried out. "It's painful."

Alexis shrugged. "It's funny. But truly, Kat, I think we have a pretty good idea of what you're looking for, and you're just going to be disappointed if you keep trying to find it with Lucas. He just is not an even match for you. He treats you like you're fragile, a baby or something, when really you're the one who has to tiptoe softly around *him*. You can't be yourself with him."

Kate looked at her best friends. Sierra nodded. Alexis was right. Her analysis was spot-on, and she hadn't even made any sarcastic comments while delivering her message. "Unless"—Alexis's eyes gleamed—"you're just looking for a guy to hook up with, in which case Lucas is your perfect choice."

"No, Lex, that's you." Kate giggled, grabbed a couple of Swedish Fish, and then got serious again. "I need more than that. I want a future. I *do* want a prince."

"You're not animated, so a real prince is unlikely." Sierra grabbed an Oreo. "But you can find someone who wants a relationship, not just a set of lips."

"I need the emotional connection," Kate confessed. "I want a boyfriend who I also respect as a friend. One who is willing to give up waterskiing for, like, ten minutes to hang out doing something fun together." She looked down, studying a pinkish stain on the futon cover. It was shaped like a heart. Kate covered it with a Swedish Fish so she couldn't see it anymore. Adam's face suddenly flashed through her mind, and Kate was struck with the same sickly feeling she'd been suffering from all morning.

When Kate looked up again, she could tell that Alexis and Sierra had been watching her. "You'll find him," Sierra said quietly.

"I know," Kate agreed. Then she stopped. She wasn't ready to tell her friends what she was feeling about Adam, because she still didn't know what it all meant. And before she could think about a silly and unlikely crush on a guy she'd disliked for years, she had to deal with the relationship she was already in.

"So . . . what? No more hooking up?" Lucas looked at Kate blankly.

That night at the bonfire was the first time Kate had seen Lucas all day. She had finally managed to pull him away from a burping contest with Turbo and Harris to talk to him about what she was feeling. Kate had carefully thought through the way she was going to word her breakup speech, but he'd cut her off right after she'd said, "I don't know if we're looking for the same thing with this relationship."

"Um." Kate was taken aback by Lucas's question. "Yeah, I guess no more hooking up."

"Too bad. You're still really hot." Lucas pushed Kate's hair behind her ear and looked at her with the same expression he had so many times before. For some reason the look had a lot less of an impact on her after those words.

Kate pushed his hand away from her head. She started to say something snippy, then realized that Lucas did have kind intentions. It was just that Kate had envisioned a very different summer romance than he had. That wasn't his fault. "It is too bad," she said finally. Then she leaned in and gave him one last hug. She breathed in the smell of sunscreen and lake water, letting the familiar scent take her back to that first kiss one last time.

As she stepped away, she noticed Adam near the bonfire with his banjo, but when he spotted Lucas and Kate together, he turned and walked back toward his cabin. Kate was relieved, since she didn't think she could handle anything more that day. Her emotions were in a rapid tailspin, and she had to get her head in order before she could let her heart lead her anywhere. And Adam seemed to have an ability to meddle with her emotions more than Kate was usually willing to allow.

Late that night, long after the last embers of the bonfire had died down and most people were in bed, Kate was startled awake. Gina was standing over her with her hands on her hips, her hair a tangled mess. "*Lucas* is at the window," she hissed.

"What?" Kate muttered groggily. "What window?"

"The window in *my* bedroom," Gina whispered. "He said he's looking for you."

Kate stumbled out of bed, quietly padding behind her sister toward the small second bedroom in their cabin. There was a tiny trail that ran behind their cabin, but no one ever used it. Frankly, it was sort of a creepy little path, and the fact that someone *had* used it made it even creepier. The lights were all off inside their cabin, so when Kate and Gina plodded into the bedroom, they could see Lucas illuminated outside by the silvery moonlight.

The window was open. Kate sat on the twin bed and said, "What do you want, Lucas?"

"Want to come out with me?" he said, with no further explanation.

"To do what?" she asked. Gina cleared her throat, suggesting that she knew full well what Lucas was looking for.

"I just thought maybe we could go down to the lake. . . . It's beautiful tonight." Kate wasn't stupid. She knew he just wanted to hook up. But it was sort of a romantic gesture—or would have been, if they'd still been together.

"Lucas, I can't," she whispered. "You need to go before you wake up my parents."

"Please?" he begged. The desperation in his voice made

her feel sorry for him . . . and more confident about her decision that he definitely wasn't the right guy.

"It's just not going to happen," she said bluntly. "I'm looking for a relationship, not a booty call."

Lucas shrugged, then turned to Gina, who was still lurking in the background, observing their conversation. "Do *you* want to come out and see the stars with me?" he offered hopefully.

"Ew!" Gina cried, covering her mouth as Kate slid the window closed and lowered the blinds.

The two sisters giggled hysterically on Gina's bed until their mom appeared in the doorway, demanding to know what they were doing up at that hour. Kate finally fell asleep in her sister's bed just before dawn, slipping into a dream where she was Cinderella at the ball. She woke up just as the glass slipper fell off her foot.

Thirteen

Love, Wisconsin

"Your parents are cute, Sierra." Kate squinted at the shoreline from her seat on the dock, watching Sierra's parents stroll along the beachfront holding hands. Sierra's mom ran playfully into the lake and splashed her husband with the cool water.

"I guess," Sierra said wistfully. "This is better than the fighting, right?"

"Of course it's better than the fighting. It seems like these few weeks at the lake have really helped them out."

"They've been going on so-called dates pretty much every night," Sierra said, rolling her eyes. "My dad keeps packing picnics to take on a hike, or taking my mom to the quarry to eat peanut butter sandwiches, or they go for milk shakes in town. It's like they're thirteen."

"I think it's great," Kate declared. "We can only hope we'll get that kind of romance with someone someday."

"Maybe *you* wish for that," Alexis said sourly. "I'd be horrified if someone tried to take me to the freaking quarry for peanut butter sandwiches. It'll take sushi in Tribeca—at a minimum—to win me over."

"Isn't it about the company?" Kate asked, leaning back in her beach chair. "Who cares where you are or what you're doing, as long as you're together?"

"Blah, blah, blah," Alexis said. "If it doesn't matter where you are or what you're doing, then why wasn't the waterskiing boat enough for you, dear Kat?"

"Come on, Lex." Kate smiled. "You know what I'm saying."

"I do, I do." Alexis lifted her sunglasses slightly so her eyes were peeking out from under the bottom of the lenses. "Speaking of waterskiing . . ."

Kate looked up. Lucas and Zack were ambling toward the boat dock, carrying their life jackets under their arms. It was already almost noon, so they were getting a late start. Lucas looked over at Kate and her friends but said nothing.

"What's that all about?" Alexis muttered.

"I hope he's a little embarrassed about last night," Kate

said. She had told Alexis and Sierra about Lucas's attempted late-night booty call. "I feel bad about the breakup," she said, subtly watching Lucas load up the boat. "I really think I caught him off guard. I hope he's not too upset."

As soon as she'd said it, Kate wanted to reel her words back into her mouth and swallow them down again. Because Harris and Turbo had just walked onto the dock with a gorgeous brunette in a teal bikini— and Bikini Girl immediately wrapped her arms around Lucas's neck as though she'd been practicing for weeks.

"Didn't take him too long to move on, eh?" Alexis was clearly trying not to laugh.

"I guess not," Kate muttered. She was torn between wanting to laugh and wanting to cry. She'd spent so much energy over the past year planning out her romance with Lucas. She couldn't believe it could all shift, just like that. Of course, Kate had deliberately given up her spot inside those arms, but she hadn't thought Lucas would recover so quickly. He had moved on—without even a glance back.

The funny thing was, Kate felt completely disconnected from Lucas as well. It was clear, watching him with this gorgeous new girl, that she and Lucas were never meant to be together . . . not in the way she would have wanted them to be. Despite that realization, Kate still felt heartbroken somehow. Bizarrely, she was able to watch Lucas caress this girl's hair and nuzzle her cheek without even an ounce of jealousy. She just didn't care.

But Kate still felt hollow inside. There was something tossing around inside her stomach, and she couldn't make it stop.

"Kate, are you okay?" Sierra leaned over Kate, blocking the sun and getting right in her friend's face. "You're all white."

Kate nodded wordlessly.

"Do you want to go up to your cabin? Maybe we should get some lunch?" Sierra looked over at Alexis, the concern evident on her face. "Kate, seriously, you're freaking me out."

Alexis stood up, holding her towel out like a cape at her sides, blocking Kate's view of the boat dock. She was clearly trying to keep Lucas and his new girl out of Kate's line of sight. "I'm thirsty. . . . Let's go," she said, stretching her towel out farther.

"You don't have to block my view," Kate said quietly. "I don't care about Lucas and that girl."

"Why the hell are you acting like such a psycho, then?" Alexis whispered. "It's as though you just took a bite of the evil queen's poisonous apple and you're falling under her spell."

"No more Disney!" she cried, remembering her dream

from the night before. "It's not Lucas," she repeated, watching carefully as Lucas got into the waterskiing boat and motored off with Bikini Girl and his ski crew.

Sierra and Alexis exchanged a look again. Sierra eventually said, "Do you feel like your romantic issues are still a little . . . unresolved?"

Kate blinked, caught off guard. "What do you mean?"

"Maybe it's time to figure out what's going on with Adam?" Sierra said this simply, without a hint of pressure.

"Adam?" Neither Alexis nor Sierra had mentioned Adam in that way since they'd first arrived in Love. . . . Had she been that transparent?

"Girl, my cousin has been waiting for you to get rid of lame Lucas the whole time we've been at the lake," Alexis said, and ran her hand through her hair, twisting the bottom into a spiral. "You *have* noticed, right?"

Kate was suddenly covered in goose bumps, despite the heat of the sun beating down on her. "But the idea of me and Adam . . . It's nuts, isn't it?"

"It's perfect." Sierra smiled, nodding.

"You guys are hilarious together," Alexis seconded. "Not to mention the fact that he clearly worships the ground you walk on. Without being a total doormat."

"But he drives me crazy!" Kate declared. "And all we do is fight."

"It's romantic banter," Sierra said, and giggled. "You love it."

Kate flopped back onto her lounge chair. "But I've totally blown it with him!"

"I don't think so," Alexis disagreed.

"I have. . . . You guys, he told me he was interested in me, and I ran."

Sierra frowned. "You ran?"

"Literally ran," Kate said. "We were out on the island, and he said he was falling in love with me, and I turned and ran like hell. I got out of there as fast as I could. It freaked me out, because I was pretty sure I was starting to feel something for him, too."

"Oh, Kate." Sierra sighed. Alexis was laughing, but covered her mouth as she always did when she laughed at inappropriate moments. "Have you said anything to him since?"

"Not really. He saw me before my pizza date with Lucas a few nights ago and told me I looked cute, but I told him not to say things like that to me."

"Oh, Kate." Sierra sighed again.

"Stop sighing!" Alexis demanded. "It's depressing. Kate, it's not a big deal. . . . If you and Adam had had a foundation built on politeness and appropriate responses, these little things would matter. But you've been completely honest with each other about everything, so it's not like he's expecting you to treat him like a porcelain doll emotionally."

"So what am I supposed to do?"

"Go get your guy!" Sierra declared. "Tell him you screwed up."

Alexis looked a little misty-eyed. "Do you really think you might want to get with my cousin? There's something sort of sick and sweet about that, all at the same time."

"I don't know what's going to happen . . . but I know I need to talk to him to figure out if we're supposed to be together. When I see him, I'm pretty sure I'll just know."

"So stop sitting here and go find him," Alexis instructed. "You're a mess, and you're not going to feel any better until you get your issues with Adam sorted out."

"Do you want us to come?" Sierra offered.

"Would you?" Kate looked at both Sierra and Alexis, hopeful. It wasn't that she was afraid to talk to Adam on her own, but it was really awkward to have to go to his cabin, and potentially run into his parents, and then what if he had changed his mind and she had to walk back to her cabin all dejected and alone and . . . "Yes, please come with me. I need you."

"Well, let's go, then. We need to make this shit happen." Alexis snapped her towel at Kate and strode down the dock.

Kate jumped up and followed. She finally felt like she was back on the right path.

"Serious warning," Alexis said as they hiked up the rocky, slanted trail that led to Adam's cabin. "My aunt is chatty."

"Lex, I know your aunt," Kate responded. After all, they'd been coming to the lake with Adam and his family for years. She'd been around Adam's mom—Alexis's aunt— a million times at barbecues and down on the dock.

"You know my aunt publicly, where she understands the rules of social conversation." Alexis nodded. "On her own turf, she's something else."

When they got to Adam's cabin, Kate immediately understood what Alexis had been warning them about. Michelle, Adam's mom, welcomed the girls in with a wave of her arm and a mouth that was moving a mile a minute. She told them to "sit, sit, sit" at the table in their little kitchenette, and almost immediately had a cup of Kool-Aid poured for each of them.

Kate quickly surveyed the cabin, and surmised that neither Adam nor his brothers were there at the moment. It pained her to have to sit there and make idle chitchat with

Adam's mom when all she wanted to do was find her guy and figure out where things stood, but she bit her lip and smiled while Michelle gave them her point of view on national politics. It was completely random, and Kate wanted to scream while sitting there patiently.

Eventually Alexis managed to squeeze a word in. "Aunt Michelle, you don't know where we can find Adam, do you?" Kate shot her a grateful look.

"Oh, of course you're looking for Adam, girls." She winked at Sierra. "But you knew he went home this morning, didn't you?"

Kate's stomach dropped straight down onto the ground beneath her feet. It felt like there was just a giant rotting hole where her insides used to be, and what was once her stomach was now just a pile on the floor of the cabin. "Home?" she squeaked out.

"Well, yes." Adam's mom nodded. "Adam's dad dropped him off at the bus station in town this morning. Apparently Adam got a text message from one of the other boys on the soccer team, and it sounded like they changed the practice schedule to start a bit early. Adam wanted to be prepared for the season, so he headed back to New Jersey."

"You sent him back alone? On the bus?" Alexis asked angrily. Kate appreciated her friend's obvious frustration.

"He just decided to go last night—a spur of the moment

sort of thing. You know Adam. . . . Boys will be boys. He caught a bus to Madison and will transfer to the express bus to New York later this afternoon. He's staying with the Blacks until we go home in a few weeks."

"What time did you drop him off at the bus station?" Kate whispered. Her voice sounded hollow, much like she felt. "Do you think he's still there?"

Michelle shook her head. "Well, no." She looked at the old classroom clock on the cabin wall, then down at her watch. "The bus left early this morning. He should be in Madison, if he isn't already on the bus to New York."

Kate stood up and thanked Michelle for the Kool-Aid. Sierra picked up their empty cups and set them in the sink.

Michelle followed them to the door, and called out after them, "Did you need to talk to Adam about something, girls?"

"Apparently not," Kate muttered. She looked through the trees and out to the lake. Kate could see her island poking out of the water, reminding her of the day when everything had changed. But Kate had blown it, and now she'd missed her chance to tell Adam that she was falling in love with him too. By the time they got back to New Jersey, too much time would have passed. "Let's get in the car," she said suddenly.

"The car?" Sierra queried.

"We're going on a road trip," Kate declared. "Let's finish this thing where it started. We're going to catch Adam on the road."

"That's my girl!" Alexis whooped. "But you know we'll have to drive faster than fifty-five if you want to catch his bus, right? Buses go slow, but not Kate-slow."

"If that's what it takes." Kate nodded, smiling. "True love takes sacrifice."

Fourteen

On the Road Again

"Dude, I've gotta pee." Alexis adjusted in her seat uncomfortably about an hour after they'd left Love. "It's serious."

"Lex!" Kate cried. "We don't have time to stop. We're already behind the bus by a few hours. We don't stand a chance of catching it anytime before Pennsylvania if we stop for a potty break."

"Okay, Mom." Kate saw Alexis smirk in the rearview mirror. "I'll just go in this OJ carton back here. If I miss at all, it's spraying in your direction."

Kate signaled to get off the interstate. "That's nasty, Lex."

Alexis shrugged. "I didn't get to go before we hit the road. This was sort of a sudden trip."

"I'm being spontaneous. I'm not going to let Adam get away," Kate said, and pulled into the parking lot of a Perkins restaurant, just off the interstate. "I need to find him now—not when we get back to New Jersey in a few weeks. I need to know if we can be together, and I don't want to wait."

"How are you going to know?" Sierra asked, unfastening her seat belt to get out of the car.

Kate followed her friends into the restaurant. "A kiss will answer that. A kiss will tell me everything I need to know. I just hope he doesn't hate me for taking this long to figure everything out."

While Alexis and Sierra hit the bathroom, Kate bought a bag of muffins. She felt guilty for using a restaurant's bathroom without buying something, and figured it was the least she could do to thank her friends for coming with her on the road. On the way back to the car a few minutes later, Sierra dug into the bag and pulled out a lemon poppy seed muffin. Alexis requested a raspberry, and both were so engrossed in their snack that neither noticed the bus that was pulling into the parking lot as they were piling into their Ford.

But Kate did. Laughing, she said, "Look! It's the Q-tip tour!"

"What?" Alexis looked up from her muffin, muttering

through a mouthful of crumbs. "What's a Q-tip tour?"

Kate put the keys into the ignition and backed out of their parking space. "The ladies from the bus trip. Remember, they were at the amusement park, and then we ran into them at our hotel outside Ann Arbor? Adam and I hung out with them playing cards?"

"That's so funny," Sierra assessed. "It's like they're stalking us."

The bus stopped, and the door opened. The three girls watched as some of the ladies climbed down the bus steps into the parking lot. Something kept Kate from driving away—perhaps it was the memory of her night with Adam, playing pinochle with Fern. Or maybe it was just that the bus tour reminded her of their road trip—when everything had seemed so much simpler, and her summer with Lucas was still just an imaginary and perfect scenario in her head. They sat there so long, with Kate paralyzed and unable to move, that a car pulled up behind them and started honking.

Startled, Kate pushed her foot on the gas, then ground to a stop again when Sierra yelled, "Adam!"

"Adam is in that bus, Kate!" Alexis was waving her muffin in the air and had turned herself completely around in the backseat to look out the back window.

Kate looked in the rearview mirror. "He's with the Q-tip tour?" she wondered aloud. Sure enough, Adam was sitting in the back seat of the bus, staring absentmindedly out the window. His dark hair was immediately obvious, in stark contrast to the white heads bobbing around next to him. Kate threw the car into drive and whipped a U-turn, causing several cars turning into the parking lot to screech to a halt to keep from hitting them.

The sound of the squealing tires made Adam look their way, and he perked up in his seat when he saw Alexis's familiar little green Ford in the parking lot beside the bus. He stood up, and they could see him hustling down the aisle of the bus toward the front door.

Kate was out of the car in an instant. She met Adam as he descended the steps of the bus into the parking lot. Her heart was beating fast, telling her that her instincts had been right. She needed to be with Adam—she was sure of it. "Your hair is too dark for the Q-tip tour," she said, grinning when she saw him. "You're ruining the effect."

"I know." He chuckled. "Um, what are you doing here?"

"We're looking for you."

"Kate, listen," Adam said seriously, looking down to watch his own feet shuffling across the gravel in the parking lot. "I was on my way home . . ."

Kate nodded. "I know. Your mom told us. How did you end up here? Why are you on the Q-tip tour?" She was so confused, and mildly freaked out. This was surely some sort of sign, bumping into Adam in the parking lot of Perkins, back on the road.

"I got off the bus about an hour east of here and hung out for a few hours, waiting for a bus to take me back toward Love. I was chilling in a rest area, and out of nowhere, Fern comes up and taps me on the shoulder. They were going my way and invited me to tag along, so I hopped onto the bus. I figured I could get a lift the rest of the way back from my dad or Alexis once I got a little closer to the resort—"

"But I thought you decided to go back to New Jersey for soccer practice. But now you're not—" Kate wasn't following. Adam was making no sense.

Adam cut her off to say, "There is no soccer practice. I just wanted to get out of Love. But I realized I'm not ready to give up yet."

"Give up?" Kate asked.

"I know you're with Lucas, but—"

"Not anymore," Kate said. She realized she should stop talking, since it seemed like Adam had something to say, and she was expertly ruining the moment.

Adam looked at her, hopeful, and started talking again. "I guess a part of me hopes that if I stick around long enough, maybe you'll realize that you're being a total idiot for not realizing that we need to be together."

"So why were you taking off on a bus back to Jersey,

then?" Kate asked, grinning. She couldn't help but tease him, just a little bit.

Adam shrugged. "I don't know. I guess I just couldn't stand seeing you and Lucas together anymore. But it only took a few minutes on that bus before I knew I needed to come back and make a fight for it . . . for you." He paused. "Okay . . . in the interest of full disclosure, I have to admit that the bus was nasty. The dude sitting in the seat next to me was picking strings of something out of his teeth and sticking them to the bus window, like little stacks of hay or something. I didn't want to be there when they dried and started to fall off the window again." Kate laughed. "But that's not why I got off the bus. I wanted to come back for you. Kate, we have to try." He looked at her seriously, studying her face for a reaction, some sign that she agreed. "I know I drive you crazy. . . . I'll wait—the rest of the summer, next year—"

"Stop!" Kate said suddenly. "Enough. That's enough." Without another word Kate grabbed Adam's face and pulled him toward her. His eyes stayed fixed on hers as their lips connected, but then Kate closed her own, so she didn't know if he was still looking at her. She didn't think so. No one could kiss like that with his eyes open. She could tell that Adam was focused on their first kiss with every part of his body. It was electrifying, a kiss unlike anything Kate had ever felt before. The parking lot faded away, the loud roaring of the bus motor behind them became a low mur-mur in the background. All Kate noticed was Adam's body leaning into her, and the beating of her own heart.

She opened her eyes slowly as their lips pulled apart. His eyes were still closed. Kate smiled. "Yep," she said, still grinning. "That definitely feels right."

"Good," Adam said, smirking back at her. "I've been saving that one for you."

Kate rolled her eyes and jokingly said, "*How* is this going to work? We're crazy to think we can be together, aren't we?"

"I'm crazy about you," Adam said, pulling her into a hug. "And *you*—you are fascinated with my charm and subtle humor, correct?"

"Correct," Kate said, laughing.

Suddenly Kate became aware of their surroundings again. She waved to Fern, who was standing by the door of the bus. Then she pulled Adam into the backseat of Alexis's car. Sierra had already grabbed Adam's bag from the back of the bus, and Alexis was in the driver's seat. They were ready to go.

As they merged onto the highway, headed back toward the resort, all Kate could think about was how romantic this scenario was. Kate and Adam's first hours together as a couple were on the road to Love. . . . She could think of no happier ending than that.

Epilogue

Happy Ending, New Jersey

"Hey, princess, what's going on?" Adam sauntered up and pinned Kate against the wall next to her locker, movie-star-style. It was the first day of senior year, and Kate was starting the year with a boyfriend. "Tell me I'm the guy of your dreams," he demanded in his mocking tone.

"I don't know about *that*," she joked, beaming at Adam. She laughed as he kissed her quickly. "Where's your locker?" she asked when he pulled away. "How far do I have to go to see my boyfriend between classes?"

"Right around the corner." Adam gestured toward the band hall. "In fact, if I remember correctly, it is in the very same bank of lockers you were in last year."

"Really?"

"Mm-hmm," Adam murmured, nuzzling her ear with his lips. They were still in that new-couple stage, and Kate loved it. "It's possible," Adam whispered into her ear. "It may be the very same locker, as a matter of fact."

Kate's heart started pounding harder as he slipped his hand into hers; a tiny slip of paper was pressed against his palm. She pulled their hands apart and twisted the piece of paper open. The words written on it were in her handwriting, and said: "hello, you, from kate."

"I found this in my locker," Adam said goofily, studying her face. "Look familiar?"

Kate smiled and held his hand tighter. "Yep," she confessed. "I left it there for you." Gazing up into Adam's smiling eyes, Kate knew for certain that she had finally found her prince.

About the Author

Erin Downing still can't figure out what she wants to do with her life (and probably never will), but she's living a pretty awesome one while she sorts it all out. A native of Duluth, Minnesota, Erin lived in England, Sweden, and New York City before settling down in Minneapolis with her husband and three kids. She is the author of the teen novel *Kiss It* as well as one middle-grade novel, *Juicy Gossip*. She's currently working on her next novel for teens. Visit Erin on the Web at www.erindowning.com.

More to love! Check out:

Royally Crushed

NIKI BURNHAM

EXACTLY SIX WEEKS, FIVE DAYS, AND NINE HOURS AGO, my mother ruined my life. And even worse, because of her, I am missing a damned good party.

Right this second, I should be over at my best friend Christie Toleski's house, getting ready to watch a parade of hot French and Australian actors (my favorite types) walk the red carpet at the Golden Globes. My friends Natalie Monschroeder and Julia (a.k.a. Jules) Jackson are already there, undoubtedly noshing on popcorn during the television coverage and discussing the plasticity of the host's face while she kisses and disses the celebs and their clothes—or lack thereof.

When Christie's parents aren't in the room, they're also

probably talking about how far Christie and her boyfriend, Jeremy Astin, went on their last date, how far she actually wants to go, and how all of them are sooooo sure David Anderson (whom I've been crushing on since kindergarten) is finally interested in me.

But no. They're doing all that without me. I know because they texted me about half an hour ago to rub it in.

Unfortunately, my failure to attend this year's let's-make-fun-of-celebrities Golden Globes party (not to be confused with our annual let's-make-fun-of-celebrities Oscar, Grammy, and Emmy parties) is because, thanks to my mother, my parents are getting a divorce and I had to move with my dad to Schwerinborg a month ago.

Yes, Schwerinborg's a real country, and yes, my friends all refer to it as Smorgasbord, even though the people here aren't even Scandinavian. The Schwerinborgians— or Schwerinborgers or whatever they're called—speak German. And we're south of Germany, not north. Not that any of my friends care where it is, other than the fact that it's very, very far from Virginia.

So why not live with my mother? After all, she has a nice apartment back in Virginia, where all the important awards shows are carried live. And even though the location of Mom's new place means I'd have to go to Lake Braddock High School instead of to Vienna West, where I've been going, I could still see my friends on a regular basis.

Hmmmm . . . how about because Mom's new apartment is also home to Mom's new *girlfriend*?

Yep, girlfriend. A super-organized, yoga-twisting, vegan Weight Watchers–devotee girlfriend named Gabrielle, who is, no kidding, a decade younger than my mother. And no, Gabrielle isn't a girlfriend like Christie, Natalie, and Jules are my girlfriends.

Gabrielle is *that* kind of girlfriend.

I haven't even had the guts to tell *my* girlfriends about her, and it doesn't take a psychology degree to guess why. It's the kind of thing that takes you a while to work up to telling someone, even your best friends. Telling them about my parents' divorce—and that I was moving to Europe with Dad—was bad enough. Popping out with, "Oh, and by the way, my mom—the woman who took us all out for manicures and facials before homecoming and has definitely seen all of you naked at one time or another when we've gone clothes shopping—yeah, well, she's announced that she's gay!" wouldn't have gone over with them very well.

I know they say they don't care whether a person is gay, and I've never heard them say one derogatory word about anyone's sexual preferences, but I'm not quite sure I want to test their beliefs yet.

And it's not that *I'm* a homophobe. Seriously. I know a

couple of gay kids at school, and they're totally cool. But this is different. This is my *mother*.

It's like the mom I knew disappeared one day and now there's another person inhabiting Mom's body. That's the really hard part. Not the what-is-she-doing-with-that-woman? part. It's that I have to wonder if she's lied to me about who she is my entire freaking life.

You'd think I'd want to find the highest turret—well, if it had turrets—of Schwerinborg's royal palace and toss myself off of it.

But no. I'm not even close to suicidal right now, even though I'm sure about a hundred hot actors look completely droolworthy walking the red carpet in their Armani tuxes and I'm missing it. (Thankyouverymuch, Mom.)

It's because Schwerinborg is completely incredible. I mean, there are definite downsides, like the fact they use mayo on their French fries, that the weather is misty and depressing all winter long, and that I can't watch the Golden Globes live. (Which, come to think of it, makes absolutely no sense—the awards are given by the Hollywood Foreign Press, and if anything's foreign to Hollywood, it's gotta be Schwerinborg.)

It's because I have a boyfriend.

I have a boyfriend who looks like the hottest of those actors, only better. More of a sweetheart, less of a male slut.

I have a boyfriend named Georg Jacques von Ederhollern, *and he is a freakin' PRINCE.*

Yep. I, Valerie Winslow, a totally boring, non-cheerleader, non-athletic, non-popular sophomore redheaded nobody from Vienna, Virginia, have officially hooked up with a European prince. A prince who knows how to kiss in the most knock-me-on-my-ass way, and who is formal and polite and looks beyond hot in a tux, but who also knows how to kick back and be cool and totally un-prince-like when we're alone, if you catch my drift.

And you wanna know a secret? Even though it's the dead of winter and he's always in sweaters and jackets, I've discovered that he has these amazing arms.

Ever see Hugh Jackman in *X-Men?* It's an old movie, but still. THOSE arms.

Okay, Georg's almost seventeen, so he's not quite X-Men caliber yet, and he's a lot more lean and wiry than Hugh Jackman, but he's headed in that direction. His arms are totally ripped and solid—the kind that other guys refer to as guns. A girl could be about to go off a cliff, grab on to those biceps just as her footing slips, and not worry for even a second she's going to fall, you know?

Yes, I know that girls probably go for Hugh Jackman—and every other Aussie actor, for that matter—because of their accents as much as their arms or other, um, physical attributes. But if his name alone doesn't make it clear, Georg *also* has an accent, and it's pretty damned sexy. (However, I will admit that if someone had told me a year ago that listening to a guy speak with a deep, German accent would make me get all gooey inside, I'd have thought they needed some serious therapy.)

But you see, the thing that makes Georg an even better boyfriend than any Hollywood actor could ever be is . . . NONE OF THEM HAS A CROWN! They do not have staff members who polish their shoes before school or ask if they'd like a Coke or finger sandwiches while studying Trig in the palace library. Georg does. And he's not the least bit egotistical about any of those things. In fact, it makes him blush if you mention it. He gets this little pink glow right along his cheekbones, and then he tries to hide his face so you can't see. It's totally cute.

Also, Georg does not care that my mother is a lesbian. He actually tells me I should try to be more understanding of her, and at the same time, he totally gets that while I really do love her, I'm completely ticked off at her for what she did to me and Dad.

Is that love, or what? You don't find that with just any guy. The arms, the accent, and even the crown are simply bonus material. He likes me for me, and David Anderson never did.

Well, unless you believe my friends, who I think keep telling me David likes me to try to make me feel better about the whole divorce thing.

Ha.

Wait until they hear about my prince. Or better yet, wait until I put them on the phone with him so they can hear his accent.

So right now *I'm* on the phone with Georg, and I can hardly follow what he's saying, because I'm so hung up on how he's saying it. All rich and Euro-like, but thankfully without even a hint of that thick nasal sound that you might expect from someone whose native language is German. Georg's voice is smooth and seductive. And it's making me wish he would hurry up and get over here so I can grab him and kiss him the way he kissed me day before yesterday, when we went to this dinner-party-reception-formal thing his father was hosting for the British prime minister here at the palace, then ditched for a while to go make out in the garden. It was icy out there, and all the plants were that generic shade of gray-green that plants get in the middle of January, but between the kissing and him whispering to me in that fabulous accent, I was totally warm. It was our second kiss, but the first serious one, and this time we both knew there'd be more. Lots and lots more.

I can't think about anything else *but* kissing Georg.

"Valerie. Are you still listening to me?"

I sit up on my bed and try to focus. It's difficult, though, when my room is maybe only five degrees warmer than the garden was and Georg isn't here to keep me toasty.

My dad and I live in the royal palace in Schwerinborg because he's the new protocol chief to the royal family—meaning he works for Georg's dad, Prince Manfred—who rules the country—and Georg's mom, Princess Claudia. He advises them on things like the proper way to address everyone from visiting Buddhist monks to the queen of England, and warns them about the fact that when they visit Egypt, they might get served pigeon but that it's perfectly safe to eat.

It's a totally whacked thing to do for a living, but since it once got me a behind-the-scenes tour of the White House (which is where my dad did his protocol thing until the überconservative, up-for-reelection president discovered Dad had married a lesbian) and it's the reason I met Georg and have gotten to hang out with him despite the fact I'm your average American fifteen-year-old, I'm not going to make even one crack about it.

On the other hand, while it might sound cool to actually *live* in a real palace, I'd much rather the royal couple hadn't offered us their, uh, hospitality. Other than the fact that Georg is under the same roof, it pretty much sucks.

Our very ritzy-sounding "palace apartment"—which is actually only three small rooms and a kitchen—is always so cold I have to wear double layers of socks, and it has the decor of a circa-1970s, never-been-renovated motel. Probably because we're in a 150-year-old section of the palace that hasn't been renovated since, well, the 1970s. We'd have been better off living a couple blocks away, in a nice little walk-up.

Preferably one with heat.

"Yeah, I'm listening," I say to Georg as I stare at my tiny, ancient bedroom window and wonder how much cold air is leaking in from outside. "You said you had two assists and a goal at the scrimmage yesterday. But I wish you'd just come over. I can follow soccer talk much better in person."

I'm totally kidding because we both know it's way too late, but still. Does he think a five-minute walk from one side of the palace—the beautiful, *warm,* renovated side, where his family lives—over to the other side, where my apartment is, would kill him? I mean, the guy's an incredible soccer player, so you know his legs work just fine.

They're very nice legs. All tight and muscular and—

Whoa.

This thought zaps my brain back to reality. I have it bad for him. Way bad. I can't stop thinking about his various body parts, and we went out—officially—for the first time, what, Friday night, and it's only Sunday?!

Maybe I'm wigged out because this is the first time I've ever had a real boyfriend (since I don't count Jason Barrows, whom everyone thought I was going out with because he kissed me on a dare in seventh grade. Puh-leeze.). Maybe it's because Georg's a prince, and no matter where he goes, he always has this prince-like aura around him.

But even so, this is not good because Georg and I are trying to keep things low-key, or at least make it look that way for the time being.

Given the way my synapses are firing right now, though, if Georg and I get within fifty feet of each other, I'm going to be all over him. On top of it making me look totally desperate, which would be bad because Georg has no idea I'm a little, um, inexperienced, it would blow the whole low-key thing out of the water.

"I know you're kidding, but if I thought we could get away with it, I would," Georg tells me. "But it's nearly midnight. My father said the fund-raiser would be over around one a.m., which means everyone will be back soon. Until your father's not suspicious about the cigarettes any-more . . . well, we have to be careful."

"I know." I twist one of my sheets into a little whorl

with my fingers, then glance at the bedside alarm clock. "I still can't believe we got busted."

We weren't even smoking them when my dad walked in on us Friday night, and we weren't going to. Really. Georg was just showing me where he keeps an emergency stash, behind the paper towel holder in the handicapped stall of the men's restroom that's below the palace ballroom. He'd even hidden them back away before my dad came in, but they'd fallen on the floor.

Major oops.

I must be pretty desperate, though, because I add, this time only half-joking, "I still think you'd be okay, if you really wanted to come over. Now that Dad's had a day to chill, he's beginning to understand that I wasn't trying to corrupt you with cigarettes."

"And get him fired."

"Exactly." Europeans are pretty lax about smoking, just not when it comes to their royalty. Apparently, Georg getting caught with cigarettes—say, by the press or something—would be a pretty big deal.

I pull the covers up over my shoulders like a cape, then cradle the phone a little closer to my ear. "I told him they were on the sink when we got there, and one of us must have accidentally knocked them off when we were, ah, *talking* in there."

If it's possible to hear someone smile over the phone, I can hear it. "Well, that's good news, at least. So he seems to think it's okay if we're going out?"

"Hey, all we're doing is engaging in a little soccer talk, right? Nothing that will jeopardize your reputation as the next leader of Schwerinborg."

He laughs, but it dies out pretty quickly, which means he's thinking about something serious. "Well, that's what I was getting to. Some of the guys were talking yesterday after we got out of practice."

"Yeah?"

"Well, remember how Ulrike's dad was at the dinner on Friday night? He must have mentioned seeing us together to Ulrike, because the guys were asking me about it."

Uh-oh. I know exactly where this is going. Ulrike is this really nice girl at my new high school who's the president of everything. One of those girls with white-blond hair and a perfect Crest smile, and who I usually write off based on her looks alone, because 99 percent of girls who look like Ulrike are just heinous. Snobby and mean and they think they're God's gift to the world. But Ulrike's actually really smart and friendly—and not just to other beautiful people, but to everyone.

On the other hand, Ulrike has this equally beautiful friend, Steffi, who's the world's biggest bitch. One of those

fake, manipulative people no one—especially naive, trust-
ing types like Ulrike—ever *get* until it's way too late.

"Let me guess—"

"Yeah, I'm pretty sure Steffi already knows we're
together." Georg sounds irritated by Steffi's mere existence
as he talks. "If not, she'll know soon. Thought we should
figure out how we're going to handle it when she asks us
about it."

Great. It's not that I really care if she knows. Maybe it'll
knock her down a peg to realize that just because she's tiny
and brunette and popular, she can't get any guy she wants.
Like Georg.

But chances are, rather than simply acting like a normal
person with hurt feelings when she hears that the object of
her crush has a new girlfriend, she'll get totally ticked off,
meaning she'll be more aggressive than usual about giving
me backhanded compliments when everyone's around . . .
making offhand comments about how I must have some
wonderful hidden traits if Georg is willing to take the time
to introduce me around the school when he's such a busy
person.

As if whatever good traits I might have aren't obvious, or as if Georg is doing me this huge favor because I'm
clearly not good enough to be around him.

Steffi's like that. You can't really pick apart anything she says as being nasty and call her on it, because she says it in this fakey-nice, syrupy way. But I know she wants me to get the message, especially because she makes genuinely nasty little remarks to me under her breath when she knows no one else can hear. She's so quiet with it, I can barely hear her.

So I say to Georg, "Well, you know how I usually deal with Steffi. I ignore her. But what do you think?"

As much as I'd like to rant to Georg about what Steffi can do with her opinions, I don't, because I know it'll only make me sound like a whiner. Georg tries to be nice to Steffi—since he's a prince, he's stuck trying to be nice to everyone or else risk his family's good reputation, which really sucks if you think about it—but he's the one guy in school who sees right through her.

And I love that about him. We have this funky-cool connection, where we just look at each other and *know* we both see the world the same way. As deranged as it is, the fact we both understand Steffi and her little games—when no one else does—just makes our connection that much stronger.

"Well, I figure we have three choices, assuming she actually asks us what's going on. First, we can play dumb. Second choice, we act like it's no big thing and say we were at the reception together because we both live under the same roof and thought it'd be fun."

"And third?"

"We come clean, and who cares if Steffi knows we've hooked up." I can hear the smile in his voice again. "And that's the fun option, because it means if I feel like kissing you between classes, I can, which definitely has its appeal."

"So what do you want to do?" No way am I making this call. I like option three, for the same reason Georg does. Frankly, a quickie make-out session with Georg—of course where Steffi can see—would totally strengthen my ability to deal with her and all her crap. But Georg knows Ulrike, Steffi, their friend Maya, and all the rest of the kids at school way better than I do. So I figure he's the one who should decide.

"I'd prefer to be honest about it." His voice has that tone that makes it sound like a *but* is coming, and it does. "But the more I think about it, the more I think it wouldn't be smart."

I make a face at the wall. Ooo-kay. Georg was the one who said he didn't care if Ulrike's father saw us dancing together, or who knew about us. And now he does?

"So I shouldn't say anything around school?" I guess it would pretty much be the gossip of the week if we confirmed it to anyone. But why should he care?

Then I realize that I'm the hypocrite of the century. I'm freaked about him not wanting to tell his friends, even though I still haven't told my friends about him, let alone about my mother and everything else. And they're thousands of miles away.

I'm about to apologize, and say we can do whatever he wants, when he says, "School isn't really the problem. It's the people outside of school. Okay, Steffi's a problem, but it's not her attitude around school that worries me. It's who else she talks to."

He gets quiet a second, and the lightbulb turns on in my head. Now I get it. Tabloids.

There's this one reporter assigned to Georg who walks about twenty yards behind him on the way to school a couple times a week. The poor guy's probably the bottom of the food chain at *Majesty* magazine. There really isn't much to report about Georg—his parents crack down on him hard, so he really can't get in any trouble, and he doesn't go out partying. And I'm willing to bet most of the world's population couldn't find Schwerinborg on a map, let alone identify its prince. Not like they could identify Prince William or Prince Harry.

But still, Georg is always careful, so that most of the reports this guy files are about fairly innocuous things, like last week's story, "Teen Prince Risking His Smile," which ran alongside a snapshot of Georg ducking out of a coffee-house on his way to school, but mostly talked about how if you drink coffee or tea for years and years, your teeth can get stained.

"Valerie, I don't want you to think I'm embarrassed to be with you, or that I don't want anyone to know—"

"Hey, no problem. Really." And I mean it. I don't exactly want to be on the front of some trashy rag either. I'm beginning to realize that keeping things low-key goes with the dating-a-prince territory, even if you weren't almost caught smoking.

"You know how I feel about you. It's just that—"

He sounds so concerned about it, I can't help but laugh. I know I shouldn't—my dad would probably tell me it's against some very important rule of protocol—but I can't help it. "I told you, no problem."

He's quiet for a sec, then says, "If I hurry, I can be over there in five minutes, stay for maybe twenty, then get back before my parents are home from the fund-raiser. I just need to watch the clock so I have a five-to-ten-minute cushion."

"And what if we get caught?"

"Have your Chemistry book out, maybe?"

This time I'm really laughing, because my dad knows— and so does Georg—that I'm a total geek and there's no way I'd put my Chem homework off until midnight Sunday. I can hardly stand to have homework that's not done by Saturday at noon.

Is it any mystery why I haven't had a boyfriend before?

His voice is low and completely hot as he tells me, "I'll be there in five minutes, like it or not."

"Not!"

Exactly four minutes and thirty-two seconds later, there's a knock at my apartment door. And I definitely like it.

To: Val@realmail.sg.com
From: ChristieT@viennawest.edu
Subject: Armor Girls

Heya, Val Pal!

Can I just say I'm totally bummed you missed the GGs last night? The red carpet interviewer was wearing a dress that was totally see-through when she stood under the lights. They kept having to cut away from her and back to the person being interviewed, which was hysterical. You'd have made tons of jokes about the woman wanting to show off her boob job.

BTW, Jules told me about your Armor Girl theory—the whole thing about *A Knight's Tale*, the movie where Heath Ledger falls for this totally shallow rich-girl-princess type and ignores the girl who makes his armor. Jules claims that you think you're only an

Armor Girl to David Anderson's knight, and that he's only interested in you until he can find a Shallow Princess.

You are WRONG.

Tonight sucks for me, but you will be home tomorrow
night, so I can FINALLY talk to you on the phone, right? I was
nice to my cousins for an entire week so my mom would let
me call you, and you haven't been there. Now you MUST be.
Because I have actually talked to David about you, and you
are so not an Armor Girl.

DO YOU GET IT YET?! YOU ARE THE PRINCESS.

I'm tired of dropping hints about this, which is why I'm
cyber-yelling. You said you could change your mind and live
with your mom if you wanted. I think you should. (I promise I
will forgive you for going to Smorgasbord.) Natalie and Jules
think you should come home too.

How often do all three of us agree on something? Seriously. Think about it. I know you told Jules that you thought
David could never really like you for you, but you are so, so
wrong. David is perfect for you. AND HE WANTS YOU.

Hugs and miss you and etc.,

Christie

PS—So what is this "unbelievable dirt" you told me about in
your e-mail on Friday night? PLEASE tell me you haven't met
someone. And if you did, get over him. He's not David.

To: Val@realmail.sg.com

From: CoolJule@viennawest.edu

Subject: You and your potential ass-kicking

Yo, Valerie!

Five very important things. Are you paying attention?? GOOD.

Number 1: Okay, I will acknowledge, after seeing last night's Golden Globes, that most of Hollywood is constructed of silicone and that the tabloids are probably correct about which celebs have had work.

Number 2: You're still wrong about the Armor Girl thing. I told Natalie and Christie about it, and they totally agree with me that you're the princess, NOT the Armor Girl, so get over yourself.

Number 3: Even Heath Ledger, may he rest in peace, was not as hot as the Schwerinborg prince Christie and Natalie and I read about on the Internet. The one the article said lives in the same palace you do. The one named Georg. (Did his parents forget the "e" in George? Or is that some bizarre Schwerinborg thing?!)

Number 4: You have still not written me back to say what happened when you gave Prince Georg, mentioned in item Number 3, my phone number and e-mail address.

Number 5: If you haven't done it yet, I'm going to kick

your ass. You're on a tight time line here, Val, because we KNOW you're coming home soon. RIGHT? So go accidentally and on purpose bump into my future boyfriend and GIVE HIM MY E-MAIL! I am not joking about the ass-kicking and you know it.

The future princess of Smorgasbord,

Jules